GOODBYE HEARTBREAK, HELLO MAY

A NOVEL

L. B. JOYCE

GOODBYE HEARTBREAK, HELLO MAY
Copyright © 2021 by L. B. Joyce

Goodbye Heartbreak, Hello May
Book 1
Print ISBN: 978-0-9600311-7-7

ALSO BY L. B. JOYCE

This book is the eighth in the series,
Twelve Months, Twelve Love Stories:

A Million Decembers

For the Love of July

February's Angel

Promise Me November

An Unexpected June

A January to Remember

September's Moonlight Serenade

Goodbye Heartbreak, Hello May

March, a Song and a Dance

* * *

Holidays in White Oaks Valley:

A Grand Slam Kind of Christmas

WELCOME TO BOOK 8!

*I would like to dedicate this book to all of you
who have been faithful readers of this series up until now.
I couldn't have arrived at this point without you.
Enjoy!*

*Love is like a puzzle...
When you're in love, all the pieces fit.
But when your heart gets broken,
it takes a while to get everything back together again.*

~ Unknown

CHAPTER 1

Our Wedding Day ~
The best day ever, the start of our forever.
~ Anonymously Yours

Darcey Hollister and Jason Bennett couldn't have asked for a more perfect wedding day.

There wasn't a cloud in the sky, the temperature holding steady in the mid-seventies. Like magic, the buds of yesterday had blossomed overnight into a riot of vibrant spring colors.

Add the sparkling blue expanse of Lake Erie in the background, and you have the ideal setting for a momentous occasion such as this.

Everyone had been skeptical when Jason and Darcey chose the first Saturday in May for their wedding day. Some had even tried to talk them into a later date. Like June… or even July.

Because, who in their right mind planned an early spring wedding in Cleveland? This was an enormous gamble, the city known for its unpredictable weather.

Believe it or not, snow was always a possibility. A look into the past would confirm this. And this didn't mean only a sprinkling of flakes here and there. No, we're talking about blizzard-like conditions.

But Jason and Darcey stayed strong and the weather gods smiled down on them with the perfect spring weekend. Beginning with the beautiful and very moving outdoor ceremony. Darcey was a gorgeous bride and Jason perfection in a tuxedo.

But it was the love they shared between them that everyone would remember of this day.

And now, after an elegant five-course dinner by candlelight, the dance floor of the Grand Ballroom was rocking. Almost everyone was dancing to the music played by the band Jason and Darcey had chosen.

They weren't as good as Jason's band, but they were a pretty close second.

When your favorite and only brother gets married, you want everything to be perfect. This meant Stephanie Bennett had been on the go for the past forty-eight hours.

Now in a desperate need of a break, what better way to do this than with a slice of wedding cake?

From the best bakery in town… Sweet Abby's.

She arrived at the cake table just as the band finished their song. In the lull that followed, she glanced over to see the bandleader take a long swig from his water bottle before he grabbed the microphone to address the crowd.

"Okay, everybody… can I have your attention? We need everyone to clear the dance floor. Except for all of you single and beautiful women here with us tonight. Because, guess what? It's time for the bride to toss her bouquet. So, come on ladies… let's see all of you out here, no excuses."

He motioned to a few of the women standing nearby. "Come on, don't be shy. Because next, we'll be calling up all the single men for the garter toss. This could be your night at finding the man of your dreams."

Stephanie rolled her eyes.

Yeah, right…

Grabbing the plate of cake closest to her, she began searching the room. There had to be somewhere she could hide.

She was not—and she was going to stand firm on this, no matter how hard anyone tried to convince her otherwise—going to be one of those women out on the dance floor, making a desperate attempt at trying to snatch up the bouquet.

At your age? Is this pathetic, or what?

And even if she caught the bouquet? From experience, she knew there was no guarantee she would be next to get married.

After all, you have proof. You caught the bouquet at Sophie's wedding. And here you are, still very single.

She edged her way over to a grouping of ornamental trees, positioning herself as far behind them as she could. The plan was no one would even notice she was missing. Darcey would throw the bouquet, enabling her to rejoin the party and eat her cake in peace.

Crisis averted.

Unfortunately, it appeared this wasn't her lucky night.

She was about to put a forkful of cake in her mouth when the bandleader made another announcement. "Okay, everyone… I've just been told by the bride one of our single ladies is missing. So, Stephanie, wherever you are, we're waiting. According to Darcey, we can't do this without you. Remember, she's the bride. So, what she says, goes."

She groaned.

Seriously? This was not good.

The prospect of being remembered as the woman who hid behind an ornamental tree at her brother's wedding reception, in order to avoid catching the bouquet? This was not a memory she wanted to be associated with.

God, no… your friends would never let you live this down. Not in a million years.

She set her plate down on the nearest table. With a big smile pasted on her face, she made her way to the dance floor.

Five minutes later, after almost being knocked over by an overly zealous woman evidently desperate to get married, the bouquet fell right into Stephanie's arms. It was a direct hit from Darcey.

It turns out she had been a star pitcher when she played softball in high school and college.

By the excited reaction of the guests, you'd think you had won the lottery.

3

But this also meant until the next wedding rolled around?

Everyone would remember her as the woman who last caught the bouquet.

The pressure was on…

Jack Buchanan had been watching all of this with interest. An all around musician in Jason's band, Banded Together, he was also one of Jason's groomsmen and partnered up with Stephanie for the wedding.

Having witnessed Stephanie's attempt to hide behind the ornamental trees in order to avoid the bouquet toss, she had his total sympathy.

He knew exactly what she was going through.

Ever since he had hit thirty, it seemed like everyone felt it was their duty to play matchmaker. There wasn't a day that went by without someone pulling him aside. They had the perfect woman for him. Their cousin, co-worker, neighbor, sister's best friend—you name it—they would make the perfect couple.

Only yesterday, the owner of the corner deli had approached him. After the usual pleasantries, he began rambling on about his niece, who had just gone through a divorce. Yeah, her four kids were a handful. But this was only because they needed an older and stable father figure in their lives. Would he be interested in something like this?

Would you be interested? Just how old does he think you are?

He frowned just thinking about this. He was pretty sure he hadn't fallen in into the category of one of the older guys just yet. Maybe in a few years, when he hit his late thirties, this would better describe him.

And four kids?

He had no experience with kids, knew little about them.

Geeesh… you never even owned a pet.

And, please… don't even think of bringing up the possibility of on-line dating. Yes, he had heard about the many brilliant matches made through these sites. He even knew a few people who swore by it.

But this wasn't for him.

So, as politely as he could, he made it known he didn't need help. He even went as far as using his age to make his point. Yes, he was thirty. This also meant he had grown comfortable with the way things were.

He knew what he wanted in his life.

He'd figure it out.

What he didn't share was he was hoping this would include Stephanie.

Jack had been waiting for his chance with Stephanie for what now seemed like forever. Going back to a little over two years ago when he joined the band. This was also about the time Stephanie graduated with her nursing degree.

That he still hadn't made his move after all this time was something he didn't even want to think about. It was when Jason and Darcey announced they were getting married, he realized he had waited long enough.

His hope was the time he and Stephanie spent together because of all the wedding events would set off some kind of spark between them.

Yeah, she'd realize what a great guy you are. The silent type, but still a nice guy.

Hadn't he made the list of Cleveland's most eligible bachelors?

Didn't this count for something?

Something you're wondering if it's more of a curse than an honor...

But it turned out he and Stephanie hadn't spent as much time together as he thought they would. Caught up in all the important details needed for the event to run smoothly, Stephanie had been like an elusive butterfly, always beyond his reach.

If they did come together, it was only to have her again go fluttering off because someone else needed her help.

And now he was running out of time, as the day would soon be over.

So, it looked like he needed to take advantage of this latest development.

She caught the bouquet?

Then his goal was to snag the garter.

He wasn't stupid. He knew the tossing of the bouquet and garter was only a fun tradition. It took more than one good catch to land the perfect marriage. So, no one really believed it could come true.

Unless you were to count the woman who almost knocked Stephanie to the floor in order to grab the bouquet. It was clear she took this tradition more seriously than most.

But, hey… a nudge in the right direction couldn't hurt, right?

He finished his drink, and after setting the glass on the table, he headed for the dance floor.

He was a man on a mission.

An hour later, Jack pulled up in front of Stephanie's condo. After he got out of the car, he ran around to open the passenger door.

She smiled up at him as she got out of the car. "Thanks so much for bringing me home. You don't have to walk me to the door. I'll be fine."

He shrugged. "No problem. I'll feel much better if I do." He chuckled. "I also don't want to hear what Jazz would have to say if he found out I didn't. We both know how seriously he takes his big-brother role."

He was about to close the car door when he noticed she had left the bouquet behind on the seat. He handed it to her. "Here, you don't want to forget this."

She hesitated before she took it from him. "Thanks." She glanced over at the garter he was still wearing on his sleeve. "It was a fun wedding, wasn't it?"

Their eyes met, with her the first to look away. She shrugged. "But just like that, the night is over. And it's time to move on."

Time to move on?

Tilting his head, he studied her for a moment. Was she trying to tell him something?

He decided even if she was, this might not be a good time to ask her what it was. After all, it had been a long two days. It was late, and they were both exhausted. So, he was silent as he waited for her to unlock her door.

She turned to him with a smile. "Thanks again, Jack."

"Sure, sweet dreams." He followed this with a brief kiss to her cheek.

And just like that, she closed the door. Leaving him alone on the steps.

For a few moments, he gazed up at the stars.

Yep, this was a night made for romance.

But, it seems, not for you.

There would be no sweet dreams for him.

He didn't understand.

Why was this so hard?

After exhaling a long, drawn out breath, he turned and ran to his car. He needed to get home and get out of this tux.

He was ready to call it a night.

Weddings were exhausting.

CHAPTER 2

One week later, on this rainy Monday morning, Stephanie finished counting the number of people ahead of her in line at the License Bureau.

It wasn't looking good.

The line was long, wrapping all the way around to the back of the room.

The last time she counted? She had been at number sixteen.

And now?

She was number thirteen. According to the clock on the wall, in the shape of a colorful map of Ohio, it had taken her about fifteen minutes to get to this point.

This meant, at the rate things were going, she could be in line for another hour.

Or, God help you... even longer.

Her frown grew deeper. This would be the same frown that had been with her all morning and had now reached the point it was almost painful. She wouldn't be the least bit surprised if it became engraved on her face.

So, as you have probably already guessed, Stephanie was not in a good mood.

She was in a lousy mood, in fact.

A very lousy mood.

And anyone who knows Steffi would be quick to tell you this was not the norm. She was by far the most optimistic and laid-back person around. This terrible mood she was in wasn't part of her repertoire.

But today?

Today was different.

Suddenly, everything was too much to handle... her job, her life, everything. And although this might come across as a little dramatic, she was wondering if she should accept things were not going to get much better.

She sighed, shoving her hands in her pockets. A glance over at the windows confirmed it was still raining. As it had been for the past two days. A soaking, steady rain.

And it was cold, not your typical May weather. No, were you to go by the saying—April showers, bring May flowers—this would be more of an early April kind of day. A far cry from last weekend, when it had been absolutely beautiful for Jason and Darcey's wedding.

Yep, today was a day best spent in your pajamas. Maybe even start up a fire in the fireplace, and nestle in your favorite chair. A cup of something hot in one hand and a good romance novel in the other.

Ah... but for you, this isn't even an option.

She sighed, glancing down at her watch. She needed to be at work in less than an hour. This would normally be her day off, but she was filling in for one of the other nurses on her floor. At seven months pregnant, her doctor had advised her to take the day off after she slipped and fell in the parking lot yesterday.

When Steffi had offered to take her shift, she hadn't planned on spending the rest of the day waiting in line at the license bureau.

But you can only blame yourself for this. Why you let Noah get to you after all this time is inexcusable.

And who is this Noah who had brought her to this state? None other than Dr. Davis. Dr. Noah Davis. Or, while flashing a smile she found impossible to resist, he had told her to call him Noah.

Last night, when out to dinner with her friends, she had glanced across the room just as he walked into the restaurant.

The smile this brought to her face had disappeared when she realized he wasn't alone. Her heart dropping to her stomach, she watched as the woman gazed up into his face, laughing at something he said. The way she was clinging to his arm sent out the obvious message she thought of him as her private property.

But it was the kiss he gave her in response that did Stephanie in.

She panicked...

She had grabbed her wallet and phone off the table. Slipping them into her coat pocket, and giving a rambling and almost incoherent excuse to her friends that she suddenly didn't feel well, she had sprinted out of the restaurant.

It wasn't like you told a lie. You did feel sick... sick and tired of being played the fool.

And it hadn't ended there. After a restless night, she woke to find her wallet hadn't made it into her pocket as she had thought. A thorough search of her car, followed by texts to her friends and a trip to the restaurant, all turned up nothing.

This explained why she was now waiting in this long line at the license bureau.

The man behind her in line was standing way too close. Enough for her to feel like he was breathing down her neck, sending a strong odor of pastrami or salami right at her. If this wasn't enough, she had been forced to listen to his annoying off-key humming ever since he got in line.

She closed her eyes.

Oh, God... enough already.

Maybe this could this be a good time to practice the breathing exercises her friend Melanie had taught her? A yoga instructor, or wellness and serenity instructor as she preferred to be called, she claimed to have a cure for everything. Ailments, moods, injuries... you name it.

How about something to make everyone disappear? Wouldn't that come in handy?

She closed her eyes, deciding it couldn't hurt to give it a try. Anything to shut out everything around her.

Breathe in... and hold...
Breathe in... hold it... then slowly let it all go...
Ahhhhh...
She did this a few times.
And?
Nothing...
But the possibility of anything happening was close to non existent since the man behind her had now moved even closer. Hoping this was his way of letting her know the line had moved up, she opened her eyes to find, no... nothing had changed.

Frustrated, she pulled out her phone. Maybe there was a message from Jason.

She hadn't talked to him since he returned from his honeymoon. And she had already left the restaurant in order to avoid Noah when Darcey showed up late for their girl's night out.

Jason had sent a text.

> Hey, we got the wedding photos. There are a lot of great shots. If you get a chance, stop over. Call me.

"Steffi?"
She looked up from her phone.
Jack was standing in front of her, a tentative smile on his face.
Her smile was just as uncertain. "Hi... fancy meeting you here. Long time, no see." As soon as these words came out of her mouth, the natural blush in her cheeks became even more pronounced.

Fancy meeting you here? Long time, no see? What kind of greeting do you call that?

She began stammering. "What I meant... well, I haven't seen you since the wedding. And then to find you here..." Her words trailed off.

A smile tweaked the corner of his mouth at her obvious embarrassment. Not that he was laughing at her. Of course not. This was only because he understood where she was coming from.

What was it they said? it takes one to know one? He liked to think this applied to him and Steffi, that they were two of a kind.

Even though this didn't seem to be working in his favor.

After he had finished his transaction at the counter and turned around, his gaze had been drawn right to her. And like every other time she showed up in his life, his nerves kicked in, his brain shut down, and he turned into a love-struck kid instead of the thirty-year-old guy he was.

Not the best combination when you want to impress someone.

This was also when he knew this time probably wouldn't be any different.

Going for a casual look, he stuffed his hands in his pockets. He cleared his throat. "I decided it was time to get a new truck. So, I needed a title transfer."

He tilted his head, studying her. "What about you?"

She began playing with her keys, swinging them back and forth. When she saw he was watching this, she dropped the keys in her pocket, blushing even more in embarrassment. "I was out to dinner last night and I must have left my wallet on the table. I called the restaurant this morning, but it was nowhere to be found. So, now I have to get a new license and all that stuff."

Jack nodded. Twice he did this. "*Ah...* that's a bummer. Must be a real hassle."

"Yeah." She sent a glance around the room before she gave a frustrated sigh. "I didn't think it would be so crowded."

He nodded again. "Yeah, I know. I feel like I've been here for hours."

A silence fell between them. One that seemed to go on and on and on. This had him closing his eyes, giving a slight shake of his head.

What the hell is the matter with you? Why did you even stop to talk to her? Because you've certainly done a stellar job of turning this into an awkward situation.

But this was something he needed to do. He was running out of chances. The time they spent together at Jason and Darcey's wedding hadn't worked out as he'd hoped. And he couldn't keep running in the other direction whenever he saw her.

Yeah, it's now or never.

While he was searching for something to say, she sent him a bright smile. "So, is the band working in the studio today?"

He nodded, relieved. Music, and anything to do with the band, was something he found easy to talk about. "Yeah, now that Jason's back, the plan is to put a wrap on our latest album. The past few months, he has been a man of action."

He grinned. "I'm pretty sure Darcey's responsible for this."

When she grinned in return, his confidence kicked in. And this is when he decided it was time to give his all. He took a deep breath. "Since I don't need to be at the studio for another hour, I thought I'd head over to the little cafe across the street for a cup of coffee. I could use a little pick-me-up on such a miserable day."

He nodded towards the windows, where they could see it was still raining. "It's a good thing it wasn't like this for Jason and Darcey's wedding."

"I know." She sighed. "It was such a beautiful wedding."

He nodded. "Yes, it was."

After they had both stared out the window for much longer than necessary, he glanced over at her, an eyebrow raised. "I was wondering... after you're done here, you would like to join me? Or I would be more than happy to wait here with you. Keep you company."

This resulted in another long stretch of silence between them. Again, not the response Jack had been hoping for. In fact, he was beginning to think this had to be the longest moment of his life.

He also wasn't stupid. He knew a losing situation when he saw one.

So, when she finally turned to him, her face scrunched up in a frown, he knew what her answer would be. "Oh, Jack... I'm sorry, I can't. I took another nurse's shift today. At the rate this line is moving, I'm wondering if I'll even make it to the hospital on time."

He nodded, trying to hide his disappointment. "I understand." Then, after a slight hesitation, he decided to give it one more shot. "I just thought after the wedding, well... it was a fun, wasn't it?"

She nodded vigorously. "Yes, it was."

Encouraged by her answer, this prompted him to say more. "Yeah, so I thought it would be nice to get together again. Dinner, coffee, whatever..."

He shrugged. "If not now, maybe another time..."

She nodded again. "Yes, maybe."

And now he had no clue what to say. This had him backing away as he began fumbling with his jacket zipper, which suddenly refused to work. Barely suppressing his groan, he gave it a hard jerk. This had him almost hitting himself in the chin. Now thoroughly embarrassed, and wanting to be anywhere else, he pulled his keys out of his pocket. Only to drop them on the floor.

He scooped them up before sending Stephanie a brief nod. And what he hoped resembled a smile. "Yeah, so good luck here. Hope you don't have to wait too much longer. Take care..."

He was across the room and out the door before she even a chance to say goodbye.

A loud snort came from behind her.

She slowly turned around.

His arms crossed, the annoying man was shaking his head.

Jamming her hands deeper in her pockets, she narrowed her eyes at him. "Yes? Is there something you'd like to say?"

Again, this wasn't something she would do, confront someone she didn't know. Especially in public and surrounded by strangers. But the way her day was going, nothing was surprising at this point.

He kept shaking his head. "Real nice. Just shoot the guy down. Would it have hurt to give him a few minutes? How many people offer to wait in line with you at the license bureau, of all places? A big fat zero, I believe. Instead, you embarrassed him in front of everyone."

Stephanie glanced at everyone around her, only to have them turning away, feigning ignorance. Except for the woman in front of her. She nodded, her dangling shoulder length pineapple earrings bobbing up and down in agreement. "Yeah, I would have no problem going for coffee with him. He was cutie."

She glanced over at the windows. "Look, he's backing his truck up right now. Looks like it's loaded, a great ride."

She winked over at Stephanie. "I'm referring to the truck, of course."

This had everyone turning around, craning their necks to take in the shiny black Ford pickup truck slowly passing by the window. Then they all turned back to her, disapproval in their gaze.

Her cheeks burning with embarrassment, Stephanie closed her eyes.

This can't be happening. Could this day get any worse?

She pressed her lips together and turned her back on the man behind her. She then stared straight ahead, zeroing in on the pot of daisies setting on the counter.

Just ignore them. You don't know any of these people. And what are the chances you'll ever run into any of them again?

Forty-five minutes later, she was running through the rain to her car. Then it was off in a race to get to the hospital, where she arrived for her shift with two minutes to spare. Her usual smile in place, no one even had a clue how terrible her day had been so far.

Nope, she was the same positive and laid-back Steffi they had all come to expect.

But only about an hour into her shift, after she had knocked over a full cup of coffee in the staff lounge and called one of her patients by the wrong name, she made her escape to the women's lounge.

She took out her phone to send a text.

She needed to talk to Jason.

> Glad you're home. Hey, can we meet sometime tomorrow? Café Latte? I need to talk to you. I have the day off. Let me know what time works for you. xoxo

She slipped the phone back in her pocket. As she left the lounge, there was a determined look on her face.

It was time to make a change in her life.

And, yes… she was serious this time.

CHAPTER 3

Once in a lifetime,
you meet someone who changes everything.
~ Anonymous

J ason Bennett finished the call he was on. After he shoved his phone in his pocket, he sauntered down the hall and into Darcey's office.

A slow smile spread across her face when she glanced up from her computer and saw him.

For a long moment, they fell into each other's gaze. Then, with a smile to match hers, he strolled his way over to her desk. Bracing himself with his hands, he leaned across the desk to give her a lingering kiss.

He was smiling as he reluctantly pulled away, his voice wrapping around her like a hug. "Hey gorgeous, I hope you don't mind my stopping by, but I needed this moment. It's been a crazy morning. I also wanted to say hi to my favorite wife before I headed over to the studio."

She smiled up at him. "*Hmm...* your favorite, huh? Well, if this is true, you can stop by whenever you want."

The look she was giving him had sent his mind scrambling, trying to think if there was any way he could get out of the recording session he was due at in less than a half-hour. He hadn't been exaggerating when he said the morning had been hectic. And he could think of nothing that would make things better than to spend time with her.

But he knew this wasn't about to happen.

He reached over to tuck a stray curl behind her ear, his fingers trailing down her cheek in a soft caress. "I shouldn't be too late. The job shouldn't take long. Of course, this all depends if everyone is ready to go. If they are, it should be an easy wrap."

After leaning in for another kiss, he tilted his head, his look suddenly pensive. "Have you talked to Steffi since your dinner with the girls last night? I know you said she left early because she wasn't feeling well."

Darcey shook her head. "Only through a text. She claimed she was fine, but wanted to know if I might have found her wallet on the table. She thought she put it in her pocket, but when she checked this morning, it wasn't there. I hope she found it."

Jason frowned. "No such luck, I guess. Jack told me he ran into her a little while ago at the license bureau. She was there to get a new one. He said she seemed sort of frazzled, not her usual self."

He sighed. "Not long after I talked to him, I got a text from Stephanie. She wants to meet at Café Latte tomorrow. She said she needs to talk to me."

His hands jammed in his pockets, he walked over to the window. For a few moments, he was silent, staring out at the rain drenched courtyard.

He turned back to Darcey, his brow creased with worry. "She seemed like her usual self at the wedding. I wonder what's going on?"

He frowned. "This better not have anything to do with that doctor... Noah, or whatever the hell his name is. I don't understand why she is so infatuated with him. He's left her hanging so many times."

Darcey had left her desk and leaning against him, she rested her head on his shoulder. "She's said nothing about him to me." She smiled up at him. "I think it's wonderful how close the two of you are.

Over the past couple of years, I've hardly talked to my brother, let alone seen him."

A smile suddenly lit up her face. "I'm so glad he flew in for the wedding with Alicia. Even though they have only been dating for about five months, they seemed pretty serious. Don't you think?"

Then she frowned. "But, my father? I'm still not happy about him and June not having a real wedding."

Jason wrapped his arm around her, pressing a kiss to the top of her head. "*Ah...* yes, I know. You're not happy they got married without telling anyone. But this is what they both wanted."

She tilted her head up at him, skeptical. "Oh? And how do you know this?"

He shrugged. "Your father and I talked for a long time. He told me they want to keep everything low key for a while. Then they plan to have a small reception in the fall."

He grinned down at her. "And, yes... we will be invited."

She leaned her head back to look up at him. "Wow... and here I was so worried about the two of you not getting along."

"It's all good, gorgeous." He framed her face in his hands, and after giving her another lingering kiss, he sighed. "I'd rather not, but I should get going. I'll see you later, okay?"

She grinned. "Okay, and after dinner tonight? We should get a start on all those thank-you notes we need to write."

He groaned. "I've got an idea. Instead, let's break the rules and send out a mass thank you email. This way, we'll get it done in record time."

Her horrified expression made him laugh. "I'm kidding, gorgeous. I've been around more than my share of weddings to know better."

At the door, he turned to blow her a kiss, mouthing the words I love you. After giving her a smile, one she knew he saved for only her, he left her office.

Back at her desk, she started thinking about Stephanie. She had surprised everyone when she left the restaurant during dinner last night. But in the text about her missing wallet, she said she was fine, coming across as the cheerful Stephanie they all knew.

Darcey glanced down at her watch. She was working on her report for the weekly meeting tomorrow morning with Elenore Cromley, the new owner of The Regency. After she finished, her plan was to stop by the studio to surprise Jason.

She rested her chin in her hand, thinking about how much she loved watching him at work. But this wasn't going to happen if she didn't stop thinking about him and get back to work.

After she refreshed her computer screen to check what she had so far, she groaned, dragging her hand through her hair. She had forgotten all about Elenore's request for new brochures. According to her, it was time to shelve the run-of-the-mill pamphlet they had put up with for so many years. She wanted to add a touch of class, keep up with the times.

She checked the time. If she wanted to surprise Jason, she needed to get some work done.

Starting now.

A short while later, she was holding the printed copy of the report in her hand.

Yes, printed copies were what Elenore insisted on for all office related business dealings. She claimed staring at a computer screen, day after day, was what had caused a decline in her vision over the past few years.

Darcey shut off her computer, and locking her office door, she left The Regency.

She couldn't wait to surprise Jason.

CHAPTER 4

"**L**adies and gentlemen, this is your captain speaking. Welcome to Cleveland. The local time is six-twenty-four, light rain is falling, and the temperature is at fifty-four degrees. A chilly day for the start of May in Cleveland."

"For your own safety and the safety of those around you, please remain seated until the 'Fasten Seat Belt' sign shows it is safe to stand. Also, since articles may have shifted during flight, please use caution when opening the overhead compartments. Have a safe trip home, and we look forward to again doing business with you in the future."

Evan Marshall watched his fellow passengers in a mad rush to exit the plane.

He wasn't feeling the same urgency. After all, there was no one waiting to meet him.

Nope... the only thing you have to look forward to is your empty condo.

There was one person who might care he was back. This would be Joe Nicholson, his partner in crime in the world of freelance photography. They had been friends since Evan took a job with the same newspaper Joe had worked for the past fifteen years.

When Evan was offered a freelance assignment for a travel magazine shoot in New Zealand, it was Joe who encouraged him to take the job. He was quick to point out, not only was he too talented to stay on at the local paper, a change of scenery would do him good.

He needed to stop feeling sorry for himself. It was time he got off the pity train he was on and joined the living again.

After all, it wasn't all about him.

He also had a lot more to say, but this about summed it up.

This had made Evan furious, their resulting argument almost developing into a full-blown fistfight. But after another setback, his life again feeling like it was spiraling out of control, Evan accepted the job.

Like Joe, he had joined the world of freelance photography.

And how was that working out for him? As of now, he had no new job prospects, and the few inquiries he'd sent out were still unanswered.

So, he had no idea what was going to happen next.

But as much as he hated to admit, especially to Joe, he was thankful for the push he gave him. Not only had his time in New Zealand been the experience of a lifetime, he had been busy twenty-four-seven. So, this gave him very little time to think about anything else.

This included Kelsie. The overwhelming grief that came upon him when she took over his thoughts had begun to lessen. And his memories were now easier to bear, bringing almost as many smiles as tears.

He glanced around to see the plane was now almost empty. About to leave his seat, he had to wait for a woman to pass by. Loaded down with more bags than should have been allowed, her long blonde hair nudged his memory, an image of Stephanie popping up in his mind.

But then… *Poof.* It disappeared.

But why does this surprise you? After all, she has no reason to be there.

He hadn't seen or talked to her in over six months. So much could have changed by now. She could be engaged or even married.

This possibility had him angrily hauling himself out of his seat and grabbing his bag from the overhead bin. After nodding his thanks to the flight attendant, he made his way to the baggage claims. There he saw the same long blonde-haired woman also waiting to claim her luggage.

Damn if this didn't have Stephanie invading his thoughts again. But this time, her image hung around.

Closing his eyes, he gave in and let the memories play.

Stephanie… what is it about her? Why can't you seem to let her go?

Yeah, her friends called her Steffi. But for him, she would always be Stephanie. He had decided this the moment she first told him her name. There had been no short cuts involved when God made her. She was perfect in every way. So Stephanie was only fitting.

It was when he arrived early to photograph the Grand Ballroom on the night of the Masquerade Ball that he first saw her. His mind trying to grasp she was real and not a figment of his imagination, he'd watched as she appeared to float from table to table, adding programs to each place setting. Her pale blond hair had shimmered like spun gold in the candlelight.

She had him spellbound.

When she had turned, their eyes meeting, the connection had been instantaneous. And from that moment on, very move, every word they shared became a permanent memory in his mind.

He liked to think she had been sent to rescue him. A beacon of light in the darkness he had been struggling so hard to leave behind.

It was a night that changed his life forever. And now, with New Zealand behind him, he'd swear she kept showing up in his mind, more than she had before.

Like now.

Watching the suitcases bounce their way past him on the luggage carousel, he thought about the last time he saw her. Not even twenty-four hours after the night of the masquerade ball, he decided to surprise her while she was working her shift at the hospital. Holding a bouquet of roses and a box with a chocolate brownie, from what she'd told him was her favorite bakery, he had stepped off the elevator to the third floor of the hospital.

He saw her right away.

She was talking to a man, his white coat indicating he was a doctor. Waiting for them to finish their conversation, he had watched as the man whispered something in her ear. But it was when he caressed her cheek with his fingertips, this intimacy between them had been enough for Evan to know it was over.

He didn't have a chance.

It wasn't until someone had reached around him to hit the button to hold the door open, he slipped back into the elevator. He glanced over seconds later to see Stephanie was no longer there.

He didn't remember the ride down to the main floor. And he only vaguely recalled the confused expression on the woman's face at the registration desk when he handed her the flowers and bakery box. After mumbling some lame excuse about allergies, he'd practically ran out of the building.

The next day, he decided Joe was right. He needed to clear his mind, find a better way to deal with what life had handed him. And to do this, he needed to get away... the further, the better. So, this is why he'd accepted the job in New Zealand.

But things don't always work out the way you think they will. Because here he was, back on familiar ground, slipping right back into the life he'd hoped to leave behind.

Why did you even think you were ready to move on?

He almost missed his bag, just barely managing to drag it off the carousel before it passed by. Then he was off to join the long line for the next available taxi.

The blonde haired woman had disappeared, nowhere to be seen.

He hoped this wasn't a premonition of what was to come.

Forty-five minutes later, he was unlocking the door to his condo.

After he dropped his bag to the floor and turned on the light, he gazed slowly around the room. Comforted by the familiarity of home, as simple as it was, he felt his whole body relax in a long sigh.

There was a bottle of wine on the dining room table. This was accompanied by a note. The almost impossible to read handwriting, more like a scribble, told him it was from Joe.

Welcome home. There's a pot roast from Beth in the fridge. Call me after you get caught up with your sleep. I might have a lead on a job for you.
Enjoy the vino, Joe

23

He took the pot roast out of the refrigerator, knowing he was in for a treat. It was a well-known fact Joe's wife Beth was one of the best cooks on this side of town. After he put the pan in the oven and hit the timer, he headed for the shower.

It was after midnight when he finally fell into bed. He thought about Joe's mention of a job. And for the first time in a long while, he found he was looking forward to what it wa about.

But this was as far as his thinking went before he fell into an exhausted sleep.

Remember, he was still on New Zealand time.

CHAPTER 5

Sometimes it's easy to love.
Sometimes it's difficult.
But at the end of the day, it's always a choice.
~Anonymous

A cross town, Jake Martin was jerked out of a sound sleep.
An unfamiliar sound filtering through his semi-conscious state, he tensed, staring into the darkness.

Something wasn't right.

Lifting his head from the pillow, he squinted over at the clock on the nightstand to see it read two-forty-eight.

This was when he realized the whimpering sound that woke him?

It was coming from Gracie.

Pressed up against him, the fabric of his tee-shirt clutched in her hands, she had burrowed her head underneath his arm as if she was trying to hide.

She pushed even harder against him, her words coming out in a muffled sob. "No, no, no... you can't do this. You can't take her... please..."

Now he was wide awake.

What the hell? Take who?

Lifting his arm, he turned to frame her face with his hands. His voice was urgent, but soothing. "Peaches, wake up, baby. You're having another bad dream."

She stilled. He watched as her lashes fluttered open. Her eyes frantically searching his face, she began to cry, big gulping sobs. Then she tried to tell him something. But she wasn't making any sense.

He pulled her against him, his lips moving in her hair. "There, there... let it all out. Whatever it is, you're going to be okay. I'm here."

Even though the tone of his voice was calm, he was worried. This was the second night in a row she had jerked him out of a sound sleep because of one of these nightmares.

But last night's dream hadn't been as bad. After he'd kissed her awake, murmuring words of comfort as he held her in his arms, she had drifted right back to sleep.

He sighed, pressing another kiss into her hair. He would never get used to these nightmares she had. Usually triggered by a bad memory, they kept coming back to haunt her. And no matter how many times he told her nothing she shared about her past would change the way he felt about her, she refused to let him in. A closed look coming over her face, she would change the subject.

So, he was powerless, only able to give as much love as she was willing to accept.

But these last two nights, the nightmares were different. There was something deeper going on, something she wasn't telling him. Something terrified her. Not only could he see this, he could feel it.

When she became still against him, his murmur fell right below her ear. "What's going on, baby? Tell me. Whatever it is, I'll do what I can to make it better."

This set her off all over again, the tears flowing afresh. But this time, at least he understood some of what she was trying to say. "Oh, Jake... I don't think you can. I'm so scared. I received a notice from the adoption agency. Bella's father is filing for total custody. He claims he's turned his life around and is ready to be her father again."

She took a big gulping breath, her hands gripping his shirt even tighter. "He tried to do this once before, but failed. According to the social worker, this time he's been able to gather a lot of support. From his employer, neighbors, family… the list goes on and on."

Her voice hardened. "I'm sure some of his contacts are part of this list. The people who owe him favors. They have a lot of experience at putting up a good front, while hiding what is really going on."

She began crying again. "Oh, Jake… even the social worker told me how worried she is. I can't let him take Bella. I know what will happen. And it won't be good."

Jake was having a hard time. He didn't understand. The thought of losing his little Bella-bee, this the nickname he'd given her, was something he thought they would never again have to worry about.

My God, with all the red tape and interviews you and Gracie went through to get the adoption finalized, how is this even possible?

Then his confusion turned to anger, followed by a sudden determination. This was not going to happen.

Not if he could help it.

He pulled Gracie closer, his words a solemn vow. "Peaches, I promise you, no one is going to take Bella away from us. No matter what it takes, we will settle this once and for all. We are a family, and we're going to stay a family."

Her eyes searching his, trying so hard to believe him, had her shaking her head. "But he's her father. This holds so much weight in the adoption process. They always give parents top consideration."

He didn't respond. This had her bottom lip quivering, bringing on more tears. "Oh, God… I'm so sorry. You don't deserve this. I've already brought so much pain into your life as it is."

He shifted, so that he was gazing into her face. There was a huskiness in his voice. "Peaches, look at me. You and Bella are everything to me. What you brought into my life is more love than I ever thought I'd have. I love you. I love Bella. And I will fight with everything I have to keep the three of us together. We'll get the best lawyers and do whatever is needed to stop this once and for all. Okay?"

She let out a long, trembling sigh before she nodded. Then she gazed up at him, her words brushing across his face. "I love you, Jake Martin. You are my rock. I still don't understand how you can love me, too." Her next words were barely audible. "It's just that I'm so afraid with the mess I've made of my life, having a baby with you is something that will never happen. And if we lose Bella..."

She closed her eyes, shaking her head. "This isn't fair to you."

He gathered her even closer. "Peaches, it's in God's hands. With his help, we'll work this out. I know we will."

Lulled by the soothing sound of his voice, his hand gently sifting through her hair, she was finding it hard to keep her eyes open. Over the past two days, the all-consuming fear of losing Bella had taken over her life. Sleep was impossible, any she got interrupted by bad dreams. Leaving her so damn tired.

She hadn't planned on telling Jake about Bella, not until she received more information from the social worker. With his restaurant experiencing one of its busiest months, for Jake, this made for long days. When he came home, he needed a night of uninterrupted sleep.

Like, now... he shouldn't have to worry about you all the time.

She reached up to give him a kiss. "I'm sorry. Go back to sleep. I'll be fine now." Curling up against him, she closed her eyes and within minutes, her even breathing told him she had fallen asleep.

But for Jake, sleep didn't come easy. Staring into the darkness, his mind wouldn't let go of what Gracie told him.

So, it was a long time before, exhausted, he also fell asleep.

And this time, he was the one plagued by bad dreams.

The blaring beep of the alarm clock had Jake searching for the snooze button. After almost knocking both the lamp and the clock off the nightstand, he finally put an end to the annoying sound.

The time was seven-forty-five, the numbers a bright red glow in the pale morning light.

He gazed down at Gracie. Curled up against him, her hand clutching his arm even in sleep, she didn't move an inch.

"I love you, peaches." When she only burrowed deeper into the blankets in response to his whisper, he placed a soft kiss on her cheek. Carefully maneuvering his way off the bed, he shut the bedroom door behind him and padded down the hall to the kitchen.

He switched on the coffeemaker. Leaning against the counter, he dragged his hands back through his hair and gave an enormous yawn.

For the next few minutes, mesmerized by the comforting sound of the coffee perking, he tried to wake up.

He felt like he had been hit by a truck. Since he hadn't slept well, his hope was the coffee would remedy this. He had a full day ahead of him.

This began with his usual early morning trip to the farmer's market for fresh produce. Then he had a late morning appointment with a new wine distributor. The woman who handled all the desserts for the restaurant had also promised to stop by in the afternoon with her newest creations.

First things first. He picked up his phone from the counter. He needed to send Sam Bridges a text. As one of his long-time friends, he'd swear Sam knew almost everyone in town. Even if he didn't know of a lawyer experienced in custody cases, he'd be able to recommend someone who did.

His first impulse had been to call Joel Kennedy, his friend and co-owner of Jake's Place. Since he had just passed the bar, he might be of some help. But he didn't want to bother him since he and Amber, his assistant chef, had finally given in to his insistence they take some time off. Only yesterday, they had returned after a two-week trip to Florida with Amber's two kids.

He smiled, thinking about Joel and Amber. If there was ever a perfect match, they had nailed it on all counts. He sensed there was an engagement in their near future.

The text sent, he began scrolling through his messages, his fingers crossed there were no additional problems waiting for him at the restaurant.

"Daddy?"

He glanced up from his phone to see Bella standing by the entrance to the room, her stuffed rabbit clutched in her arms. She sent him a big smile.

Setting his phone on the counter, he held out his arms.

She came running across the room, and after he scooped her up in a hug, he planted a big kiss on her cheek.

He was smiling as he brushed the hair back from her face. "Hey, sweet Bella-bee, what are you doing up so early?"

Snuggling in even closer, she gazed up at him. Her brows scrunching up in concentration, she shook her head. "I don't know."

She held up her stuffed rabbit. "Maybe Bunny woke me up?"

His expression just as serious, he nodded. "You know what? I bet he did. *Hmm...* maybe he's hungry?"

He held the rabbit up to his ear. "Let's see what he has to say."

With Bella's gaze fixed on his face, her eyes huge, he didn't move. Then, after nodding once or twice, he handed her the rabbit.

He gave another nod. "Ah... just as I suspected. He wants his breakfast."

He watched Bella laugh as she gave the bunny a big hug. And this is when he decided it was time to make some changes in his life. He wanted to spend more time with her and Gracie.

And there was no reason he couldn't start now.

Since Amber was back in town, and the workaholic she was, he would ask her to take over the morning trip to the market. Wasn't she always insisting she could do a better job at this? Well, today would be her chance to prove her claim.

Still holding Bella, he began walking out of the kitchen. "I have an idea... how would you like to make a trip with me to the bakery down the street? We'll pick out something for breakfast, surprise mommy. Does this sound like a good idea to you?"

Her eyes growing big with excitement, she nodded. "Can I get a donut? With sprinkles?"

He smiled. "I think we might be able to swing that."

Grinning from ear to ear, she wrapped her arms around him and planted a big kiss on his cheek. "I love you, daddy."

Jake wasn't one to cry. But this was one of those moments he came pretty close.

His resolve was now stronger than ever.

Give up Bella?

Never.

CHAPTER 6

J oe Nicholson was sitting in his car in the Café Latte parking lot. Since he wasn't due to meet Evan for another twenty minutes, he thought he'd call into the office before making the trek into the cafe.

Frustrated beyond all get out, he sighed, running his hand through his hair.

He needed to vent. Big time…

This latest assignment he was on? It was really testing his patience.

Why was it every single damn celebrity he'd ever worked with— this numbering about a dozen—had this I'm-more-important-and-you-better-not-forget-it kind of mindset?

Well, he had news for them.

They weren't. Not by a long shot.

Nope, all that glitz and glamour? You want no part of it… they can keep it.

And now, after spending the last ten minutes trying to explain this to Susan, the society page's head editor, he realized complaining wasn't going to do him a damn bit of good. The story, including his photos, were to be featured in next Sunday's edition of the paper.

No excuses. And the photos better be good.

Of course, she had to remind him no one forced him to take this job. He should be happy. He was getting paid almost triple for this shoot. There was also the recognition the job could bring him.

Again, this was only if the photos were acceptable.

He rested his head back against the seat and closed his eyes. "Yeah, I hear you. And, yeah… I know it's a great opportunity, fantastic money. But you know I don't usually take on this kind of job. I'm at my best when I'm working on genuine stories. Stories about real people. Stories that can change people's minds, and make them look beyond the bubble they're living in. I have no desire to chase after some hotshot celebrity who has graced us with her presence while filming some low-budget movie here in Cleveland, mind you."

When Susan started right in again, repeating almost word for word what she had already said, he zoned out, his mind wandering.

He wondered… who had been the one to decide it would be a great idea to get phone calls in your car?

Well, whoever it was? They were dead wrong. Driving was and should be the only activity of the person in the driver's seat. Weren't there enough distractions in life without adding a phone to the mix?

Closing his eyes, he shook his head.

Damn… he missed the days when he first started working. That feeling of relief when he made his escape to the privacy of his van after a long day. Hoping to shut out the rest of the world, he'd slide in his favorite CD and crank up the volume almost as loud as it could go. Maybe even sing along. Or he'd simply sit back and enjoy the solitude. No need to answer to anyone.

But now? He swore people called just to call. To let you know every damn thing that happened in their life. Where they were, what they were doing, who they were with.

Blah, blah, blah…

Then they felt the need to take a photo to back it all up and prove their point.

Yep, these days he'd swear he spent more time on his damn phone than he did taking photos.

Like now…

This had him ending the call and heading for the café.

He could really use that cup of coffee.

Ten minutes later, Evan walked into Café Latte.

After spotting Joe sitting at the table in the far corner, he sent him a wave. Then he put in his order at the counter.

As he waited for his coffee, he gazed around the small cafe. From what he could see, nothing much had changed.

He averted his gaze from the display case filled with homemade pastries the café was known for. He didn't want to know if they still had the giant peanut butter cookies that were Kelsie's favorite.

Closing his eyes, he let out a long, steadying breath. Kelsie had loved anything peanut butter. Cookies, cakes, pies, candy... you name it. She had even insisted on a peanut butter wedding cake.

He smiled at the memory. He hoped there was an unending supply of peanut butter up in heaven. And if there wasn't? He'd be willing to bet Kelsie would make that happen.

He was still smiling as he set his cup on the table where Joe was sitting. Settling in the chair across from him, he sent him a big grin. "Hey, long time no see."

"Back-at-cha. It's good to see the smile on your face."

Leaning back in his chair and stretching out his legs, Evan nodded. "Yeah... coming here brought back a lot of great memories." He sent another glance around the room before he slowly shook his head. "I wasn't sure how I would feel..."

Relieved, Joe nodded. "Great memories, that's what I like to hear." He studied Evan more closely. "I was wondering if you were even coming back. How did it go? Everything good? You're good?"

After a long drink of coffee, Evan shrugged. "Yeah, I guess. Everyone seemed happy with the outcome. A learning experience, for sure. We were on the move every day, so it was almost too easy to get the results I did."

Joe gave a slow nod. "*Sooooo*... I take it this means you're glad I convinced you to go?"

He hesitated, studying Evan for a few seconds before he continued. "Did you get that new outlook on life? Put some of the past at rest?"

Evan's mouth twisted in a wry smile. "I can't believe I'm about to say this, but yes, you were right. Now I finally feel more like myself, ready to take on each day. Some memories won't ever go away, but now I can at least look back and smile most of the time."

A look of relief flashed across Joe's face. "Good. That's great. Mission accomplished then."

He leaned more comfortably back in his chair. "Before I forget, Beth wants to know if you can come for dinner Friday night. She wants to hear all about your trip. She meant to ask you when you called to thank her for the pot roast."

He smiled, shaking his head. "I swear, she has become a whirlwind in the kitchen, cooking up a storm. Now in her fourth month, she's always hungry. Which is fine with me."

He patted his stomach. "But at this rate, it won't be long before I'm bigger than she is."

"Yeah, sure, Friday is good. I have nothing going on." Evan chuckled. "I thought it was strange when she randomly asked me if I like ribs, but didn't expand on that. Thought maybe she was just hungry or something. Again, when is the baby due?"

"Late October. I swear, she's started worrying about everything. Her biggest concern right now? She's afraid the baby might decide to make an appearance on Halloween. Me? I couldn't care less when it happens, as long as we get a healthy baby in the end."

He held up his hand. "And, no... before you even ask, we didn't find out the sex. We want to be surprised. I can't tell you how many times we've been asked this."

Evan was shaking his head. "I'm still trying to imagine you as a dad."

Joe chuckled. "Yeah, same here. But I'm sure I'm not the first guy to think this."

He sent Evan a sly glance. "So, what about you? Any New Zealand beauties catch your interest while you were there? You can't tell me it was all work and no play. And even if you try, I'll have a hard time believing you."

After another drink of his coffee, Evan shook his head. "Nope. Just wasn't into that."

He shrugged. "Not ready yet, I guess."

Joe's answer to this was a big grin. "Well, a warning here... Melody in human resources has been asking about you. She wanted to know when you were coming back. I think she's planning to ask you to be her date for the annual Cleveland's Elite banquet next Wednesday night. An event you better mark on your calendar and plan to attend, since you are now looking at one of the chosen elite who's up for an award."

He nodded at Evan's raised eyebrow. "Yep, they nominated me for the photos I did for the article in the Cleveland Here and Now magazine."

Evan held up his hand for a high five. "Congratulations. I'm impressed. But not surprised. You're more talented than you give yourself credit for. And Melody? Sorry, I'm sure she has her good points, but I can't get past her type A personality. She's exhausting. Everything about her runs at high speed."

He sat straight up in the chair, his gaze glued to the entrance of the café. "*Whoa... it can't be...*"

After Joe turned to see what caught Evan's attention, he glanced back at him. His head tilted, he searched his face. "What's up? See someone you know? Is it the blonde? The one who just walked in?"

Evan looked right at him, but Joe would be willing to bet he didn't see him. He looked like he was in a trance. Reaching over, he slapped his hand down on the table in front of him. "Hey, pay attention... what's up?"

Startled, Evan made a grab for his cup. After taking a big gulp of coffee, he shrugged. "Nothing, not a thing. For a second, I thought I saw someone... I mean something." He shook his head. "But it turns out I was wrong."

Now Joe wasn't stupid. Something? It was more like someone had set off this reaction in Evan. And ninety-nine percent of the time, and again he'd be willing to bet on this, the someone turned out to be a woman.

So why should this time be any different?

He looks like he just saw a ghost, for God's sake.

After he sent another glance over at the customers in line for their coffee, he turned back to Evan. "Is it Jason Bennett's sister? The blonde? Do you know her?"

"Uh, who?" Avoiding Joe's gaze, Evan's attention was now centered on his coffee cup. He began inspecting the Café Latte logo printed on the side of the cup as if it was, by far, the most interesting design he had ever seen.

Watching him, Joe groaned. "Come on, you know who I'm talking about. Jason Bennett, the musician. The band leader of the group, Banded Together. That's his sister who just walked in. I think her name is Steffi. Do—"

Evan's head jerked up. His expression almost threatening, he cut him off. "Stephanie... her name is Stephanie. Not Steffi."

Joe leaned back in his chair, sending him a wary glance. "Yeah... okay, then. Steffi... Stephanie... whatever you want to call her. I take it this means you know her?"

"Maybe." After this one-word answer, Evan sent another glance over at the crowded counter. Then he picked up his cup and finished off the rest of his coffee. Pushing away from the table, he started to stand. "I should get going. I've got a lot of things to do and..."

Joe jumped out of his chair, his hand going to his shoulder to stop him. "Hey... sit."

Evan opened his mouth. To then shut it, shaking his head.

Joe pointed to the chair. "I mean it. Sit."

Sinking down into the chair, Evan closed his eyes.

This was followed by a long silence. Finally, Joe cleared his throat. "Do you want to tell me what's going on?"

He waited.

After another silence, Evan began to talk.

Without a lot of detail, because this was just the way he was, he told Jason about Stephanie... from when they first met the night of the Masquerade Ball and ending when he made a surprise visit to where she worked. Only to find her practically in the arms of another man.

A wry smile on his face, he glanced over at Joe. "Some surprise, huh? Instead, the joke was on me."

Joe shook his head. "*Ah...* not what a guy wants to see. But now I get why you were so eager to get out of town."

He shrugged. "I can't say I don't blame you for taking off. I would have done the same thing."

Evan shook his head. "I thought she was different… maybe the one to give me a reason to join the living again."

He stared into space, a smile spreading across his lips. "That night, after the ball ended, determined not to let her out of my sight, I asked her to go to this wine bar with me. We talked about everything. Even after the wine bar closed, we sat in my car in the parking lot, still talking. Neither one of us wanted the night to end. The sun was about to come up when we finally parted. This is when I made the promise to call her."

He groaned, dragging his hand through his hair. "The second promise I made to her. Only to break it again. I'm such a jerk."

Joe cleared his throat, his intention to contradict him on this. But Evan was on a roll. After keeping this bottled up inside for so long, nothing was going to stop him from letting it all out.

He stared down at his cup, shaking his head. "Then when I saw Stephanie with this other guy, it suddenly all felt so wrong, like I was cheating on Kelsie. I guess I still wasn't ready to let her go."

Joe was quiet. And a little uncomfortable.

He would be the first to tell you, he was a cut and dried kind of guy. No frills. Definitely not. He was also bad with any kind of discussion dealing with love or any of that relationship stuff. The whole idea of this was enough to make him cringe.

But somehow, in the short time he had known Evan, he'd unofficially taken him on as his own special project.

The kid had needed help. Big time.

At thirty, he was far from a child. But the little information he volunteered gave Joe the impression his childhood hadn't been good. And his family? He ignored any mention of this, only to volunteer he had been on his own most of his life.

This was until he met Kelsie. She had been his saving grace, his reason for living. To then lose her so suddenly and so tragically? This had been almost more than a person could expect to endure. For months after, he had struggled through one day at a time, his only goal to survive.

As he studied him, Joe again felt the need to help him. He cleared his throat. "So, you basically turned into one of those guys who say they're going to call, yet never does. Leaving the poor girl wondering what happened. Not what I would expect from you."

When Evan didn't respond, his gaze fixed on his cup, Joe nodded. "Hey, I'm not one to take the woman's side, not when a friend is involved, but did you ever think you may have misread the situation?"

Still refusing to meet his gaze, Evan began tapping the cup on the table.

Joe grabbed the cup and set it out of his reach. After he sent another glance over at Stephanie, he groaned, dragging his hand down over his jaw. "And seriously? Take another look at her. The woman is gorgeous. That being said, with this life-changing moment you claim the two of you had, why are you still sitting here with me? You need to go after her."

"I don't have to look at her." An exasperated sigh coming from him, Evan pointed to his forehead. "As crazy as this may sound, I have every single feature of her engraved right here. Believe me, it's a constant reminder of how stupid I was."

"I don't get it. Then why aren't you making your move?"

Evan's silence had Joe taking it one step further. "*Ah...* I see. It's still about Kelsie, isn't it?"

His head jerking up, Evan shot him a warning glance.

But Joe refused to back down, meeting his gaze head on. "You told me you've finally come to terms with what happened. So, it's time you move on. You know damn well Kelsie wouldn't want you to put the rest of your life on hold because she's gone."

Evan briefly closed his eyes. "I know. But what if —"

Joe cut him off. "There are no guarantees in life. But you can't let this stop you from going after what you want. You get knocked down, you get back up. Then you move on. You keep doing this and one day, everything will fall into place."

About to add more, he hesitated.

Evan raised an eyebrow, the ghost of a smile touching his lips. "What? You're on a roll, so go ahead... say it."

Joe grinned. "I haven't steered you wrong yet, have I?" Then his expression turned serious. "Remember that day you refused to take a photo of that girl in the hospital? After you told me why and left my office, I sat there for a long time, thinking about Kelsie and her brother. How life can change in the blink of an eye. That same night, I asked Beth to marry me. And look at us now... we're about to have a kid. All because I took a chance."

His smile growing, Evan shook his head. "At least something good came out of what happened."

"Yeah, you gave me the push I needed." Uncomfortable with this share your feelings kind of conversation, Joe sent a glance around the room. "*Hmm*... it looks like Steffi... excuse me, I mean Stephanie... is here to meet her brother. He just walked in."

He looked over at Evan, an eyebrow raised. "This could be your chance. It's a beautiful spring day. And you know what they say... this is when a young man's fancy turns to thoughts of love."

Evan burst out laughing. "What? A young man's fancy? Where did you get that from?"

Joe shrugged, embarrassed. "Hell, I don't know. I read it some-where. Think of this as goodbye heartbreak, hello May. Sort of like an update to an old saying. Whatever it takes you to make your move."

Evan was shaking his head. "*Whoa*... not so fast. I'm not going to go charging over there, only to make a fool of myself. I need to think this through." He leaned back in his chair. "In the meantime, you can fill me in on this job you hinted at. If I'm going to start taking chances, I'll need some back up... starting with a job." He shrugged. "I can't, as you would say, make my move until I at least have something to offer, right?"

Joe was well aware of the furtive glances Evan was sending over at Stephanie. The look on his face said it all. He shook his head. "I think you're stalling."

Evan shook his head. "Nope, just cautious. I don't want to make any more mistakes."

Joe grinned. The kid was in deep. Which meant he was going to need his advice. And he had the perfect person to help him with this.

When he got home, he was going to ask Beth what she thought.

She loved this kind of thing.

CHAPTER 7

She thought he was the one for her.
But it turned out she wasn't the one for him.
~ Anonymously Yours

Café Latte was having a good day, almost every space in the parking lot was taken. Once Stephanie parked her car, she checked for Jason's SUV. Even though it looked like he hadn't arrived yet, she decided to wait for him inside.

Within minutes, she was holding a tray with two cups of coffee, a strawberry muffin for her, and a cinnamon and raisin bagel for Jason. Snagging the last table, she pulled out her phone to check if Jason had left a message he'd be late.

Nope, no message.

But there was a call from a number she didn't recognize. She checked her contact list to see it was from Jack.

He had also left a voicemail.

Jack? Why would Jack be calling you?

She was just about to listen to the voice mail when Jason plopped down in the chair next to her. He reached for a cup, holding it up to her in a salute. "Hey... here's looking at you, kid."

He said this using his best Humphrey Bogart impersonation. But even with all the talent he possessed, his attempt was a sad one.

It was pathetic, in fact.

Stephanie laughed. "Hey to you, too. Not to be mean, but that was pretty bad. I think you should stick to your singing."

Sending her an exaggerated frown, he reached for the bagel. "I take it this is for me?" At her nod, he began slathering it with butter. Raising the bagel to his mouth, ready to take a big bite, he paused at her look of disapproval.

He frowned. "What? I'm hungry. I've had nothing to eat since breakfast."

She shook her head. "The bagel is fine. It's all that butter you piled on. It's not fair you can eat like you do and still be in such good shape. If I did the same, I'd weigh a ton."

He raised an eyebrow. "Maybe you should… eat like me, that is." He peered more closely at her. "Because it looks like you've lost weight. Have you?"

He didn't want to sound too concerned, but he was finding this a little hard.

She looked exhausted, dark circles under her eyes. This, along with the baggy sweats she was wearing and her hair pulled back into a messy ponytail, didn't add up to the Stephanie he knew.

Avoiding his gaze, she shrugged. "Most of the time, I'm too busy to eat. And when I get home from work, I'm so exhausted, I'd rather sleep than eat."

His worried look had her jumping in to explain. "Lately, it's been so hectic on the floor because we've had so much going on. So, I never get to leave on time."

He opened his mouth to say something, but she cut him off. "It's not only me. All the staff has been busy."

Okay, maybe she was exaggerating a little. Maybe more like a lot, since their patient count was down right now. But this was for the best, since she was finding it so hard to concentrate, her mind drifting off to other things.

Like this latest thing with Noah…

But she wasn't going to tell Jason this. He would be on this in a second, piling all the blame on Noah.

And as much as you'd like to deny this, he would be right…

And when she wasn't working? When she got home from work, after eating a bowl of cereal—or whatever else she could heat in the microwave—she was more than content to settle on the sofa and watch old movies or re-runs on TV until she fell asleep.

Lately, she seemed to be sleeping there more than she did in her bed. It was easier.

She frowned.

This isn't normal. And this isn't you. You need to get out of this funk you're in. You're to the point you've probably seen almost every Hallmark movie ever made.

Jason had set his bagel back on the tray. He leaned back in his chair, frowning as he studied her. While she refused to look at him, fixated on the muffin she was crumbling with her fingers.

He nodded towards the muffin, or what was once a muffin. "You know those are to eat and not to play with, right?"

She didn't even give him a dirty look, only shrugged.

This meant it was time for him to get serious and find out what was wrong. As her big brother, this was his job.

After a fortifying gulp of coffee, he cleared his throat. "Hey, Steff… talk to me. Tell me what's going on. You haven't been yourself for the past few weeks. Even Jack noticed this. He told me he saw you yesterday?"

"Jack?" Then she nodded. "Oh, yeah… I ran into him at the license bureau. Well, it's more like he came over to say hi as he was leaving." A frown flitted across her face. "I need to apologize the next time I see him. I wasn't very nice. It wasn't one of my better days."

Before Jason could respond, she started right in about the drama of losing her wallet. How she had contacted everyone, her friends and even the restaurant, hoping someone had found it after she left.

But no such luck.

She then told him about the long line at the license bureau. Even including a detailed description of the annoying guy in line behind her and how he wouldn't stop whistling. All information was all delivered non-stop.

She had just launched into the list of credit cards she had to cancel when he reached over, pressing his fingers to her mouth. "Stop. All of that is fixable. I'm more concerned about you. I know from experience, when you babble on like this, something's wrong."

She frowned, while mumbling something about him being ridiculous... she didn't babble.

Trying not to smile, he leaned back in his chair, his arms crossed over his chest. "So... what's going on? Darcey told me you left dinner early last night because you weren't feeling well. Are you sick?"

For a moment, she only stared at him. Then, pushing the pile of crumbs aside, almost sending them flying off the table, she shook her head. "Sick? Yes, I guess you could say that. Yeah, I'm sick... sick of everything."

Watching as she began blinking to keep the tears from spilling over, he reached for his coffee and took another big gulp.

Uh, oh... you know you can't handle it when she cries.

Like every other man on the face of the earth, the sight of tears was enough to make him want to take off and run. Unless they were happy tears, something he knew was far from happening at the moment.

He frowned.

This better not have anything to do with that damn doctor.

He cleared his throat, the calm tone of his voice a contrast to the irritation he was feeling. "This isn't about your doctor friend, is it?"

Refusing to meet his gaze, she gave a faint nod.

He groaned, raking his hands back through his hair. "Steff, come on... this isn't like you. What is it with this guy that he has you so rattled? Falling in love has its trials—I, for one, know how this goes—but you shouldn't be so miserable. You both need to be on the same page."

He abruptly stared into space, a thoughtful expression on his face.

Stephanie dropped her head down in her hands. "Oh my God, you're not already composing a song in your head about this, are you? Because if you are, I swear, I'm leaving."

Proof of what she said, she made a grab for her phone.

He put his hand on her arm. "Stop. You're not going anywhere."

After she sank back into her chair, she sighed. A very long and dramatic sigh. Her natural blush now a darker shade of anger, she tossed her phone back on the table. "Don't treat me like a child. I'm not five."

He was quick to call her on this. "Well, you're sure acting like you are."

When she refused to comment, he leaned closer. "I assure you, I wasn't thinking about music…"

She glared at him. "No?"

"No." He shook his head. "But can I give you some advice? From a guy's perspective?"

She sighed. "I guess…."

"He's never going to change. Never No matter what you think. Proof of this is how he conveniently left out the part about being engaged. And if his fiancée hadn't come for a surprise visit, who knows if he ever would have? I know he told you some heartbreaking story about why they called off the engagement. But with his track record, I bet that's not true either."

He nodded. "If he lied to you once, he's going to do it again. And as long as you keep letting him think he's getting away with it, his lies will just get bigger and bigger."

Trailing her fingers through the pile of crumbs that once made up her muffin, she was silent. Then she sighed. "I don't know why I'm telling you this, but the reason I left the restaurant was because I saw him come into the restaurant with another nurse from the hospital. I know nothing about her since she works on another floor. But the way she was hanging all over him, it was obvious it wasn't the first time they had gone out."

This had Jason frowning. "Man, this guy is something else. I wonder how long it will be before everything catches up with him?"

Little did he know she was about to give him even more of a reason to dislike Noah. Avoiding his gaze, she shrugged. "What upset me the most was he had asked me if I wanted to do dinner with him the same night, at the same restaurant. But I told him I couldn't, since it was our girl's night out."

She began fingering the muffin again. "So, why did he pick the same restaurant when he knew I was going to be there?"

Tapping his fingers against his cup, Jason was silent. Not because he had nothing to say. Oh, no... he had plenty. But he didn't trust what might come out of his mouth.

He was furious. The more he heard about this guy, this Dr. Noah, or whatever the hell his name was, the more he wanted to meet him.

He wanted to talk to him, face to face. See if he could figure him out. He would only need a few minutes. This would be more than enough time to straighten him out, knock some sense into him.

The bottom line? He wanted to send the message, loud and clear, he needed to stay the hell away from Stephanie.

She deserved better... so much better.

He sighed. "Steff... when is the last time you took some time off? Went on a vacation?"

He already knew the answer to this. It would be a big indisputable never. Stephanie was a giver. She was happiest when she was making other people happy, even if this meant she had no time for herself. And she was probably never going to change.

The muffin in front of her now beyond recognition, she pushed it away. She shrugged. "Where would I go? And who would you suggest I go with? Everyone has things to do... jobs, families, a life. A life a lot more exciting than mine, I can assure you."

He almost smiled at her mournful expression. But knowing this wouldn't go over well, he reached over to give her arm an encouraging pat. "Come on... I'm sure there must be somewhere you've always wanted to go. Somewhere fun. Where there is no Dr. Noah or Davis or whatever you said his name is."

She made a face at him. "You know what his name is."

He debated whether he should even bring up what he was about to suggest. "How about Chicago? Go visit your friend, what's-her-name?"

She laughed. "You've always had such a problem with names. Or maybe it's that you don't want to remember. And you're suggesting I go to Chicago? Wow... I would think this would be the last thing you would want me to do."

He reached over, brushing his knuckles over her cheek. "Hey… I want you to be happy. I hate seeing you like this."

He sat back in his chair, studying her.

Again, she grew wary. "You make me nervous when you get that look on your face. Like you're about to say something you know I won't like. Just say it."

He smiled. "Well, I don't know if you've noticed this, but Jack has had this thing for you, for I don't know how long. If he asked, would you consider going out on a date with him?"

Dumbfounded, she stared at him.

When *you saw Jack at the license bureau, he did say something about getting together. But you didn't think he was serious. you did agree with his suggestion they get together again.*

Then she narrowed her eyes. "Wait a minute… have you already talked to him about me? Is this why he called?"

This surprised him. "He called you? *Hmm…*."

She groaned, closing her eyes. "Jazz, what did you do? Please don't tell me the two of you were discussing how pitiful I am."

He was shaking his head. "Believe me, I did nothing of the kind. I know better than to do something like that. The only time your name came up was when he mentioned he saw you at the license bureau."

He realized she hadn't heard a word he said.

Her eyes huge, she looked like she had seen a ghost.

Twisting around in his chair, he scanned the room. There didn't seem to be anything unusual going on. But, since he didn't know what he was looking for, he turned back to her. "See someone you know? Someone from the hospital?"

For Stephanie, time had come grinding to a stop.

She closed her eyes. Then, after she took a deep breath, she opened them again.

It was definitely him.

Evan…

For six months, she had wondered if she would ever see him again. And now, here he was. Less than thirty feet away, if even that.

Someone you know? More like someone you thought you knew.

Turning to Jason, she shook her head.

She needed to leave. Before Jason started asking questions.

She stood, making a wild grab for her purse. "I need to go. I told the kids I was going to surprise them with a new cookie tomorrow. But I'm almost out of flour. So I need to stop at the grocery store." Her laugh bordered on hysterical. "And as everyone knows, you can't make cookies without flour."

She leaned over and pressed a kiss to his cheek. "Thanks for meeting me here. After I talk to Jack, I'll send you a text to let you know why he called."

Slow to react, if only because he was so surprised, he watched as she headed for the door. Then he got his wits together, and scrambling to his feet, he took off after her.

He caught up to her just as she was about to get into her car, slipping between her and the car door. His arms crossed and his feet planted firmly on the ground, he had no intention of letting her leave until he found out what was going on.

She turned her back to him.

Dragging his hand through his hair, he groaned. "Steff, come on... look at me. What happened back there that had you hightailing it out of the café? Or should I ask *who* was it you saw?"

Imitating his stance, she glared right back at him. "Jason, you're exaggerating. I didn't, as you said, hightail it out of the café." She shrugged. "Like I told you, I have things to do. So, move out of my way."

He didn't move. Nor did he respond. From experience, he knew he only had to wait before she would break down and tell him everything.

Sure enough, she caved. "It's not a big deal. I thought I saw someone I know sitting at a table in the back of the café."

She sent a furtive glance back at the café, bringing him to do the same. Then he looked back at her. "And who would this someone be?"

She sighed. "Evan... his name is Evan. We met the night of the masquerade ball. Silly me, I thought we hit it off. But, after spending most of the night together, talking about everything imaginable, why wouldn't I? We had even made plans to go out again."

Her voice grew angry. "But guess what? I never heard from him again. What a surprise, huh?"

She was trying to squeeze around him to get into the car. Hoping to distract him, she gave him a bright smile. "So, if you don't mind, I'd rather not discuss this anymore. And I was serious about the grocery store. I need to leave."

She made her move. Slipping inside the car, she pulled the door shut.

Undeterred by this, Jason tapped on the driver's window, motioning for her to open the window.

She groaned, dropping her head down on the steering wheel.

She loved Jason. And she knew he meant well. But she didn't feel like dredging up what happened that night. She wasn't in the mood.

She shot a look over at Jason. The stubborn expression on his face told her he had no plans to leave.

After a very long and dramatic groan, she lowered the window halfway. "I've told you all you need to know. Enough to understand why I don't want to talk about this now." She shrugged. "Because at this point? What's the use?"

He was trying not to smile. Not that he found what she said amusing, but did she have to be so dramatic?

Resting his arms on the top of the window, he nodded. "*Hmm...* I see. So, do you have any idea why he didn't call?"

She turned her head to face him, rolling her eyes. "Jason, come on... do men even need a reason? From my experience, it sure seems like they don't think they do."

A faint smile touched her lips. "Even though I was so sure he would." She ducked her head. "I know you think I'm crazy, but with him, it seemed different... so right."

Again, he nodded. "No, I understand."

Her head came up, a surprised look on her face. "You do?"

He nodded.

Yeah, of course you do. With Darcey, you felt the same.

A sudden frown creased his brow. "He isn't already engaged or married, is he?"

After sending him an irritated look, she shook her head. "No, at least he wasn't that night. But with my luck, he could be married by now. With six kids."

She hesitated. "He was once engaged, though. But a week before the wedding, he lost his fiancée in a motorcycle accident. This happened about a year ago. They were high school sweethearts."

Jason shook his head. "Damn, that had to be hard. No one should have to deal with a blow like that."

She nodded. "I could see he was still having a hard time with this. And again, I know you'll think I'm crazy, but I felt like I was the one who could help him. "

She gazed up at him, her hopeless expression tugging at his heart. "I've convinced myself the reason he never called was because he's not ready to start up with someone new." She frowned. "Or, maybe like almost every other guy I've known, he changed his mind."

Jamming his hands in his pockets, Jason shrugged. "Hey, look what happened to me. Three years went by before Darcey and I found each other again. So, don't give up on him yet."

He glanced over at the café, then back at her. "You realize there's a simple solution to this. You could ask him. It's not too late, you know."

Horrified, she sputtered out her response. "Are you insane? I can't go back in there. And what would you suggest I do? Confront him? Demand an explanation?"

He chuckled. "No, that would send the poor guy running right out the door. I was thinking more like a simple hi, how have you been, kind of greeting. Why not take a chance? You wouldn't believe the things I did to win Darcey back."

For a few seconds, she seemed to consider this. Then she sighed. "*Ah...* but your situation was different. You had a history. You already knew you were in love. Where I don't have a clue what Evan is thinking. Or if he even remembers that night."

She glanced down at her baggy sweat pants. Embarrassed to see a few lingering crumbs from her muffin, she brushed them away. She shook her head. "Nope, I can't. I'm certainly not looking my best right now."

She checked her watch. "I need to go. I don't want to be up the whole night making cookies. Again, good bye, Jason."

She closed the window, a clear message their conversation was over.

After he watched her drive away, he headed for his SUV, reaching into his pocket for his keys.

They weren't there. Which meant he must have left them on the table in the café.

But this was okay. This would give him the opportunity to introduce himself to this Evan, maybe get an idea of where he was coming from. He knew Steff would have a fit if she knew he was doing this. But he didn't care. He was her big brother, and it was his responsibility to look after her.

You need to keep her safe from guys like Evan and Noah. Being a guy, you know damn well what's going on in their minds.

He wasn't an expert on matters of the heart, and probably never would be. But he knew Stephanie. And everything about her wistful expression when she talked about Evan led him to believe she was pretty serious about the guy.

You hope to God this Evan feels the same.

And if he didn't?

Well, he must be a damn fool.

He was whistling as he headed back to the café.

CHAPTER 8

"**N**o."

Evan shook his head.

An assignment for a photo shoot at the Children's Hospital?

The same hospital where Stephanie worked?

Why the hell would Joe think this is something you'd want to do?

He shook his head again. "Absolutely not."

Joe groaned, dropping his head down on his arms. When Evan greeted this with only silence, he lifted his head just enough to stare over at him. "Come on, man... what's the big deal?" He grinned, sending him a wink. "Think of all the nurses... all those hot, beautiful nurses, right under your fingertips, waiting for a guy like you to take care of. "

Receiving only a raised eyebrow from Evan, he persisted. "Okay, so forget about them, since it's obvious you're already set on Stephanie."

Evan groaned. "You are getting way–"

Holding up his hand, Joe cut him off. "Hey, don't think you can renege on that, since you've already made it clear how you feel. And this is okay. Believe me, I'm pulling for you."

When Evan started shaking his head, Joe groaned. "Okay, then look at it this way. This could be your chance, the perfect opportunity to make your move and patch things up with her. Forget what you saw when you tried to surprise her. Just because you saw her with this guy didn't mean it was serious. Or what are the chances she's even still with him? After all, that happened months ago."

He stopped to shake his head. "And can I give you a little advice here? Forget about surprises until you get to know her better." At Evan's puzzled look, Joe nodded. "Trust me, I know what I'm talking about. And it's a big hospital, so what are the chances the two of you will even run into each other?"

Evan shook his head.

What are the chances?

He'd be willing to bet they would be pretty good. Somehow, they would end up in the same place at the same time.

Again, call it destiny... fate... or whatever the hell you want to call it. He wasn't sure what it was, only that it was there.

And this made him a little nervous.

Joe was beyond trying to understand. He was so sure Evan would jump at the opportunity to take on this job. Not only could it be a tremendous boost to his career, the pay was excellent. So, unless the guy had lots of extra cash stashed away, he needed a job. He had bills to pay, just like everyone else.

So, this was a win, all the way around.

Hell, if you didn't already have so much going on right now, you would've nabbed the job for yourself.

Evan's reluctance had him deciding to go with another tactic. "Do you know who Elenore Cromley is?"

Evan shook his head.

Joe took another gulp of his coffee, to find it was cold. He shuddered. "I need more coffee, but that can wait."

He cleared his throat. "What can I say about Elenore Cromley? If ever there was such a thing as a queen here in the city, she would be the one to wear the crown. Her husband's family made millions, maybe even billions, in the steel industry. But he died about thirty years ago. This left her with more money than any one person could spend in a lifetime. Since they never had kids or any close relatives, she has devoted her life to helping others, the Children's Hospital coming in at the top of her list. She funded an addition to the hospital, a combination community center and museum showcasing the hospital's history over the past one hundred years. And now she wants to turn one wall—and this is an immense wall, about thirty-feet high—into a collage of oversized photos depicting the everyday operations of the hospital."

He sat back in his seat, pointing his finger over at Evan. "This is where you come in. If she likes your work, this could lead to even more jobs. Take The Regency for example. She just took that over, too."

He grinned. "The same party center, again may I remind you, the Cleveland's Elite banquet is going to be held. And don't worry about a ticket. I reserved one for you."

After making a mental note to change the ticket count to two in case things worked out between Evan and Stephanie, Joe began searching his pockets. He pulled out a business card. Tapping it on the table, he glanced over at Evan. "But back to Elenore. She told me she's planning to update all The Regency brochures, catalogs, etc. And for that, what do you need?"

He nodded. "Bingo... a damn good photographer."

He held up the card. "This could be your ticket to success. Elenore has connections not only in Cleveland, but everywhere. And if she likes you, which I'm pretty sure she already does after the great things I said about you, good things will happen."

He pushed the business card across the table to Evan. "Here... I hope you don't mind, but I told her you would call her by the end of the day. This is her contact info. Just to warn you, she is a person who wants everything done yesterday. And she's one hell of a stickler for details."

He sat back in his chair. "So, what do you think?"

Evan was thinking he should have stayed in New Zealand. He had received a decent job offer from a local magazine right before he was to return home, but he turned it down. At the time, it hadn't seemed like a good idea.

Now you're thinking maybe you were wrong.

Why had he been so quick to return home? In New Zealand, there had been no pressure. The only thing required of him had been to take photos. Lots and lots of photos. His choice, his call. The more, the better. A skill that came naturally to him and required very little thinking.

This temporary reprieve from his life back in Cleveland had led him to believe he had moved on, grown stronger. But everything he thought he had left behind was now coming back to haunt him.

Starting with Stephanie. Look at how even a glimpse of her had been enough to throw him off, sending his world tilting out of control.

He dragged his hand through his hair, sending another glance in her direction.

She was gone. He missed his chance.

This is when he realized what a fool he was. She was the reason he had returned home. If only to apologize for breaking another promise. To make things right.

One more chance, this is all you ask. Think of it as your final at bat. You strike out, you're done...

"Evan... hey, are you still here?"

Evan blinked.

Joe was studying him, a concerned look on his face.

He shrugged. "Okay, I'll do it."

Once it registered Evan had given him the answer he was hoping for, Joe reached over to shake his hand. "This is great. I know you won't regret it."

And even though Evan's handshake wasn't as enthusiastic as he'd like, Joe was fine with this.

Hell, this would come in time.

After all, hadn't he been right about New Zealand?

Now he had to work on getting him and Stephanie back together...

CHAPTER 9

"Are you afraid to fall in love?" She asked.
"I'm afraid of being the only one who falls," He replied.
~Anonymous

After sending a glance around the busy coffee shop, Joe stood, nodding over at Evan's empty cup. "Give me your cup. I'll get refills before the after-work crowd shows up, and it gets even crazier."

Cups in hand, he turned and almost ran right into Jason.

After he set the cups back on the table, he smiled, shaking the hand Jason offered. *"Whoa...* sorry about that. I wan't paying attention. Too focused on getting more coffee, I guess. But, hey... how's it going? I heard you got married?"

Jason grinned. "Yes, I am now a married man. For almost two weeks. So, things are good. A little hectic, but good. And I heard you're going to be a father soon, right? Congratulations."

Joe nodded. "Thanks. Eighteen weeks and counting."

Jason glanced over at Evan. His expression guarded, he held out his hand. "I don't believe we've met. Jason Bennett."

"Evan Marshall." Jason's tight grip, lasting a little longer than necessary, was enough to let Evan know he had already formed an opinion of him.

And it wasn't a good one.

Damn... yeah, no explanation necessary here.

Sensing the tension between them, Joe cleared his throat. "Evan is a colleague of mine, also a freelance photographer. He just got back from a six-month assignment in New Zealand and is ready to get back to work. If you're ever in need of another photographer, I can vouch for his work."

Jason took a few seconds to think about this before he nodded over at Evan. "We're always on the lookout for new photographers for the band. If only to keep things fresh. Album designs, publicity shots and all that. And now that The Regency is under new management, they might also be in need of a photographer. My wife, Darcey, would be the person to contact. Would you be interested in either of these?"

Surprised at Jason's requests, Evan hesitated. First the killer hand-shake, and now an offer of a job? He hadn't even seen any of his work. So, if this was his way of keeping an eye on him, he was up for the challenge.

You've got this.

Reaching into his pocket, he pulled out one of his business cards. He knew Joe was loving this, since he was the one who had talked him into getting the cards. He handed it to Jason. "Sure, here's my card. Check out my website so you can get an idea of what kind of work I do."

"Great." Nodding, Jason slipped the card in his pocket. Then he hesitated, studying Evan for a brief moment before he spoke. "It's too bad we didn't meet before the wedding. We had a dickens of a time finding a photographer given the little time we had to work with. But something tells me wedding photography isn't your thing. You know, all that commitment and stuff."

He turned to Joe. "I need to get going. Make sure you take care of that wife and soon-to-be baby of yours."

He nodded over at Evan. "Nice meeting you. I'll be in touch."

Joe and Evan watched him walk away before Joe chuckled. "I believe you've been warned. Something tells him wedding photography isn't your thing? All that commitment and stuff? If this wasn't a don't-mess-with-my-sister-or-else kind of threat, I don't know what it was."

He shook his head. "When it comes to his sister, Jason Bennett is one protective guy. So, you better up your game. For God's sake, whatever you do, don't mess up again. Because if you do, you'll not only have Stephanie to contend with, you'll have Jason right there to back her up. Not something you want to happen, trust me. He's got a big following around here. He can do no wrong as far as the female population is concerned."

He grinned. "And a good thing you got those business cards, huh? Didn't I tell you? Stick with me, kid. You won't go wrong."

He picked up their cups and headed for the counter. Leaving Evan wondering what the hell he had gotten himself into.

Again? New Zealand is looking really good to you right now.

But at the same time?

He was starting to feel alive again.

Stephanie had been aimlessly wandering around the grocery store for the last twenty minutes.

She came to a dead stop. She was in the wrong aisle. Unless she had a dog or cat she didn't know about. Something that was now beginning to sound very appealing.

Pets don't run off on you. Make promises they don't keep. They don't judge or question every move you make. No, they worship the ground you walk on. Always ready to give you their undivided attention. They love you for who you are.

Traits she had found most men seemed to lack.

Yeah, maybe it was time to get a dog. Though a cat might be a better choice, since she was rarely home.

She gazed over at the cute little kitten calling out to her from the label on the can of cat food.

She shook her head.

You don't need a pet. You can't even keep your own life in order.

She gave a frustrated sigh. This mood she was in? It was all Evan's fault. Just when she accepted she would never see him again, he shows up at Cafe Latte.

And now she was second guessing herself all over again.

You should have taken Jason's advice and gone over to talk to Evan, gauge his reaction. Instead, now you're right back to where you were six months ago.

Wondering what she did wrong.

Well, enough was enough. She was going to sweep both Noah and Evan right back where they belonged, in the past and best forgotten.

"Excuse me, can I sneak by?"

Stepanie glanced over to see a woman was trying to maneuver her cart around her. After she moved out of her way, she tossed a bag of flour into her basket.

How was she to know there was a hole in the bag?

It exploded, sending a shower of flour over everything, including her. Before she could count to ten, the manager, assistant manager, three stock boys and about ten curious customers had gathered in the aisle to assess the situation.

It was the license bureau all over again.

After trying to shake the flour out of her hair and brushing it off her clothes, she grabbed another bag of flour. Mumbling her apologies, she almost ran to the checkout counter.

She just wanted to bake cookies.

Was this too much to ask?

It was almost midnight when Stephanie took the last tray of cookies out of the oven.

She was just about to crawl in to bed when she remembered Jack's voicemail. Phone in hand, she settled in to listen to his message.

> *"Stephanie... Jack, here.*
> *I hope you got everything straightened*
> *out with your license, and you didn't*
> *have to wait too long in line.*
> *But the reason I'm calling... I was*
> *wondering if you would like to be my*

date for the Cleveland Elite Awards
Banquet next Wednesday night. A
score I did for a Cleveland documen-
tary film received a nomination.
I know it's a weeknight, and you
might not have the night off. And I'm
not giving you much notice. But if
you're free, this would be great. If you
can't? It's not a big deal. Let me know
what you think. I'll talk to you later."

She looked up from her phone. She liked Jack, she really did. He was a great guy.

But there was no spark... no sudden rush of anticipation. Or that breathless, he's the one feeling.

But perhaps she was asking too much?

She wanted to be with someone who could make her feel the same way she felt that night of the masquerade ball.

And how did that work out? Fizzled out on you, didn't it?

Irritated at this observation, she slapped her phone down on the nightstand and turned out the light. She pulled the quilt over her head, something she always did when she was feeling overwhelmed, and closed her eyes.

Five minutes later, she sat up and tossed the quilt aside. Hugging her knees to her chest, she stared into the darkness.

Should you be worried?

Because what if she never found such a man? They were all taken? Or what she was looking for had been right in front of her? Which meant she might have been searching for the wrong kind of love all along.

She groaned, dropping her head to her knees.

Slowly raising her head, she nodded. Her mind was made up. Before she left for work tomorrow, she was going to call Jack and tell him she would love to be his date. This would give her a chance to get to know him better.

Who knows? He might be what she didn't even know she was

looking for. Maybe they just needed more time.

Life was not the perfect fairytale every woman dreams about. The story one finds in every romance novel. After all, those were fiction.

Settling back under the quilt, she closed her eyes.

She needed to get some sleep or it would be a long day tomorrow.

At about the same time, Darcey added the final sealed and addressed thank-you note to the stack in front of her. She leaned back in her chair, a satisfied smile on her face. "That should about do it. Now we only have to take these to the post office."

She glanced over at Jason. His chin resting on his hand, his eyes were closed.

"Jason?"

His head jerked up. Wild eyed, he stared at her. "What? Are we done?" He sent a guilty glance over at the finished cards on the table. "So, who are we thanking now? And for what?"

She laughed. "Relax. We're done. Or should I say, I'm done."

He groaned, dragging his hand through his hair. "I'm sorry, gorgeous." He glanced down at his watch. "But look how late it is. It's after midnight."

She leaned over to press a kiss to his cheek. "I know. I'm tired, too. Come on, let's go to bed."

Jason was almost asleep when Darcey crawled into bed, settling next to him.

She leaned over to peer into his face. "Are you asleep?"

Unable to stop the smile tweaking the corner of his mouth, he pressed a kiss to her nose. "Well, if I was, I'm not now. What's up?"

She was smiling. "You never told me about your meeting with Stephanie? What did she want?"

He tried to hide his groan with an enormous yawn. She was going to want all the details. This meant any chance of sleep could be a long time coming.

He gave her a hopeful look. "Can't it wait until tomorrow?"

Pressing another kiss to his cheek, she shook her head. "Please?"

After a long sigh, and she had settled next to him, he gave her a very brief version of what Stephanie had told him about both Noah and Evan. And how he got to meet Evan when he went back inside the café for his keys.

This led to a flurry of questions. Most of these about Evan.

Starting with… what did Jason think of him?

You thought he seemed like a pretty nice guy. But then, you only talked for a few minutes.

Did he think Stephanie really likes him?

From the way she talked about him, you'd say yes.

What did he look like? Was he cute?

Cute? Hell, you don't know. You're not all that sure what a woman means by cute when describing a man. He looked normal.

Could he be the one?

Again, she seems to like him. And if he helps her forget all about this doctor, then you're all for it.

And now what was Jason going to do to help things along?

He gave her a long look, one that should be enough to let her know he'd rather do nothing. He met the guy, wasn't that enough for now?

She waited.

He groaned. "Oh, geeez… I don't know. I think I should lie low on this one. Steff made it very clear she didn't want my help."

His brow furrowed. "There's one thing that bothers me. How he left Steff hanging, never called like he said he would. But Joe mentioned something about how he just returned home after six months in New Zealand for a photo shoot."

He shook his head. "Though you and I both know from experience that shouldn't be an excuse. You can call anyone, anywhere, these days."

He grinned. "She had that dreamy look in her eyes when she talked about him. I remember you were like that. Couldn't get enough of me."

She tried not to smile, but failed. "*Hmm*… yes, I'll admit I fell for you. Literally, I did."

Her face scrunched up with worry, she gazed up at him. "But what do you think will happen next? What are the chances of them getting back together?"

A guilty look appearing on his face, Jason cleared his throat. "Ah, ha... how funny you should bring that up. Because I asked him if he'd be interested in doing some photos shoots for the band. And maybe The Regency. Thought it would be a good way to keep an eye on the guy."

She sat straight up on the bed, staring down at him in disbelief. "What? Jason... you already have a photographer. And Elenore Cromley has to approve a photographer for The Regency. You can't just give him the job."

He shrugged. "I know. But is it that big of a deal? I thought it might somehow be a way to get Steff and Evan together. No pressure involved." Then he groaned, running his hand down over his jaw. "Hell, I don't know what came over me. But at the time, it seemed like a good idea. And if you had seen Steff's face. She looked so sad. I guess I wanted to make things better."

Even though Darcey was shaking her head, she was smiling. "You are such a true romantic and I love you for this." She backed this up with a big kiss before she settled back against him.

After a brief silence, she sighed. "I guess I'll need to do a lot of fast talking if Elenore finds out about this."

"*Ummm*... yeah. You can do it, gorgeous. I have faith in you."

She was smiling. *Gorgeous*... it didn't matter how many times he called her this, it got to her every time.

She reached up to kiss him again. "I really do love you."

"And I love you, too." Already on the edge of sleep, this was only a murmur.

But for Darcey, it was enough.

They were both sound asleep in no time.

CHAPTER 10

S tephanie drove into the hospital parking lot. She had no sooner pulled into a space and turned off the ignition, when her phone dinged.

Thinking it was a text from Jack, responding to her about the awards banquet, she checked her phone. It was from Elenore Cromley.

She read the text. Puzzled, she read it again.

> Stephanie, please meet me in the new wing at three-thirty. I have a project I'd like you to take on.

A project? What kind of project?

She groaned. The last thing she wanted, the last thing she needed right now, was another project. From experience, she knew whatever Elenore had in mind? It was going to involve a lot of work. And a lot of time.

Time you don't have.

She pulled out a large container from the backseat. Filled with the Snickerdoodle cookies she had made last night, a recipe she chose because of its five-hundred-plus rave reviews online, she headed for the hospital entrance.

She glanced over at the clock in the reception area. She would now have only about twenty minutes to hand out the cookies to the kids before she had to meet with Elenore.

This had her walking even faster. Deciding not to wait for the elevator, she headed for the stairs. By the time she pushed open the door to the third floor, her mind was made up.

Elenore could wait. The children came first. Wasn't she always reminding everyone of this?

After she dropped off a plate of cookies at the third-floor coffee station, she made her way to where the children would be waiting. As soon as she walked into the room, they all came running over to greet her, clamoring for cookies.

Laughing, she held the container up and out of their reach. "Okay, okay... but before I pass these out, who wants to guess what kind of cookie I brought this time?"

For the next few minutes, she forgot all about Elenore Cromley.

Evan hit the elevator button for the third floor of the Children's Hospital. He was relieved he was the only occupant.

This would give him a little extra time to calm his nerves.

He didn't like to be rushed.

About an hour ago he'd checked his phone to see there was a message from Elenore Cromley. This was in response to the message he'd left on her voicemail yesterday after his meeting with Joe.

She had started right in by telling him how pleased she was to hear he was interested in the job and she wanted to meet with him as soon as possible.

This would be at her office on the third floor of the Children's Hospital. He was to check in at the nurses station and someone would escort him to her office.

This afternoon would work best for her. But since she was giving him such short notice, she would leave the time up to him.

He'd stared down at his phone, shaking his head in disbelief.

She certainly didn't give you the option to refuse, did she?

Since Joe had given him the lowdown on Elenore and what to

expect, he knew it would be in his best interest to meet up with her as soon as possible. So, in less than twenty minutes, he had showered, got dressed and was out the door.

Now leaning back against the wall of the elevator, his heart pounding like a jackhammer in his chest, he closed his eyes and took in a deep breath.

He didn't know why he was so worked up about this. The interview process wasn't new to him. Over the course of his brief career, he had sat through more than his share and now viewed them only as another learning experience.

It had taken a while, but he eventually figured it out. If he was meant to get the job?

It would happen.

Maybe your uneasiness has nothing to do with the job. Instead, it's all about where the interview is.

Watching the numbers blink for each floor, he tried not to think about the last time he had used this same elevator. All of his hopes and dreams disappearing when the doors opened.

He frowned. He didn't need a repeat experience of that.

Not today.

The elevator came to a stop, the doors sliding open. After a glance up and down the hall, relieved to see no sign of Stephanie, as instructed, he headed for the nurses station.

Deep in conversation, the three nurses on duty didn't even notice he was there. It was only when he cleared his throat, they became silent, all eyes on him.

A bit unnerved, he smiled. "Hi, I'm Evan Marshall. I'm here to see Elenore Cromley. I was told someone could show me to her office?"

The eldest of the three came from behind the counter, gesturing for him to follow her. "Hi Evan, I'm Caro. Elenore told me you'd be stopping by this afternoon."

She smiled up at him. "So, you're a photographer, huh? Well, just so you know, Elenore is very excited about this photo collage. This community room project is something she has been planning for years."

As they walked down the hall, she kept up a constant chatter, mostly about the new wing and how amazing it was. Finally coming to a stop, she pointed to a room off to the right. "That's Elenore's office. The door is open, so this means you're free to go in."

Before she turned to leave, she sent him a wink. "Good luck. And remember... sometimes Elenore may seem overbearing, but she means well."

He frowned as he watched her walk down the hall. He was a getting a little worried. This was the second warning he had received about Elenore Cromley.

First Joe, and now this Caro?

How bad could this Elenore be?

But, come on... he should be able to handle her. It wouldn't be the first time he had to deal with a demanding client and had still nailed the job. So, why should this time be any different?

He took a deep breath and started to walk into the room, where he almost collided with the person who was leaving. Evan recognized him as the man he'd seen with Stephanie the last time he had been in the hospital.

But this time he caught the man's name on his security tag as he brushed by, stopping briefly to mutter an angry apology before he went striding out into the hall.

Dr. Noah Davis.

Evan glanced over to see an elderly woman, whom he assumed was Elenore, standing by the window. She was frowning down at the folder she was holding.

When she looked up to see him, she set the folder on her desk and held out her hand. "Hello, I take it you're Evan? Let me apologize for Dr. Davis's behavior. I had hoped to introduce you, but as you just witnessed, he was in a bit of a hurry." She shook her head. "I've found some of the hospital's most gifted staff members can also be the most temperamental. But you haven't come here to listen to my opinion of this. So, please... sit and we'll get started."

Once they were both seated, she studied him, the intensity of her gaze making him squirm.

Finally, she smiled. "So, tell me all about yourself. What is it that makes Evan Marshall the man he is?"

Unprepared for such a question, it took him a few moments to come up with the answer he thought she might be looking for.

He cleared his throat. "Well, as you already know, I am a photographer, a career I take seriously. Just recently, I decided to go freelance. This will give me the option to be more selective about the work I choose. Before I start each job, I always do as much research as I can in order to–"

She cut him off. "No, no... that information is on your resume or your website. I'm more interested in who you are as a person... where you grew up, your family... all of what made you the man you are today."

Clasping her hands together in front of her, she gave him an encouraging smile. "Like you, I like to be selective. But more on the personal level. I find this tells me so much more about the person... who he is and what I can expect. Along with what they expect of me."

He shifted uneasily in his chair. Personal?

You don't do personal.

No, this wasn't something he felt comfortable with. Until now, sharing anything about his personal life was the one thing he had made a point of keeping off-limits. And so far, he had done a pretty good job at this.

Except with Stephanie.

The words flow unchecked when you're with her. You feel like you can tell her anything.

At first, this had upset him. This wasn't how it had been with Kelsie. There were so many things he had been hesitant to share with her, unsure of how she would react.

Or maybe it was more like he didn't want to disappoint her. Instead, he had tried to live up to the perfect man she thought he was.

He shook his head.

And you are far from perfect, that's for damn sure.

"Evan?"

Elenore's polite cough had him snapping to attention.

He cleared his throat. "I was born in Cleveland but spent my childhood in Atlanta. My teenage years were a little rough. I was one of those kids who thought they knew everything, and this, along with my attitude, got me in trouble more times than I'd like to admit. When I turned eighteen and was out on my own, I returned to Cleveland."

He smiled, shaking his head. "For the next few years, I went from job to job. I tried everything, making just enough money to survive. Then I guess you could say I grew up, got serious about my life. Since photography has always fascinated me, I set out to get a degree. I got a scholarship, studied hard, and now here I am."

"And your parents? Have you kept in touch with them?"

He shrugged. "I never knew them. They died when I was born."

"You never knew them..." Slowly, she repeated this.

This had him feeling obligated to explain. "They were in a car acci-dent... the driver of the other car had a heart attack and went left of center, hitting them head-on. My mother was almost nine months pregnant with me. They were able to save me, but my parents and the other driver didn't make it."

Elenore seemed so upset by this, Evan tried to reassure her. "Please don't be upset. It's okay. Really it is. I can't grieve for someone I never knew."

She nodded. "But who took over your care? Someone from your immediate family?"

"My aunt and uncle. The only other living relatives of the family." He shrugged. "Though, it turned out to be more of me raising myself. Let's just say they didn't get along. There were a lot of angry words exchanged, doors slamming, and all that. Not the happiest atmosphere for a kid..." His voice trailing off, he thought about what he told her.

They didn't get along? This was putting it mildly.

How many times had he hidden away in his room, trying to block out the sound of their fighting? Or he would sneak out of the house, hoping to find someone to hang around with until he knew it would be safe to return. His uncle had finally stormed off in a rage, or the alcohol had left both him and his aunt in a stupor.

A brief time-out would always follow these episodes. Then some-thing else would set them off, and the fighting would start up all over again.

Unfortunately, this vicious cycle hadn't ended until the day he came home to find his aunt had been the one to leave this time. And they never heard from her again.

Shaking off these unwanted memories, he sent Elenore a bright smile. "When I was about twelve years old, my uncle got into a fight with a neighbor, and the police were called. After that, I spent my time in a series of foster homes until I turned eighteen."

"And your aunt and uncle? What happened to them?" This came from Elenore in almost a whisper.

He shrugged. "I've had no contact with either of them since then. So, I don't know if they're still even around." He hesitated, slowly shaking his head. "To this day, I still wonder why they had agreed to take me on."

Elenore's distressed expression worried him. He needed to stop talking. That he had even told her what he had, made little sense. Not only had he dug up memories he had spent so long trying to forget, sharing this kind of information certainly wouldn't help him get the job.

He sent her a brief smile. "Please don't feel bad for me. In the end, I think I turned out okay. I'm sure there are a lot of kids who have experienced so much worse."

He watched as she almost angrily began shuffling the papers in front of her. Only after she stacked them into a pile and slapped them down on the corner of the desk, almost sending them over the edge, she glanced over at him, her eyes bright.

"You will be perfect for the job. I have already checked out your website and was more than impressed with your work. But most of all, I believe with everything you have already experienced in your life, you'll be able to connect with the children and your photographs will reflect this."

A smile flashed across her face. "You also came highly recommended by Joe. Since I've had the pleasure of working with him quite a few times, I know I can trust his opinion."

She extended her hand. "So, if you want the job, it's yours."

Shocked at her quick decision, it was a few seconds before Evan reached across the desk to shake her hand. "Thank you, Mrs. Cromley. I promise I will do my best to not disappoint you."

Her grip just as firm, she nodded. "I know you will. And please, call me Elenore. This is what all of my friends call me."

He smiled. "Okay, Elenore it is."

She sat back in her chair and removing her glasses, she gave them a quick wipe with her handkerchief before she smiled over at Evan. "Thank goodness we got that all sorted out. Now we can get right to work. I have already chosen an assistant for you. She is one of the best nurses we have. She will be able to answer any questions you have. And help you see the kind of image we want to promote to the public."

Evan tilted his head, puzzled. "An assistant?"

Elenore sighed. "Yes, even though I trust you, I'm afraid we can't let you wander around the floors on your own. This is because of the recent security measures the hospital put in place. All temporary non-visitors, and this would be you, now need to be accompanied by a member of the staff. I hope this won't be a problem."

Her expression was downright threatening. "You must always remember, everything we do is for the children, each and every one of them. Their trust in us can never be broken."

Evan nodded. "Yes, ma'am. I promise I'll never forget this."

She smiled. "Good. And don't worry, I can't imagine you'd be unhappy with my choice of assistant. She's not only smart and compassionate but also beautiful."

She glanced down at her watch. "I asked her to meet us in the new wing, and she should be here in about fifteen minutes. So, why don't we plan on heading there right now. This will give you the chance to check out the space you'll have to work with."

About to stand, she hesitated.

She reached for her phone. "If you will excuse me for a few minutes, I have a quick call I would like to make. You will find a coffee station right down the hall. If I'm not mistaken, you will also find homemade cookies made by one of the members of our staff."

She sent a wave towards the door.

"So, please... help yourself. I'll join you as soon as I can."

CHAPTER 11

Things work out best for those who make the best of how things work out.
~Unknown

Deep in thought, it was the hot coffee overflowing the cup and onto his hand that had Evan letting out a little yelp. After a quick glance around to see no one had witnessed this, he mopped up the spill.

He took a cautious sip from the full cup.

Seriously, what is wrong with you?

Was he losing his mind, or what? Why was he still so nervous, as though something unexpected was about to happen?

You need to relax. You already got the job, remember? It's yours... you nailed it.

Yeah, it had turned out to be one of the easiest interviews he'd ever sat through. He had only one concern, and this was he had little experience working with kids.

But he was more than willing to take on the challenge.

He could handle this.

How hard could it be?

After all, he was an excellent photographer.

A damn good one at that.

Yet they hadn't even discussed this in the interview.

Maybe this is the reason you feel so uncertain?

He was still trying to figure out how Elenore had managed to get him to open up, sharing with her almost his whole life story. It seemed his vow to keep the less desirable details of the past to himself had flown right out the window.

At the same time, he got the feeling she already knew more about him than she was letting on.

The cup halfway to his mouth, he paused, his brows knitting in a frown. But who gave her this information? Maybe Joe?

Lost in thought, he reached for a cookie from the plate on the table and took a bite.

Whoa…

He held up the cookie and studied it before he finished it off. With the crunchy cinnamon sugar coating on the outside, and a soft vanilla cake-like texture inside? This alone was addictive.

But add in the little hint of chocolate sprinkled here and there? He'd swear it was like an explosion of flavors in his mouth.

Hands down, it was the best cookie he had ever tasted.

He sent another glance over at the cookies. From what he could see, there were at least a couple dozen piled on the plate. If he were to take another one, no one would even notice it was gone.

After a quick glance up and down the hall to find it was deserted, he did just that.

Hey, he was hungry. Not at all surprising, since he had skipped lunch in his rush to get to this interview.

He had just popped the last of the cookie in his mouth when Elenore's voice came from behind him. "So, what do you think? Pretty good, huh? Well, today is your lucky day. Because in a few minutes you'll be able to compliment the baker in person."

She checked her watch. "Give her about another ten minutes and she should be here. I can't wait for the two of you to meet. Her name is Stephanie… Stephanie Bennett. But here at the hospital, she goes by Steffi."

Evan slowly swallowed what was still in his mouth. That he did this without choking, or worse yet, spitting it all over Elenore, was a miracle.

His mind racing, he stared down into the empty cup.

Her name is Stephanie. Remember? No shortcuts with her.

Thinking he had said this aloud, he glanced over at Elenore.

The look on Evan's face had Elenore worried. If she had to guess, she'd say he was in shock. Concerned, she watched as he carefully set his empty cup on the table.

His voice came out in a loud croak. "Stephanie? Stephanie Bennett?"

Now even more worried, she rested her hand on his arm. "Yes, Stephanie Bennett. My goodness, do the two of you know each other?"

Running his hand back through his hair, he continued to stare at her.

Do you know each other? You thought you did. Only to find after those brief yet perfect hours you shared, you didn't know her at all.

Adjusting her glasses, Elenore peered more closely at him. Then she frowned. "Oh, my... you do, don't you? And it didn't end well."

She frowned. "I hope this won't be a problem? Whatever happened has since been resolved and you are now friends."

His mind still trying to process this new information, his response was slow to come. "Friends? Yes, we were... until... well, you know how things go. We lost touch, and I didn't call... and I still like Stephanie. I do..."

His voice trailing off, he shrugged. "Don't worry, we'll be okay. I'm sure we'll be able to put the past behind and everything will be fine."

He laughed, this coming out much harsher than he intended. "Can't always expect that happy ending, right? I, for one, can attest to this."

A look of comprehension flashed across Elenore's face. She nodded. "Good. I like it when people get along. It makes life so much easier, don't you agree?"

Her point made, and not waiting for an answer, she began walking down the hall, gesturing for him to follow. And even though she talked non-stop, mostly about the grand opening and all the work still needed to be done, he didn't hear a word.

How could he? His mind was in a turmoil, trying to deal with this new development.

It didn't seem possible. Out of all the staff here at the hospital, what were the odds Elenore would choose Stephanie?

Look at the difficult time you had when you saw her yesterday in Café Latte? And now you'll be working together?

He frowned. This was all Paul's fault. He never should have let him convince him to take this job. And he was going to make sure he told him this.

But first things first. Ten minutes. This was how much time he had to get it together before Stephanie joined them.

A mere ten minutes...

You're in big trouble.

While Evan was wracking his brain, scrounging up the right thing to say to Stephanie when he saw her again, Elenore was dealing with a few problems of her own.

The interview had turned up something she hadn't expected, jogging her memory in a most unsettling way. Then there was this recent development with Stephanie and Evan.

With the Grand Opening less than three weeks away, everything needed to stay on schedule. Any delays or interruptions weren't even an option.

The bottom line? She didn't want any surprises.

Elenore pulled open the double doors at the end of the hallway. She walked into the room before she turned to Evan. "Here it is, The Peter F. Cromley Community Room. My dream has finally become a reality."

With a grateful sigh, she sank into the folding chair set up by the door. She sent Evan a brief wave. "Go... check it out. I'll wait here."

She watched as he strolled around the room, taking it all in.

She smiled. He was such a handsome young man. He had this brooding artist vibe going on, fitting in so well with the scruffy, unshaved look so popular these days.

She could only imagine how disgusted Peter would be with this trend. The one time she had tried to convince him to grow a mustache many years ago, when they were at the height of popularity, he had flat out refused.

He had been horrified, claiming this gave men a shifty, untrustworthy look. Pirates had mustaches. As did most criminals. Look at Rhett Butler in Gone with the Wind, he had reminded her. A scoundrel through and through.

A wistful smile curved her lips. Even after all these years, there wasn't a day that went by she didn't think of him. He would be so excited about this new addition to the hospital, and so proud to have it named after him.

After blinking back a rare tear, she continued her inspection of Evan.

He was tall, a little over six feet. Muscular, but not to the extreme. Enough to show he cared about his appearance and worked out on a regular basis. His dark auburn hair was wavy and slightly on the longer side, almost halfway to his shoulders.

But it was his face she found so interesting. It was such an expressive and kind face. Unfortunately, this was almost over shadowed by the hint of sadness in his eyes. A rich chocolate brown, they looked as though they had seen more than their share of heartache. Definitely more than any man should have experienced at this young age.

As if he knew she was checking him out, he turned around and walked back to join her. Then he smiled, a smile so genuine she knew she had made the right choice in hiring him. She could trust him to get the job done on time.

And he would do it well.

But then there was Stephanie…

She was worried about her.

Not about her work. No, Stephanie was by far one of her favorite staff members. Her dedication to the children was beyond what was expected. She couldn't think of a single person who would have anything bad to say about her.

But over the past few weeks, there had been a change in her behavior. Her usual enthusiasm had faded. Her smiles weren't as bright, and she gave them out less often. She wasn't the Stephanie they all knew and loved.

Elenore was pretty sure the charismatic and handsome Dr. Davis was the reason for this. She hoped she was wrong, because the possibility Stephanie had fallen for Dr. Davis's charming demeanor did not set well with her.

Elenore wasn't blind. Nor was she deaf. She was very proud of her ability to know almost everything that went on with the members of the staff. And from what she had observed of Dr. Davis, even though he was a wonderful doctor and destined for greatness, he had a lot to learn.

Starting with the proper behavior required of his professional standing.

Over the past few months, his priorities had shifted. The man was insatiable. To him, women were fair game. She would be willing to bet he had either dated or flirted outrageously with every single female staff member. And this was after he had only been with them for about a year.

But now Evan had come on the scene. That he and Stephanie had a past could make things very interesting.

Elenore wasn't a matchmaker. In fact, the idea had never even entered her mind. But she did believe everything happens for a reason. That she had chosen Evan and Stephanie to work together was no accident. Call it fate, or whatever… this was a plan set in place by a much higher power, and beyond their control.

She glanced up at Evan and gave him a big smile. After he helped her up, she pulled a sheet of paper from her notebook and handed it to him. "This is a sketch I made to showing my vision for the final project."

She began walking towards the wall in question. "Come, let me give you a better idea of what I have in mind."

CHAPTER 12

As had happened every other time Stephanie walked into the recently completed hospital wing, she smiled.

The formal name, as noted on the plaque hanging over the immense stone fireplace, was the Peter F. Cromley Center.

This was in honor of Elenore's late husband, Peter Francis Cromley. But the staff had already christened the room with a different name...

The Sunshine Wing.

This was because on a sunny day the forty-foot domed glass ceiling, besides making the room seem even larger than it was, turned the room into a golden oasis, light filling the room.

No cost or amenities had been spared in the design of this addition. The individual stations along the outside of the room offered every kind of activity a child could want, from outdoor play sets to a library filled with books for every age group. There was even a small theater, an artist's studio and a full working kitchen.

And if the room needed to be used for a special event? With one touch of a button, the stations would disappear behind a series of panels as they slid together to hide everything from view.

Only one section of the room still appeared to be unfinished, the entire wall a blank canvas.

And this was where Stephanie found Elenore, surprised to find she wasn't alone.

Deep in conversation, neither Elenore nor Evan noticed when Stephanie entered the room.

It was when she was only a few feet away, Elenore turned to greet her with a big smile. "Stephanie, I'm so glad you could make it on such short notice. Evan and I were just discussing the layout of the photos he will be taking. You're just in time to give us your input."

But Stephanie hadn't heard a word she said. Instead, she had become completely still. She couldn't move, her gaze fixed on Evan, who had turned to face her.

A hesitant smile on his face, he held out his hand. "Stephanie... it's been a while, hasn't it?"

These words had no sooner came out of his mouth when he closed his eyes, a low groan passing his lips.

God, no... did you really just say that? It's been a while? What kind of greeting is that?

But that he even managed a response was an accomplishment. Though it might have been better if he'd said nothing at all, using the time to get his wits together now that she was actually standing right in front of him.

He only knew he'd give almost anything to have the chance to start over again.

And what would he say?

He'd start by saying exactly what was on his mind. That she was as beautiful, if not more so, than the last time he saw her. Then he would tell her how he still remembered everything about the night of the masquerade ball.

Every single moment... every smile... every touch... every word...

He'd also make sure to let her know how he'd kept every one of these memories safely tucked in his heart. Because they were what gave him hope one day he could trade them in for the real thing.

Yes, every emotion he'd experienced the night of the masquerade ball was still with him.

And now?

With her standing right in front of him?

They were even stronger than before.

If this wasn't love, he didn't know what it was.

Stephanie stared down at the hand Evan was holding out to her. And even though everything inside of her was screaming this is what she'd been dreaming about for the past six months, and she'd be a fool not to meet him halfway?

She couldn't.

Her gaze darted over to where Elenore was watching them, her expression hopeful. And this was when she did something she knew she would later regret. Something so childish and clearly not the best way to go about impressing Elenore Cromley.

She took a step back and, clasping her hands behind her back, she sent Evan a curt nod.

"Evan..."

And that was it.

Just one word. No handshake. No smile.

And definitely no eye contact.

A look of surprise crossing Evan's face, he slowly dropped his hand.

This was followed by a long silence that made the moment even more awkward than it was.

Elenore realized if she didn't say something, this unspoken battle between Evan and Stephanie could go on forever. So, after clearing her throat to get their attention, as usual she didn't mince words. "It's obvious the two of you have met before, and for whatever reason, it didn't end well. But I've always been a firm believer in second chances. So, I suggest you both take this opportunity to leave the past behind and make a new start. Life is too short to hold a grudge. Can you both agree?"

Evan mumbled a yes.

While Stephanie responded with only a curt nod.

Relieved, though she had a feeling this truce was only temporary,

Elenore pulled two sheets of paper out of the folder she was holding. She handed one to each of them. "I want you to read through this carefully. It is a list of everything that needs to be done for the grand opening. I am giving the two of you free rein and I expect you to work as a team. This means even if one of you falls short, the blame will still go to the both of you."

After scanning the list, Stephanie glanced up at Elenore, her face scrunched up in disbelief. "Do interviews with the media? I can't do this. I'm not good at public speaking. And I know nothing about photography. I—"

Elenore silenced her with a wave of her hand. "This is why you have Evan to help you. And vice versa."

She glanced at the clock above the entrance to the room. "Now, if you'll excuse me, I need to go. I have a meeting with the head of laundry." She frowned. "She always has something to complain about. I can't even imagine what it is this time."

Then she gave them a big smile. "If you have questions, you know where my office is."

Evan and Stephanie watched her walk out of the room. It was only when the squeak of her heavy soled rubber shoes eventually faded, Stephanie whirled around to face Evan. "Was this your idea?"

A little surprised, not only by the angry tone of her voice but also the accusing look in her eyes, he took a step back, shaking his head.

Whoa... you don't understand... what's happening here?

This was not the Stephanie he remembered from that September night. Not even close. An angel, a mystical fairy and a beautiful mystery woman, all rolled into one... this is the memory he had kept with him. She had him believing in miracles, daring to dream of a second chance at love.

No, this was a very different and angry Stephanie.

And you're not sure of how to deal with her. Or, if you should even try...

Afraid if he moved too fast, this could set her off, he slowly slipped his hands in his pockets before he studied her more closely.

Everything about her was more exquisite than he remembered. Except for her eyes. There was a caution he didn't remember from before.

This is when it hit him. Literally, it was like a punch in the gut.

Was he the reason for this?

This had him moving closer, his voice hesitant. "Stephanie... It's so good to see you."

This only had her backing away, her hands clenched at her sides.

She kept shaking her head. "Oh no, you don't... there's no way you can talk yourself out of this. Because whatever you have to say, I'm not going to believe you. Why should I? You've already proved how easily you break the promises you make."

She paused, briefly studying him. "But do you want to know what bothered me the most?"

When he so, so slowly shook his head, she continued. "I thought you were real, one of the good guys. I told you things about myself I've never shared with anyone else. All because I liked you... *really* liked you."

Then she shrugged. "But I guess I can't put all the blame on you. I'm just as much at fault for being such a fool."

He cleared his throat. "No matter what you think, I'm sorry. I am so very—"

She cut him off, ignoring his apology. "This is ridiculous. We have nothing to talk about. It's also obvious you don't need help with this project. And I don't want to be the one to help you. But since Elenore has done so much for everyone here at the hospital, I will do as she asks. Just don't expect me to be your friend. Now, if you'll excuse me, I need to get back to work."

She turned and began walking briskly towards the door.

He took off after her.

"Stephanie, wait. Before you leave, no matter how you feel about me, you're right. We have no choice but to see this through. This means we need to discuss what's next, compare our schedules and decide how often we should meet. Since you're required to be with me at all times because of hospital security rules, we need to come up with a plan. I'm sure you noticed this underlined in red."

When she glanced over at him, a puzzled expression on her face, he raised an eyebrow. "That is, if you actually read the complete list?"

The look she sent him was angry... but also guilty.

No, she hadn't read everything on the list. But this was only because after she read the opening paragraph, the words—work closely together at all times—had almost sent her into a panic and she stopped reading all together.

While he'd obviously read every word.

Proof of this, he pointed to the paper. "Right here… number six states because of the strict security guidelines within the hospital, any outside vendor, which I assume would be me, can't be on the floor without a certified staff member."

He glanced up from the list. "And you are a certified staff member. Hand-picked by Elenore, may I add. So, no matter how you feel, we need to stick together."

He folded up the paper and stuffed it in his pocket.

He waited.

When she had nothing to say, he cleared his throat. "*Sooooo*… whatever works for you. My schedule is pretty open."

She finally glanced over at him, giving a frustrated sigh. "Oh, I don't care. My shift goes from three to eleven. So, maybe four would work? Or seven? It's hard to pick a time because it's impossible to predict what the day will bring. Around here, things can change rather quickly."

He took time to think about this before he nodded. "Okay, let's plan on tomorrow around four. After that, we'll take each day as it comes."

She frowned. "Do you really think this is going to take more than one day?"

He hesitated. If he were to be honest? Yeah, he could probably get enough photos in one day. But for him, the photos were no longer his chief priority.

This didn't mean he was planning to skimp on the quality of his shots. Of course not. He would never let this happen. He was too much of a professional to let his personal life interfere with his work.

But he was now a man with a goal… one that could very well turn out to be life changing. He was going to do whatever was necessary to win Stephanie back.

Even if you have to drag this on for days.

Yep, he was in for the long haul.

So, in answer to her question, he nodded. *"Hmm...* from experience, I've learned it's best to go with the flow. Forget about the time. I like to shoot as many photos as I can. I don't want to later find I missed something because I was in a rush just to finish."

He had proof of this... the photos he took the night of the masquerade ball. When he had gone through them the following day, he had been so disappointed to find he had taken so few photos of Stephanie. Had he known that night would become only a memory, he would've taken more.

But maybe this was a good thing. You might have completely forgotten the reason you were even there... to take photos of the actual event.

A smile tweaked the corner of his mouth. "I would love to show you the photos I took the night of the masquerade ball. How I captured some of the magic of that night."

She almost smiled. Then she caught this, frowning instead. "Yes, for some people, I'm sure it was a night to remember. Where for others? Unfortunately, it turned out to be only a dream."

She sent him an accusing glance. "I should know. But now, I need to go. I will see you tomorrow. At four."

She turned, almost taking off in a run down the hall.

He groaned. That she couldn't wait to get away from him certainly wasn't a promising start.

He called out. "Stephanie..."

At first, he thought she was going to ignore him. But after a slight hesitation, she finally turned to look at him.

He smiled. "Elenore said you made those cookies? They're amazing, the best cookies I've ever had. I'm embarrassed to say I got greedy and took more than one. But, to be perfectly honest? I'm not the least bit sorry, they were that good."

For a long moment, she merely stared at him. Then, he wasn't sure, but he liked to think she smiled before she continued down the hall.

A sliver of hope filling him, he headed for the exit.

"Evan... do you have a minute?"

This voice becoming all too familiar, he turned to see Elenore beckoning to him from her office

He groaned, briefly closing his eyes.

Why do you have a feeling this can't be good?

His hands in his pockets and a tentative smile on his face, he slowly sauntered into the room.

She sent him a big smile in return, waving her hand towards the chair. "Please, have a seat."

Once he made himself comfortable, she clasped her hands together on the desk, a curious expression on her face. "Well? How did it go? Did the two of you come up with a plan?"

Suddenly feeling like he was back in grade school and about to be reprimanded by his teacher, a situation he'd experienced more times than he'd like to admit, Evan nervously cleared his throat. "A plan? Let's just say we're still trying to work things out. But don't worry. Unless we're hit with some major catastrophe, I'm sure we'll have no problem pulling it off."

Her eyebrow raised, she almost smiled. "Let's hope 'pulling it off' is exactly what happens. And how did it go with you and Stephanie?"

"Me? And Stephanie? We'll be fine. Any background info or stories she shares will give me a deeper perspective into hospital life." He smiled. "This can only lead to great photos."

She laughed. "Oh, Evan... I was referring to the two of you as a couple, not how well you'll work together. I'm not blind. I've been around long enough to know when two people are attracted to each other." She was shaking her head. "My goodness, the chemistry between the two of you is electric. What makes it even more obvious is the way you look at her."

She nodded, pressing her hand to her heart. "Your eyes show what you feel for her right here."

She leaned forward, intently searching his face. "But I feel there's something you did to lose her trust. So, tell me... what happened?"

He dragged his hand down over his jaw, stifling a groan. It was obvious Elenore had no plans to let up on this. So, he needed to come up with a believable explanation. One that didn't have him coming across as a complete jerk.

He sighed. "Let's just say I broke a promise. Two, as a matter of fact. I fixed the first one, but I still have a lot of work with the second. Between you and me, I consider it's a miracle she's even talking to me."

He sent a longing glance out into the hall. This wasn't a discussion he wanted to have right now.

No… you're not open to any more input. It's bad enough you've already had to listen to Joe's take on the whole subject.

He let out a long, drawn out breath. "But don't worry, I'll figure it out."

She peered at him over the top of her glasses. "I hope so. And I hope this happens soon. Because I think the two of you have a lot in common, probably more than you know. You also make such a striking couple. In fact, this brings up something else I'd like to run by you. A favor of sorts."

He sent another wistful glance out into the hallway before he smiled, trying to hide his uneasiness.

Elenore sat back in her chair. She knew exactly what he was thinking. Yes, she could be demanding. And she knew some people didn't like that she never hesitated to speak her mind. But she had learned not to let this bother her.

At her age, the only person she needed to please was herself.

She held his gaze. "I am having a dinner party this Saturday night, a black-tie event. I guess it's what you would call my annual appreciation dinner for the board members. This year made even more special, their support turning my dream of a community room into a reality. I've found people always appreciate an extra pat on the back."

She shrugged, her brow furrowed in a frown. "Some more than others."

She sent him a big smile. "Since I've decided to appoint you and Stephanie as ambassadors for this project, I'd like you to be at this dinner. Your job will be to get the younger generation involved, something we so desperately need."

She shook her head. "I fear the group I've worked with for so long is now getting too old and set in their ways. Change doesn't come easily to them." She sighed. "But then, the same applies to me."

Sitting up straighter in her chair, she raised an eyebrow. "So, are you on board?"

Knowing he really had no choice but to agree, this is what he did.

It was only after she filled him in on the details of the dinner party and he had left her office, something she said suddenly registered.

A black-tie event?

So... this meant a tuxedo, right?

This means you'll need to rent one again. Even though after the masquerade ball, you vowed this wouldn't be happening.

Maybe it was time to throw in the towel and get one of his own? Since he needed to wear one again for the awards dinner Joe asked him to attend next week.

But he'd worry about this later. Briskly running down the steps to the main floor and pushing open the door, it was a relief to breathe in the fresh spring air.

Once he was in his car, he gazed up at the third floor of the hospital. Raking his hand through his hair, he sighed. This job was turning into a lot more than he expected.

But on the bright side?

It was also a guarantee he would be spending time with Stephanie.

But one more mistake? Or another broken promise?

You'll lose her for good this time.

CHAPTER 13

All our dreams can come true
if we have the courage to pursue them.
~Unknown

After her dramatic exit, Stephanie headed for the nurses station. Relieved to see no one was around, she sank down in a chair and closed her eyes.

The way her heart was beating so hard and out of control, you'd think she had just finished running a marathon.

Hoping to slow things down, she decided to once again put some of those yoga breathing exercises to work.

And again, she got nothing. If anything, she felt more anxious than before.

After making a mental note to tell Melanie she needed to come up with some new moves, she signed into the computer. It was time to get her mind off Evan and back on her job.

She spent the next few minutes of staring at the current patient stats before she groaned, dropping her head in her hands.

You can't let this guy get to you. Remember? He already had his chance, and he blew it.

She didn't understand.

Was there was some kind of sign hanging over her head? Advertising only guys like Noah and Evan need apply for her affection? You know, the break-your-heart-and-have-no-intention-of-sticking-around kind of guys.

Lifting her head, she muttered out loud. "Well, from now on, you're done with men. Every single one of them. For good."

An annoying laugh came from behind her, one she'd recognize anywhere.

It was Lucy. One of the full-time nurses on the floor, she was known as the biggest gossip on staff. This was something she was quite proud of, claiming it as her way of keeping everyone on their best behavior.

Leaning against the counter and crossing her arms over her chest, she peered down at Stephanie. "So? Did I just hear right? You're done with men? *Hmm...* I find this hard to believe. Especially after what I just saw."

She grinned. "Come on, give... who is this gorgeous man who seems to have appeared out of nowhere, leaving you so rattled?"

She tapped her finger to her mouth, mulling this over. "Though I'm sure I would react the same way if he had shown up to see me. He's definitely easy on the eye."

After a nonchalant shrug, Stephanie peered even closer at the screen. Maybe if she ignored her, Lucy would stop asking questions and leave.

Who are you trying to kid? You know darn well this won't happen. She wants information. The more scandalous, the better.

She sighed before mumbling her response. "He's a photographer. Mrs. Cromley hired him to take photos for a collage she wants to have on one wall of the new wing."

Lucy wanted more. "But why you? Are you into photography, too? Or just pretending, using this opportunity to get to know the guy better."

Stephanie shot her an annoyed look. "No, believe me, the only photos I take are using my phone." She sighed. "You know how strict they are about security here. Since this means he's not allowed to wander around the hospital on his own, Mrs. Cromley asked me to be his escort."

Lucy's eyes grew wide. "Escort?"

Then she laughed. "*Hmm*... how convenient for both of you."

Her face now almost up to the computer screen, hoping to hide that she was blushing, Stephanie almost barked out her response. "Ok, so maybe using the word escort was a bad choice. But I'm sure you know what I meant. Think of me as a glorified tour guide, someone to answer questions he might have about the patients or the hospital. Or, I don't know... whatever else he needs to know."

She groaned, dragging her hand through her hair. "I assure you, this is not something I want to do. If there was a way to pass the job on to you? I'd do this in an instant."

Lucy was nodding. "*Hmm*... and how were you chosen for this? Do you know him? And what do you think Noah will have to say?"

Stephanie closed her eyes.

Okay, this had gone a little too far. You need to put an end to this conversation.

In one swift move, she pushed away from the desk. She stood, glaring over at Lucy. "Yes, I know him. I met him a few months ago. But this has nothing to do with why he is here. Mrs. Cromley set this up, and why she chose me is just as much of a surprise to me as it is to you."

Searching for her phone, she almost shoved Lucy into the counter to grab it from under a pile of papers. Ignoring her shocked expression, she slipped the phone in her pocket and walked away, her voice coming out extremely loud in the silence. "And Noah? Or, as its only proper, we should refer to him as Dr. Davis? What he thinks of me, doesn't matter."

She waved her hands in the air. "Nor do I care."

She stormed off down the hall, unaware the one and only Dr. Davis was standing only a few feet away and had heard every word.

Almost in shock, he and Lucy stared at each other

Lucy was the first to speak. "Well... that was, uh... interesting, wasn't it?" She aimed a bright smile at him. "So, is there something I can do for you, Dr. Davis?"

Staring down the hall where Stephanie had disappeared, his mind trying to process what brought on her angry outburst, Noah's glance over at Lucy was a bit distracted.

Then, after shaking his head, he handed her a folder. "I just received this. A new patient of mine and Dr. Carlyle's will arrive on the floor in about an hour. Post-surgery, and in need of extra care for the next few days. Can you check the report to verify all the information is correct and a room will be ready in time?"

As she began reading over the patient's medical file, he whipped out his phone and began scrolling through his messages. This was all for show, since he couldn't even read what was on the screen, his mind still reeling with what he had overheard.

Never had Stephanie referred to him in such a furious tone of voice. That this upset him was understandable.

Now, he had only caught the end of Stephanie and Lucy's conversation. But this was enough to let him know if he wanted to keep Stephanie in his life, he needed to up his game a little.

He glanced up from his phone, his eyebrows raised. But, come on... he was finding it hard to believe she meant what she'd said.

What he thinks about me doesn't matter. Nor do I care.

He shook his head, a knowing smirk on his face. There was no way she believed this. And even if she did? He was confident he'd be able to change her mind. A couple of smiles, a few lingering looks, and one or two evasive promises would have her right back where he wanted her.

He just needed to be careful. Content with the no commitment vibes they had going on, he had no intention of taking their relationship any further. But, having grown comfortable with her companionship, he didn't want to tell her this and risk losing her for good. The way she became so flustered when she was around him was also an enormous boost to his ego.

He glanced over at Lucy. What the heck was taking her so long? He wanted to leave. It had been a long day.

He cleared his throat. "Well?"

Her eyes still on the folder, she didn't even look up as she began walking away. "Everything seems in order. I'll make sure everything is ready to go, Dr. Davis."

"Thanks, Lucy. I'm leaving. So, have a good evening."

She finally glanced over at him. "You're leaving for the day? Any special plans for tonight?"

When he didn't answer, only kept walking, she leaned against the counter.

She was smiling as she called out to him. "Okay, then... whatever you do, I hope it's a good one."

It had been over an hour since Elenore ended her meeting with Evan and Stephanie.

Since then, she had spent most of this time in her office, the phone to her ear.

She sent another wistful glance out her office window. It had turned out to be a beautiful afternoon, all sunshine and blue skies. Not a day one should have to spend inside, held prisoner by a cell phone.

Yes, she could set her phone to speaker mode. This would enable her to finish up some of her paperwork, maybe even move around a bit, rack up some steps, get her blood flowing.

But speaker calls didn't set well with her. She didn't like that every word of the conversation was available for everyone to hear.

Not that she had anything to hide. But since she was never shy about speaking her mind, there was always that slim chance she might say something she'd later regret.

"Hello? Are you still there?" Coming back on the line, the woman from city hall had the information Elenore was looking for. After she promised she would send out a copy of right away, Elenore ended the call.

She leaned back in her chair, and removing her glasses, she massaged the bridge of her nose. Then she stared down at what she had written on the notepad in front of her.

So... now what? Even though you're not responsible for what happened, you feel an obligation to do something.

She was in a quandary. She had always been one to do the right thing. But at this late date, she wondered if it would be better to leave things as they were.

Well, until she had the report in her hands, there wasn't much she could do.

Time to go home.

She grabbed her purse and keys, locked the office door, and headed for the elevator. Maybe she would have a glass of wine with her dinner tonight. After the events of the day, she deserved one.

She also had a lot of thinking to do.

CHAPTER 14

The next afternoon, Evan pulled into the hospital parking lot with fifteen minutes to spare before he was to meet Stephanie. He didn't want to be late, so he had given himself extra time.

After he signed in at the reception desk, he took the stairs up to the third floor. As he approached the nurses station, he saw someone seated at the counter. A woman, her head down, was typing on the computer.

He slowed his steps, a smile spreading across his lips.

Stephanie...

Engrossed in what she was working on, she didn't even notice he was there.

But this was okay. He didn't mind waiting.

Cautiously leaning against the counter, so as not to disturb her, he watched her fingers flying across the keys. More like attacking them, he'd have to say. He wondered what she was so worked up about.

After she read what she'd typed, she groaned, raking her hands through her hair. Then she pressed her finger down hard on the delete key, erasing everything.

Fascinated, he listened as she began mumbling to herself. "Come on… what are you doing? Just finish this. Then you need to get yourself together. You've let yourself get all worked up about seeing him again, and he hasn't even shown up yet. You can't start letting him make you crazy. Remember? He's not worth it."

Then she mumbled something else, bringing him to move even closer in order to catch what she said.

"Yeah, keep telling yourself this."

At first, this had him smiling.

Whoa… this is fantastic. Because it sure sounds like she's talking about you, doesn't it?

The more he listened, the bigger his smile…

And you have her all worked up? To the point she can't stop thinking about you? Going as far to make her crazy?

In this case, crazy was good, right?

But then, and this was an enormous blow, did she just say what he thought she did? He wasn't worth it?

He frowned. This wasn't what a man wanted to hear.

At least, not this man.

It was time for him to announce his presence. Before she had even more to say about him, something he didn't need to know.

He cleared his throat.

Her reaction was a flashback of what happened when she caught her first glimpse of him the night of the masquerade ball. Startled, she lifted her head to find her face only inches from his. Giving a little shriek, she came diving out of her chair. Her hand hit the cup of coffee she had set next to the computer, sending the entire contents splashing across the counter and right down the front of her scrubs.

Her mouth wide open in shock, she stared at him.

Then she came to life. After glancing down at the coffee dripping down the front of her, she jerked her head up and glared at him. It was a look threatening enough to have him take a step back.

Her voice came out in a hiss. "Now look what you've done, sneaking up on me like that. What were you thinking?" She grabbed a roll of paper towels from under the counter and shoved it at him. "Hurry… you need to help me clean this up."

Without another word between them, they began mopping up the spill. Though, if Evan had his way, there was a lot he'd like to say. Starting with... why was she putting all the blame on him? He did not sneak up on her. He had gone out of his way not to startle her. Was it his fault she always seemed to over-react?

Nope, he wasn't the one at fault here.

Absolutely not.

But he wasn't stupid. Voicing his opinion, no matter how right he thought he was, would not go over well. He had learned from an early age to tread carefully when faced with anger, be it coming from a man or a woman.

But more so when it was a member of the opposite sex.

This went back to when he was in the sixth grade. It hadn't been his intention to embarrass a girl in his class when he teased her about her braces. This had been his way of flirting, having harbored a crush on her, braces and all. So, the slap she gave to his face had been a complete surprise. Then, to make things worse, she went crying to the teacher, and he ended up with five days of an after-school detention.

So, yes... he had learned his lesson very early in life. If in doubt, it was best to shut up and wait for things to cool down.

And Stephanie? How was she coping with this?

Now that she had time to calm down, she was feeling a little foolish. But when she had glanced up to find him so close, his smile aimed right at her? Was it even a surprise she reacted like she had? Any woman alive would have done the same.

But this was trivial compared to the possibility he may have overheard her talking to herself.

She glanced over at him. The smug look on his face led her to believe he had. So, to avoid even looking at him, she frantically began wiping at the coffee stains on her scrubs.

This is when Evan noticed the pattern of the fabric, a whimsical design of dancing puppies and kittens.

A smile spread across his lips.

Hmm... maybe you can make a little joke about this? Lighten the moment?

He cleared his throat. "So, I guess you could say we have a case of 'it's raining cats and dogs' going on here."

She looked up from her scrubbing, sending him a puzzled glance. He cleared his throat again, giving a pointed look at her scrubs. "I, *ah...* I was referring to your uniform... you know, the cat and dog pattern. And the coffee... well, that would be the rain. I just thought... but, never mind..."

His voice trailing off, he shrugged, wondering why he had even brought it up.

But then she rewarded him with the tiniest of smiles before she threw the rest of the used towels in the wastebasket. This had him moving closer, a tentative smile on his face. "Stephanie, I'm sorry. I didn't intend to startle you. Honest, I didn't. I only wanted to let you know I was here, since I'm earlier than expected."

Almost holding his breath, knowing what he was about to do could very well work against him, he reached over to brush his knuckles along the curve of her jaw. When she didn't pull away, almost leaning into his touch, this had his next words coming out easy. "I guess I'm eager to get to work on the project. And to spend time with you."

Her fingers trailing over the same spot he touched, she closed her eyes. This simple contact, as brief as it was, had sent her spiraling right back to how she felt the night of the masquerade ball.

How is this guy able to get to you like this?

"Stephanie... hey, are you okay?"

She blinked, dropping her hand to her side

He was so close. This had her flustered, her heartbeat soaring into high gear. In a panic, she backed away.

A dangerous move... at least for her, it was. She bumped into the chair and lost her balance.

He reached out to grab her arm, his gaze briefly holding hers. "All right there?"

It was only when she nodded, he let go of her arm.

And darn if he didn't aim another one of his smiles right at her. "It appears my presence is causing nothing but trouble." He backed away. "Maybe it would be best if I left, even for a few minutes. I can get you another cup of coffee or something. This will give you time to calm down."

As soon as these words came out of his mouth, he knew she was going to take them all wrong. But then again, he wouldn't blame her.

What the hell made you come out and say something like that? Makes you look like you're a little full of yourself, doesn't it?

Sure enough, her expression alone was more than enough to let him know what she was thinking. Unfortunately, this didn't stop her from feeling the need to share this aloud. Her hands going to her hips, she glared at him. "Don't flatter yourself. What happened here has nothing to do with you. It just happened. And now, if you will excuse me, I'm going to go change into another uniform. While I'm gone, please try to stay out of trouble."

Her lecture finished, she picked up the wastebasket and walked away.

Now Evan wouldn't be able to tell you why he felt the need to go after her. That she took the wastebasket with her was something he had no reason to question.

But for some strange and unexplainable reason, this is what he did. Breaking into a run, he almost skidded to a stop next to her. "Hey, what are you planning to do with the wastebasket?"

Stephanie turned to him, a puzzled look on her face. She glanced down at the full wastebasket, then at him. She didn't understand.

Why did he even care?

She shrugged. "If you must know, I'm planning to empty it. We're not supposed to have trash piling up in the nurses station. But again, thanks to you, this is what happened. So, I'm only trying to follow the rules."

This wasn't entirely true. But she certainly didn't want him to know she really had no clue as to why she was now holding the wastebasket. She honestly didn't even remember picking it up.

Obviously, he had her so riled up she wasn't thinking clearly.

Evan held out his hand. "Here, let me take care of that for you. You just worry about changing into a dry uniform."

Maybe he saw his offer of help would be a way to redeem himself. Or a way to make up for the fiasco of the coffee spill. But, for whatever reason, he just couldn't let it go.

She shook her head. "Nope, I've got this under control." She swung the wastebasket out of his reach at the same time he made a grab for it. Furious, she held on even tighter. This resulted in a brief tug of war between them before they both let go at the same time.

This sent the wastebasket barreling through the air before it slammed into the tile wall with a colossal bang. They watched in disbelief as the contents went shooting in all directions, sending papers, cups and whatnot everywhere. It was almost as if a mini-tornado had passed through, leaving a paper trail of destruction in its wake.

In shock, they gazed around at the mess before they stared at each other. It was the sound of voices that had them turning to see almost the entire third floor staff, along with one of the hospital's security guards, bearing down on them.

The horrified look on Stephanie's face had Evan jumping into action. He jerked his head towards the hallway. "Go... just go. Now... I'll take care of this."

When she continued to stare at him, her mouth working as if she wanted to say something, he put his hands on her shoulders and pointed her in the right direction. "I mean it... Now, go..."

So, she took off in a run down the hall.

Evan glanced down at his watch again.

Stephanie had been gone for only about fifteen minutes? How was this possible? Because it seemed like so much longer.

After his very brief and simple explanation of what happened, leading everyone to believe he was the one at fault, the mess had been cleaned up in no time. Everyone then went back to work.

Unfortunately, there was one nurse who seemed to think he needed her company.

Her name, she told him, was Lucy.

As soon as she had opened her mouth, Evan knew she was the type of woman he usually tried to avoid.

This wasn't because he thought he was too good for her. Or there was something wrong with her. No, she was quite attractive and had a pleasant smile. Along with a very outgoing personality.

Maybe a little too outgoing?

She just wasn't his type.

If there was such a thing as his type.

Remember Melody? The woman in human resources Joe claimed had been asking about him?

Yep, Lucy and Melody were two of a kind. Since Lucy introduced herself, she hadn't stopped talking. Her endless questions and comments, coming one right after the other, had him wishing he could take off running.

She also had this way of inching closer to him, or placing her hand on his arm. And no matter how many times he backed away, or shrugged his arm from her hold, she came right back at him, moving even closer.

She was deep into a very detailed description of a party she was throwing on Saturday night, giving him every reason why he should stop by, when he saw Stephanie walking towards them.

Thank God...

Lucy also saw this. Her hand possessively resting on his arm, she sent Stephanie a bright smile. "I was trying to convince Evan he should come to my party Saturday night. I would have liked to tell him you would also be there, but you always refuse my invitations."

She glanced over at Evan, shaking her head. "Stephanie has made it very clear she's not a party kind of girl. Isn't this right, Steff?"

If only to look busy so she wouldn't have to answer her, Stephanie began gathering up all the papers on the desk. After she shoved them in a folder, she looked up to see both Evan and Lucy were watching this, waiting for her response.

She sighed. "That's not true, Lucy. I like parties. But I'd much rather hang out with my close friends than with a bunch of people I don't know."

Crossing his arms over his chest, Evan nodded over at Lucy. "I agree with Stephanie. So, I guess that means I'm not much of a party kind of guy either. I've also just learned this Saturday won't work for me. Or for Stephanie."

He sent Stephanie a wink. "It appears we already have something going on that night."

Stephanie glanced over at him, confused. "We do?"

He nodded. "Yes… an invitation we can't refuse. I'll fill you in later."

He glanced down at his watch. "But right now, we've got work to do. You need to make your rounds. And I need to start taking some photos."

He sent Lucy a smile. "It was nice talking to you, Lucy. I hope your party is a great success."

He took hold of Stephanie's arm, giving her no choice but to go with him to the elevator.

Her forehead creased in a frown, Lucy watched until they got onto the elevator.

She couldn't figure them out. And this was driving her crazy. She liked to think she was quite the expert on love and relationships.

Even though Stephanie had made it very clear she didn't like the guy, Lucy didn't believe this for a minute. From what she had seen so far, the chemistry was there, but something was holding them back. And she was determined to find out what it was.

And if it did turn out to be nothing serious? She was going to stake a claim on Evan before someone else did. Like she had told Stephanie, he was a keeper.

It just wasn't fair. Why were the good ones always taken?

After a long and dramatic sigh, she reached for the papers Stephanie had put in the folder. She groaned when she saw what a mess she had made of them. It was going to take her forever to put everything back in the right order.

Stephanie could say whatever she wanted, but it was obvious Evan had taken over more of her mind than she let on.

CHAPTER 15

The first sigh of love is the last breath of wisdom.
~ Anonymous

O nce they were in the elevator, Stephanie moved as far away from Evan as she could. Since the elevator was the original model from when the hospital was built over seventy-five years ago, this added up to about a foot and a half.

If even that.

And even if it was five times this, for you, it still wouldn't be enough.

This had her moving even further into the corner.

Her gaze fixed on the doors, her voice seemed to come out extremely loud in the small space. "So, are you going to let me know what you meant when you told Lucy we already have plans for Saturday night?"

Noting she was still flustered, he tried not to smile. Casually slipping his hands in his pockets, he glanced over at her. "I don't know if I should. At least not until you promise to be a little nicer to me. Or at least act like you tolerate my company."

She glared at him. "Promise? You toss that word around quite a bit, don't you?"

When he only sighed, shaking his head, she persisted. "Unless you only used that as an excuse to get out of Lucy's party."

She tossed her head. "You should go. You might enjoy it. I'm sure you would be a hit with all her friends."

He nodded. *"Hmm... I might just do that. It could turn out to be fun."*

In the silence that followed, he glanced over to see she was frowning. She also looked like she was about to cry. His smile disappearing, he was quick to reassure her. "But to be honest, that's not something I'd want to do. Nor am I interested in meeting any of Lucy's friends."

Hell, no... this is the last thing you want to do.

He began fiddling around with his camera, adjusting the lens and, who knows what else, completely ignoring her. Yes, he had a habit of doing this when he was nervous or unsure about something. And right now, he'd have to say he was a little of both.

Watching him, she gave a frustrated sigh. "Well? Are you going to tell me? And if not, why did you even bring it up?"

He appeared to be confused. "Oh, are we back to talking about Saturday night?" Then he grinned. "I'm sorry. But for some reason, and even though it always seems to get me in trouble, I enjoy teasing you. If you had pigtails, I'd sneak up behind you and give them a yank. You know, just to show that I like you."

She stared at him, dumbfounded.

Reaching over, he pressed his fingertip to her lips.

"It's all good, sweetheart. And about Saturday night? I think I'm going to leave it up to Elenore to give you the details."

Sweetheart?

In order to ignore this, because it probably didn't mean anything, she tried to focus on what he said about Elenore. She groaned. "Oh my God, another one of Elenore's plans? This is what always happens. She sets her mind on something, and you don't have a chance."She sent him a guilty look. "I'm not criticizing her. Not after all she does for everyone here at the hospital. But sometimes? Well, let's just say, working with her can be a real challenge."

He was still smiling. He was getting a kick out of how flustered she was, her cheeks flushed, her eyes flashing with fire. It was enough to make him want to push the lock button on the elevator, pull her into his arms and give her a kiss that had her clinging to him for dear life.

Weren't elevators known as the perfect setting for romance? The chance to share a passionate kiss. All the while, hoping you won't get caught?

Yeah, you wouldn't mind this happening…

But speaking of elevators, was it his imagination, or had they even moved yet? He knew the elevator was old.

Which meant it was slow. But not this slow.

She was still scowling at him, her cheeks now even more flushed. "What are you grinning about?"

Unable to lose the smile, he shrugged. "I'm sorry. Carried away with my thoughts, I guess. Wondering if this is some kind of little rendezvous you planned? Hoping to get some alone time with me in the elevator? Or did you forget to hit the button? Because we seem to be at a standstill right now."

She dove over to hit the button to the fourth floor, sputtering out her answer. "Trust me, this was not a plan. The last thing I want is to spend more time with you. Certainly not in a small space like this."

He nodded. "*Hmm…* not much of a compliment. And I think the space is quite cozy. Makes one think of romance. Taking a chance one normally wouldn't consider."

A suspicious look on her face, she edged closer to the doors.

Where she remained until they opened, and scooting out into the hall, she headed for the nurses station, with him trailing behind.

He watched as she grabbed a folder off the counter and began leafing through the contents. Once, twice, three times, she did this before she stilled, staring off into space.

Evan found this interesting.

Was she still back in the elevator? Wondering what could have happened?

Because he knew he was…

This had him more at ease, his confidence soaring. He cleared his throat. "I'm very disappointed in you."

Her mouth falling open, she turned to him. "What?"

He nodded at the scrubs she had changed into, frowning at the familiar sports logo printed all over the fabric.

He shook his head. "The Yankees? Please, out of all the choices you must have had, you chose the Yankees? How could you? Where's your loyalty to Cleveland?"

Slapping the folder shut, she gave a huffy sigh. "Believe me, this was the best I could do. All the other choices were men's sizes and too large for me. And, to put your mind at rest, I wouldn't dream of wearing these in public. My friends would disown me." She sent him another glaring look. "And, must I remind you, the reason I'm even wearing these is all because of you?"

She began walking away, her words coming over her shoulder. "Come on... let's go."

For a moment, he didn't move. He was a little disappointed. Once again, his attempt at a little humor didn't work.

Well, he wasn't giving up yet.

He took off after her. If only to slow her down, he put his hand on her arm. This is when he saw she was crying. Or close to it.

Yep, those were tears pooling in her eyes.

Oh, geez… this isn't what you wanted to happen.

He groaned. "Stephanie… please don't cry." And even though he wasn't sure why, he apologized. "Please, I'm sorry. I didn't mean to make you cry."

She jerked her arm from his hold. She wanted to tell him she wasn't crying. At least not yet. The tears were there all right, ready to fall. But she had no plans to let this happen.

And to be honest? She wouldn't be able to explain why they were even there.

Stuffing his hands in his pockets, he sighed. "Stephanie, please… the last thing I want is to make you unhappy. Would you like me to tell Elenore this won't work? I'm sure she'll have no trouble finding someone else to take the photos. No job is worth seeing you like this."

This sent her tears out in a flood.

Maybe he was right. But now she felt awful. Why should he lose this job? It would certainly be easier to replace her. Any of the other nurses would jump at the chance to take her place.

She only knew things couldn't stay the way they were. At the rate they were going, they might accidentally kill each other.

She took a deep breath. "You're right. But it seems I'm the one who is the problem. So, I'll talk to Elenore. Let her know I can't do this."

"Can't do what?" This inquiry coming from behind them, they both whirled around.

Only a few feet away, Elenore was shaking her head. She frowned. "You aren't thinking of bailing out on me, are you? Because this could be a big problem. Must I once again remind you of the tight deadline we're on?"

It took a few seconds for Stephanie to find her voice. "Mrs. Cromley..."

"Stephanie, please... its Elenore, remember? While working together on this project, there is no reason for us to be formal with each other."

Stephanie took a deep breath. "Okay, then... Elenore, we..." she nodded over at Evan, "and by we, I mean Evan and I, we decided... well, we thought..."

Her words trailing off, she sent Evan a desperate look.

Evan put his hand on her shoulder, giving it a gentle squeeze before he sent Elenore his most charming smile. "I believe what Stephanie is trying to say is she's a little nervous, knowing how much this new wing means to you. But don't worry, neither one of us plans to bail out on you. I promise you this."

Stephanie just barely managed to not roll her eyes. Again, here he was with the promises. She was wondering if he even knew what the word meant. Otherwise, he wouldn't use it so freely.

Think of the heartache this would have saved you.

Elenore peered at Evan over the rims of her glasses. "I'm going to hold you to this promise... both of you. And please, let's make sure there will be no more mishaps like what happened on the third floor a short time ago, okay?"

She nodded at the guilty look Evan and Stephanie shared. "Yes, I heard all about that."

Shaking her head, she turned to leave. Then she came to a stop, turning back to them. "One more thing, since I won't be around the rest of the week to remind you, don't forget about Saturday night."

After frowning over at Evan, Stephanie shrugged. "I'm not sure I know what you mean?"

Elenore gestured to Evan. "*Ah...* you haven't told Stephanie yet, have you? Since I should have left here long before this, I'll leave it to you to give her the details. But to refresh your memory... my house, cocktails at six-thirty, dinner at seven. If you can show up a little early, this would be nice. And please, no more shenanigans. I expect both of you to be on your best behavior."

With what was almost a smile, she left.

Stephanie twisted away from Evan's grasp.

Her arms crossed, she glared at him. "What happened there? I thought we had an agreement?" Then she slapped her hand to her forehead. "Oh, now I remember... a promise from you doesn't mean anything."

He groaned, dropping his hand to his side. He didn't understand. He thought he had handled the situation quite well. Hadn't he done an excellent job of smoothing things over? Reassuring both her and Elenore there was nothing to worry about?

Everything was good, crisis averted.

Why couldn't she see this?

He cleared his throat. "I don't know. I really don't. But I think we both knew this would happen, so why fight it?"

She ignored this. "Will you please tell me what's going on with Saturday night?"

After giving a long and dramatic sigh, because, hey... he knew darn well how she was going to react, he filled her in about the dinner. Along with Elenore's reason for inviting them.

Speechless, she stared at him.

Ambassadors? You and Evan? What did this even mean?

She shook her head. "No, no, no... I can't do this. Absolutely not. She is asking too much."

After giving her a long look, not sure what to say, Evan picked up his camera and began explaining the importance of lighting and the time of day when taking a photo. He then gave her more information than she would ever need, even going as far to point out all the different settings.

Then he glanced at his watch.

She took this as he didn't care how she felt. Or worse yet, since she'd made it very clear she had no plans of attending the dinner, he was relieved. And now he wanted to get to work and finish the project as quickly as possible. The less time he had to spend with her, the better.

This made her angry.

Evan wasn't thinking like this at all.

He figured his best option would be to get to work, stay low, and wait it out, hoping once she thought things over, she'd change her mind. This was the way he usually worked out his problems.

There was one thing he knew for sure... he would not be attending the dinner without her.

He watched as she appeared to struggle with what she wanted to say. Then, after a long, frustrated sigh, she took off down the hall, her words floating back to him. "I see we only have about two hours before you have to leave. So, if you want to salvage something of this day, follow me."

He had to break into a trot to keep up with her.

For the next two hours, while Stephanie took care of her patients, Evan trailed behind, snapping photos.

And the entire time, she ignored him.

Pretty sure this was her way of trying to avoid any discussion about Elenore's dinner party, he followed her cue and did the same. It was when she was escorting him to the elevator, he finally brought up the subject. "You do know Elenore isn't going to take no for an answer, don't you?"

This earned him a curt nod.

He peered more closely at her. "So, can I assume you've thought it over and you'll go?"

She gave another nod, avoiding his gaze.

They were both silent until the elevator doors opened and he got in. He sent her a tentative smile. "Okay, then... this is good to hear. And now, about tomorrow... same time?"

She waited until the doors had almost completely closed before she gave him an answer. "Yes, tomorrow... same time."

When Evan walked out of the elevator onto the main floor, even though he wasn't sure if he had a reason to smile, he was.

Because, honestly? Today turned out a lot better than you thought it would.

And Stephanie?

She was walking down the hall when she spun around and made a mad dash towards the exit. She practically flew down the two flights of stairs, pushing open the doors to the main floor just as Evan was about to walk outside.

She called out to him. "Evan... wait."

He turned, his brow furrowing in concern when he saw her. "Stephanie... is something wrong?"

Out of breath, she came to stand in front of him. "No... nothing... nothing's wrong. I... I only wanted to say, well... I'm sorry I've been so crazy and everything."

She shrugged, giving him a tentative smile.

For a moment he was silent, his look searching. Then he reached over, and brushing his knuckles over her cheek, the smile he gave her sent an unexpected warmth through her.

This had her moving even closer.

Unknowingly, he did the same. "Hey, its okay."

The need to touch her again, he reached over to tuck her hair behind her ear. "But thanks for telling me."

After a few awkward seconds, he cleared his throat. "Again, it's all good. I'll see you tomorrow, okay?"

She nodded.

Then she turned, almost taking off in a run to the elevator.

Though he had no reason to wait, he stayed until the elevator doors were about to close.

He waved.

And, with what he'd swear was an actual smile on her face, she waved back.

He pushed open the door and headed for the parking lot.

He was grinning like crazy.

CHAPTER 16

S tephanie pushed open the door to the Chic Boutique, the jingling bells announcing her arrival.

She had decided to stop in before she went to work. An event like Elenore's dinner party was deserving of a new dress.

If only as a confidence booster. *Right?*

"Hey, Steffi..." Sophie waved to her from the back of the boutique. "I'll be on this call for a few more minutes, so look around. Our newest arrivals are on the rack by the dressing room. See if anything catches your eye. Check out the blue cocktail dress. It's gorgeous. When I saw it, I thought it would be perfect for you."

Stephanie sent her a wave before wandering over to check out the cocktail dress. She took it off the rack and held it up to her in front of the mirror.

As usual, Sophie was right. The dress was stunning.

Though it might be too much? The beading along the neckline wasn't her style. She liked simple lines, dresses that flowed when she walked. Chiffon and soft jerseys in pastel shades.

She looked down at her scrubs, the random stains on the front.

But then what would you know? Look at you... this has become your signature look.

Because, honestly? She didn't have a clue what to wear for this dinner party. The guest list alone was enough to scare her. Made up of who's who in the Cleveland's society pages, the cost of one of their outfits was more than she spent for clothes all year.

She stared at her reflection in the mirror.

It also didn't help that socializing didn't come easily to her. She wasn't good at making conversation. Her mind would always go blank at the most inopportune of times.

With a sigh, she hung the dress back on the rack. If only she could just be herself. Like when she was with the children.

She was looking through another rack when Sophie joined her, a big smile on her face. "I'm so glad to see you. We were all so worried when you left during dinner." She peered more closely at her. "Are you better now?"

"Yeah, I'm fine. At least I was until I woke up the next morning to find I had lost my wallet. It was not one of my best nights."

Sophie shrugged. "Oh well, as long as you're okay now."

She grinned. "Now, what brings you here? Do you have a hot date coming up? Met a new man you want to impress? Whatever it is, we'll take care of it."

Stephanie laughed. "I hope. I have to attend this dinner party on Saturday night. Hosted by none other than Elenore Cromley. She gave me the job of assistant to this photographer she hired. His photos are to be featured in a collage on one wall of the new wing of the hospital."

Sophie tilted her head, a confused look on her face. "I didn't know you were into photography. Is this a new hobby?"

Stephanie laughed. "No, to both. You know how strict they are with security at the hospital. Which means they don't want someone wandering the floor by themselves, taking photos. This wouldn't go over well with either the kids or their parents. So, my job is to act as a buffer, I guess."

Sophie nodded. "*Hmm...* so, this photographer... is he cute? Young? Available?"

The blush that spread across Stephanie's cheeks was more than enough to give Sophie her answer.

She grinned. "*Ah...* then I want to hear everything, every single detail. And don't think you can brush me off, because you can't. I know you too well to let that happen."

Stephanie almost groaned aloud.

Oh, geeez... maybe coming to the boutique wasn't such a good idea? You know how relentless Sophie can be.

She grabbed a dress off the rack. A mix of tulle, sequins, and feathers, there was a definite rainbow theme going on. After fluffing out the tulle, sending a shower of glitter everywhere, she held the dress up against her. She glanced over at Sophie. "So, what do you think? Is this me, or what?"

Since this was a dress Sophie knew Stephanie would never wear, not even on a million dollar bet, she took it from her and hung it back on the rack. "*Hmm...* hilarious. But not your style." Crossing her arms over her chest, she peered more closely at her. "Why am I getting the impression this guy must be pretty special? You want to impress him. And if so, what's the problem?"

Stephanie sighed. "If I tell you, will you promise to keep this between us? Until now, Jason is the only person I've confided in. But I always have to be careful with how much I tell him since he can be so protective. I swear, he thinks any guy who comes within a few feet of me as a potential evil villain, out to kidnap me."

She shrugged. "But I need advice...."

Sophie laughed. "Yeah, older brothers can be like that. I see it all the time with Chester, with how he acts with Carrie and Livy. But enough about them. I want to hear more about this new guy of yours."

She grinned. "So, come on... spill..."

So, Stephanie told her everything. Beginning with how they'd hit it off the night of the masquerade ball, he'd promised to call, but never did. And now, after she'd accepted she'd never see him again, they were expected to work together on one of Elenore's projects.

She gave a frustrated sigh, running her hand through her hair. "But the magic has disappeared. We're no longer the same people we were. Most of what comes out of my mouth is so nasty or hurtful. Then I feel awful and end up apologizing. I feel like I'm turning into some kind of crazy person."

She looked so miserable, Sophie reached over to give her a hug.

"Oh, boy… you could never be nasty. I'm sure this is only your defensive side kicking in, guarding your heart. But, whatever the case, it sounds to me like you've got it bad. As my Uncle Paul would say, you've fallen for the guy… hook, line and sinker." She scrunched up her face. "At least I think that's what he said. Whenever he started lecturing me about boys, I tuned him out."

She laughed. "The poor guy, becoming a guardian of three kids, it couldn't have been easy for him. But back to you? It's going to be okay. It's all good."

She smiled at Stephanie's puzzled look. "Yes, because from what you've told me, I'd be willing to bet he's got it just as bad."

She sighed. "Love can do a number on a person."

Someone had entered the boutique, setting the bells ringing. After spending a few minutes with them, Sophie returned to Stephanie. "This is what we're going to do. We'll find you the perfect dress. You'll look so amazing, there will be no chance of him disappearing again."

Her head tilted and her finger to her lips, she studied Stephanie. "*Hmm…* what you need is a sophisticated, yet sexy look. So Evan won't be able to keep his eyes off of you. What's your favorite color? Or should I ask, what color makes you feel good when you wear it?"

Stephanie shrugged? "Gosh, I don't know… nothing too bright?"

She didn't really have a favorite color. She wore neutral shades. This way, she didn't stand out. The last thing she wanted was to draw attention to herself.

Sophie tried not to look too horrified. This went against everything she believed about fashion. A woman should always aim for a look that made her stand out. Not in a garish way, but enough to show she was confident with who she was.

Never, *never* should a woman feel the need to blend into the woodwork.

Gesturing for Stephanie to follow her, she made her way over to a rack of dresses. After a quick search, she pulled out a tea length pale blue chiffon dress that appeared to float from the hanger. She checked the tag for the size, and held it up for Stephanie's inspection. "What do you think of this? A classic and very feminine look. And with the low cut back, there is just enough sexiness to make the mind imagine so much more."

Stephanie studied the dress.

Hmm… make the mind imagine more? Is this what you want?

She sent Sophie a tentative smile. "I'm not sure? Yes, it's beautiful. But maybe a bit too much?"

But Sophie had already started for the dressing room. "Let's wait to see how it looks on before you decide. I think you're going to love it."

As usual, Sophie was right. Stephanie fell in love with the dress the moment she saw herself in the mirror. She did a slow spin, watching the skirt float around her in a cloud of fabric before she smiled over at Sophie. "This would be the perfect dress to dance the night away."

Sophie's eyes lit up. "There's going to be dancing?"

Stephanie laughed at her excited expression. "I doubt it. I imagine this dinner will be a very quiet and formal affair." She did another spin, gazing at her reflection before she sighed. "Maybe someday if I'm lucky…"

Sophie was smiling as she unzipped the dress so Stephanie could change back into her other clothes. "Well, since it sounds like it won't be a late-night affair, ask him to take you out dancing afterwards. And don't say you can't do this. Because you can. The way you look in this dress should give you the confidence you need to do anything you want."

She gave Stephanie a gentle push towards the dressing room. "Now go get changed. Then we'll decide on accessories. I have to say, this was an easy sale. A perfect fit, too.

Almost as if the dress was waiting for you."

She winked. "A promising sign, wouldn't you say?"

Later that afternoon, when she stepped out of the elevator on the third floor to report to her shift, the first person Stephanie saw was Evan.

Sprawled out in a chair in the visitors' lounge, his chin resting in his hand, his eyes were closed.

Her rubber-soled clogs silencing her approach, Stephanie walked over to him. Thinking he had dozed off, she studied him. He looked completely at ease, his facial features relaxed. The usual cautiousness she had come to expect had disappeared.

When the corner of his mouth lifted in a smile, she wondered if he was caught up in a dream.

It's obvious you're not in it. There's no way. He'd be frowning if you were.

There was only one other person in the lounge. An elderly woman, she smiled over at Stephanie. When Stephanie smiled in return, she leaned forward in her seat and nodded towards Evan.

She spoke in an exaggerated whisper. "Is he a friend of yours? If so, you're a very lucky woman. He's such a nice young man. We chatted a bit on the elevator."

She smiled. "I'm waiting for my granddaughter. She volunteers to read to the children on Thursdays. Bethany is her name."

Stephanie smiled. "I know Bethany. The children love her."

"We love her, too. And here she comes now." The woman came to her feet. "In a few months, she'll have her driver's license. I'm going to miss bringing her here once a week." She nodded over at Evan again. "If you haven't already, grab on to him. He's a keeper. Trust me, life moves too fast. You don't want to look back and regret the chances you didn't take."

After watching Bethany and her grandmother get on the elevator, Stephanie glanced down at her watch.

She didn't want to be late. Cautiously moving even closer to Evan, she reached over and brushed her fingers down his cheek.

She whispered. "Hey, Evan... wake up."

Though his eyes were closed, Evan wasn't asleep.

When he'd checked in at the nurses station only minutes before, he was told Stephanie hadn't yet reported for her shift.

So, he chose to wait in the visitor's lounge. Right next to the elevators, this was a guarantee he'd see her as soon as she arrived.

Even before she began chatting with Bethany's grandmother, he sensed her presence. He was also aware she had been checking him out.

This explained his smile.

It was only when she touched his cheek, he opened his eyes. Reaching over to link her fingers with his, he also whispered. "Hey... I'm awake." Then he grinned. "So... I hope you listened to what that nice woman had to say about me. A nice young man? A keeper? All very complimentary. And, I assure you... all very true."

Though she tried, she couldn't hide her smile. "Don't let her comments go to your head. You're lucky I didn't set her straight. After all, she knows nothing about you."

He raised an eyebrow. "And you think you do?" He shook his head. *"Hmm... it looks like I've got my work cut out for me."*

Coming to his feet, and still holding her hand, he gazed down at her. Then he peered at her even more closely, a smile spreading across his face.

This made her nervous.

What did he see? Did she have a smudge or something on her nose? Her hand going up to her face, worry gathered in her eyes. "Is something wrong?"

He let go of her hand, and crossing his arms, his smile grew bigger. "I'm wondering... is this sudden sparkle you've got going on all for my benefit? If so, it wasn't necessary."

For a moment, she could only stare at him. What was he talking about?

Then it hit her... the dress in Chic Boutique. The one with all the glitter and feathers. When she left the boutique, evidently she'd taken some of that sparkle along with her.

She hoped there weren't any feathers floating in her hair. The possibility of this had her patting her head to check.

When she realized he was watching this, she shook her head. "I have no plans to impress you. So, don't flatter yourself. I stopped at my friend's boutique to find a dress for Saturday night and I must have picked up the glitter from there."

He nodded, slowly he did this. *"Ah... a new dress.* For someone who was so insistent they wanted nothing to do with this dinner party, I find your purchase of a new dress very promising. I look forward to seeing it. "

He frowned. "I guess this means I should step up my look, too."

She shrugged. "You do whatever you want. It's not like this is a date." The possibility he would have something to say about this, she quickly changed the subject. "So, what do you think? Should we chance it? See if we can get something accomplished without getting in to any more trouble? I only have so many uniforms."

This had him looking at her scrubs. It appeared puppies and kittens were a popular choice for her. He grinned, reaching over to trace one puppy with his finger. "Well, I guess we can't do much worse than we already have."

She laughed.

And just like that, he was spiraling back in time… six months ago and on the night of the masquerade ball.

Her laugh…

He had fallen in love with her laugh the very first moment he'd heard it. Like the music of a million tiny little bells, it seemed to float around them, everywhere. Bringing every inch of him to attention, but in a good way.

It healed him.

Filled him with peace.

He'd swear it was the laugh of an angel.

It was the same laugh he had kept tucked away in his memory, along with the hope he would hear it again someday.

And damn, if it doesn't look like your prayers have been answered.

Unprepared for the sudden rush of emotion hitting him, and not quite able to deal with this, he reached for his camera and began adjusting the settings. As there was a good chance he'd make a mess of things with the state he was in, he shut off the camera before sending a furtive glance over at Stephanie.

She was studying him, a concerned look on her face. Then after glancing at her watch, she gave him a bright smile. "I'm willing to try if you are. But this means we need to get started."

Filled with a sudden tenderness, he reached over to tuck her hair behind her ear. "I bet we'll nail it, beautiful."

Beautiful?

And this time, there wasn't even a chance of hiding her smile.

CHAPTER 17

The problem is not the problem.
The problem is your attitude about the problem.
~ Anonymous

Evidently, some things just aren't meant to last.

The special moment Stephanie and Evan shared only a short while ago? This was now only a memory.

It seems they had reverted right back to their previous behavior.

Yes, they were arguing. It was an all-out angry and almost shouting kind of argument.

Much to the amusement of the staff manning the third-floor nurses station, they watched Stephanie go storming by. With Evan following close behind.

Once they were at the elevator, she whirled around to face him. Her hands went to her hips. "Okay, you are now free to leave. And again, no... you do not need to pick me up tomorrow night. I am perfectly capable of driving myself."

Gazing up at the ceiling, Evan let out a long groan. "For God's sake, I don't understand you at all."

He reached over to push the elevator button. To then hit it again, much harder, before he looked over at her. "I was only trying to be nice. And what I thought would make sense. But I'm certainly not going to keep arguing with you about something so ridiculous. If driving by yourself is what makes you happy, fine. I guess I'll see you at Elenore's tomorrow night when you get there."

After he stepped into the elevator, Stephanie made it a point to wait right before the doors closed to get in the last word. "Yes, this is what I want. And don't you forget it. Good... bye..."

The sound of Lucy's laugh coming from behind her, Stephanie turned, her eyes narrowed in anger. "Don't even start..."

Lucy stepped back, her hands going up in surrender. "Whoa... take it easy. We're just innocent bystanders here. If you don't want any input, then you should conduct your arguments in a more private place."

She leaned against the counter, shaking her head. "But, Steff... what are you doing? Trying to drive the man away? Because this is what it looks like."

Stephanie opened her mouth to respond, but then closed it just as quickly. Judging by the evasive smiles of the other two nurses manning the station, she had already made a fool out of herself. So why make things even worse?

All because of a man. An annoying, overbearing and arrogant man...

Her hands clenched at her sides, and giving a huffy sigh, she turned on her heel and went storming off to the staff lounge.

She wanted to be alone.

She needed to calm down.

Relieved to find the lounge was unoccupied, she sank down on the sofa and closed her eyes.

She didn't understand...

What happened to the magic she and Evan had shared that September night? Or had there even been such a thing? Maybe she had let herself get too caught up in the series of events, and what she'd thought was a fairy tale kind of beginning was only something she'd dreamt up in her imagination?

Because, if there had been any kind of connection between them, it had disappeared.

She was a Cinderella who had not only lost her shoe, but every-thing else that went along with it.

A faint smile curving her lips, she sighed.

Everything about that night had been so perfect.

And now?

Nothing was right. And the only thing they seemed to have in common would be to disagree with just about everything.

Someone came into the lounge. She opened her eyes just enough to see who it was.

Lucy.

Oh, please... you don't want to hear what she thinks about all of this.

She stayed completely still, watching as Lucy poured out a cup of coffee. After she leaned against the counter and took a sip, she started right in. "Wow, Steff... this guy has you rattled, doesn't he?"

When Stephanie had nothing to say, she laughed. "Okay, so I'm going to take your silence as a yes. I have to tell you, it's been very entertaining watching this new Stephanie. Never did I think I'd see this kind of behavior coming from you because of a man."

She smiled. "It's almost like watching our own private soap opera unfolding right before our eyes."

After taking another sip of coffee, she was silent for a few moments before she continued. "But would you like to know what I think?"

No, no... you don't.

About to voice this aloud, Lucy didn't give her the chance. On a roll, it was clear she intended to have her say. "You, my dear, are going about this the wrong way. This is not the way to win yourself a man."

Stephanie rolled her eyes, confident Lucy couldn't see this, since they were still closed.

But come on, who talks like this? Win yourself a man?

Lucy, it seems. And there was more. "I don't like to meddle, but your childish behavior is proof the two of you deserve each other. You need someone to step in and set you straight. Otherwise, you're going to make a real mess of things. So, may I give you a little advice?"

Stephanie groaned.

No, you don't want to know what she thinks. If you're going to screw up, you'd rather do this on your own.

But since she knew Lucy had no plans to leave her alone until she said her piece, she gave a faint nod.

Lucy grabbed a cookie from the plateful on the counter before she settled in a chair. "Okay, I'm getting the impression this is not the first time you've had something going with this lover boy of yours. Am I right?"

This had Stephanie lifting her head to glare over at her. "Evan... remember? His name is Evan. And he is not, as you just called him, my lover boy. There is nothing going on between us."

After another bite of her cookie, Lucy nodded. "*Hmm...* if you say so. But this Evan... my guess is he did something that made you angry. Maybe he stopped calling... cancelled at the last minute. Or you suspected he was losing interest. Whatever, your mind sent the message to break it off, forget about him. Am I right?"

Stephanie gave a reluctant nod.

After popping the last piece of cookie in her mouth and washing it down with the rest of her coffee, Lucy shook her head. "*Hmm...* just as I thought. But this isn't an easy to do if your heart has already decided otherwise. And it's clear, with the way you've been acting these past few days, you've fallen head over heels in love with the guy."

She held up her hand, stopping Stephanie's protest. "*Ah, ah, ah...* hold on, I'm not finished yet. Because there's a big but here... and this is you don't trust him. You try, but that little voice in your head won't let you. And because you don't want to get hurt again, you take it out on him." A deep frown creased her brow. "And the next thing you know, he gets that glazed look in his eyes, or stares over your shoulder in order to avoid any contact with you. He stops calling and your imagination has him already in love with someone else."

Her laugh was bitter. "Yeah... and you're back to dinner for one. Deleting any mention of him from your phone."

She snapped her fingers. "And *Poof...* you're back to square one. Angry with every single man on the earth."

Worried Lucy was going to share all of her past relationship fall outs, Stephanie opened her eyes and sent her a direct look. "So, what's your point?"

Throwing her empty cup in the trash, Lucy shrugged. "You need to go easy on the guy. It's obvious he likes you. Otherwise, he wouldn't still be hanging around."

She frowned. "Trust me, I've been there, so I know the signs. And if you don't give him some slack? There are plenty of other women out there that will. If I hadn't just started dating Brian, I'd be one of them."

A faint smile flitted across Stephanie's face.

She wouldn't have a chance. You've seen Evan search for the nearest exit at just the sight of her.

She stood, sending Lucy a bright smile. "Well, as much as I appreciate your advice, I need to get back on the floor. I've been neglecting the kids as it is, spending so much time with this project of Elenore's." She frowned. "I would think Evan had more than enough photos by now. But he told me he likes to take as many as he can, time isn't an issue."

Lucy groaned, throwing her hands up in the air. "Seriously, Steff? You are so naïve. What more do you need? Of course, he should have finished up by now. But has it occurred to you he might be stalling in order to spend more time with you?"

She flounced out of the room, leaving Stephanie to enjoy the silence she so desperately needed.

A few minutes later, she left the lounge. She was ready to get back to work.

Until she almost ran right into Noah.

"Whoa... slow down." With his phone still to his ear, Noah grabbed Stephanie's arm to steady her. After ending his call, he moved closer, smiling down at her. "Hey, what's your hurry?"

"I need to relieve Katy." This came out in a mumble. Which was a mistake, because this meant he had to lean in closer.

He searched her face. "Come on... give me at least a few minutes. I've hardly seen you, and when I do, you go rushing off before I can even say hello. What have you been up to these past few days?"

She shrugged, avoiding eye contact.

Undeterred by her reluctance, he braced his hand against the doorjamb and right above her head.

This left her with no choice but to look right at him.

He flashed one of his heart-stopping smiles, his voice dipping lower. "I miss our little chats."

She zeroed in on his security badge.

Dr. Noah J. Davis.

Remember, to you he is Dr. Davis, nothing more...

He gave a long sigh. "Stephanie? Are you avoiding me? Because it sure seems like you are."

Avoiding him?

Why don't you tell him, yes, this was exactly what you've been doing?

Since this could only lead to more questions, or worse yet, an unpleasant awkwardness between them, she shook her head. Then she gave him a bright smile, pointing at her watch. "Just busy, that's all. In fact, I'm already late for my shift and I'm sure Kara is wondering where I am. She should already be on her way home right now."

He shrugged. "Don't worry, I just came from there. She was in the middle of playing dominos with the kids, so I'm sure she won't notice if you're a little late."

His mouth curved into a teasing grin. "You can tell her you were consulting with your favorite doctor." His gaze roamed over her face. "I'm still your favorite, aren't I? Please don't tell me I'm not."

She gazed up at him, searching his face for some kind of sign. Letting her know he really cared what her answer would be.

But she saw nothing.

And this is when it hit her...

Jason was right.

Noah was never going to change. She had been holding on to the dream she could be the one to change him. But she realized this wasn't what she wanted at all.

Feeling as though an immense burden had been lifted from her shoulders, she gave him her brightest smile. "Oh, Dr. Davis, I believe you are everyone's favorite. But if you'll excuse me, I really need to get back to work. Have a nice evening."

Proud of how she had handled the situation, she ducked under his arm and continued down the hall.

"Steffanie? One more thing..."

She turned, a determined look on her face. If it was his intention to sweet talk her into something, she wasn't interested.

Sure enough, his arms crossed over his chest, he sauntered over to her. He gave her a smile that, at one time, would have sent her heart beating out of control... or at least a little faster. "I wanted to let you know I'm looking forward to tomorrow night."

"Tomorrow night?" She was puzzled. Did she forget something? Missed a memo?

Then it clicked. He was talking about Elenore's dinner party,

Oh, no...

He nodded. "Yep... Elenore told me that you would also be there as a guest. I'm sure it will be an interesting evening. I'll see you then."

With a brief wave, he hurried on his way.

This was the absolute last thing she wanted to hear.

She pushed open the door and headed for her car.

She would worry about this tomorrow.

CHAPTER 18

Stephanie was running late.

This had all started with her afternoon hair appointment, scheduled over three months ago.

When she'd arrived, it was to find a group of high school girls had taken over the salon. A loud and giggling group of ten, they were getting their hair styled for prom.

This meant everyone in the shop, including her long standing and favorite hair stylist—and the only person she trusted to do her hair—was running behind.

After she finally arrived home almost two hours later than planned, she was unlocking her front door when she saw her next-door neighbor running towards her, waving like mad.

She wanted to know if Stephanie could watch her sleeping four-month old. After she had settled the infant down for a nap, she remembered her seven-year-old needed to be picked up from dance class.

She promised this would only take about fifteen minutes.

Stephanie, being Stephanie, had agreed.

And the fifteen minutes had turned into almost triple that amount of time.

So, after a rush to get ready, she gave one last check in the mirror.

Stephanie wasn't one to dwell on her appearance. She brushed off most of the compliments she received, becoming extremely embarrassed when someone told her she was beautiful.

This was a touchy subject between her and Jason, irritating him to no end.

He claimed she was crazy.

But tonight? She didn't know if it was the dress or her new haircut, but even she had to admit she looked pretty good.

It had to be the dress. It would make anyone feel beautiful.

She grabbed her pashmina, turned out the lights and locked the door. Then she ran out to her car as fast as her heels would allow.

Before she pulled out of the parking lot, she checked her GPS. Barring any unforeseen problems, she should arrive for Elenore's dinner party right on time.

According to her GPS, Stephanie's drive was now down to nine minutes.

The sudden sound of a horn coming from behind her, she glanced in her rearview mirror to see a van was approaching at a high rate of speed. In disbelief, she watched as, the horn still blaring, the van veered to the right of her. Then it picked up speed, scraping against the side of her car before swerving over into her lane in front of her. She gripped the wheel and, holding on tight, slammed on the brakes.

But the outcome was inevitable. The van clipped her bumper, sending her car in a spin and over into the next lane.

Horrified, she watched as the bumper flew through the air, where it hit the pavement and skidded to a stop in the intersection almost thirty feet away.

And the van? It picked up speed and disappeared into the traffic ahead.

In a state of shock, the sound of the crash still echoing in her ears, she rested her forehead on the steering wheel. She closed her eyes, telling herself to breathe.

A man was knocking on her car window. "Hey... are you okay? Can you open your window?" The panic in his voice had her lifting her head. She opened the window and, even though she was shaking, she nodded. "I'm okay. More in shock than anything else. Though it doesn't look good for my car."

The man gave a big sigh of relief. "Thank God you're okay. And the car can be fixed." He shook his head. "I swear, the driver of that van had to be drunk or high on something with how fast he was traveling. I hope someone was able to get his license number."

At the sound of approaching sirens, he smiled. "*Ah...* it sounds like someone already called the police. I'll stay long enough to give a witness statement. But then I have to leave. Is there someone you can call? Because I don't think your car is drivable."

She could call Jason. Or one of her friends. And at last resort, she could call Evan.

Though this might not be a good idea.

Since you did refuse his offer to drive... and then there's Kelsie. This might be too much of a reminder of that time in his life.

Surely it wouldn't come to that. So she nodded. "Yes, I'll be fine. And thank you for your offer to stay. You have already been more than kind."

She checked her watch. It was almost seven.

It looked like she was going to be late for Elenore's dinner party.

Really late.

The cocktail hour had ended and dinner was about to be served.

Evan glanced down at his watch. It was pushing seven, and only three minutes since he'd last checked the time.

This meant Stephanie was now forty-five minutes late.

You don't understand... where is she?

He lifted his glass to his mouth, surprised to find it was empty. This was a sign of how worried he was. He rarely drank.

And if he did? He could usually stretch out a drink to last the whole evening.

He set his glass down and, shoving his hands in his pockets, sauntered over to the window. Maybe he'd get lucky and Stephanie's car would be coming up the driveway.

Nope. There was no car in sight.

He gazed down at the floor, exhaling a long breath.

You need to stop. You're overreacting. She's fine. Just because she is a little late doesn't mean something has happened to her.

"Evan, do you have any idea what might be keeping Stephanie?"

He jerked his head up to find Elenore was standing next to him. Concern furrowing her brow, she was peering at him over the top of her glasses.

He cleared his throat. "I, *ah*... I wish I knew. But I'm sure there's a good reason she's not here yet."

He gave her a reassuring smile. "She has my number. If there's a problem, I'm sure she'll call."

As if on cue, his phone vibrated in his pocket. He pulled it out, Stephanie's name jumping out at him from the screen.

He sent Elenore a smile. "*Ah*... it looks like we're going to get our answer right now. It's Stephanie."

Seated in the waiting room of the police station, Stephanie was staring down at her phone.

She didn't understand. How was it every number she'd tried, starting with Jason's, went right to their voice mail?

Was no one answering their phone tonight?

This meant she was down to her last choice.

Evan...

She closed her eyes, and taking a deep breath, she hit his number.

He answered on the second ring. "Stephanie? Where are you?"

At the sound of his voice, she was momentarily at a loss, not sure of where to start or what to say. His abrupt greeting worried her. She couldn't shake the feeling he was going to have a hard time with what she was about to tell him.

"Hello? Stephanie?"

The anxiety creeping into his voice had her response coming out in a rush. "Evan, I was in an accident. A van ran into the side of my car and..."

Evan had stopped listening. His eyes closed, he felt as if the air had been sucked out of him, his gut clenching in response. Her words had sent him spiraling back into a time and place he never again wanted to experience.

His response came out in a gruff bark. "Where are you?"

Thinking his anger was directed at her, she tried to explain. "I'm sorry. I'm at the police station, not too far from Elenore's house. My car had to be towed and since I refused to go to the hospital, they wouldn't let me leave on my own, so–"

He cut her off. "I'll be there in about ten minutes, fifteen at the most. Just stay where you are. Okay?"

"Okay... But Evan, everything is okay. I'm okay. So, please don't..." This was when she realized the screen on her phone had gone dark. He had already ended the call.

She could still remember the grief in his voice when he told her about the call he received about Kelsie's accident.

Slowly shaking her head, she closed her eyes.

And now you're making him relive it all over again...

This was Evan's worst nightmare.

After he ended the call with Stephanie, he stared down at his phone. Suddenly, he had no idea what he should do, every possible emotion flooding his mind to the point he couldn't think.

She claimed she was okay. But he wouldn't be able to believe this until he saw her with his own eyes. He needed proof she was still in one piece, not a scratch on her.

He groaned, dragging his hand through his hair. Why the hell hadn't she gone to the hospital?

She's a nurse, for God's sake... she should know better. She could have a head injury and not even know it.

"Evan, is everything all right?" The concern in Elenore's voice was enough to bring him back to life. After he gave her a brief explanation, with the promise he would call with an update as soon as he could, he ran out to his car.

The drive to the police station was pure torture. He felt like everything inside of him was churning, almost to the point he felt sick.

Flashbacks of Kelsie's accident took over his mind, coming one right after the other.

He didn't even realize he was speeding until he almost flew past the police station. Quickly slamming on the brakes, he made the turn into the parking lot.

In only seconds, he was out of his car and sprinting to the station entrance.

CHAPTER 19

You can always feel safe in my arms.
Because I'll never let you go.
~ Unknown

A slow night at the Shaker Heights Police Station, Stephanie was the only person in the waiting room.

Huddled in one of the beat-up metal folding chairs facing the TV mounted up on the wall, the ten minutes she'd been waiting for Evan now felt like an eternity.

She had forgotten to grab her pashmina out of her car before they towed it away. And now, with the air-conditioner turned on full blast, she was cold.

A miserable, shivering cold.

She closed her eyes, wrapping her hands even tighter around the small styrofoam cup of coffee they'd given her, grateful for even the little warmth it provided.

A loud alarm buzzed, the sign someone had been granted the right to enter the building. This had her opening her eyes, sending a hopeful glance over at the door.

Evan....

Their eyes met and within seconds, he was standing in front of her, his gaze roaming over her, everywhere.

He wanted to make sure she was all right. *Really* all right. He had already decided if he saw anything that led him to believe she wasn't, he would whisk her off to the hospital. No matter how much she protested.

She gave him a tentative smile.

Exhaling a long sigh of relief, he sank into the chair next to her. For a few moments, they sat in silence. He was trying to regain his composure, or at least slow the pounding of his heart. While she decided to wait, unsure of what to say.

It was after a loud laugh came from the office behind them, he turned to her. His gaze searching, his voice was strained. "Are you sure you're okay? Maybe you should go to the emergency room to get checked out. Just to be safe. Because you–"

Stephanie pressed her fingers to his lips, shaking her head. This was what she hadn't wanted to happen. Especially since it was because of her. At the same time, she couldn't believe how glad she was to see him. She wanted to put her head on his shoulder, ask him to put his arms around her, hold her close. If only so she could sink into the strength and comfort she knew he would provide.

Instead, hoping to ease the haunted look still lingering in his eyes, she gave him a bright smile. "No, I'm okay. Really, I'm fine. I tried to tell you this when I called because I didn't want you to worry. But you hung up too quickly."

Gripped by this sudden need to touch her, if only as proof she was really okay, he brushed her hair back from her face, tucking it behind her ears. "What happened?"

His gaze never left her face as she gave him a summary of the accident. Then she shrugged, her mouth curving into a wry smile. "It was all so crazy. I didn't have time to even think about what happened until I found myself here, waiting for you. One officer said my guardian angel must have been watching over me. There could have been a car in the lane next to me. Or someone might have been crossing the intersection...." Her voice suddenly trailing off, she closed her eyes.

Oh my God... what is wrong with you?

She put her hand on his arm. "Oh, Evan... I'm so sorry. I didn't mean... I never–"

"It's okay. I'm fine." Abruptly coming to his feet, he held out his hand. "Come on, let's go."

He was far from fine. This was all too familiar, bringing back memories he didn't want to relive But, he wasn't going to tell her this. It wasn't her fault he was having such a hard time.

When she took his hand, and he realized she was shivering, he removed his tuxedo jacket and draped it over her shoulders.

She pulled the jacket more tightly around her, giving a long sigh of relief as she sank into the warmth left from his body heat. Gazing up at him, she smiled. "Thank you. It's so cold in here, and I left my pashmina in my car. With everything so crazy, I forgot all about it."

She frowned. "It was a Christmas gift from Jason and one of my favorites."

A pashmina?

He had no clue what this was... maybe a jacket or something? So, his only response was to take her arm to lead her to his car.

This wasn't because he didn't care... of course, he did. For all he knew, this pashmina might have some kind of special meaning. She did say it was a gift from Jason.

But right now, he could only focus on one thing, the only thing that made sense to him. This was to whisk her off to a place where he could keep her safe. Later, he would figure out what to do about this missing pashmina.

You'll buy her a new one if necessary. Hell, you'll buy her one for each day of the week.

He closed his eyes, shaking his head.

You're crazy. If you don't get a hold of yourself, you're going to scare her. Let it go. She's not Kelsie.. she will be fine.

Pashmina, or no pashmina.

He gave her hand a gentle squeeze. "Tomorrow I'll see if I can get it for you."

Thinking this was the last thing he'd want to do, she shook her head. "*Oh, no, no...* please don't worry about it. I don't expect you to–"

Her words cut short when she stumbled over an uneven section of the parking lot, she grabbed onto him for support. Now even more rattled, she started right in with a long and detailed apology. "I'm sorry. It's these shoes I'm wearing. I've found the only thing they're good for is making a fashion statement. Definitely not for navigating uneven parking lots."

She chattered on, unable to stop. "I'm not used to wearing heels this high. So, when I do, I have to learn how to walk in them all over again. I've grown too comfortable wearing my work clogs. Or tennis shoes. For work, those are the best choice."

His silence, along with the closed expression on his face, had her falling silent. But she got it. It was bad enough he had to come to her rescue. And now he was expected to listen to her lecture on the importance of the proper footwear?

This is when the events of the night finally caught up to her. On the verge of tears, she watched as he unlocked the passenger door of his car.

The door opened, he turned to her. Huddled deep in his jacket and her eyes closed, her face was scrunched up as though she was trying not to cry.

She looked absolutely miserable. And just like that, something gave way inside of him, a tenderness washing over him. That he was responsible for her distress was the last thing he wanted to happen.

You need to fix this.

He moved closer. His thumb brushing over her cheek sent her lashes flying open. "*Hmm…* If I'm not mistaken, on a night not too long ago and in a parking lot very similar to this, uneven and filled with potholes, I shared a dance with a woman wearing these same shoes."

He nodded down at her feet. "This was after she claimed she couldn't dance. But I soon found out how wrong she was. She was a beautiful dancer. The memory of that dance is one I'll keep forever."

He remembers your shoes?

Now, as a woman who loved shoes—but then again, what woman doesn't—Stephanie zeroed right in on this. A smile curving her lips, she searched his face. "You remember my shoes?"

He moved even closer. "*Ah...* there is so much I remember about that night. That it came at a time I was in such need of hope in my life made it even more memorable." He shook his head. "It was a night every man dreams of... a chance encounter with a beautiful woman. You might say it was magical... enough to make one believe in fairytales."

Her lips parted, Stephanie stared at him. Yes, she would agree. Indeed, it had been an evening of magic. But she didn't understand... if this is what her remembered, why had he never called?

And, if it hadn't been for Elenore, they wouldn't be together now.

So, no... there was no magic involved.

She shook her head. "I'm not sure if I–"

At the loud crunch of gravel, they both turned to watch a car pull into the parking lot, the headlights passing over them like searchlights in the night.

Evan moved to shield her from the blinding light before he smiled down at her. "*Whoa...* I believe this is a sign we should leave. Come on, let's get out of here."

Unfortunately, this meant Stephanie would have to wait until later to get her answer.

Evan started up the car and turned the heat on full blast before he glanced over at Stephanie. "Once we get you warm, we'll decide what we should do next."

She sent him a grateful smile. "It was so cold in the waiting room. And again, thank you for coming to my rescue. Never did I think I'd be sitting in a police station tonight, waiting for someone to come get me."

As soon as she said this, she wished she hadn't.

Sure enough, a frown creasing his brow, Evan began tapping his fingers on the steering wheel. "And to think this may have been avoided if you had accepted my offer of a ride." A smile tweaking the corner of his mouth at her resigned expression, he nodded. "Yep... I may be right on the mark with this, wouldn't you agree?"

She shrugged. For some unknown reason, she didn't want to give in to him. At least not yet. "You don't know this for sure. Anything could have happened. What is it they say? Everything happens for a reason…"

He chuckled. "*Hmm…* yes, I'll give you that. But in this case?" He gave her a long look, slowly shaking his head.

She sighed. "Okay, I'll admit I should have let you drive. Next time–if there is a next time–I'll think more carefully about my decision. Especially when it concerns you."

"Oh, don't worry, there will definitely be a next time." Mumbled under his breath, this had been intended for his benefit only. But when her swift glance showed he'd voiced his thoughts aloud, he whipped his phone out of his pocket and began scrolling down through his list of contacts. "I need to call Elenore. I promised to report back to her. Since dinner was about to be served when I left, it's safe to assume we've missed out on that. So, what do you propose we do?"

Still mulling over his comment about a next time, she stared at him, a bemused look on her face. "*Umm…* maybe let her decide?"

He hit Elenore's number. "Okay then, let's see what she has to say."

While Evan was on the phone, Stephanie had time to think about what he said.

> "*Oh, don't worry, there will definitely be a next time.*"

Maybe she heard wrong?

Because his behavior until now certainly hadn't sent the message he wanted to spend more time with her. But to be fair, she hadn't given him much of a reason to feel this way.

So, do you blame him?

She sighed, and closing her eyes, she rested her head against the back of the seat.

Honestly? She didn't know what to think anymore.

After he ended his call with Elenore, Evan glanced over at Stephanie.

She certainly didn't look like she was ready for a night of socializing. At least not at a formal dinner party with people she didn't know.

He peered over at her. "Are you sure you are okay? I know I already said this, but maybe we should get you checked out. Just to be on the safe side."

"Again, I'm fine. Honest." Then she shook her head. "Okay, so maybe I'm not fine. I'm upset. And so embarrassed I made a mess of the whole evening." She followed this with a long and dramatic sigh. "But why am I even surprised? Nothing ever turns out the way I'd hoped."

Amused at this sudden outburst, he rested his arms on the steering wheel, studying her before he spoke. "*Hmm...* don't you think you're being a little hard on yourself? I wasn't there to witness what happened. But from what you told me, you weren't the one who was driving like a maniac, running into other vehicles. So, there's no reason to blame yourself."

When her only answer was a faint shrug, it was his turn to sigh. "You also might be interested to know Elenore was relieved to hear you're okay. She made it quite clear, even though she would love to have us stop by, she would understand if we bowed out the rest of the evening. There will be other times, she said."

He frowned at the thought of this. Other times? What had Elenore meant by this?

You have the feeling, for you, it's nothing good.

He'd always considered himself as a behind-the-scenes kind of guy and his intention was to keep it this way. He had no desire to get involved in any kind of high society events.

There was also another time during their conversation Elenore had him confused. She had rambled on about how she wished she could change the past. But since this wasn't possible, she wondered if there was a way she could make things right. But first, she needed to find the best way to go about this.

And she was telling you all of this because?

He had assumed she was referring to the new hospital wing. From what he knew about the project, this was her baby and a long time coming.

So, he did his best to assure her there was no reason to worry. At least not on his part. More than satisfied with the photos he had taken so far, he was confident her wall of memories would turn out just fine.

He glanced over at Stephanie at the same time a tear slipped down her cheek. One solitary little tear. But it was almost enough to send him into a panic.

Tears had been an almost constant companion to him over the past several months. A reminder of what he tried so hard not to think about, they would pool in his eyes at the most unexpected time. Even with his emotions now more under control, it still took very little to set him off.

Tears from Stephanie fell right into this category.

He reached over, brushing away the tear with his thumb. "Hey, come on... it's not the end of the world. It's just dinner. With a bunch of pretentious people who we have nothing in common and will probably never see again. Elenore did suggest we could stop by for dessert. But I'll leave this up to you. Whatever you decide, I'm game."

Stephanie thought about this before she gazed over at him. "It would be the right thing to do, if only for a little while."

Evan was having a hard time. Caught up in her eyes, brilliant from her tears, that she was so unhappy he wanted to comfort her. Or at least make her smile.

He slipped his fingers under her chin and tipping her face to his, he was unable to hide the huskiness in his voice. "Like I said, it's all up to you."

A smile slowly spreading across her face, she reached over to straighten his bow tie. "Don't you think it's only right we at least make an appearance? Take this opportunity to show you off?" Shaking her head, she trailed her fingers down over the buttons of his shirt. "Because, I've got to hand it to you. In your tux, you look very handsome."

Pleased with what she said, he caught her hand, linking her fingers with his. "You think so, huh? This is good to hear, since I finally broke down and purchased one of my own. I figured if Elenore is serious about this ambassador title she's given us, you and I may be attending more of these events in the future. So I'll need to look my best."

Before she could respond, he lifted her hand to his mouth. After pressing a slow kiss to her fingers, his voice dropped to a low, sexy drawl. "And you... you look absolutely stunning. But then, you always look beautiful. Even in your hospital scrubs. Maybe even more so because of the love you put into everything you do."

That these words came so effortlessly out of his mouth was a novel experience for him. Flattery had never been one of his best traits. He was more direct, a man of few words.

But one look into Stephanie's eyes?

He became a different man. Confident.

Maybe even a little daring.

This had Stephanie all flustered. "Thank you. And you're right, I do love you."

Pure panic flashed across her face. "*Oh, no, no, no...* that didn't come out right. I meant to say I love what I do, not I love you. Not that I don't like you, because I do, but..."

Her protest faded as he moved closer, his whisper brushing across her jaw. "*Hmm...* it's okay. I sort of like what you said."

She had now gone so still, he would swear she wasn't even breathing. His mouth hovered over hers. "And I know we're in the parking lot of a police station, not where I would have planned to kiss you for the first time. But after what happened tonight, I need this. If only as proof you're here. And that you're okay..."

After the slightest hesitation, but not enough to give her the chance to protest, he claimed her mouth in a slow, sweet kiss.

It was the perfect kiss.

And, if you were to ask, they would both tell you it was a kiss long overdue.

For Evan, this was a life-changing moment, a second chance at love. This didn't mean Kelsie would no longer be a part of him. Because she would... always. But now he knew there was more than enough room in his heart to love again. And who better to do this with than the beautiful woman he was with?

He brushed his thumb across Stephanie's cheek, watching as her lashes fluttered open.

His voice was gentle. "Hey... are we okay?"

Caught up in his eyes, she nodded. "Yes, yes… we're okay."

He shook his head, a chuckle escaping him. "I'm beginning to believe there's a lot more to parking lots than they're given credit for. What do you think?"

She would have to agree.

Definitely…

CHAPTER 20

You would think Stephanie and Evan were celebrities with the enthusiastic welcome they received from the guests gathered around the table at Elenore's dinner party.

Once seated, and their dessert placed in front of them, the conversation around the table turned to Stephanie's accident.

Only one guest was quiet.

This would be Dr. Davis.

When Elenore had invited him, she let him know he would be in the company of a very impressive gathering of guests. Long-time board members and prominent leaders in the community, the combined wealth of the group was staggering.

Noah got the message, assuring Elenore he would be on his best behavior.

And up until now, he was.

Since here was nothing he liked more than an appreciative audience, true to form, he'd piled on the charm. Entertaining everyone with stories about his internship days, he had them hanging on his every word.

Yeah, you may have embellished a bit, but this was only to make things more interesting.

But unfortunately, his time in the spotlight had come to a halt when Evan and Stephanie arrived.

This put Noah in a terrible mood.

It was a well-known fact he was a man who had the tendency to want what he couldn't have. Even he admitted to this. And nowhere was this more obvious than when the object of his desire was a member of the opposite sex.

Let's just say he liked the thrill of the chase.

If someone were to call him out on this, he'd deny it, claiming his actions were only because of his competitive nature. He was a man who enjoyed a challenge. Was it his fault, after he accomplished his goal, he became bored, ready to move on?

But along came Stephanie…

From the very beginning, she intrigued him. Never having met anyone like her before, he still wasn't sure if she was shy, or simply playing hard to get. Either way, her elusiveness had him wanting her more.

And that he was the one doing the chasing? This was a whole new experience for him.

Now lounging back in his chair, taking in the bits and pieces of conversation flowing around the table, his gaze shifted over to Stephanie and Evan.

He was not happy with what he saw. The brief glances they shared, along with Evan's protective manner, made him wonder if there was more than just a friendship between them.

Or, it could very well be a temporary bond they shared because of the accident. Yeah, maybe Stephanie needed someone to lean on. And Evan just happened to be around.

As a doctor, you know how these things go. People react differently when faced with a trauma.

He studied Evan more closely.

He didn't understand.

What did Stephanie see in the guy? He was a freelance photographer, for God's sake. No doubt one of these artsy-free-spirit-and-live-in-the-moment-types. His head in the clouds and content to fritter his life away taking photos.

He made a grab for his glass of wine, draining what remained in one gulp. This was when he realized a silence had fallen over the room, the discussion of Stephanie's accident had gone as far as it could go.

So, why not use this opportunity to find out more about this Evan? See what his game was.

He cleared his throat.

Once he had everyone's attention, he casually reached for the wine decanter. As he began filling his glass, he sent Stephanie one of his most charming smiles. *"Hmm…* Stephanie, I'm so disappointed you didn't come to me. I would have been more than happy to bring you here. And who knows? This might have altered the series of events tonight."

He set the wine decanter back on the table and glanced over at Evan. He frowned, slowly shaking his head. "I guess I assumed since the two of you are collaborating on this photo project, well… never mind what I thought."

He sat back in his chair and, after taking a drink from his glass, he sent Stephanie another smile. "But, that you escaped unharmed, this is all that matters."

All eyes were now on Evan and Stephanie.

Evan wasn't stupid.

He knew exactly what Noah was insinuating. But he was also a little confused. Why this sudden attack? Noah knew nothing about him. Heck, they had met for the first time earlier this evening.

Yes, they had crossed paths while he was taking photos at the hospital. But once he'd recognized him as the doctor he saw with Stephanie last September, he had gone out of his way to avoid him.

He glanced over at Noah. His arrogant smile was all the motivation he needed. If this was a test, he was up for the challenge.

Casually fingering the stem of his water glass, he nodded over at Noah. "You're absolutely right. I should have insisted–"

Interrupted by the loud clink of metal against china, he glanced around the table. He saw all eyes were on Stephanie, who had just set her spoon down on her plate much harder than necessary.

Her voice broke the silence, coming out much louder than she intended. "Dr. Davis, I think you're making way too much of this. It was my choice to drive. Evan offered to pick me up. In fact, he offered more than once. But I refused, a move I assure you I now regret."

She sighed. "It's obvious I had no plans of getting into an accident, and as you said, I was lucky it wasn't worse than it was. But if you don't mind, I'd rather we not talk about this anymore. I'm sure there are so many other interesting topics we can discuss."

There was complete silence.

Stephanie wasn't sure why she had reacted so strongly. Dropping her gaze to the serving of Crème brûlée in front of her, she could feel the blush rising in her cheeks.

You did it now. It looks like you need to bring up one of those interesting topics you just suggested. And fast…

Re-arranging her napkin on her lap, she sent Elenore a bright smile. "This is so delicious." Then her gaze darted over to Evan. "Don't you agree, Evan?"

Even though Evan was feeling pretty good about how Stephanie had come to his defense, the look she sent was enough to let him know she was angry about something. With him right there at the top of her list.

He would know. He had been on the receiving end of this same look quite a few times over the past few days.

Damn… maybe coming here wasn't such a good idea after all.

He grabbed his glass and took a big gulp of water. Then he nodded. "Yes, yes… it is. One of my favorites, in fact."

The glance he sent Elenore bordered on desperation. "*Umm…* I'm afraid it's slipped my mind… what is it called again?"

Elenore patted her mouth with her napkin to hide her smile before she responded. "It's Crème brûlée. I'm glad to hear you like it, Evan. It's my favorite, too. I've found it's always a crowd pleaser."

In an attempt to get the conversation rolling again, she directed her next comment to a guest at the table. "So, Marjorie, how is your garden? I bet it's coming along nicely with all the rain we've had."

This had everyone joining in the discussion of gardening. Most notably, the challenge of dealing with the unpredictable Cleveland weather.

Evan took this chance to send a glance over at Stephanie.

Hmm... still not good.

She was staring down at her Crème brûlée as though she didn't know what to do with it.

He reached for her hand and gave it a gentle squeeze.

Right now, the state of Cleveland's weather was the least of Stephanie's worries.

She was mad. *More like furious.*

And all this anger was directed at Evan and Noah.

She didn't appreciate that they were discussing her as though she wasn't even present, their comments insinuating she wasn't capable of taking care of herself.

So, yes... she was angry.

But then Evan reached over to give her hand a gentle squeeze, the warmth of his grip enough to calm her.

She glanced down at their hands. Then she looked up at him and smiled.

Unfortunately, Noah witnessed this. This had him even more irritated. Again he cleared his throat, pleased to see he got a faster response this time. Almost eager, he would have to say.

Yeah, you've still got it.

Little did he know this was because Elenore's dinner parties were usually a very formal, almost regimented kind of affair. Bordering on boring. So tonight, this exchange between Evan and Noah was an interesting addition. Even exciting. The subject of gardening could wait.

Noah directed his question to Evan. "So, I'm curious... how does one go about becoming a professional photographer? Are there special classes you had to take? Or are you self-taught?"

Evan had already put their last conversation behind him. Now taking a cue from everyone else around the table, he was happily enjoying his Crème brûlée.

At least, up until now, he was. So, the glance he sent over at Noah was more than a little annoyed.

Self taught? Seriously? What is this guy's problem?

He scooped up the last of his dessert. After wiping his mouth with his napkin, he tucked it next to his plate. He did all of this slowly, as if he had all the time in the world.

This wasn't because he was trying to come up with a response to Noah's question. No, he was thinking about how he would really like another serving of Crème Brûlée.

Give him a break... He and Stephanie had missed dinner. So, it was understandable he was hungry. But since he knew the chance of getting another dessert was slim, he was more than happy to play along with this latest attack from Noah.

What Noah didn't realize, even though Evan came across as a laid-back-and-go-with-the-flow kind of guy, he was never one to back down from a challenge. And since he still wasn't sure what kind of relationship Noah and Stephanie shared, this was as good a time as any to let him know he was up against some stiff competition.

He nonchalantly draped his arm along the back of Stephanie's chair, his fingers just barely grazing her shoulder. Hoping this would send Noah the sign Stephanie was no longer available, he nodded over at him.

"I graduated from Yale with a BFA. Then I got an MFA in photography in case I eventually want to teach. When I decided on a career in the arts, I knew I needed to go about it the right way. Yale rates at the top for their photography program."

He shrugged. "I couldn't afford the tuition on my own, so I applied for a scholarship and I guess you could say I got lucky. It was a great experience. Even though I sometimes wonder if all the traveling I did after I graduated might have taught me more than what I learned the four years I spent at Yale."

This was not what Noah wanted to hear.

The guy had to be kidding, right? Yale?

Come on... he found this hard to believe. Was a college degree from such a prestigious school really necessary to become a photographer? It made little sense. In fact, it seemed to be a little extreme. These days, anyone could take professional quality photos using their cell phone.

But with Evan's latest revelation, Noah now had nothing else to work with. Nor was he to find it mattered. The attention around the table had now swung back to Evan, everyone bombarding him with questions about his travels.

To hide his irritation, he pulled his phone out of his pocket and began scanning through his messages. He pounced on the first text requiring a medical related response, deciding to use this as his excuse to leave. After mumbling something about duty calling, he sent his goodbyes around the table, thanked Elenore for her hospitality, and he was out the door.

Once he was in his car, he began scrolling through his contact list.

The night was still young.

Elenore leaned back in her chair and slowly gazed around the table.

Aside from Stephanie's unfortunate accident, she was quite pleased with how the evening had turned out. She would rate it as one of the most interesting dinner parties she had hosted in a very long time.

She sighed.

Lately, the dinner topic always seemed to gravitate towards the subject of everyone's declining health. This resulted in the usual discussion about prescriptions and insurance costs, sometimes even the exorbitant cost of funerals. Not the most enlightening of conversations.

But with the age of her guests averaging somewhere around eighty, this wasn't surprising. Set in their ways, they didn't hesitate to speak their minds. This turned every new project into an ongoing and frustrating battle.

She frowned. Change didn't come easy to this group.

Even she recognized the need to keep up with the times. And this was why she had asked Evan and Stephanie to be a part of this dinner. It was time for the current generation to take over, bring a much-needed breath of fresh air into the group.

She glanced down at her watch. It was almost nine, a time in her mind signaling the party should end. It had been a long week, leaving her more tired than usual. That tomorrow was Sunday, with no plans or pressing engagements, was a huge relief.

She tapped her spoon against her water glass. Once she had everyone's attention, she sent a smile around the table. "I am so glad you could make it tonight, some a little later than others. But that you escaped unscathed is all that matters."

After she sent a nod over to Stephanie, she resumed speaking. "I also hope you enjoyed your dinner. As usual, the caterers did a fantastic job. They definitely outdid themselves with the Crème brûlée." She followed this with a wink in Evan's direction."

Her expression turning serious, she clasped her hands together on the table in front of her. "No doubt you're tired of listening to me carry on about the community center. But as you all know, for me, this has been a long time coming. And I'm beyond thrilled to report we're finally on the home stretch."

She waved away the enthusiastic applause before she continued. "I'm sure you would also agree we are in dire need of more young people to help spread the word about the programs we've put in place. I'm not talking about monetary donations, but hands-on volunteering. This would be so beneficial for the children who are in our care."

She gave a nod to Evan and Stephanie. "For that reason, I've appointed Evan and Stephanie as honorary ambassadors for this project."

She sent Stephanie a smile. "Stephanie is an excellent example of everything we're looking for as a volunteer. Her dedication as a nurse is beyond exemplary."

Her glance shifted to Evan. "And even though I've known Evan for only a short time, I know he's the kind of young man we want on our side. Together, I believe they will do good things, inspiring others to do the same."

She stood, bringing everyone else to do the same. "And with that being said, I would like to thank all of you for coming tonight. And please remember to drive safely."

In her typical Elenore fashion, this was her way of making it very clear…

The evening was over.

CHAPTER 21

Thinking of you keeps me awake.
Dreaming of you keeps me asleep.
Being with you keeps me alive.
~ Anonymous

Evan chuckled as he watched Stephanie fasten her seatbelt.

She responded with a tentative smile.

He shook his head. "Exactly what happened back there? I'm beginning to think Elenore has us signed up for something much bigger than we were told. A mission, of sorts. I wonder if anyone else at dinner knew what she was planning? Or if they approve?"

Stephanie shrugged. "I don't know if it matters what they think. She always has the last word with most of the hospital projects. And remember, I warned you. This is what she does. She convinces you to go along with her plan before you even know what you're getting yourself into."

Then she laughed.

Again, the sound of a million tiny little bells surrounded him, bringing a smile to his face. He'd swear it was something you would expect to hear in an enchanted forest.

Now, this wasn't a sign he's a believer in fairy tales. Or fate... or even destiny. He had given up on those a long time ago.

But can you blame him? Until now, his life certainly hadn't been what one would consider a prelude to a happily ever after.

"Evan..." Stephanie was waving her hand in front of his face. "Where did you go? Come back to me."

He blinked. Then he reached over to brush his knuckles along the curve of her jaw. There was a huskiness in his voice. "I haven't left. No, I'm right here."

He shook his head, a bemused smile on his face. "I've kept your laugh tucked away in my mind ever since the first time I heard it. It makes me happy, thinking only good things are possible. My hope is I'll be able to hear it more often."

Stephanie didn't know what to say. A thank you didn't feel like it was enough. So, she leaned over to press just the hint of a kiss to his cheek before she responded. "I hope so, too."

This had Evan smiling as he started up the car. About to pull out onto the main road, he glanced over at her. "I don't know about you, but I'm starving. Would you like to stop somewhere for a bite to eat?"

"That would be nice. I'm hungry, too." She grinned. "And remember, we've already both agreed we're dressed for a night out."

He nodded. "Yes, we have. And I know the perfect place."

She waited for him to say more, but he didn't. Curious, she glanced over at him. "So, is that all you're going to tell me?"

He tilted his head, thinking about this before he nodded. "Yes, I think so."

She couldn't help but smile. "Not even a hint?"

He shook his head. "Nope, you'll just have to trust me."

"I do." And for some odd reason, these two simple words came out more seriously than she intended. Almost as if she was taking a vow, promising him much more than he was asking.

This had her in a panic.

What are you doing? It wasn't like he was asking you to marry him. He just wanted to know if you were hungry. For food... and only food.

She turned to stare out the passenger window. If she tried to explain, there was a good chance she would only make things worse.

Yeah, you would wind up asking him to marry you instead.

This possibility had her gaze even more intently focused on the passing scenery.

Busy merging onto the freeway, Evan was clueless, having noticed nothing unusual about what she said. Now in the lane of his choice, he linked his fingers with hers, resting their hands on the console. He was feeling pretty good with the direction the evening was going. But there was something still bothering him. He cleared his throat. "So, I'm a little curious..."

Oh, dear...

Her smile was cautious. "Yes?"

"This Dr. Davis... what's he all about? I don't know, maybe it's my imagination, but I got the impression he doesn't like me. Which makes little sense, since tonight was the first time we actually met."

He sent her a sidelong glance. "Do the two of you have a history together? Is he someone special to you?"

She stared at him, her lips parted.

A history together? Someone special?

She'd give anything to tell him, no... there was no history between them, a claim she knew Noah would be quick to second. This would suggest a commitment on his part. Again, this wasn't his style.

And special? At one time, well... yes, she would admit to this. She had even gone as far to think maybe he was 'the one' for her. Now she knew better.

Evan squeezed her hand. "Stephanie?"

One look in his eyes was enough to know she could be nothing but honest with him. She sighed. "Noah... I mean, Dr. Davis, has been a part of the staff for only about a year and he's an excellent doctor. The children all love him."

A smile tugged at the corner of his mouth. It was obvious she was trying to skirt around the question. He nodded. "*Ah...* Yes, I've noticed how the children light up when he enters the room. But so do most of the female staff."

Then, as she was so prone to do when she was nervous, she began talking fast, her words tripping over each other. "Yes, I'm pretty sure almost every nurse at the hospital has had some kind of crush on him at one time or the other. As my friend Sophie would say, he's a big-time player. He can be very charming in order to get what he wants. But this all changes when something better comes along."

She shook her head. "But I honestly believe he thinks he's doing nothing wrong. A telltale sign of a true player."

Player? An interesting choice of word, for sure.

Evan was nodding. "*Hmm...* doesn't sound good. And, player? I don't believe I've ever heard of this."

His first roommate at Yale—who had made it clear from day one he came to Yale to party, not study—would fit into this category. How many times had he been in the awkward position of having to cover for him. Or worse yet, forced to listen to the long and intimate details shared by one of the many heartbroken women, who came searching for him after being cast aside.

Yeah, not a lot of good memories with that guy. It wasn't a surprise when he flunked out of the program the first year.

Stephanie shrugged. "A player is someone who backs off from any talk of a serious relationship. When he first arrived, Dr. Davis was engaged, but then he broke it off. And who knows what will happen next? His actions make it pretty clear he intends to play the field." She shook her head. "No, commitment is not part of his plans."

His eyes on the road, Evan nodded. He found this to be very encouraging. Because even if Stephanie had fallen for this doctor's so-called charms, this was now in the past.

And his surprise visit to the hospital? Well... this no longer mattered.

You would think this would be enough to reassure him. But Noah's behavior at Elenore's dinner party still worried him. It was of a man staking his claim, confident of getting his way. So, maybe it wasn't completely over between them?

The only way you're going to find out is to ask her

But it turned out this would have to wait when Evan turned off the main road and pulled into a parking space. He shut off the ignition and smiled over at Stephanie. "So, what do you think?"

She peered out through the windshield, immediately recognizing the sign over the entrance to the small building in front of them.

The Glass and Grape.

She looked over at Evan, a huge smile spreading over her face. "Oh, Evan...."

He was grinning. "So, I guess this meets your approval? I thought this could be a start at getting back some of the magic we once shared."

She nodded. "Yes, this is perfect."

His grin even bigger, and feeling very pleased with himself, he got out of the car. After he came around to open her door, he held out his hand. "Come on, let's get this evening started."

CHAPTER 22

E van folded his napkin and tossed it on the table. His mouth twisted in a grimace, he reached up, running his finger under his collar.

He was so damn uncomfortable.

This might be a good time to remind you of how much he hated tuxedos.

Remember, he wasn't a formal attire kind of guy.

Though he really couldn't complain, since this was only the second time in his life he had to wear one. Kelsie's brother's wedding had been the first.

But now, the prospect of having to wear one again in only a few days for Joe's awards dinner was something he didn't even want to think about.

You, in a tuxedo twice in the time span of less than a week? How did this happen?

He tugged at the collar again.

He must have tied the stupid bow tie too tight. Or buttoned the wrong buttons. Or it was possible the shirt was the wrong size. He didn't know what the hell was wrong, only that it was getting harder to breathe.

Maybe this was an exaggeration. But he'd swear the collar kept getting tighter by the minute.

Thank God you broke down and ordered one, tailored to fit.

He made a mental note to call first thing on Monday morning to make sure the order would be in before Wednesday, as promised. This was the night of Joe's awards banquet.

Again, formal wear wasn't his thing

Unbeknownst to Evan, Stephanie had been watching his ongoing struggle. As he was about to give the collar another tug, she put her hand on his arm.

When he glanced over at her, she smiled. "May I?"

He nodded. He didn't know what she was planning, but her smile was enough to have him agree to whatever she had in mind.

She reached for his tie and gave it a good tug until it came undone. At his sharp intake of breath, she stilled, a question in her eyes. He nodded, his gaze never leaving her face as she undid the top two buttons. When she pushed open his collar, the brush of her fingertips over his bare skin sent every single cell in his body on high alert.

She was so close. This was taking every ounce of control he had to keep from leaning in a little more to press a lingering kiss to the pulse racing at the base of her neck. Then he would capture her mouth in a kiss. A kiss even more passionate than they shared in the parking lot of the police station.

He blinked.

What are you doing? You're getting way ahead of yourself here...

But the memory of how her mouth felt on his wouldn't leave him. So warm, inviting... her lips so soft.

So, it was a moment of desperation that had him catching her hand and placing a slow, open-mouthed kiss to her wrist.

This had Stephanie's voice coming out all breathless. "So, I take it you feel better?"

Still holding her hand, he smiled. "Yes, much better. Thank you." He shrugged. "I'm sorry. I guess I'm not a tuxedo kind of guy."

"It's okay. At least now you look more comfortable." She smiled. "Even sort of reckless, I'd have to say."

"Reckless?" He smiled, liking the sound of this.

You can do reckless if this is what she'd like.

He shrugged. "*Hmm*... I've never thought of myself as reckless. But if this is the type of guy you'd like, I'd be more than willing to give it a try."

Her expression turned serious. "I would never expect you to change just for me."

She hesitated, her next words so soft, he almost didn't catch them. "And I like you just the way you are."

He leaned closer. "Stephanie–"

"Another glass of wine for either of you?"

Their server was standing next to the table, a big smile on her face. "Or maybe you were you thinking of trying one of our dessert flights? With five different mini desserts big enough to share, you get to try a little of everything. So, how can you go wrong? I guarantee you won't be disappointed."

Stephanie began shaking her head, no. "Oh, I don't..."

"That would ..." While this came from Evan.

He laughed. "I know you're going to say we already had dessert, but this comes with a guarantee. How can we refuse? I say we go for it."

Before she could respond, the server nodded over at Evan. "Okay, one dessert flight coming up."

Stephanie watched her leave before she shook her head. "You're going to spoil me."

He leaned back in his chair. Fingering the stem of his wineglass, he smiled. "I'd be more than happy to spoil you. I'd think this is something a reckless kind of guy would be good at. And come on, if I did, would this be such a bad thing?"

He watched as the blush in her cheeks grew even more pronounced before she shrugged. "I don't know? No one has ever asked me this before."

A look passed between them, one that had them both reluctant to look away. He was the first to speak. "So, let me be the first."

She wrapped her hands around her wine glass. After gazing down at the wine remaining, as if she hoped it would provide the words she was looking for, she glanced up at him. "Can I ask you something?"

The seriousness of her expression had him a little wary, but he nodded. "Sure."

"Why didn't you call? Was it something I did? Or said? I thought… well, I felt like we had some kind of connection, the start of something special that night."

He groaned, closing his eyes. His plan had been to bring this up, but it never seemed like the right time. His reason for running away— and yes, this is exactly what he had done—now seemed so childish. And now that she beat him to it, he felt like a jerk.

He took a deep breath. "*Ah…* let me start by saying it was rather stupid move on my part. The day after the masquerade ball, I got this crazy idea to surprise you at work. Even though it had only been a few hours, I wanted to see you again. But when I got off the elevator, you were with Dr. Davis, or Noah… whatever."

He began fingering his napkin, smoothing out the creases as he spoke. "The two of you looked so, well… I guess I'd say friendly?"

He frowned. "Maybe more than friendly. At least this is what I saw. So, I left. When I got home, I accepted a job offer for six months in New Zealand. After what I saw, I figured there was no reason for me to stay here."

He shoved the napkin away, meeting her gaze. "When I came home, I still couldn't stop thinking about you. But I figured too much time had passed. You had moved on."

He shook his head. "Joe, a colleague of mine, asked me to meet him at Café Latte about a job. And, while we were there, you walked in. This is when I realized I wasn't ready to give up on us. So, when Joe told me about the hospital project, I thought this was a sign. A second chance, of sorts. And, well… you know what happened next."

He shook his head. "I should've tried to talk to you at Café Latte. Even if only to say hi. But, to be honest? I was scared. So, I convinced myself I needed more time to think about what I wanted to say."

She studied him, not saying a word. Then she sighed. "Oh, Evan… I saw you at Café Latte. I was there with Jason. But like you, I was afraid. And when you came to the hospital that day in September? What you saw was Dr. Davis doing his thing. I'm sure you've noticed how he acts with all the nurses."

She gave him a wistful smile. "I wish you had stayed. Instead of leaving without talking to me."

He leaned back in his chair, running his hand through his hair. "I'm sorry. But it seems I lose my ability to think where you're concerned. Kelsie used to say—"

A stricken look on his face, he shook his head. "I'm sorry... I didn't..."

She placed her hand on his. "Please don't feel you can't talk about Kelsie. She was a big part of your life and always will be, if only in your memories. I would love to know all about her."

He was silent, staring down at their hands. Then he lifted his head, meeting her gaze. "What I was going to say, Kelsie always said my one fault was my tendency to act too quickly on my emotions instead of taking time to think things through."

A grin began to spread over her face. "So, let me get this straight. You're telling me you only have one fault? *Hmm...*"

Now he was grinning, too. "I know you'll find this hard to believe, but I like to think she was right. I'm a pretty nice guy once you get to know me."

Their server appeared at the table with the promised dessert flight, bringing an end to their conversation. Instead, inspired by the delicious assortment, the subject turned to Evan's lack of kitchen skills. Stephanie was laughing at something he said when a family passed by their table, the father pushing one child in a wheelchair.

Evan turned to Stephanie, a thoughtful look on his face. "That family reminds me of something I've been wanting to ask you. It's about one of your patients. Nathan, the young boy in a wheelchair who is always by himself. I've tried to talk to him, but the most I've gotten so far is a yes or no answer. If I'm even lucky enough to get that."

Stephanie sighed. "Believe it or not, he is so much better than he was a few weeks ago. He is the only survivor of a car accident. His mom, dad and older sister didn't make it. This happened when they were on their way to pick up a puppy that was to be his birthday gift."

She sighed. "And now, the only family he has is his aunt. The first three weeks after the accident, she was with him twenty-four seven. But now, as Nathan's sole provider, she doesn't want to lose her job, so she visits only when she can."

She shook her head. "But don't feel bad. He talks to no one. Even his aunt. I think it will take a long time for him to accept what happened."

Evan shook his head. "The poor kid. I can't even imagine what he's going through right now. He probably blames himself for what happened. But I'll keep trying to talk to him, get him to open up. The last time I was with him, I almost got a smile out of him."

Stephanie was smiling.

He smiled hesitantly in return. "What did I say now?"

She was shaking her head. "Nothing. But I'm beginning to think Kelsie was right. You are a nice guy."

A glimmer of hope filling him, he linked their fingers together. "I know I haven't given you much of a reason to trust me, but give me a chance. I promise not to disappoint you."

Holding his breath, he waited.

When she nodded, he closed his eyes, relief pouring through him.

Evan wasn't sure what just happened between him and Stephanie, but whatever it was, it had changed everything.

At least for him, it had.

This woman, this vision of pure beauty, and everything good, was all he needed in his life.

"Evan?" She sent him a tentative smile. "Are you okay?"

Overwhelmed by his thoughts, he was at a loss for words. Then, gazing down at their hands, he smiled. "Yes, yes, I am."

In an attempt to hide his muddled state, he nodded toward what was left of their dessert. "So, the verdict is still out on these. Should we go for it and try the last one?"

She nodded. "Yes, definitely. It would be a shame if we didn't."

Then she sent him another one of those spell-binding smiles that had him ready to promise her the moon, along with all the stars in the sky. "Thank you for making this night turn out so much better than it began. This is perfect.

He grinned. "Hey, again, this is what we nice guys do. We aim to please."

He glanced around at the now almost empty room before he looked back at her. "*Hmm...* it looks like once again, we'll be the last to leave."

He reached for his fork. "Since you insisted we save this one dessert until last, would you like the first taste?"

He was grinning.

Since it was chocolate?

He already knew what her answer would be.

CHAPTER 23

With you, I know everything will be all right.
Even when it all looks so wrong.
~ Anonymously Yours

I t was a beautiful Monday morning.

Abby Kartell peeked into the porta-crib set up next to the counter at Sweet Abby's. Carefully tucking the blanket around the now sleeping Madeline Rose, she tip-toed away from the crib.

She glanced down at her watch. If she was lucky, she should have at least a couple of hours to get some work done while Madeline Rose napped.

First on her agenda was the large cake on her worktable. Waiting for the final coat of frosting and fondant decorations, it was for the annual Cleveland Law Enforcement Banquet. It was to be delivered tonight.

There were also two small cookie orders, waiting for their finishing touches.

With Kevin on day five of a seven-day road trip with the team, she was running behind. Not that she was complaining, but she was really looking forward to his return.

Pouring out a cup of coffee from the just brewed pot, she sighed after she took a much needed sip. Was it her imagination, or did it always seem like her orders seemed to double while Kevin was away? Not that she expected him to help with her, but he was a god-send with Madeline Rose.

Now that she was walking, more like running, she was constantly on the move. Who knew a toddler could get into so much trouble.

She smiled, thinking about the bond between Kevin and Madeline Rose. Since she first made her appearance in the world, Madeline Rose had him wrapped around her little finger. When he was home, she followed him everywhere. And when he left without her, she threw a fit, eventually crying herself to sleep.

A sudden cry from Madeline Rose, followed by silence, had Abby hurrying into the pantry to get the fondant decorations and tub of frosting for the cake.

It was time to get to work.

She began slapping frosting on the cake.

Stephanie turned the huge SUV into the parking lot of Sweet Abby's, bringing it to a jerking stop. Her rental car until her car was repaired, she wasn't quite used to driving it yet. Much bigger than her little car, she felt like she was driving a semi.

Not that she had ever driven a semi.

Now, there's an idea for you. If you were a truck driver, you would have less stress, travel the country and see the sights at the same time.

Since she was stopping by unannounced, she was glad to see Abby's SUV parked in front of Sweet Abby's.

She needed to talk to someone.

You need advice. Before you goof up a chance at something good.

Not that she and Evan had any kind of relationship. No, it was more like they had been thrown together through no action of their own. This had them tip-toeing around each other, not a clue of what they were doing.

So, yes... she desperately needed some guidance.

When she walked into Sweet Abby's, the first thing she saw was the porta-crib set up next to the counter. Hoping this meant Abby had brought Madeline Rose with her, she headed in that direction.

"*Shhh.... please* don't wake her." This loud whisper had her stopping dead in her tracks. She glanced over to see Abby almost dive out of her chair, her finger to her lips.

They shared a hug before Stephanie responded, also in a whisper. "I hope it's okay I'm here." She glanced over at the porta-crib. "Did she just fall asleep?"

Abby nodded. "Yeah, thank goodness. She has been a wild thing the past few days, into everything. Moody, cranky... you name it. Her answer to everything has been a resounding no. I think she misses Kevin. So, my hope is she tired herself out enough to take a nice, long nap."

She pulled Stephanie into another hug. "I'm so glad you stopped by. I heard about your accident. Thank goodness it wasn't worse and you're okay. I heard your little car didn't do as well. But that can be fixed."

She returned to her seat at the table and, after piling another generous scoop of frosting on the cake, she glanced up at the clock. "I have about four hours to get this cake done and delivered. So, I hope you won't mind if I keep working while we talk."

She nodded towards the counter. "There are cookies over there, and I just brewed a fresh pot of coffee. So, help yourself."

After Stephanie picked out a cookie and poured out a cup of coffee, she sat next to Abby. She took a big bite out of the cookie. Closing her eyes, she gave a long sigh. "Oh, Abby... your cookies are just so good."

About to take another bite, a big smile lit up her face. "When I get married, something I'm doubting will ever happen, I want you to make me a cookie cake. No cake, only cookies. Maybe in the shape of a cake."

"A cookie cake..." Her head tilted, Abby thought about this before she nodded. "*Hmm...* you just might be on to something. And I bet you anything I'll be making this cookie cake for you sooner than you think."

The cake frosted to her satisfaction, Abby sent a curious glance over at Stephanie. "So, what's the reason for this visit? I feel all this nervous energy coming from you. Is there something you want to talk about?"

After slowly tracing the rim of her cup with her finger, Stephanie finally met her gaze. "I'm not good at this. I don't know what to do."

When this was all she had to say, Abby nodded. "*Umm...* I think I might need a little more information than that." After peering more closely at Stephanie, she grinned. "Is it possible this could be about a man? A man who is also a photographer? His name is Evan, I believe."

About to take a sip of her coffee, Stephanie almost dropped the cup. Incredulous, she stared at Abby.

Abby laughed. "You should know by now what you tell Sophie is fair game. She can't keep a secret for the life of her. Thanks to her, I know you and this Evan were both invited to a dinner party given by Elenore Cromley. This was why you bought a dress from the boutique. And we both know, if there wasn't a man involved, and a special one at that, you would have made do with what you could find in your closet."

She pointed over to a tray of fondant stars. "While we talk, can you hand me those fondant stars? One at a time?"

After working in a companionable silence for a few minutes, Abby sent her a grin. "With your help, we'll finish in no time. And we can still talk about the important things. Like the dress you picked out. According to Sophie and her aunt, it was a perfect fit. And you looked amazing."

Stephanie smiled. "I love the dress. But amazing?" She shook her head. "I don't know about that. This dress would make anyone look good."

She sighed. "Every time I go to the boutique, I want everything I see. They always have such beautiful things. In fact, I'm tempted to call Sophie and have her put this sheer white gauze top on hold for me. It's so pretty. The hem and the neckline are both trimmed with embroidery and—"

Abby cut her off. "Enough about the boutique. I want to hear about Elenore's dinner party. Or did you decide not to go after your accident? Tell me everything."

Stephanie filled her in on the chain of events that made up the evening. Beginning with Evan picking her up at the police station, and ending with their late dinner at the Glass and Grape.

Abby sat back in her chair, inspecting the cake. After re-arranging a few of the decorations, she sent a thoughtful glance over at Stephanie. "Why do I feel you're not telling me everything? At least not the important stuff."

Comprehension dawned on her face. "Oh my gosh, this is because you like him, don't you? I mean, you really like him."

Stephanie nervously tucked her hair behind her ears. "I do... but then I don't. Because even though he seems interested, I can't let go of the feeling this won't last."

She meticulously began folding and refolding her napkin in order to avoid Abby's calculating look.

Watching this, Abby sighed. "I take it this is because he never called like he promised?"

Stephanie's mouth dropped open in surprise. Then she laughed. "*Oh, geeez...* Sophie told you about that, too? There are no secrets with this group, are there?"

Abby shook her head. "Nope. But think of this as a good thing. It shows how much we care about each other. Sophie also told me Evan was engaged and what happened to his fiancée." She sighed. "How awful this must have been for him, a break-up of the worst kind. No warning, with so much left unfinished."

Determined to keep working, she pointed to the next tray of fondant decorations. "Now, while you hand those to me, you can tell me what Evan said when you asked him why he never called."

When this met with only silence, she glanced over at Stephanie. Intently focused on the tray, it was obvious she didn't want to answer.

She sighed. "Steffie?"

Stephanie smiled over at her. "Wow, these flags you made are really amazing. And the police badges, they're so realistic. How did you put the names on? The printing is so small..."

Abby raised an eyebrow. "*Umm...* the fact you're trying to avoid my question leads me to believe you didn't ask him, did you?"

Stephanie sighed. She really didn't want to tell Abby about Evan's reason for not calling. Then she would also have to tell her about Noah, something she didn't want to do. Jason was the only person she had confided in about Noah. And she wanted to keep it that way.

She shrugged, trying to sound nonchalant. "I did. He thought I was already in a relationship with someone else."

At Abby's puzzled expression, she sighed. "He came to visit me at work and when he saw me talking to one of the doctors, he took it the wrong way. So, he left. For the next six months, he was in New Zealand on a photo shoot for a travel magazine. When he got back home, Elenore offered him the job at the hospital. She didn't know we had met before."

She shrugged. "And now, here we are."

Abby shook her head. "Sounds like a horrible misunderstanding to me. But I'm willing to bet what happened with his fiancée also plays a big part in all of this. It must have been a shock to find he had feelings for someone new. A betrayal of sorts. Unable to handle this, he ran."

She shook her head. "You need to give him the benefit of the doubt, Steff. Give him another chance. When will you be seeing each other again? Did you make plans?"

Stephanie glanced down at her watch. "In about two hours when I report for work." She sighed. "Though I'm not sure how much longer he'll be coming to the hospital. He's already taken a ton of photos. I would think he'd have more than enough by now."

Abby smiled. "Sounds to me he doesn't want to leave. He wants to spend more time with you. If only to make sure you won't be hanging around with any more doctors."

Then she sent Stephanie a sly grin. "But now let's move on to something even more interesting... has he kissed you yet?"

A smile curved Stephanie's lips. "Yes. And this makes everything so difficult. I can't even explain what that kiss did to me, only that it completely changed how I feel about him. I'm pretty sure he felt the same."

Abby nodded. "Even more of a reason you need to stop worrying and enjoy the moment." Her look was stern. "I mean it, Steff. Lighten up."

Stephanie stuck her tongue out at her before she picked up her empty cup and took it over to the sink. After a quick peek into the porta-crib, she whispered over to Abby. "It looks like she is still sleeping." She smiled, shaking her head. "Such a little angel."

Met with Abby's skeptical expression, she grinned. "Come on, she can't be that bad."

Abby laughed. "Trust me, behind that angelic vibe she gives out is a little whirlwind waiting to wreak havoc in our lives. I'm open to you babysitting her anytime. So, you can see her in action."

"I would love that. But right now, I need to get going."

Abby smiled. "Okay, but I want to say one last thing. And this is I hope Evan realizes how lucky he is, out of everyone in the world, he found you. You're the best, Steff. And you deserve the best."

She walked with Stephanie to the door, giving her a hug. "Thanks for stopping by... I really appreciated your help. And keep me posted."

Two hours later, Abby had accomplished everything she had set out to do. The cake and cookies were decorated and packed in the car, ready to be delivered. And Madeline Rose was awake and in a very cheerful mood.

On her drive home, listening to Madeline Rose's chatter, her thoughts drifted to Stephanie and Evan. She really hoped they worked things out between them.

She was eager to meet him.

CHAPTER 24

It was now late afternoon, a time when the kitchen of Jake's Place was bustling with activity, the rush on to get ready for the night ahead.

But today it was unusually quiet.

In need of some alone time, Jake Martin had ordered his staff to take a break.

He was also feeling a little guilty. Not in the best of moods, his temper had surfaced more times than he wanted to think about.

After shoving the last tray of cut up vegetables in the commercial sized refrigerator, he leaned against the door, giving it a hard shove with his shoulder. It slammed shut, the loud bang echoing in the silence.

Still leaning against the refrigerator, his eyes closed, he didn't move.

If only he wasn't so damn tired. To the point he didn't trust himself to finish the rest of the prep work for tonight's menu offerings. With the way things were going, he wouldn't be surprised if he left out an important step or ingredient.

He glanced down at his bandaged thumb. Flexing his hand, he winced at the pain.

Hell, look at you. You nicked it pretty good when you were chopping up those onions.

More like almost sliced off the tip. It was still throbbing.

Amateur... you're a damn amateur. You know better.

He let out a frustrated groan.

"Hey, are you okay?"

He jerked away from the refrigerator, glancing over to where the voice had come from.

It was Amber.

Standing a few feet away and holding a tray piled high with rolls just out of the oven, there was a concerned look on her face.

He reached up to massage the back of his neck, a sheepish half grin, half grimace on his face. "Sorry, I'm beat. I haven't been sleeping very well. Got a lot on my mind, I guess."

She set the tray down on the counter. She crossed her arms over her chest, and her head tilted, she studied him. "You want to talk about it? Because lately, it seems like even though you're here, your mind is somewhere else."

She sent him a tentative grin. "Or maybe, like the rest of us, you're about to lose it with how busy the restaurant has been these past few weeks. I can't believe reservations are still at their all-time high."

She glanced over at the door leading to the restaurant. "In the last hour, we had to turn down at least a half dozen requests for tonight." Her grin had faded. "But on a more serious side, I'm more worried about what you're going to goof up next."

She sent a nod to his thumb. "Exhibit A... I can't remember the last time you cut yourself prepping vegetables."

He shrugged.

She sighed, and walking right past him, she went over to the table and chairs set up in the corner. She pulled out a chair, and turning to him, she pointed to it. "I think it's time we take a break. While I pour each of us a cup of coffee, I want you to sit. Then, you can tell me what's going on."

He opened his mouth, only to close it when she held up her hand, nodding toward the chair. "Nope, I will not take no for an answer. Like I said, sit."

His exhaustion winning over, he almost fell into the chair. When she returned and set a cup of the steaming coffee in front of him, he sent her a faint smile. "Thanks. Sometimes I wonder where I'd be at this point if it wasn't for you."

Another faint smile flitted across his face. "I can't believe I'm going to say this out loud, and to you of all people, but hiring you was the best decision I ever made with the restaurant."

She grinned. "I know. Just make sure you never forget this important fact. But right now? Drink your coffee, let the caffeine do its thing.

She peered more closely at him. "When is the last time you ate?"

He stared up at the ceiling. Dragging his hand down over his jaw, he exhaled a long, drawn out breath. "Geeez... I can't remember. This morning maybe?"

She sighed. "Why am I not even surprised?"

She pulled open the refrigerator door, where she began searching the shelves. "I'm going to find something for you to eat... something nutritious. Talking can wait, at least for a little while."

With the rays of the late afternoon sun falling across the room and Amber doing most of the talking, they snacked on the cheese board she put together.

A longer than usual silence fell between them before Amber looked right at him, her eyebrow raised. "So, are you going to tell me what's going on?"

After he leaned back in his chair and stretched out his legs, Jake's response came out after a long sigh. "Gracie got a call the other day from social services..."

He then told her about Bella's father's unexpected request for sole custody. And how they were now at the mercy of the state, waiting for the social workers' decision.

He told her how worried he was about Gracie, afraid she was on the verge of a nervous breakdown.

She wasn't eating or sleeping. And if she did happen to fall asleep? She was plagued by nightmares.

This meant he wasn't sleeping either.

Amber was confused. "But I thought you already adopted Bella?"

Jake crumpled up his napkin, throwing it on the table. "Yeah, that seems to be the million-dollar question here. The only explanation they've given us is Bella's father now claims he wasn't in his right mind when the adoption papers were filed."

He shoved his fingers through his hair. "Hell, there hasn't been a day in his life this guy has been in his right mind. Anyone who knows his track record should be able to pick up on this."

He shook his head. "Sorry, but I'm having a hard time making sense of this. Joel and Sam both gave me the number of the same lawyer who specializes in cases like this. But he told me there isn't much he can do until we get more information from social services."

His brow furrowed in concern. "I'm so afraid Gracie will try to fix this on her own. She keeps trying to convince me once she talks to Bella's father, he'll realize Bella is better off with us. But I find this hard to believe. And more importantly, it's way too dangerous."

Abruptly coming to his feet, he glanced down at his watch. "Speaking of Gracie, I've tried to call her twice in the past two hours, but she didn't answer. So, I want to make a quick trip home to make sure everything is okay. I could be worrying for no reason, but..."

Amber gave him a quick hug. "Go... and don't worry about us." She smiled. "Remember me? Your best hire decision ever? Hey, between the two of us, we've got this place so organized it could run without us."

He raised an eyebrow. "I don't know about that..."

She waved her hand towards the door. "Just go. And make sure you give both Gracie and Bella a big hug from me."

After she watched him leave, she began clearing the table. Halfway to the sink, she sent a glance around the kitchen.

She sighed.

Even though they might be organized, there was still a lot of work to be done.

Almost on cue, the door opened and the rest of the staff burst into the kitchen and headed right to their stations.

She watched as they began working, joking around with each other.

Hmm… maybe you and Jake have it more together than you thought?

Ten minutes later, the comforting sounds of a well-run kitchen filling the room, all her worries disappeared.

Just like you told Jake… you've got this.

Jake pulled his jeep into his condo parking space, a sense of foreboding filling him when he saw the space next to his was empty.

There was no baby blue Mini Cooper parked there.

Damn…

But just because her car wasn't there, didn't mean something was wrong. She could have gone out somewhere with Bella. To the grocery store. Or maybe they went to the park. The playground there was Bella's favorite.

Yeah, you're probably getting worked up over nothing.

He shut off the ignition. He was going to go inside. If she wasn't there, he'd leave her a note asking her to call him. Just to let him know she was okay.

Then he'd head back to the restaurant. Where he should have stayed in the first place.

He got out of the jeep, went running up the steps, and unlocked the door.

Silence greeted Jake when he entered the condo. Then he noticed was the note on the hall table. This sent his heart plummeting to his stomach.

Gracie sent texts, not notes. If she left him a note, it was about something she was too shy or worked up about to say to his face.

His favorite was the note she gave him on their wedding day, a list of all the things she loved about him. He had tucked it in his wallet for safekeeping.

He set his keys down on the table, and for a moment or two, he eyed the note, reluctant to even touch it. He finally picked it up.

Jake,

I'm sorry, but I couldn't sit back and wait for something to happen.

I know where to find Bella's father, so I went to talk to him. Please

don't worry, I'll be fine. Bella is with Elaine.

Love, Gracie

She had added the time at the bottom of the note… one-forty-five. This was about three hours ago.

He now understood why she hadn't answered his calls. Gracie had never lied to him, and never would. But if they talked, he'd convince her to tell him where she was. Then he'd go after her.

When he looked up from the note, he saw Bella's stuffed rabbit, Bunny, on the sofa. Since Bella took Bunny everywhere she went, this told him Gracie must have left in a hurry.

He raked his hands through his hair, giving a long, frustrated sigh.

Don't worry? Was she out of her mind? How can you not worry? What she's doing is dangerous… beyond dangerous.

Hadn't she told him enough of what went on in her past to know this? Give him every right to be upset?

And now she thought it was okay to go fix this on her own?

This could lead to a terrible ending.

So, dammit, yes… he was mad.

Furious…

He crumpled up the note and went striding into the kitchen, his intent to throw it in the trash. His hand raised in mid-air, he shook his head.

He couldn't throw it away. What if—heaven forbid—this was the last contact he ever had with her? Leaning against the counter, he groaned, closing his eyes.

Now, remember… he was exhausted. He wasn't thinking clearly. He was also scared. So, that he'd become so worked up was to be expected.

He opened his eyes and read the note one more time. After smoothing out the creases, he folded it up and slipped it in his pocket.

First things first... he was going to check on Bella, ask Elaine if she wouldn't mind watching her for a little while longer.

Then he would decide what to do about Gracie.

Jake was on his way to Elaine's condo when he saw the familiar baby blue Mini Cooper come racing through the parking lot. He stuffed his hands in his pockets, watching as Gracie pulled into the space next to his jeep.

He couldn't believe how relieved he was. Yet, he was still so unbelievably angry. Which made little sense.

She was here.

She was safe.

Wasn't this all that mattered?

Her heart feeling like it had lodged in her throat, Gracie peered through the windshield at Jake. At first, he appeared to be glad to see her. But this had changed.

Now he looked mad... an expression so unfamiliar to her.

During her drive, she had kept up a constant prayer. This was that he hadn't come home worried because she hadn't answered his calls. Then she'd confiscate the note she left. After she thought about what she wrote, she realized how upset he would be. And now she wished she'd never written it.

This didn't mean she regretted her decision to go see Bella's father.

No, absolutely not.

After hearing nothing from the social worker, she knew she had to do something... anything. Otherwise, she would have gone crazy with worry. And now that there was a glimmer of hope, the only thing she wanted was to run into the safety of Jake's arms.

Cautiously emerging from her car, she remained where she was. She searched Jake's face, hoping for some kind of sign. Any kind of sign.

But there was nothing, his expression unreadable.

Her hands shaking, she stuffed them in her pockets and moved a little closer.

She swallowed. "Hi."

When he only gave a curt nod, the sudden rush of tears in the back of her eyes had her blinking like crazy. If they fell, she knew there would be no stopping them.

She moved even closer until she was only a few feet away.

When his response to this was only more silence, a deep fear traveled through her. This was not typical of Jake. Never once had he given her the silent treatment. Even when angry, he was always one to talk things out in a calm and rational manner.

She swallowed again. "Did you... did you get the note I left for you?"

He fished the note out of his pocket. After he held it up for her to see, he stuffed it back into his pocket.

He finally spoke, his voice cracked with emotion. "I almost threw it away. But I couldn't. Only because I couldn't clear my mind, thinking it could be the last thing I'd ever get from you."

He searched her face before he took a deep breath. "Peaches, how could–"

Before he could finish, everything she wanted to tell him came pouring out, her words tripping over each other. "I'm sorry, I'm so sorry. I know you're mad at me, but I had to do something, Jake. I couldn't sit back and wait for them to come and take Bella. I couldn't. I know how the system leans towards placing children with their actual parents. They don't see the complete story sometimes."

Running her hand through her hair, she took a deep, gulping breath. "I thought if I talked to her father, I'd be able to convince him it would be better for her to stay with us. But when I got to his apartment complex, there were police cars all over the place. I didn't want to attract any attention, so I stayed in my car and out of sight, watching. It was after about an hour, I saw the police bring him out of the building in handcuffs and they drove away."

She closed her eyes. "I tried to not get my hopes up, but when I called the social worker to tell her what happened, she told me this was fantastic news, at least for us. This could put an end to any of his claims for Bella in the future."

She gave a long, shaky sigh. "But for now, we're back to waiting again, since they can do nothing until they have an official report in their hands. But at least we have more reason to hope."

She searched his face. "So, please, please don't be angry. Because I had to do this." Her voice rose in a sob. "And after everything that's happened, I don't think I could take it if you were mad at me, too."

In one swift move, he pulled her into his arms. His face buried in her hair, his voice was husky with emotion. "Oh, baby... I'm not mad at you. At least not now, I'm not. At first? Yes, I was furious. But only because I was so damn scared. The possibility of something happening to you is one I never wanted to experience again. I love you, I need you... Bella needs you."

He leaned back and framing her face in his hands, the intensity in his gaze held her captive. "Remember? We're a team. There is nothing we can't fix as long as we're together. I will always have your back. Forever and always, peaches." His look was fierce. "I want you to promise you won't do something like this again on your own."

Her nod led to his kiss, sealing her promise.

A sudden wave of tenderness washed over him. He smoothed her hair back from her face, his whisper brushing over her brow. "Right now, the first thing we're going to do is go get Bella. Then I'm going to make dinner for all of us. After that, I'll need to go back to the restaurant..."

When she opened her mouth to protest, he put his finger to her lips. "Shh... listen to me. This will only be as long as it takes to make sure everything is on track for the night. Trust me, the only place I want to be tonight is with you."

She nodded, allowing herself to sink into the promise of what he was offering. In his arms and her head resting against his chest, she was comforted not only by his strength, but by the steady beat of his heart. And all the fear and anxiety she had been carrying with her over the past few days slowly began to fade away. Leaving her beyond exhausted.

Muffled against his chest, her words were barely audible. "I'm so tired. So, *so*, tired."

He pressed a kiss into her hair. "I know, baby. I am, too. So, starting right now, we're going to let it all go... leave everything in God's hands."

After he pressed another kiss to her forehead, he reached for her hand. "Come on, let's go get Bella." He smiled down at her. "So, what would you like for dinner? Pasta? Pizza? It's your call, peaches."

Remember... for Jake, food was a cure, a celebration... and a way to soothe the soul.

It was also his way of showing his love.

Silence greeted Jake when later that night—much later—he made it home. He had been delayed at the restaurant much longer than he expected when one oven abruptly quit on them. It was only after a lot of trial and error, they got it up and running again.

But now it was almost midnight.

He turned out all the lights and checked their bedroom to find Gracie was asleep. Bella was curled up next to her, sleeping just as soundly.

He carried Bella to her room, covered her with the quilt and turned on the nightlight. He was halfway out of the room when he remembered Bunny. Retrieving the stuffed rabbit from beneath the quilt on their bed, he tucked it next to Bella.

He got undressed and brushed his teeth in record time. Once he was in bed, with Gracie in his arms, he pressed a kiss to her cheek. His words were a soft murmur in her ear. "I love you, peaches."

He'd swear she mumbled the same. And even if she hadn't? As tired as he was, he was smiling. Safe in his embrace and a perfect fit against him, this was all he needed.

She was his destiny.. His soulmate... His world...

Within seconds, he, too, was sound asleep.

CHAPTER 25

Just because it looks like I let you go, doesn't mean this is what I wanted.
~ Anonymously Yours

Completely sold out for the Annual Cleveland's Elite Awards Dinner, The Regency's Grand Ballroom was humming with activity on this Wednesday night.

Dessert and coffee had been served, followed by the announcement the awards ceremony would be starting shortly.

Stephanie and Jack were seated at a table with Jason and Darcey, Paul and his wife Sasha. Along with two other members of Jason's band and their dates.

Stephanie smiled up at Jack as he set a glass of wine in front of her. She hadn't wanted another glass of wine, but he was so insistent, she had finally accepted his offer.

He began apologizing before he even sat next to her. "I'm sorry if it took so long. I think everyone wanted to get a drink before the awards ceremony starts." He frowned. "I should have asked you earlier."

"Oh, no... this is fine. Thank you." She grabbed her glass and took a sip. Relieved to see the worried expression leave his face, she took another sip, followed by another.

This was not good... not good at all.

Stephanie wasn't a big drinker. One glass of wine usually did it for her. But tonight, with the very generous-sized glasses, this number was leaning closer to three.

So it was understandable she was feeling a little desperate.

It was official... the night was a mistake. She never should have agreed to be Jack's date. To be fair, she couldn't put the blame all on him. He was the perfect gentleman, attentive to all her needs.

Maybe too polite. And more attentive than one should be.

She sighed. He was trying too hard, and instead of finding this flattering, she only grew more uncomfortable as the evening wore on.

From the moment he'd arrived at her condo to pick her up, the evening began to go downhill. They began apologizing for almost everything they said. This leading to long periods of silence where they didn't talk at all.

So, she was now more than ready for the evening to end.

She sent a glance over at Jason.

Her pained expression coming across as a desperate plea for help, he sent her an encouraging smile before he nodded over at Jack. "Hey, Jack... give us the scoop before this awards ceremony gets rolling. Do you know any of the other nominees? Do you think you have a chance?"

The two men fell right into talk of scores, acoustics, and all the other slang of their trade.

Grateful they didn't expect her to join in, Stephanie began gazing around the room.

She froze.

Oh, no... please say it isn't so...

She squinted to get a better look. If only to make sure she wasn't imagining things.

Or the wine is starting to play tricks on you.

Nope. It was definitely him.

Evan...

Seated at a table about twenty feet away, he was in conversation with the woman next to him. And though she knew nothing good would come from watching them, Stephanie couldn't bring herself to look away. When the woman put her hand on his arm and leaned in closer, Stephanie reached for her wineglass and took a big gulp.

"Are you okay?"

She almost dropped the glass before she sent Jack a guilty smile. "Yes, I'm fine. I was people-watching. Wondering if anyone I know is here tonight."

He leaned back in his seat. "I'm sorry, no doubt this is boring for you. If it's any consolation, the awards ceremony should be starting in just a few minutes."

He pulled a program out of his pocket. "I picked this up for you. My category falls about halfway through the list. And after they finish handing out the awards, I believe there will be dancing."

He gave her a big smile.

Jack liked to dance. Any kind of dance, slow or fast. As a musician, this was understandable. He found everything came easier to him when music was involved. There was no need to talk, because the music did the talking for him. And having danced with Stephanie a few memorable times in the past, he believed they moved quite well together.

Dancing?

Stephanie nodded. And before she could stop herself, she sent another glance over at Evan, bringing Jack to do the same.

He turned back to her, and after studying her for a moment, he gave a slow nod. "*Ah... I see.*"

Determined to change the subject, she gave him a big smile. "I bet you're excited. I hope you win." Then she laughed. "But, what am I saying? Of course, you're going to win." She held up her glass in a toast. "So, let me be the first to congratulate you."

He chuckled, tipping his glass to hers. "I hope you're right."

She picked up the program and, leafing through it, began asking Jack questions. She was going to ignore Evan was even in the room.

Easier said than done...

After listening to the non-stop chatter of the woman seated next to him during dinner, Evan needed a break.

Using the excuse he wanted to get a drink, he headed for the bar.

Okay, so he lied a little.

He didn't really want a drink. But, hey... a man could only take so much.

When he saw they were about to start the awards ceremony, wine-glass in hand, he began making his way back to his seat.

He slowed his steps, confused.

Stephanie was seated at a table not too far from his.

How did you not notice her before? Why was she here? And more importantly, was she here with a date?

He could see Jason was at the same table. Maybe someone from his band was up for an award? Or possibly Jason himself? This would explain Stephanie's presence.

All very simple and believable, right?

Wrong.

He watched as a man approached Stephanie and placed a glass of wine on the table in front of her. Once he was seated, in what Evan saw as a very protective manner, he rested his arm along the back of her chair, smiling at something she said.

His jaw clenching in response, Evan took a deep breath. He needed to calm down. After all, he had no reason to be upset.

You have no claim on her, remember?

But his imagination took over, his mind going right into overdrive, thinking the worst.

Was this another boyfriend she neglected to tell you about? And was this going to keep happening? Because you don't think you can handle much more.

He didn't know he was frowning until Joe came to stand next to him, resting his hand on his shoulder. He laughed. "Hey, what's with the serious face? You put on a tux, and suddenly you're trying to pull off this mysterious man about town look. Or is this the most eligible bachelor pose you're going for? Either way, I hate to be the one to tell you this, but you're at the wrong event."

He moved closer, lowering his voice. "Sorry about the woman next to you. She is a friend of Sasha's and just went through a messy divorce. Since you decided not to bring a date, Sasha thought a night out would do her some good." He frowned, shaking his head. "She definitely called that wrong. The woman has been drinking non-stop since she got here."

Evan shook his head. "Yeah, she seems to have a lot of issues. But who are we to judge?" Then he grinned. "I'll be the first to admit I'm not your man about town type of guy. That I even went out and bought this tux is something I'm still trying to wrap my mind around. I hope you realize the sacrifice I made just to be here for you tonight."

Joe grinned back at him. "Well, keep in mind a woman loves a man in a tux. Which means I did you a favor by forcing you to buy one." His focus shifting across the room, he gave a nod in that direction. "Hey, did you see who's here?"

An attempt to pull off a look of indifference, Evan shrugged. "Yeah, when you sent me the text about the extra ticket, I considered asking her to be my date, but thought it was too late. I guess I made the right decision. It's too late, all right. On all counts."

He sent a glance over at Stephanie. "I thought things were going pretty good. But now?" He shook his head. "I'm not too sure. If anything, I'm more confused than before. Like I somehow missed out on the rules of the game."

Joe gave a half grunt, half-laugh. "You got that right... it's all a game. With a hell of a lot of luck mixed in. But if she's the one, you better get ready to fight for her. Even then, there's no guaranteed win."

He sent a nod over at Jason. "Especially when you have big brother looking over your shoulder, ready to step in."

After this subtle warning, he turned to talk to someone who had come over to congratulate him on his nomination.

Evan thought about what he said.

Fight for her? Yeah, he could do this.

As they say, nothing worth fighting for comes easy.

And Stephanie was more than worth the fight.

For Stephanie, the awards ceremony passed in a blur. Somehow, she had clapped at all the right times and came up with the right comments. And she had been genuinely happy for Jack when he won the award for his category.

But this was all overshadowed by her awareness of Evan. That he was so close made it hard for her to concentrate on anything else. This had her sneaking a glance over at him every chance she could get. And it was during one of these times she found herself caught right up in his gaze.

Even with the distance between them, she could see the question in his eyes. Gripped by this overwhelming urge to go to him, instead she sent him a smile.

If only to let him know he had no reason to worry.

Holding her breath, she waited. But after barely a nod, he turned away.

Her heart now beating a mile a minute, she sat back in her chair and sent a glance around the table. She was now the only occupant. Summoned for official photos as soon as the awards ceremony had ended, Jack still hadn't returned. Everyone else had left for the dance floor.

She closed her eyes. She wanted to go home.

You can't do this.

Maybe a quick trip to the women's lounge would help, give her time to regroup.

Out of sight, out of mind, right?

She stood, and was reaching for her purse, when there was a light tap on her shoulder. She turned, her heart leaping to her throat.

Evan was standing in front of her, his expression unreadable.

He held out his hand. For what felt like an eternity, their eyes locked, they didn't move. Then he took a step closer. "Please?"

Stephanie put her hand in his and, without another word, he led her onto the dance floor. Filled with a sudden recklessness, he twirled her around before he pulled her back to where she belonged... in his arms. He didn't know what it was, but there was something about holding her against him that had him feeling powerful.

Like he could do anything... even dance.

When she rested her head on his shoulder, he closed his eyes, impulsively pressing a kiss in her hair.

This simple gesture was when Stephanie realized how deeply she had fallen in love with him. These were the only arms she wanted to hold her close. Not only when they danced, but through whatever journey life had waiting for them.

How was it possible, in such a short time, everything about him had become so familiar? Addicting, even?

The brush of his whisper in her hair. The hard, masculine strength of his body against hers. The familiar scent of his cologne. Then there was the possessive, yet gentle way his hands drifted down her back to pull her even closer. As if he planned to never let her go.

All of these had now become a necessity in her life, daring her to dream of so much more.

He is everything you hadn't known you wanted until now.

But she could feel a tension radiating from him. As though he was fighting an inner battle with his emotions, not sure of what he wanted to say. Or wanted to happen next.

So, it was up to her to make the first move.

She gazed up at him, her smile uncertain. "I didn't expect to see you. At least you never mentioned you would be here tonight."

He merely nodded.

Taking a deep breath, she pushed on. "Jack—he is a member of Jason's band—well, he sort of asked me to be his date tonight. He was nominated for one of his soundtracks. Which he won."

Sort of?

He wondered... what did this even mean?

He finally responded. "*Hmm...* He sort of asked you, huh? I'll have to congratulate him then, on what is surely a successful evening for him on all accounts."

Was it only her imagination, or did he sound amused?

The latter was confirmed when his voice dipped to an exaggerated whisper. "I'm referring to his category win, of course. Over the past few weeks, I've learned how getting a win in this town can become very competitive. Be it personal or professional."

He leaned back, his gaze traveling over her face. "*Ah...* but this is okay. I'm more than up for the challenge."

He gave a slow nod. "Yes, like most men, I play to win."

She peered up at him, confused. Was he talking about the award? Or was he talking about Jack?

If he was referring to Jack, she needed to make him understand he had no reason to worry. She would be the first to agree Jack was a catch. Handsome, smart and extremely talented, he would make some woman very happy.

But it would never be her. She wanted romance. Desire. Passion. She would never find this with Jack.

Nope, he doesn't even come close to making you feel the way Evan does.

She gazed up at him, an earnest expression on her face. "I've known Jack for a long time. He is such a nice guy. Any girl would be lucky to be with him. Even as a friend. Which is what Jack and I will always be… friends. Good friends, but again, just friends…"

She dipped her head, her words trailing off in a sigh against his shirtfront.

"*Hmm*…" When this was his only response, she sneaked a glance up at him.

A smile tweaked the corner of his mouth, his whisper brushing across her cheek. "I get it… friends."

Filled with a sudden happiness, she gazed up at him. "And, you?"

"Me?" Her smile, and the way she was gazing up at him, her eyes shining like stars, for a moment he was at a loss for words, unsure of what she was asking.

She nodded. "Yes, you. Are you also here for a friend?"

He didn't quite know how to answer this. All of this talk about friends had him confused. And more than a little worried.

Not that he didn't trust Stephanie. Or thought she wasn't being honest with him. No, after spending the past several days together, he could usually tell what was going on in her mind just by watching her face. Before the words even came out of her mouth.

It was everyone else he had a problem with… the Noahs, the Jacks and all the other men drawn to her fragile beauty. There was an aura about her that had them lining up to be with her, take care of her. Even fight for her, if the need arose.

You should know… you're one of them.

He almost groaned aloud. Was he a fool, or what? He should be enjoying this time with her. A moment making it easy for him to believe everything between them was as it should be. Instead, he was worrying about something that could very well be all in his imagination.

Come on… she agreed to dance with you. So, enjoy it.

As if she knew what he was thinking, she sighed, resting her head back on his shoulder. He lowered his head, the huskiness of his voice settling right below her ear. Enough, he noted, to send a shiver through her. "Yes, I'm also here for a friend… Joe. An amazing photographer, he was nominated for photos he took for a local Cleveland magazine. But unlike your friend, he wasn't as lucky tonight. He didn't come out a winner."

"Oh, no… I'm so sorry." She gazed up at him, her expression so tragic it took everything he had to keep from swooping in to capture her mouth in a kiss.

But as appealing as this was, he was pretty sure kissing another man's date in full view of everyone at an affair such as this would not be a good move.

And Jason would be the first to remind you of this. No doubt he has his eye on you at this very moment.

This had him sending a quick glance around the dance floor. Sure enough, Jason was dancing with his wife. Almost as if he sensed he was a person of interest, he looked over, his gaze narrowing. The message he sent was more than clear.

He didn't approve.

Message received, Evan was the first to look away.

Damn… it looks like you're already in trouble. Asking Stephanie to dance when she came with Jack has to be a big strike against you.

He frowned. Speaking of Jack, where was the guy? He should have cut in by now.

Hell, if you were Jack, you wouldn't have let Stephanie out of your sight to begin with.

Well, it was Jack's loss.

His words were a whisper in her hair. "*Ah…* don't be sad. I assure you, Joe can handle losing for once. As it stands now, he has a shelf full of awards and trophies. And as talented as he is, I'm sure there will be a lot more wins for him in the future."

She nodded her head against his chest.

A silence fell between them before he guided her in a spin, this one more daring. His gaze traveling over her, he was smiling as he pulled her back into his arms. "I don't think I've told you yet how beautiful you look. But again, you always look amazing."

Now she was smiling, too. "Thank you, but I think you're only being kind. Since this is the same dress I wore for Elenore's dinner party."

He gazed down at her, shaking his head. "Well… then I would have to say maybe it's not only the dress, but everything else about you."

Flustered by his compliment, her response came out more than a little breathless. "I can say the same about you… so handsome, the perfect cut of your tux, your bow tie, everything…" Her brow suddenly creased in a frown. "I guess this means you no longer need my help with your bow tie. Or anything else."

He shook his head. "*Hmm…* I disagree. I definitely need your help. More than you can imagine." A smile tweaked the corner of his mouth. "In case you've forgotten, I'm not a hundred percent perfect."

Her mouth dropped open right before she burst out laughing. This had him twirling her around, this time pulling her even closer once she was back in his arms.

He was smiling as he rested his cheek in her hair, the familiar sound of all those tiny little bells wrapping around him, carrying him away to a place he never wanted to leave. So, when she leaned back to gaze up at him, the kiss he gave her was inevitable.

Brought on by a moment worthy of nothing less than such a move.

Evan was the first to notice the music had come to an end. Lifting his head, he saw he and Stephanie were about the only couple still lingering on the dance floor. He stepped back, lowering his arms to his sides.

There was the hint of a smile on his face. "I believe the dance has ended. Thank you for sharing it with me. If we keep this up, I believe we'll eventually get quite good at it."

Her gaze slowly traveling over his face, she nodded. "I think you're right."

Then take a chance… be my dancing partner for life.

Stunned, he'd almost let this slip out, yet at the same time wishing he had, he reached for her hand. "Here, let me escort you back to your table."

They both glanced over to see Jack had returned and was talking to Darcey and Jason. The quick glance he sent in their direction confirmed he knew they had shared a dance. And possibly even more.

This had Evan shaking his head.

Hmm… you still don't get it. Did the guy not care?

Stephanie had taken a step back. "Oh, no, no… that's not necessary. But thank you for the dance. And, the… well, you know. It was nice." After a slight hesitation, she reached up to kiss his cheek.

He watched her walk away, jamming his hands in his pockets to keep from going after her.

Because he'd really like to ask her what she meant by that.

Nice? It was nice?

Nice wasn't the message he had been trying to send when he kissed her.

He groaned, dragging his hand through his hair.

He was so damn confused.

He searched the room, looking for Joe.

It was time for him to go home.

Jack pulled his car up to Stephanie's condo.

It had been a pretty quiet drive.

Stephanie couldn't stop thinking about the kiss Evan gave her, wondering what it meant. While Jack had finally come to accept, no matter what he did, Stephanie would never be his.

Surprisingly, he was okay with this.

Love shouldn't be this hard.

Right?

He put the car in park and turned off the ignition. Drumming his fingers on the steering wheel, he smiled over at her. "So, you and I… I guess we just don't have it, do we?"

A stricken look on her face, Stephanie opened her mouth, to then promptly shut it when he laughed, shaking his head. "Don't worry, I'm all right with it. After all, we did try."

She put her hand on his arm. "I'm so sorry. I like you, I do. But you deserve better. Someone who loves you, really loves you."

"I feel the same about you." After a slight hesitation, he sighed. "I want someone to look at me the way you were gazing up at the guy you were dancing with. As though he's the most important person in your life."

He raised an eyebrow. "I take it you know each other well? Because the vibes he sent were of a man who was staking a claim on the woman he loves."

"His name is Evan Marshall. A freelance photographer, I met him at the masquerade ball last September." A faint smile touching her lips, she shrugged. "But then we lost touch, I guess. And, to be honest? I don't have a clue what's going on with the two of us. Sometimes it seems as though all we do is argue. Other times it's wonderful, like it was when we first met."

"*Hmm*... the kiss he gave you on the dance floor certainly didn't come across as an argument."

Even in the dim interior of the car, he could see the color rising in her cheeks. He smiled. "Sorry, I don't want to tell you what to do, but maybe you should dive in. Enjoy the moment. Let go of any trust issues you have going on."

She stared at him, again in shock.

He shrugged. "I know, I'm the absolute last person to hand out relationship advice. But I'm sure I wasn't the only one who noticed the chemistry between the two of you. And if you're anything like me, you're spending too much time doubting and analyzing everything instead of taking that leap of faith."

He grinned. "And now that I know I don't have a chance, I want you to be happy. Even though this means it will be with someone else."

Stephanie was smiling. "I'll take your advice. And I feel the same about you." Then she tilted her head, her expression thoughtful.

This had him worried. "*Uh, oh*... why do I have this feeling, whatever you're about to say, I'm not going to like it?"

She grinned. "Just hear me out, okay? Her name is Savanah Jackson. She's from Texas. She moved here about a month ago because the Cleveland Ballet offered her a contract. I met her at a yoga class my friend offers and she is so nice... and so beautiful."

Pleased she had thought of this, she was nodding. "I'm serious, Jack. She would be perfect for you. She's a dancer, you're a musician..."

Laughing, Jack threw his hands up in protest. "Oh, no you don't... stop right there. I've had enough blind dates to know they're not for me. If I'm still not married by the time I'm forty, maybe I'll feel differently. But right now?"

He shook his head. "Nope, definitely not an option."

She sighed. "It was just a thought." She sent him a teasing glance. "You could come to the class. You know... so you can see for yourself how beautiful she is."

He was already out of the car, still shaking his head. When he opened the passenger door, her attempt to say something died at the warning look in his eyes.

But at the same time, he was chuckling. "Nope, Yoga is right up there with blind dates. Not my thing."

She laughed. "You know what they say... never say never."

Stephanie watched Jack run to his car, stopping to wave once more before he drove away.

As she closed the door, she was smiling.

She had a feeling they were going to be the best of friends.

CHAPTER 26

C hris Gardner tossed his napkin on the table and sat back in his chair, a look of satisfaction on his face. His suggestion to Carrie they stop by Jake's Place for dinner had turned out to be an excellent idea.

The day had been hectic for both of them. But they also had a reason to celebrate. When Carrie went in for her check-up earlier in the day, according to her doctor, the baby could arrive any time now.

Chris smiled as he watched Carrie eat her dessert, digging into it with the enthusiasm of a child.

Just to be clear, this was actually his dessert she was enjoying. This would be the salted caramel and vanilla swirled chocolate mousse, one of the restaurant's signature desserts. When they had ordered their dinner, the server let them know they were down to the last two servings.

If they were interested, they needed to let her know.

Carrie had jumped right on it, insisting they take both. He didn't want her to eat alone, did he? This just didn't seem right.

When he laughed, shaking his head, she had been quick to remind him, if the doctor was right, this could be the last time they went out to dinner for a long time.

After she had finished her dessert, the wistful look she sent him was enough to have him hand over the rest of his. Now watching her, he wondered if this had been her plan all along.

But he was okay with this. Hell, as far as he was concerned, she could have all the desserts she wanted. And, as she so often reminded him, she was eating for two.

After she had scooped up every spoonful of mousse, she set her spoon down on the table and sent him a big smile.

He chuckled. "So, did that hit the spot? You better not forget how I so generously shared with you. And I expect you to return the favor in the future."

She grinned. "Last night, when I couldn't sleep, I made an enormous pot of my Aunt Evelyn's clam chowder. Enough for at least three meals. Will this be payment enough?"

He slowly shook his head. "*Hmm*... I don't know."

Then he reached across the table to gather her hands in his, a serious expression on his face. "Are you okay? I'm worried you're not getting enough sleep. Over the past few weeks, every time I wake up in the middle of the night, you're gone, doing who knows what. I swear you've cleaned and reorganized every single item we own. You need to slow down, princess. Starting with taking some time off from work. Sam and I are more than capable of keeping the office up and running."

She sighed. "I know." She sent him a sheepish grin. "I actually fell asleep at my desk today when you and Sam made that run to the Shaker sight. If June hadn't come in to ask me about a purchase order, I might still be there, sound asleep."

She shrugged. "But as soon as I get into bed, I think about what needs to get done before the baby comes. Then I'm wide awake. I'm probably ruining your sleep, too, aren't I?"

"Don't worry about me. I'm fine." His smile was so tender she could feel the beginning of tears in the back of her eyes.

He linked his fingers with hers. "I love you, princess. Please, I want to make things easier for you from now on, okay?"

She nodded. "I love you, too. And I swear, I'm all for going to bed. I'm exhausted. More tired than I've ever been."

She grinned. "From now on, you're the boss. I'll agree with what-ever you say."

He sat back in his chair, shaking his head. But he was also grinning. "Ha… why do I have a feeling this isn't going to happen?"

He reached for the bill left by the server. "Let me take care of this and we'll head for home. Then you can hop right into bed. Maybe even sleep in tomorrow."

She shrugged. "We'll see. I have to finish up the…" The warning look he gave her had her words trailing off as she leaned over to give him a quick kiss. "Sorry. You're the boss. I'll sleep in."

Carrie wasn't exaggerating about how tired she was.

She fell asleep even before Chris pulled out of the parking lot of Jake's Place. He had to wake her out of a sound sleep fifteen minutes later when they arrived home.

But unfortunately, four hours later, she was wide awake, staring up at their bedroom ceiling. Slowly easing herself off the bed and strug-gling into her robe, she padded quietly out into the hall and down the steps.

She turned on the light, her gaze traveling around the spotless kitchen. And even though she knew exactly what to expect, she opened the freezer door to check out the large assortment of covered containers.

She was very proud of herself. She had prepared enough food to carry them over for at least the first couple of weeks after the baby came. After one last look, she closed the freezer door, a satisfied smile on her face.

You're turning into another Aunt Evelyn, cooking up a storm. Who would've ever thought you'd come to this?

She turned out the light and wandered down the hall to the baby's room. Her arms wrapped around herself, she gazed around the recently finished room.

She was in love with how they had decorated the space. Since they had decided not to find out the sex of the baby, they had painted three walls of the room a pale fern green.

The remaining wall was a hand-painted mural of a whimsical forest scene with trees and flowers. Baby animals of all kinds peeked out here and there between the foliage.

She wound up the mobile over the crib. After it had dwindled to a stop, she settled herself in the hand-carved rocking chair that had been used by three generations of Chris's family.

It was so hard for her to believe she would soon be carrying on this tradition, rocking her child to sleep in the same chair his mother had used with him and his sister, Emily.

She gripped the arms of the chair when another wave of tightness rolled through her belly. She wasn't too concerned, since this had been happening all evening. And since it really wasn't painful, she had decided to wait a little longer before telling Chris.

It was probably only false labor.

Her eyes closed and slowly rocking back and forth, she fell into a restless sleep.

A long, rolling pain, traveling across her stomach and unlike any pain she'd ever felt before, is what woke Carrie. For a few moments, disoriented, she wondered where she was, what was happening.

Then she closed her eyes, her intention to go back to sleep.

But this wasn't meant to be. Another wave of the same pain, almost as if all the muscles in her stomach were fighting each other, had her sitting up straight in the chair, more awake than she'd ever been.

She heard Chris's alarm go off. Knowing this meant he would soon come to find her, she rested her head against the back of the chair and closed her eyes.

Slowly rocking back and forth, her hands cradling her baby bump, she waited.

After Chris finally found his phone to turn off the alarm, he sat on the edge of the bed for a few minutes.

He yawned, massaging the back of his neck.

He didn't have to look over at the other side of the bed to know Carrie wasn't there. He shook his head.

Why are you surprised? You knew this would happen.

After another enormous yawn, he headed down the hall. He had a pretty good idea where to find her.

Just as he thought, she was in the baby's room, curled up in the rocking chair.

But she wasn't asleep. In fact, she looked like she was wide awake.

He leaned down to press a kiss to her cheek. "Did you get any sleep at all? Come on, let's get you back to bed."

She shook her head. "I don't think..."

He stopped her with a kiss. "Hey, what happened to me as the boss? I make the rules and you agree? Starting with you going back to bed and taking the day off so you can get some rest."

She kept shaking her head.

This is when he realized what was happening. His eyes never leaving her face, he reached for her hands, grasping them tightly in his. "Princess? Are you... do you think..."

She smiled to reassure him. "The contractions started a while ago. They weren't too bad at first, but now they're a lot stronger and... *oooooh...*"

She squeezed her eyes shut and, gripping his hand with a strength she didn't know she possessed, she rode out the contraction to the end. Then she slowly sank back down into the chair. Her lashes fluttering open, her smile was much fainter this time. *"Wow...* that was a strong one. Something tells me this baby is in a hurry to come into the world."

With a look of pure panic, Chris gazed wildly around the room.

He started for the door. Then, running his hand through his hair, he turned back to Carrie.

He opened his mouth. But his voice refused to cooperate. So, he cleared his throat and tried again. "Okay, first things first... we need to stay calm. We know what to do, we've got this. If we stick with what we planned, we'll be fine."

He nodded, if only to reassure himself. "Yes, starting with you... your job will be to stay right here. As soon as I get dressed, I'll come back and help you out to the car. We'll wait until we're on the way to the hospital to let them know we're coming."

More than happy to let him take over, she watched him disappear down the hall. Then she closed her eyes, bracing herself for the next contraction. Never in her life had she been so scared and excited at the same time.

It was baby time.

Later, Chris would tell everyone it was a good thing they knew what they were doing, since they made it to the hospital with less than an hour to spare.

Welcome to the world,
Natalie Suzanne Gardner.
Born on May 24th at 8:32 am
7 pounds, 6 ounces 19 inches

Parents - Carrie and Chris Gardner

The nurses all claimed it had been a long time since they had experienced such an easy delivery for a first-time birth.

They were also quick to assure Chris he shouldn't feel embarrassed. He wasn't the first husband to pass out in the delivery room. What mattered was he had completely recovered by the time Natalie made her entrance into the world, and he had witnessed the miracle of her birth.

And yes, they all agreed... she was absolutely perfect.

Carrie could hear one of the nurses talking to someone out in the hallway. Recognizing the voice, a smile spread across her face as she watched Chester walk into the room.

A big grin on his face, and holding a huge stuffed teddy bear, he made his way over to her. After he set the teddy bear in the chair next to the bed, he held out his arms. "May I?"

Once he had Natalie settled comfortably against him, he began strolling around the room, talking softly to her. After a few minutes, he glanced over at Carrie. "She's beautiful, kitten. Absolutely beautiful."

He smiled. "But with you as her mommy, I expected nothing less."

He peered more closely at her. "And how are you doing? You're okay?"

She nodded before she rested her head back against the pillows. "I'm fine. Still trying to take it all in. And so amazed Chris and I made this perfect little person."

He smiled. "Yeah, it really makes you believe in miracles, doesn't it?" After a quick glance around the room, he looked back at her, a curious expression on his face. "By the way, where is Chris?"

She laughed. "I seriously don't know. He handed Natalie to me, threw on his jacket and, after mumbling there was something he needed to get, he ran out of the room. I'm surprised you didn't cross paths, since he left only about five minutes ago."

"Maybe he had to make a call or something." He smiled down at Natalie. "I can't wait to introduce this little beauty to Trevor and Hudson. They have been talking about their new cousin non-stop. Even offering to give her some of their toys."

He grinned. "I'll have you know that's an enormous sacrifice on their part."

He nodded over at the stuffed bear. "They insisted we get this bear. You should also know they both said you were going to have a boy."

They both turned to watch as Chris came running into the room, almost skidding to a stop when he saw Chester. After he shrugged off his jacket, he sent Carrie a guilty smile. "Sorry, there was something I had to do."

Before she could even respond, he grinned over at Chester. "Hey, good to see you. So, what do you think?"

"Like I told Carrie, she's beautiful. And I know the two of you are going to knock it out of the park as parents."

He chuckled, shaking his head. "Believe me, there are going to be many times you'll wonder what you got yourself into. But it's all worth it, a thousand times over. And you can always call me or Sophie if you need advice."

He laughed. "Not that we're experts or anything. But we've done okay so far. At least the boys are still alive and kicking."

"Here you go, back to daddy." He handed Natalie over to Chris and, after patting him on the back, he went over to Carrie and pressed a kiss to her cheek. "I'm going to take off. Sophie is planning to come a little later. When I left, she warned me as soon as I got back, she was heading for the mall to do some shopping for baby clothes."

He paused by the door. "Try to get some rest while you're here. Because once you leave, it will be a long, long time before you get a good night's sleep."

He grinned. "Oh, and about the bear... I know it's huge. But consider yourself lucky I only brought one. They wanted to buy two, one from each of them."

With a wink, he was out the door.

After Chris settled the still sleeping Natalie back in the bassinet, he sat on the edge of the bed next to Carrie.

He leaned over to give her a kiss. "Hey, make some room for me, okay?"

Once he settled in next to her, he pulled a small box out of his pocket and placed it in her hands.

She looked over at him, a big smile on her face. "For me?"

He gave her another kiss. "Yes, for you. But after watching you give birth to Natalie, it doesn't even come close to what you deserve for what you went through. You are an amazing woman, Carrie Gardner."

She opened the box. "Oh, Chris... it's beautiful."

"Here, let me put it on you." He took the necklace out of the box. Hanging on a sterling silver chain were three diamond studded heart pendants. Two were the same size, the third a smaller version between them.

He pressed another kiss to her cheek. "We were two hearts, and now we are three. I love you so much, princess."

"I love you, too."

Chris pulled the bassinet closer so they could watch Natalie's every move, marveling at this new little person they had created. And even though this wasn't what they planned, they fell asleep in each other's arms.

This was how the nurse found them when she made her rounds.

From what she could see, they didn't need her help.

They had this.

CHAPTER 27

It's better to lose your ego to the one you love,
than to lose them because of your ego.
Your ego won't take you anywhere.
~Unknown

T he moment Stephanie stepped off the elevator on the third floor, she sensed something wasn't right. Instead of the usual everyday hustle and bustle, there was only an eerie silence.

She was concerned, but at the same time, relieved. She was late. What she had planned as a quick stop to buy a gift for Natalie Suzanne, Carrie and Chris's new baby daughter, had taken much longer than expected.

She signed in for her shift and was checking the patient files on the computer when the sound of loud voices floated over to her.

Loud and angry male voices. Coming from the direction of Elenore's office.

Her intuition was telling her, and she really hoped she was wrong, Evan was part of the reason for this.

"Hey, Steff..."

She glanced up to see Lucy striding towards her, a huge grin on her face.

After plopping down on the chair next to her, she laughed, shaking her head. "Well, well, well… it looks like lover boy is stirring things up, messing with the big doctor."

She nodded toward Elenore's office. "They've been going at each for a while. Be honest with me, is this something the two of you cooked up together? If so, what were you thinking? You know Dr. Davis doesn't like it when someone questions his authority."

Stephanie groaned.

Just as you thought, Evan is involved.

She sent a glance over to where the angry voices had now stopped. Resisting the urge to tell Lucy to stop referring to Evan as lover boy, as this would only encourage her to do it even more, she gave her a big smile. "I assure you, I have nothing to do with what they're arguing about."

Lucy shook her head. "I bet Elenore is fit to be tied right now. You know how she hates any kind of conflict."

It was at this very moment Elenore came out of her office. When she saw Stephanie, she waved. "Stephanie, you're just the person I'm looking for. Can you join us for a few minutes?"

Lucy snickered. "Oh, boy… seems like you may be more involved than you're letting on. Why else would she be giving you the royal summons? *Hmm…* why do I have a feeling this is going to get really interesting?" She laughed. "And all because of a puppy."

Already on her way to Elenore's office, Stephanie came to a stop. Puzzled, she turned to Lucy. "Puppy?"

Lucy grinned. "Yes, a puppy. A furry black and white bundle of cuteness. The kids are ecstatic. But you know as well as I do, animals aren't allowed unless they have been trained to work as therapy dogs." She scrunched up her nose. "I wonder, is there such a thing as a therapy cat? I know they have therapy horses, but–"

Stephanie groaned. *"Lucy…"*

Lucy shrugged. "Sorry, back to your Evan. It appears he's a man who doesn't like to follow the rules."

She sent Stephanie a sly grin. "You're one lucky girl. Who doesn't love a man willing to bend the rules a bit? Especially when it comes to a romp in bed." Resting her chin on her hand, a dreamy smile touched her lips. "A masterful man. A man who wants to please his woman, keep her coming back for more."

She sent a sly glance over at Stephanie. "Is this what attracted you to your Evan?"

Stephanie's usual blush was now off the charts. She could actually feel the heat rising in her cheeks. Angry and embarrassed, her response came out much louder than she intended. "I don't know what you're talking about. Now, if you'll excuse me, I need to see what Elenore wants. No doubt it's something to do with the photos."

Pursing her lips, Lucy nodded. "*Hmm*... I guess you'll soon find out, won't you?" She waited until Stephanie walked away before she called out. "And, Steffi?"

Coming to a halt, Stephanie closed her eyes, waiting.

"Methinks you doth protest too much." Lucy followed this with a big grin. "In case you're not up on the classics, this is from Shakespeare. It means you're ignoring the obvious. But, go ahead... make all the excuses you want if this will make you feel better."

Too angry to even respond, Stephanie went marching down the hall to Elenore's office.

Obviously, Lucy didn't know what she was talking about.

And even if she did?

It wasn't any of her business.

A heavy silence greeted Stephanie when she entered Elenore's office.

Sprawled out in a chair, his arms crossed, Evan was staring down at the floor. While Noah was standing by the window, his phone to his ear, muttering to himself.

Seated at her desk, Elenore sent Stephanie a relieved smile. She gestured to the chair next to Evan. "Stephanie, please have a seat. Then maybe you can help me understand what happened here. What do you know about this situation with the puppy?"

With both Evan and Noah watching her, Stephanie shook her head. "I'm sorry, but I'm lost. I don't know what you mean."

Elenore sighed. "Evan brought in a puppy for Nathan, one of our patients. He told me this came about after a conversation the two of you shared."

Stephanie glanced over at Evan. His expression giving nothing away, she nervously ran her hand through her hair. "Yes, Evan and I had talked about Nathan. He told me he wished there was some way he could help him. But a puppy wasn't—"

Coming to his feet, Evan cut her off. "Can I say something here?" Getting a nod from Elenore, he began pacing back and forth, anger rising in his voice. "After our talk," here he nodded over at Stephanie, "I had a chance to talk to Nathan's aunt when she came to visit him. She told me the breeders were still holding the puppy for him. But she didn't have a contact number, nor did she have the money to pay them. So, I offered to take care of it and bought Nathan the puppy. End of story."

He quit his pacing, turning to Elenore. "My God, the kid needs something. He lost his whole family, left with his injuries as a reminder of what happened. He has to be scared to death, wondering what's coming next. This is more than enough for anyone to handle, let alone a little kid."

He shrugged. "I'm sorry if I broke the rules, but I only wanted to help."

He glared over at Noah. "And you need to get a grip. I don't know why you're making such a big issue about this. As though I've committed a major crime."

Noah glared right back at him. "There are rules and regulations that need to be followed. This is a hospital, not a kennel. You can't bring animals in here and let them run all over the place, doing who knows what, just because a patient says this is what they want. What's next? A pony?"

"Again… It's. A. God. Damn. Puppy." This coming through gritted teeth, Evan's expression was furious.

The strained silence that followed had Noah nervously checking his watch before he sent a glance over at Elenore. "Are we done here? I need to get back to my rounds."

She waved her hand towards the door. "Yes, go."

But Evan had no intention of letting Noah leave without his final say. He called out to him. "Before you go, you know damn well this isn't about the puppy. Because in the little time I've been here, I've seen how popular you are with the kids. Which leads me to believe if you knew something like this would help, you would be all for it. No, it's me you have the problem with."

Already at the door, Noah came to a halt. He turned, and for a long, tense filled moment, the two men glared at each other.

Then Noah gave a sharp laugh. "You're crazy."

He turned and went charging out of the room.

No one seemed to know what to say.

It was Evan who finally broke the silence. Clearing his throat, he turned to Elenore. "Again, I'm sorry. I had no idea this would cause such an uproar."

A wry smile on her face, Elenore shrugged. "I know this. But you do realize what you did was against the rules. The only animals we allow are those trained as service or therapy animals. I know we're dealing with a harmless little puppy, but you should have asked someone before you decided on your own."

She nodded over at Stephanie. "Like Stephanie."

Stephanie vigorously shook her head. "I swear, I knew nothing about this. If I had, I would've explained to Evan the hospital's rules. Then we wouldn't have had this problem. Dr. Davis has every reason to be concerned."

As soon as this came out of her mouth, she knew she had made a terrible mistake. The words had come out all wrong, not at all what she wanted to say. Even though she hadn't intended to side with Noah, this was exactly how it sounded. And now, she would give anything to take back every single word.

She glanced over at Evan.

Slowly running his hand through his hair, he had a funny expression on his face. Disbelief, anger, and resignation all rolled into one. He gave a slow nod. "I see. It appears I've been wrong all along, haven't I? I guess I should have seen this coming."

Stephanie knew Evan was no longer talking about the puppy. She sent him a pleading look. "Evan... I didn't mean—"

He interrupted her. "No, you don't need to explain, Stephanie. You're absolutely right about what you said."

His next words were directed to Elenore. "Unless you decide otherwise, I will take on the responsibility of telling Nathan the puppy can't stay."

Elenore shook her head. "Give me time to think about this. I'd like to talk to Nathan's aunt before I decide what to do."

She sat back in her chair. "I'm curious, how did you know where to find this puppy?"

Evan shrugged, a wry smile on his face. "I went by the little information his aunt gave me. Along with some amateur detective work. I felt like I had to help the kid."

For a few seconds he was silent, struggling with what he wanted to say. Then he glanced over at Stephanie. Her head bowed, she was staring down at her hands.

This had him giving a long sigh. "I think I've overstayed my welcome, and it's time for me to leave. I've already taken more than enough photos and edited the best ones. Once you choose the photos you like, and they're enlarged, we'll start positioning them on the wall. You also asked if it would be possible to add lighting from behind, so I contacted a guy who specializes in this. But until the prints are ready, there is no reason for me to be here."

He walked over to Elenore, extending his hand. "Again, thank you for entrusting me with this project. And please call if you have questions."

After another glance over at Stephanie, the look he gave Elenore was resigned. "I must say, this has been an eye-opening experience."

Without a word to Stephanie, he turned and walked out of the room.

"Stephanie, are you all right?"

Stephanie jerked her head up in response to Elenore's inquiry. For a few seconds, she gave her a blank stare. Then she shook her head, her voice rising in a sob. "*No, no, no, no...*"

She jumped out of her chair and headed for the door. There she came to a sudden stop, turning back to Elenore. "I need to talk to Evan. I'll be right back, I promise."

And she was gone, running down the hall.

Elenore gazed around her now empty office. After removing her glasses, she massaged her forehead, a weary sigh escaping her.

She didn't understand this younger generation. There was always so much drama. Didn't they even try to talk things out?

Stephanie and Evan? They were a train wreck.

She shook her head.

Even if they didn't know this, they desperately needed her help.

Evan pushed open the door leading to the stairs. He was about to start down the steps when Stephanie caught up with him.

She grabbed his arm. "Evan..."

He spun around, and for a moment, he stared at her. Then, shoving his hands in his pockets, his expression became guarded. Whatever she had to say, he didn't think he wanted to hear it.

No, as far as he was concerned, there was nothing more to be said.

She had made her choice... and it wasn't you.

So, his nod was curt.

She swallowed. "Evan, please listen to me. About what I said, I didn't mean–"

His plan to remain silent? It didn't have a chance. Running his hand through his hair, he gave an exasperated sigh. "I don't understand what happened back there. Why didn't you stick up for me? You and I talked about Nathan when we had dinner at The Glass and Grape. How he needed something positive in his life. If I recall, we both agreed a puppy would be a good option. And yes, it wasn't just me. You were right there with me on this decision."

His laugh was bitter. "I guess I misunderstood? But why am I even surprised? Because lately, when it comes to you, it seems like I'm wrong about almost everything."

She was shaking her head. "Evan, please... I'll admit I agreed a puppy would be good for Nathan, but never did I think you'd run with it. You should have checked with Elenore first. Or with me. You know how strict the hospital is. And I'm sure Dr. Davis is only upset because of his concern for the kids. Whatever you may think of him, he is a hundred percent dedicated to his work."

He was silent. Then, closing his eyes, he gave a long, resigned sigh. "Stephanie, I'm sorry. I'm done. I can't keep doing this."

A nervous laugh escaping her, she searched his face. "I don't understand what you're trying to say. You can't keep doing what?"

He shook his head. "You and me. I'm beginning to think you don't know what you want. And until you figure it out, it might be best if we didn't see each other."

She opened her mouth to say something, but he cut her off. "No, let me finish. Jack... Noah... every time I turn around, one of them shows up, pushing their way between us. This has me feeling like I need to be on guard all the time, wondering if I should be worried."

Then he drew in a deep breath before simply gazing into her eyes. "I don't want to share the woman I love."

For the longest moment, they didn't move. He couldn't believe he had let his true feelings slip. While she wasn't sure if she'd heard right.

The woman he loved?

Her silence leading him to believe she didn't feel the same, his voice was weary. "I think we need to take a break. Because, whatever we're doing right now, it's not working. Maybe it's a trust issue... you still don't trust me, and it appears I don't trust you. I don't know. But if we don't have that, we don't stand a chance."

No, no, no, no...

Stephanie's heart was pounding so hard and so loud she couldn't think. So, even though there was so much she wanted to say, she couldn't. The words just wouldn't come.

So, what else was there for Evan to do but leave?

Dragging his hand through his hair, he let out a long, resigned sigh. "Okay, then... I guess I'll see you around. I hope you find what you're looking for."

He turned, starting down the stairs. Then he stopped. Within seconds, he was next to her, and pulling her up against him, his mouth came crashing down on hers in a deep, bruising kiss.

He poured everything he felt for her into the kiss.

Just as quickly, he let her go. But before he started down the steps, he had one last thing to say. "Nice was not what I intended when I kissed you on the dance floor. If this is how you felt, maybe this kiss will have you thinking differently."

He went running down the stairs.

Closing her eyes and holding on to the railing for support, she listened to the sound of his feet hitting the stairs. It was only when she heard the door to the main floor close behind him, her fingers going to her lips, she slowly sank down onto the steps.

She began blinking like crazy, determined not to cry.

But this was one time her tears couldn't be stopped.

Stephanie couldn't tell you how long she sat on the steps. It was only when the maintenance man stopped to check on her as he passed by, she finally returned to Elenore's office.

Her light was off, the door was locked.

So, she headed for the nurses station. Only one member of the staff was there. Unfortunately, this was Lucy.

She glanced over at Stephanie, her eyebrows raised. "Are you feeling better?"

At Stephanie's blank expression, she shrugged. "Mrs. Cromley said you weren't feeling well. And you might need a little time before you go back on the floor. If you're looking for her, she already left for the day."

Slipping her phone in her pocket, Stephanie gave her a bright smile. "Okay, then. I guess I'll talk to her tomorrow."

After watching her walk away, Lucy shook her head.

She'd swear... this whole thing with Stephanie and Evan?

It was more dramatic than any soap opera.

CHAPTER 28

I t had been almost a week—five days and ten hours, to be exact—
since the meeting in Elenore's office about the puppy.

 This was also when Evan had last seen Stephanie.

The longest five days and ten hours of your life.

True to his word, he had stopped in at the hospital only when
necessary.

And not once had he seen even a hint of her.

This was concerning. Because the photo wall was now finished.
Which meant his time at the hospital was done.

Strolling over to where Carl, the lighting technician, was busy
packing up his gear. Evan grinned at him. "It looks like we did it,
huh?"

After sending a glance over at the finished wall, Carl nodded. "Yep,
everything is working like we planned. This means my work here is
done. Any problems pop up, you know where to find me."

After he gave Evan a few more pointers, he gathered up the rest of
his gear and was out the door.

Evan glanced down at his watch. It was almost four-thirty. Since he
had promised Elenore he would let her know when the wall was
finished, he sent her a text.

Then he flipped the switch to turn off the lights. He wanted to see her expression when she turned on the lights and experienced the illuminated wall for the first time.

He had to hand it to Carl. The result was nothing less than amazing.

Through a magic of his own, he had programed the lights to come on one photo at a time and in no particular order. Once all the photos were lit, the lights dimmed before turning off completely. The sequence then repeated all over again. This happened every ten minutes, each time the photos coming to life again in no particular order.

He grabbed one of the folding chairs rented for the open house and set it by the door. Once he was seated, he stretched his legs out in front of him. He gazed around the room, a satisfied smile on his face.

You nailed it. Big time.

Yeah, he was proud of the work he did for this project. If anything, it was comforting to know even if he had screwed up the rest of his life, his photography skills were still there for him.

Massaging the back of his neck, he groaned. Who was he trying to kid? He didn't give a damn about the photos. Or anything else.

Stephanie... she was all mattered. She was all he could think about. But look what a mess he had made of things... going crazy on her, ruining the chance of anything between them.

Yeah... crazy is exactly how you acted. Out of control and completely unacceptable.

And now?

He didn't have the slightest idea of what to do next.

Hell, does it even matter? It's obvious she's gone out of her way to avoid you the past few days, making it clear she wants nothing to do with you.

He had hoped to see her when she reported for her shift. If only for a few minutes. So, they could at least get a start on talking about what happened. But she was nowhere to be found.

He'd swear she had completely disappeared. That this was because of him, was something he didn't even want to think about.

He glanced down at his watch again. His groan echoed loudly in the large room when he saw not even five minutes had passed since he last checked.

Well, he had promised Elenore he would wait for her until five.

So, this is what he was going to do.

Then he'd go home.

Not that he was in a hurry.

After all, it wasn't like someone was waiting for him.

Elenore couldn't remember that last time she was this tired.

More like exhausted.

She had been on one phone call after another since early this morning. Now late afternoon, she was more than ready to go home.

She gazed down at her list, every item now highlighted in yellow.

This was an excellent sign. She had touched base with everyone who had an integral part in making the grand opening a success.

Her list included the caterers for the appetizers, Abby of Sweet Abby's for the cookie favors, and the florist who was providing the table centerpieces.

There was also the disc jockey, a son of one of the members of the board. He had just started up his business, but he swore he would play the perfect music. Since Jason's band wasn't available, she could only keep her fingers crossed this disc jockey would come through on his promise.

She had also confirmed with Louise, the owner of Chic Boutique, they would deliver the dress they were altering for her on Friday at the latest. Since this was a special occasion, a new dress had been required. It was important she looked her best.

All of her plans were finally coming together. And again, fingers crossed, everything was right on schedule.

She had one last thing to do, and this was to confirm the local senior high school student volunteers had been measured for their tuxedos.

Yes, she knew a valet rarely required a tux and she might have gone overboard with her request. But the way she looked at it, if the rest of the volunteers were in formal attire, they should be, too.

This was her way of adding a bit of elegance to the event. And if anyone disagreed?

She didn't care. If she wanted everyone all decked out in formal wear, well, then... so be it.

"Mrs. Cromley, you need to go home. It's getting late." This coming from one of the maintenance men, as he passed by her office, was a reminder Evan had promised they would finish the photo wall today. And when this happened, he would call her.

She picked up her phone to see he had sent a text about five minutes ago.

> Wanted to let you know everything is ready for your inspection. I should be here until around five. I think you will be very pleased. Because I know I am.

She looked at her watch.

It was four-thirty.

Filled with a sudden burst of energy, she cleared her desk, stuffed her phone in her purse and, after locking the door to her office, she briskly started walking over to the elevator.

She felt like a kid on Christmas morning.

CHAPTER 29

All the talent in the world won't take you
anywhere without your teammates.
~ Anonymous

When Elenore walked into the community room, the room appeared to be empty, the lights turned off.

Disappointed, thinking Evan had already left, she turned to do the same.

But the signature squeak of her rubber-soled shoes was enough to jar Evan out of his preoccupied state.

"Elenore, wait…" He stumbled to his feet, almost knocking over his chair. Making a grab for it, he set it down in front of her. "Please have a seat."

Once she was settled, his hand going to the light switch, he smiled. "Are you ready?"

Her expression a mix of nervousness and excitement, she nodded. "Yes, I'm as ready as I'll ever be."

He flipped the switch.

And the lights did their thing.

"Oh, my…" Her hand going to her heart, and a look of awe on her face, she watched the play of lights as they began highlighting one photo after another.

It was only when the sequence started up again, she gazed over at him. "Oh, Evan... this is better than I could have ever imagined. You are a genius."

Then, in a move so unlike her, she came to her feet to give him a big hug. "Thank you. Thank you so much. It's beautiful. Everyone is going to love it. How could they not?" She turned to watch again, shaking her head. "It's absolutely mesmerizing. Almost as if the photos are floating."

A photo of Stephanie and a patient sharing a hug came into view. Clasping her hands together, Elenore smiled over at Evan. "That's exactly the kind of photo I was hoping for. It shows what we do here at the hospital, all the heart and soul we put into our work. I'm surprised Stephanie approved of this. She usually avoids being in the spotlight."

Their eyes met, hers questioning, Shoving his hands in his pockets, he shrugged. "*Umm...* maybe because I didn't ask her?"

Then he shook his head. "She hasn't seen it yet."

Elenore frowned. "Oh, dear... you two are still not communicating? What happened to the promise you made to me?"

Running his hand through his hair, he heaved a frustrated sigh. "It's not Stephanie. It's me. I might have said some things I shouldn't. And now? I'm not sure how to fix it."

She peered more closely at him. "And what exactly was it you said?"

He hesitated, because honestly? He wasn't sure if he wanted to share with Elenore what he now realized was another moment of his stupidity. Something that seemed to happen too often when he was with Stephanie.

Let's face it, you're surprised she's even still around.

But since he had no plan in place, what did he have to lose? He gave Elenore a brief account of what had happened the last time he was with Stephanie.

Then he waited.

It was obvious by her frown, Elenore wasn't happy with what he told her. Sure enough, she shook her head. "Oh Evan, what is wrong with you? You have to know what you accused Stephanie of is something she would never do."

When he didn't respond, she peered more closely at him. "Could it be this is more of a problem with you? You're still not ready to accept something good is happening in your life?"

His sigh was heavy. "I don't know… maybe? But, look at me… I have nothing to offer. Stephanie. No past… no family. Not only that, I have no proof of who I am, or where I came from."

Now he was on a roll, his voice trembling with anger. "And what could I possibly know about love, since I had so little during my childhood? When I finally did find what I thought would be a future with Kelsie, in an instant, it was taken from me. So, I figured maybe this was something I was destined never to have again."

His laugh was sharp. "Hell, what it comes down to, I'm what you could call a misfit. So, can you blame me for being a little wary?

Slowly sinking into her chair, Elenore stared into space, her response barely audible. "That wasn't what I had planned. Never did I want it to be like that."

At Evan's puzzled glance, she closed her eyes. "Your childhood. They promised you would be taken care of, given the best."

She gazed up at him, wringing her hands. "It was my responsibility to help, make amends for what happened. I never thought…" Her words faded into silence.

Evan was confused.

What kind of promise? Make amends for what? And why did she feel responsible?

He brought over another chair to sit next to her. He searched her face, his anger now replaced with concern. "Elenore, what are you talking about? Why would you feel responsible?"

She closed her eyes, a deep sigh coming from her. "It was my husband Peter who was driving the car that crashed into your parent's car. The coroner's report said he had a heart attack. This is what made him lose control."

She shook her head. "At the time, I was in shock over losing Peter so suddenly. But when I heard the only survivor was a newborn, a baby boy, now under the care of an aunt and uncle, I paid all the hospital bills. Since they didn't seem to have the resources to cover the additional cost of raising a child, I also gave them a large sum of money to help out. The plan was there would be enough to last through the college years."

Her eyes pleaded with him to understand. "I tried to keep in touch. But your uncle discouraged this. I thought this was because he still blamed me for the accident. So, I finally stopped trying. Then one day, I was told they were gone, leaving no forwarding address. It was as though they had disappeared off the face of the earth."

She frowned. "Instead of giving them the money all at once, I should've doled it out in yearly stipends. I never thought... well, I guess I trusted them to do the right thing."

His head bowed and his arms resting on his knees, Evan was at a loss. That she was still hanging on to this guilt for something that wasn't her fault, brought on a renewed anger towards his uncle.

This was an emotion he'd thought he put aside a long time ago.

He glanced over at her, a resigned smile on his face. "My guess would be my uncle thought gambling would be a way to make the money grow. But he must have lost it all instead. Because most of my childhood memories are of arguments about money, and how there never seemed to be enough."

When this only had Elenore shaking her head, he tried to reassure her. "But this is all in the past. So, please don't blame yourself. Like I told you in my interview, I've moved on. I'm okay with it now."

Elenore didn't believe this for a moment.

She was angry... so, *so* angry.

Yes, she would be the first to admit she had her faults. She was opinionated. Bossy, too. And, yes, she could also be very stubborn. But there was one trait she was most proud of, and this would be her honesty.

That Evan's aunt and uncle had used the money to satisfy their own needs, when it was intended for an innocent child entrusted in their care?

This made her livid.

But since she couldn't fix what happened, she needed to do whatever she could to make things right. She would start by giving Evan the report she recently received regarding the whereabouts of his aunt and uncle.

She put her hand on his arm. "There is something you need to know. The day of your interview, when you told me about your childhood, I suspected who you were. So, I had my lawyers investigate. They found your uncle died almost ten years ago. But your aunt had tried to get in touch with you this past March."

He frowned. "March... that's when I was in New Zealand."

Elenore nodded. "*Ah...* that explains why you never got back to her. Unfortunately, with all the problems involving the guardianship over the years, the most they would give me was your aunt's last known address. This is in Atlanta. But there's no promise she is still there. It's up to you to decide what you want to do with this information."

Evan's first impulse was to tell her he wasn't interested. He was done with that time of his life. When his aunt left, he had been devastated. And when he'd finally accepted she wasn't coming back, he had vowed to never forgive her.

A weariness crept into his voice. "*Geeez...* I don't know. It doesn't make sense. Why would she want to see me now? After all these years?"

Elenore shrugged. "Maybe to make amends? Tell you why she never came back? Or maybe she'll be able to give you information that will help you move on with your life." She put her hand on his arm. "It's always best to make peace with the past. Holding a grudge will only hurt you in the long run."

He bowed his head, staring down at the floor. After a brief silence, he looked up, a resigned expression on his face. "Okay, I'll do it. Do you have the information with you?"

She couldn't believe how relieved she was, how much she needed this. If only to let go of her own guilt about what happened.

She reached into her pocket and, pulling out an envelope, handed it to him. "Good, I was hoping you would. And after the community room dedication is over, you and I will have a long talk. I plan to make this up to you, give you what you deserve. It's only–"

Abruptly coming to his feet, he stopped her in mid-sentence. "No, you owe me nothing. That you would even feel responsible for what happened is unthinkable. It was an accident. Your husband didn't have a heart attack on purpose."

She shook her head. "But I believe nothing is by chance. You, me, Stephanie… we were all brought together for a reason. So, yes… we will talk. I insist."

Again, he was silent for a few moments before a slow smile curved his lips. "Okay, but you won't change my mind."

"We'll see." She held out her hand. "Now help me up. And then you can walk me out to my car. It's been a long day and I need someone strong to lean on."

He turned out the lights. With her still holding on to his arm, they headed for the elevator.

She began chattering away about the grand opening. Then she suddenly changed the subject. "It's important you patch things up with Stephanie as soon as you return from Atlanta. Promise me you'll do this. Before you do anything else."

She sent him a sidelong glance. "You do believe in fairy tales and happy endings, don't you? Because I truly believe there is one waiting for the two of you."

He grinned. "Thanks to you, I'm starting to believe in a lot of things."

Elenore had already started up her car when she opened her window to call out to Evan.

The expression on her face, one he'd become very familiar with over the past few days, was a sign he was about to get a lecture.

Sure enough, she started right in. "If you go to Atlanta, you are planning to tell Stephanie, aren't you?

He thought about this before he shook his head. "I'm not sure."

Taking this as a no, she sighed. "At least tell her you'll be gone for a short time. And—this is very important—let her know you will definitely be coming back. She needs to hear this from you."

He smiled, sending her a mock salute. "Yes, ma'am. I will."

He watched as she backed out of her parking spot, only to come to another stop and open her window again. This time, she was smiling. "I forgot to tell you. We let Nathan keep the puppy. The change in him has been miraculous."

Her frown momentarily returned. "Not that I condone what you did. But this is one time we decided it couldn't hurt to bend the rules a bit."

"This is great news. I'm glad I was of some help." He grinned. "I also promise to follow the rules in the future."

She sent him a thumbs up and drove away.

Once Evan was in his car, he leaned back and closed his eyes.

He was glad it all worked out with the puppy. But now he had bigger things to think about... like, why had his aunt tried to contact him?

Should he be worried?

Yes, you should be very concerned.

But Elenore was right. It was time to put the past behind for good.

He needed—what was it they called it—closure?

Geeez... Closure? Next thing you know, you'll be talking about getting therapy.

But he was tired of being haunted by the past, ready to get on with his life.

His hope was this would be with Stephanie.

Evan was about to start up his car when he changed his mind.

There was something he needed to do.

He headed back into the hospital. After he sprinted up the stairs to the third floor, hoping no one saw him, he made his way to Nathan's room.

Yes, already he was breaking the rules.

He hadn't signed in at the nurses station.

And he was without an escort.

But for this one time, he was willing to take this risk.

He found Nathan watching the TV mounted on the wall in his room, the puppy curled up and sound asleep on the bed beside him.

When he saw Evan, he actually smiled. It wasn't a big smile, but that it was even the hint of a smile was a major improvement.

Evan reached over to pet the puppy. "I just heard this guy gets to stay with you?"

Nathan nodded, another smile flitting across his face.

"Ah… that's great news. Did you give him a name yet?"

Nathan nodded again. "Oreo."

Evan laughed. "Since his fur is black and white, I'd say you picked the perfect name."

After he ran his hand through the puppy's silky fur a few times, he glanced over at Nathan. "I wanted a puppy when I was your age. But the person who promised to get me one went away."

He hesitated, searching for the right words. "I can't even imagine what you're going through right now, losing your mom, dad and sister. So, I thought if I got you the puppy, even though it's from me, this might make you feel a little better. And I promise you… things will get better. Because you still have so many people here who love you."

He nodded toward Oreo. "And this little guy? He'll be your best friend. You'll be able to tell him anything—when you're sad, or happy, or just mad at the world—and he won't tell a soul. He'll only love you more than he did before."

Nathan gazed up at him. "Did you ever get a puppy?"

"No. And I really wanted one. I already had the name picked out… Crackers." Evan smiled, shaking his head. "But I'm okay with this now. Just knowing you have your puppy makes me feel good."

He watched Nathan's face scrunch up, his bottom lip beginning to quiver in his fight to contain his emotions. But he lost the battle. Tears streaming down his face, the grief he had been holding inside came out all at once.

So as not to hurt him, Evan cautiously sat next to him on the bed. He put his arm around him and, without a word, held him while he cried.

He knew this was just the beginning of Nathan's slow journey towards healing.

Never had he thought this would be a healing moment for him, too.

Only two staff members were aware of what happened between Evan and Nathan. The first was Lucy. Surprisingly, she told no one.

And now, back at the nurses station, she was having a hard time thinking about anything else.

Every time someone walked by, she looked up, disappointed when it wasn't Evan.

Just as she was about to give up hope, she glanced up to see he was on his way to the elevator.

She called out to him. "Hey, Evan..."

He groaned. He wasn't in the mood. This is why he had tried to sneak by her, hoping she wouldn't see him.

She better not start in with a lecture about rules.

After all, some rules are meant to be broken.

Like now.

He had stayed with Nathan until, exhausted from his emotional outburst, he fell asleep. And now he only wanted to go home.

A smile pasted on his face, he walked over to her. "Hey, how's it going?"

She shrugged. "I'm hanging in there."

After she checked to make sure no one else was around, she leaned closer. "Don't worry, I'm not planning to tattle on you. I only wanted to tell you what a good thing you did for Nathan. Not only getting him the puppy, but what you said to him."

Here she had the grace to look embarrassed. "I was right outside his room and I heard you."

Evan nodded. "*Ah...* I see."

She drew her finger across her lips. "But mum's the word. I'm just so happy he gave way to his grief. Now he can start the recovery process."

She gave him a thumbs up. "You did good."

He was smiling as he began to walk away. "Thanks for the vote of confidence."

She nodded. "Sure, anytime. And Evan?"

He came to a stop, his eyebrow raised. "Yes?"

"I don't know what happened between you and Stephanie, but whatever it was, don't give up. She has been miserable these past few days. She loves you more than you could possibly know."

For a few moments, he was silent. Then a smile touched his lips. "That's good to know. Because I love her, too. More than she could possibly know."

He turned and left.

When the computer screen began to blur, Lucy blinked, trying to hold back the tears.

She hoped Stephanie realized how lucky she was.

And who was the second member of the staff who knew what Evan and Nathan shared?

That evening, when Nathan's aunt came to visit, she noticed the change in him right away. After he told her about his conversation with Evan, she called Elenore to tell her the good news.

Elenore also told no one. She knew this was what Evan would want.

And deep in her heart, she knew this first step towards healing hadn't been for Nathan alone.

No, Evan had needed it just as much, if not more.

After a drive free of the usual evening rush hour, even with a quick stop at the deli for takeout, Evan made it home in less than forty-five minutes.

An hour later, he had booked his flight, and was searching for his carry-on bag. He had to hurry if he hoped to get to the airport in time.

Yeah, this had been a quick decision. But he was feeling optimistic.

He was about to do what he should have done a long time ago

He would be quick to remind you... it was all about closure.

CHAPTER 30

"Don't worry about it."

Evan shrugged off the server's apology when the coffee she was pouring sloshed over the brim of his cup and on to the counter.

He didn't need any more coffee. Since he was pretty sure this was part of the reason for his increasing nervousness, he should have refused her offer of more, two cups ago.

But he didn't have the energy. So, she kept refilling his cup, and he kept drinking it, as awful as it was.

It certainly isn't up to par with Café Latte's brew. What you would give for a cup of their coffee right now.

He watched her clean up the spill, wondering what had brought her to this state. Working at an all-night diner, in a less desirable part of town, couldn't have been her first choice. If he had to guess, he'd say she was in her early twenties, the dark circles under her eyes and pale complexion hinting at a hard life.

It didn't help she was also very pregnant.

Besides the elderly man sitting at the other end of the counter watching the news on the small TV mounted on the back wall, Evan was her only other customer.

He sighed, and closing his eyes, he tried to shut out the sound of the TV. He was exhausted and the day hadn't even begun.

His trip had started out with a red-eye flight from Cleveland to Atlanta. When he had booked the flight, it seemed like a good idea. His thinking was the early arrival would give him an entire day to contact his aunt before he needed to return to the airport for a seven-thirty evening flight back to Cleveland.

But now, with morning still a couple of hours away, he was regretting his decision. It didn't help the rain greeting him upon his arrival had now turned into a steady downpour.

He took another sip of his coffee, grimacing at the taste.

Things were not looking good...

And he had no one to blame but himself.

But this was okay.

Because, honestly?

He wasn't expecting much.

When the morning commuters began crowding the sidewalks, Evan knew it was time to leave the diner.

He took one more gulp of his now cold coffee. After tucking a twenty-dollar bill under his cup for a tip, he picked up the one item he never traveled without... his camera.

His mood had improved from earlier.

His time spent in the diner had produced some great candid shots, the style of photography he enjoyed the most. As he headed for the door, he patted his pocket, the crinkle of paper confirming he still had the owner's address.

He had promised to send him some prints to display on the walls of the diner.

The rain had tapered off to a slight drizzle. The fresh air bringing on a sudden burst of energy, he decided he would walk the fifteen blocks to the address Elenore had given him. This would also give him the opportunity to get in some more shots. Some of his best shots had been taken on rainy days, and the urban setting offered even more possibilities.

Moving at a brisk pace, he noticed a change in his surroundings as he came closer to his destination. The buildings had seen better days, the rare patches of grass were unkempt, and the sidewalks filled with litter.

He finally arrived at Orchard Towers II, the address he had been given. A six-story weathered brick building, it looked like it was one of the original structures when the city had first come into existence. Unfortunately, nothing remained of the former grandeur that once housed the city's more prominent and wealthy families. Now a wild overgrowth of ivy completely hid the faded brick and crumbling facade, giving the building an almost haunted look.

After taking more shots of the building than he needed, Evan sprinted up the stairs to the main entrance. He found what he was looking for... Apartment F.

Momentarily concerned when he saw this was the only apartment without a name, he tentatively hit the call button.

He waited.

Nothing.

So, he hit it again.

Still nothing.

He groaned, running his hand through his hair.

Well, what did you expect? Not really a smart move to show up unannounced.

Obviously, he hadn't thought this out as thoroughly as he should have.

In his mind, he had pictured his aunt answering the door, excitement lighting up her face when she saw it was him. Then they would spend some time together. After he made sure there was nothing she needed and they promised to keep in touch, he would return to Cleveland as planned.

This would give him closure... or whatever the hell they called it. But it now looked as though there was a possibility this might not happen.

His good mood now a thing of the past, for a few moments, he did nothing. Then he decided he was going to wait it out. Someone would eventually come along and be able to help him out.

Right?

He leaned against one of the large pillars flanking the entrance and, pulling out his phone, checked his messages. There was an inquiry about an upcoming photo shoot for a new restaurant opening in the fall.

But nothing from Stephanie.

He sighed, slipping the phone back in his pocket.

Why do you have this feeling you're in for a long wait?

Four hours later, Evan was about to lose his mind.

Since he didn't want to leave the area in the chance he might miss someone leaving or entering the building, he had spent the time wandering up and down the block, taking what he'd swear were close to a hundred photos.

He had checked his messages about a dozen times.

And, no... there still wasn't any message from Stephanie.

So, with more photos than he could possibly use, and his phone battery running low, he was wondering if he should call it quits. He would get a ride back to the airport and try to get an earlier flight home.

After all, he tried.

He sighed, glancing down at his watch.

He would wait for fifteen minutes.

Then he would leave.

Twenty minutes later, Evan watched as a woman began walking up the sidewalk leading to the building.

When she saw him, she came to a stop. Tilting her head, she gazed up at where he was sitting on the top step.

She sent him a cautious smile. "Hi, is there something I can help you with? Or are you waiting for someone?"

He came to his feet. "Hello... and you are?"

"My name is Julie. *Umm*... just Julie."

He smiled. "*Ah*... well, just Julie... hopefully you can answer a few questions for me. Starting with, do you know Mary Marshall? I am her nephew and I was told this is where I could find her."

She peered more closely at him. "May I ask why?"

After he explained the reason for his visit, she nodded. "And your name?"

"Evan… Evan Marshall."

When he saw what suspiciously looked like a hint of tears pooling in her eyes, warning bells went off in his head.

This wasn't a good sign.

She slowly came up the steps, and putting her hand on his arm, her voice was filled with sadness. "I'm sorry, your aunt passed away a little over a month ago. She had been sick for quite a long time. I'm so, so sorry."

He opened his mouth, but nothing came out. He'd swear it was like a punch in the gut. Or, as if someone had suddenly slammed a door in his face.

This wasn't the result he was expecting.

If this is closure, you don't want it.

After a silence that seemed to drag on forever, Julie's voice finally filtered into Evan's consciousness. He tried to focus on her face, trying to take in what she was telling him.

"Your aunt lived in the apartment next to mine, and even though she was friendly, she discouraged any kind of closeness. It was only when she became sick, she shared a little about her past life. How she had one regret, and this was leaving you. So, this was why she decided to reach out to you. When you didn't respond, she entrusted me with the key to her safe deposit box. I was to give it to you if you eventually tried to make contact. I have the key, the box number and the name of the bank, everything you need."

He briefly closed his eyes. "I was out of the country. If I had known…" His voice trailing off, he shoved his hands in his pockets, his gaze going anywhere but at her.

Julie was shaking her head. "No, it's not your fault. She told me I was to let you know she accepts all the blame. She knew she should have contacted you long before this. So please, please... don't feel guilty."

When he had no answer to this, she moved towards the door to the building. "Again, I'm so very sorry. I'll go get the key." She hesitated. "Unless you don't want to be alone? If so, you're welcome to come inside."

He shook his head, attempting a smile. "No, I'll wait here. Don't worry. I'll be fine."

Fine?

You're far from fine...

Julie returned within minutes, handing Evan the key.

After she gave him directions to the bank, she searched his face, a worried look on hers. "Are you going to be all right? Because I would be more than happy to go with you."

He glanced down at the key in his hand before dropping it in his pocket. Then he glanced up at her and slowly shook his head. "I'll be fine."

He impulsively reached over to give her a hug. "Thank you. I'm glad my aunt had you as a friend."

She smiled. "Me, too."

He went running down the steps. As he started down the sidewalk, he looked back to see she was watching him.

She waved.

After returning the wave, and blinking back the threat of tears, he began walking faster.

He thought he'd prepared himself for the possibility of this happening. But now he realized how wrong he was. Instead, he now had so many unanswered questions, regrets, what ifs, and whys.

He could only pray the key he now had in his possession would bring him the answers he needed.

When Evan walked out of the bank an hour later, he had a sealed envelope tucked inside his jacket.

When he'd opened the safe deposit box and saw the solitary envelope, he had been filled with an overwhelming sense of loss. Along with a sudden anger.

How was it possible a person's life could come down to this? Sealed inside a single envelope?

Unable to get up the courage to open the envelope, he had sat in the silent vault, memories of his childhood, his aunt and uncle, and a few times he really didn't want to remember, playing in his mind.

Finally taking the envelope from the safe deposit box, he left the vault. Once he filled out the required paperwork, the envelope was his.

And now his only goal was to catch the earliest possible flight he could.

It had started to rain again. Pulling up the collar of his jacket, he began searching for a taxi.

He wanted to go home.

Only then would he open the envelope.

Hopefully, he wouldn't have to do this alone.

CHAPTER 31

Always remember -
we are the masters of our own destiny.
~ Unknown

I t was the start of rush hour.

Lost in his thoughts, his fingers drumming on the steering wheel, it was a few seconds before Jack realized the light had turned green.

A horn sounding behind him, he glanced in his rearview mirror.

For God's sake, what's your hurry buddy? Give me a break.

And even though he knew the guy couldn't see him, he sent a threatening scowl in the mirror. Right before he stepped on the gas, sending his car shooting right through the intersection.

A very immature gesture…

Yes, he was well aware of this. But it had been a long day, and he wasn't in the mood. He was beat. After being cooped up in the studio for almost nine hours, he still had a mishmash of tunes playing in his head.

Since Jason had returned from his honeymoon, he had the band working on so many projects, Jack would swear he didn't even know what day it was anymore. Jason put all the blame on Darcey. He claimed she inspired him.

Jack knew this pace wouldn't last forever. And like his dad had always been quick to remind him, any chance to up his financial security was something he should never lose sight of, no matter how young he thought he was.

But making lots of money wasn't cutting it for him anymore.

You want more… someone to share your life with. You're tired of being on your own.

He'd had the crazy thought this might be with Stephanie. But after he watched her dancing with this Evan, a guy who had shown up out of nowhere, and no one seemed to know anything about him, he knew she would never be his.

He had played at a lot of weddings and wrote enough songs to know the signs of someone who was in love.

Stephanie's heart was with Evan. And it was more than obvious Evan was hers for the asking.

So, it looked like he was back to square one.

Yep, just you and your music.

Thank God he at least had that…

The car in front of him made a slow turn into the Café Latte parking lot. Without even thinking, Jack followed him and pulled into the first available parking space.

Coffee might be just what he needed. And even though he wasn't a dessert kind of guy, he could never pass on one of their sour cherry scones.

This is if they had any left at this late hour. He'd swear they were addicting.

Go figure…

The café was unusually quiet on this late Wednesday afternoon. Taking advantage of this, Ellie Cook was taking a quick inventory of the available baked goods.

She was talking to herself. "*Hmm...* it looks like we'll be okay. Not the best selection, but enough to carry us through until closing tonight."

At the sound of someone clearing their throat, she glanced up from behind the display case to see it was Jack.

Patiently waiting at the counter, he was smiling. This was the first time he had seen Ellie since she left Cleveland over a year ago for an internship at Ohio State. He missed her ever-present smile and cheerful banter.

She gave him a big smile. "Jack... how have you been?"

"Ellie... it's good to see you. I'm good, doing my thing, keeping busy. What about you? And why are you even here? Shouldn't you still be in Columbus? Or has your internship ended?"

She shook her head. "I'm home on a break. They need extra help here since Laurel, the café owner, just had a baby. So, I volunteered to come in for a few days."

When she saw him glance over at her left hand, she grew flustered, averting her gaze. "So, still the usual? Regular coffee, no cream or sugar, and a sour cherry scone?"

Noting her unease, a slight frown marked his features. He thought for sure she would be engaged to her boyfriend, Michael, by now. The one time he had met him, he came across as a nice guy.

Ellie and he had seemed like a perfect fit.

Goes to show you, when love pushes its way in, you never know what's going to happen.

"Or maybe you want something else today?" This coming from Ellie, he shook his head. "No, what you said is fine."

Then, unsure of what to say, he was silent, watching as she put the scone in a bag.

She was the first to speak. "Looks like today is your lucky day since this is the last cherry scone. They are by far our most popular pastry. They're usually gone by noon."

"Oh, no. Is that really the last cherry scone? Tell me it isn't so."

This disappointed comment, coming from behind him and followed by a long and dramatic sigh, was enough to have Jack turn around, a smile tweaking the corner of his mouth.

This is when he'd swear everything around him came to a grinding halt. His heart pounding in his chest, he could only stare at the woman standing in front of him.

The vague thought entered his mind this must be what it felt like to be hit by Cupid's arrow.

It had zinged his heart, all right. But in a wonderfully amazing way.

He wanted to say something, if only to ask her name. But the most he could manage was a smile. So, this is what he did… he smiled like he had never smiled before in his life. While drinking in every single detail.

She was by far the most beautiful woman he had ever seen. She was exquisite. Definitely out of his league, she was a woman he would never even think of approaching. Let alone try to start up a conversation.

Her hair was the shade of a rich, dark espresso. Pulled back in a loose bun, wispy tendrils framed her face. This had him wanting to reach over and tuck these behind her ears, maybe even trail his fingers over the satiny softness of her cheeks. The possibility he might lose his mind and do this, he clenched his fists to his sides.

Her face was a classic oval, a face artists dreamed of painting. A molten chocolate brown, her eyes were wide and expressive. Soft and tempting, her mouth begged to be kissed.

He'd give anything, starting with the sour cherry scone, to experience such a kiss.

But you already know it would be amazing.

When he saw his inspection had brought a faint flush to her cheeks, he cleared his throat, relieved to find his voice was ready to join him. "Hello."

Yeah, it wasn't a lot, but at least it was a start.

"Hello." She took a step closer, her move graceful as a gentle breeze.

He briefly closed his eyes.

What the hell is wrong with you? A gentle breeze? Thank goodness you didn't say that out loud. What's next? You're going to recite poetry to her?

Actually, this was something most people didn't know about him.

Fascinated by the whole concept of poetry, he had fooled around a bit, writing a few lines himself.

And he could write volumes about this woman.

If he had to guess, he would say she was a dancer. But not just any dancer.

No, a ballerina.

The kind of ballerina everyone imagines in their mind... all beauty and grace.

Not that he knew much about dance. Or ballerinas. His sister had taken dancing lessons. Forced to sit through far too many of her recitals, what he remembered most was a lot of tulle and glitter. Along with a fair share of falls and missed cues. This invariably ended with a lot of dramatics and tears. Not at all the dancer this woman would be.

No, she would be perfection.

He just blurted it out. "You're a dancer."

She tilted her head, a look of surprise flashing across her face. Then an almost teasing smile curved her lips. "Yes, I am. And you? Are you also a dancer?"

She had moved even closer, the scent of her perfume pulling him in. A combination of lemon, jasmine and musk, it awakened his senses. Filling his mind with the possibility of long walks in the moonlight and sizzling summer nights of passion.

Again, what's going on with you? Just look at her. You don't have a chance.

He slowly shook his head. "No, I'm a musician." Then he completely surprised himself with what he said next. "I would say this means you and I are a perfect match, no? You need music to dance. And I need inspiration to write the music. I believe this is how all great love stories start."

Surprised, and even more relieved this hadn't sent her running out of the café to get away from him, he grew bolder, sending her a grin. "After all, we've already found out we have the same tastes in scones. So, imagine the possibilities."

She laughed. "But you know nothing about me. I might be a terrible dancer."

His gaze leisurely traveling over her, he slowly shook his head.

"No, something tells me, as beautiful as you are, you're an amazing dancer."

He watched the color deepen in her cheeks. Amazed this was because of something he said, he was filled with a sudden determination.

You are not going to let this woman get away.

And how did he plan to go about this?

He hadn't a clue.

Ellie, who had been watching this take place, was getting more frustrated by the minute. What was Jack's problem? Why wasn't he making his move? The chemistry between them was undeniable, so what more did he need?

Enough was enough.

She cleared her throat. When Jack glanced over at her, she sent a pointed look at the bag with the scone.

He gave her a blank stare. Then, comprehension flashing across his face, he grabbed the bag off the counter.

He held it out to the woman. "Here, I believe this scone belongs to you."

She shook her head. "Oh, no… I can't possibly take it from you. I can easily find something else."

Still holding out the bag, he smiled. "Please… I insist."

She began searching through her purse. "Then let me at least pay you."

He shook his head. "No, absolutely not. My treat."

She finally took the bag from him. "Okay. And, thank you."

The smile she gave him sent a warmth through him he couldn't describe. It was a smile that had him wanting more.

You'd do anything to spend the rest of your life making her smile.

But again… this wouldn't even have a chance of happening if he let her leave without finding out what her name was.

He moved closer. "You're more than welcome. Maybe one day you can return the favor. Or we can share a scone and some conversation."

He smiled. "By the way, I'm Jack."

Her smile abruptly disappeared, panic filling her face.

Puzzled, he watched as she began backing away. Avoiding his gaze, she mumbled her response. "I have somewhere I need to go, and I can't be late. Again, thank you for the scone."

She turned, and after almost running into an incoming customer, she slipped outside.

Jack was in shock.

He was also a little in denial. This wasn't what he'd expected. Was it something he said? Had he been too forward? Too familiar?

Slowly dragging his hand back through his hair, he turned to Ellie. "Do you know her? Or, at least, know her name?"

She shook her head. "No, I don't. But I've only been filling in since yesterday." She waved her hand towards the door. "What are you waiting for? Go after her."

So, this is what he did.

As he went sprinting out of the cafe, he tried not to think about his behavior. Because, seriously... had he lost his mind? Chasing after a woman he knew nothing about? This wasn't something he'd do. Or even think about doing.

But, for whatever reason, crazy or not, he felt like he had no choice... it felt right.

She was his destiny.

He came to a halt in the middle of the parking lot, scanning the cars and anywhere else she could have gone.

He came up with nothing.

This is when, believe it or not, he began searching the ground, thinking she may have left some kind of clue behind.

And what are you expecting to find? A glass slipper? You're losing it, buddy... you need to get a grip.

After one last glance around the lot, he made his way back into the café

Crouched down in driver's seat of her car, Savannah Jackson stared at her shaking hands. Her heart was also beating so hard, and so loud, she was afraid it was going to leap right up out of her chest.

Closing her eyes, she tried to slow her breathing.

The door to the café suddenly flew open. Slipping even further down in the seat, she watched as a man came running out, slowly scanning scanning the parking lot.

It was him.

For a brief moment, she thought of making herself known. If only to thank him again for the scone. Then she'd apologize for running out on him.

But the consequences of what could happen if she did?

This was so overwhelming to her.

Instead, she watched as he walked back into the café. Then, cautiously inching her way back into a sitting position, she started her car and drove out of the parking lot.

Jack shook his head at Ellie's hopeful expression.

She sighed, reaching over to pat his hand. "Oh, Jack... I'm so sorry."

He shrugged, and after leaning back against the counter, a silence fell between them. Ellie didn't know what to say, while Jack was trying to figure out where he went wrong.

He heaved a frustrated sigh. "Please don't tell me I imagined what happened. There was definitely something between us, right? A connection of some kind?"

She nodded. "Yes, I'd say there was definitely something there."

Then she gave a short laugh. "But maybe I'm not the one to ask."

Aware of his concerned glance, she grabbed a cup and filled it with coffee. After slapping on a lid, she slid it across the counter to him, her smile overly bright. "Now, how about your scone? I know we still have blueberry and cinnamon."

He shrugged. "Sure, you pick."

He watched her put a scone in a bag before she rang up the sale. All while she chattered away about nothing.

But she had no reason to worry. He had received her unsaid message loud and clear. Any talk about her and Michael was off limits.

When he realized there was now a line of customers behind him, he picked up his scone and coffee. "Well, I better be on my way. If I don't see you before you go back to Columbus, I wish you the best."

She gave him one of those big smiles he remembered. "Thanks. And I'll keep my eyes open while I'm here. You know… just in case a certain person comes in again. And don't worry, I have a good feeling about this."

As he walked out of the cafe, he decided Ellie's comment was proof he had every reason to feel optimistic. But this also meant he had his work cut out for him.

He needed to figure out a way to find this woman again.

Then he was going to marry her.

He stopped right in the middle of the parking lot and, raising his face to the sky, he yelled out. "It's official. You've gone absolutely insane."

Laughing, he headed for his car. This is when he saw two elderly women, who were on their way into the cafe, had turned to stare at him.

He responded with a big smile and a wave. "Have a wonderful day, ladies."

After he got in his car and turned on his favorite audio track, he started the drive home.

Believe it or not, he was in a great mood.

And he had every reason to be.

He had found the love of his life.

As Savanah began the drive home, she replayed every single detail of the last fifteen minutes in her mind. Twice, maybe three times, she did this.

What happened back there in Café Latte? This encounter wasn't something she'd normally encourage. She didn't have the time, nor did she have any interest in finding a man.

Not now. This would be absolute craziness.

Her mother would be the first to remind her of this. She needed to concentrate completely on her dancing right now. Any distractions were to be avoided. She had worked too hard and for so long to let her heart fool her into thinking she could have both.

That her mother had even suggested she take this new yoga class was still a mystery. But this was probably only because she thought it might help at relieving stress from all the new changes in her life.

She only hoped with her twenty-sixth birthday coming up in a few months, her mother would finally realize it was time to step back and let her run her own life.

Mistakes and all.

A faint smile touched her lips.

But now… this man…

He was so handsome. And the way he looked at you. Like he thought you were the most beautiful woman in the world.

She wasn't used to this kind of attention. From her early childhood, compliments had been discouraged. Unless they were regarding her dancing. And those had to be earned.

As she pulled into the parking space in front of her condo, reality kicked in. It would be best if she forgot what happened. Planned out to the smallest detail, her life was no longer her own. There was no room for a man like him.

But, try as she might, she couldn't stop thinking about his smile.

A man like him in your life?

She couldn't even imagine…

CHAPTER 32

I t was already past midnight when Stephanie got home from work. After changing into her pajamas, still hyped up from the events of the day, she made herself a cup of chamomile tea.

She picked up her phone. Tomorrow was her day off, so she wanted to see what they were forecasting for the weather.

Who are you trying to kid? You don't care about the weather. This is an excuse to see if Evan sent you another message.

Nope, nothing. No new message... no missed call.

Just nothing...

She pulled up his message from yesterday.

> I will be out of town for a couple of days.
> There's something I need to do. I'll call you
> when I get back.

She looked up from her phone.

He didn't give you much to go on, did he? But after what happened when you last saw him, you're surprised he even sent this.

Was she worried? Of course she was. How could she not be?

Look what happened the last time he promised to call? Months passed before she saw him again.

If this happens again, you and he are finished… done… and this time you're serious.

She shook her head, her sharp laugh coming out loud in the silence. How many times in the past had she already said this?

Again, you're pathetic.

She tossed her phone on the counter. She should go to bed. But knowing she wouldn't be able to fall asleep, even with the help of the chamomile tea, she decided she might as well do something productive.

She glanced around the kitchen, her gaze zeroing in on the chocolate chip cookie magnet on the refrigerator. It was a gift from one of her former patients.

Cookies…

She would bake a batch of cookies. And she knew exactly what kind.

She opened her laptop and pulled up her own recipe for Cinnamon Chocolate Chipperdoodles. The same cookies Evan told her were now his favorite.

After she put her phone in reaching distance in case he called, hating she was even doing this, she began setting out the cookie ingredients.

This was when she decided to double the recipe. Then there would be more than enough cookies for the children and for Evan.

She stilled, gazing into space.

What if you never hear from him again?

This brought on an angry shake of her head. This would be his loss. And the cookies certainly wouldn't go to waste.

She glanced over at the phone again, willing it to ring.

Of course, this didn't happen.

Frustrated, she threw the butter and sugar in the mixing bowl. With a jerk, she flipped the switch harder than she should have, all the way to high speed. This sent a spray of sugar over everything.

Muttering to herself—blaming everyone and anything she could think of for the tragedy her life had now become—she cleaned up the mess.

Then, in one swift move, she turned off her phone.

There ya go… now you can forget all about him
And of course, we all know she didn't believe this.
Nope… not one bit.

Evan was not a happy traveler.

He was mumbling to himself, something he always did when he was over-tired. But, come on… if they didn't land this plane soon, he was going to march up to the cockpit and tell them he would land it for them.

Of course, this wasn't something he would do. But after circling over Cleveland for the last thirty-five minutes—no, make that thirty-eight minutes now—he'd be willing to bet all the other passengers would cheer him on.

And what was the reason for this unexpected delay?

Not a single member of the flight crew had a clear-cut answer for this. The captain's one and only announcement had been brief… he and the crew had everything under control. There was no immediate danger and they would land as soon as possible. Everyone was to remain patient and keep their seatbelts fastened until advised otherwise.

Patient… yeah, right. Unfortunately, you're not in the mood for patience.

He closed his eyes. It had been a long twenty-four hours and the only thing he could think of at this point was sleep.

The elderly man in the seat next to him gave another snort-like snore. Once the plane had become airborne and he'd realized Evan was in no mood for conversation, he had closed his eyes and slept through the entire flight. Evan now wished he had done the same.

If he had slept at all, this had come only as a quick cat nap at the airport. And with his current state of mind, it hadn't been enough to do him any good. He also hadn't showered or had a decent meal. His one culinary highlight had been the hot dog he purchased from one of the food trucks he passed after he left the bank.

But right now? This felt like it had happened weeks ago.

The only thing he wanted was to walk into his condo, crawl into bed, and give in to his exhausted state. Only then would he be able to think clearly about everything that had happened.

God knows, your mind needs a reprieve from what you've learned on this trip.

He patted his jacket, reassured the envelope was still there. Then he gazed out the window at the panoramic view below of Lake Erie and the city of Cleveland. The Terminal Tower, already lit up in the colors of red, white and blue for the upcoming Memorial Day weekend, was like a beacon in the night.

It was also a comforting reminder he was home.

The captain's voice traveled through the plane. "Okay, folks... they have given us permission to land. So, keep those seatbelts fastened and let's do this."

It was only when the wheels of the plane made the long-awaited bump on the runway, Evan let out a long sigh of relief.

The prospect of home was looking better by the minute.

You would think at two-thirty in the morning, the Cleveland airport wouldn't be busy. But considering the run of bad luck he had experienced over the past few days, Evan wasn't surprised to find the place swarming with people.

He was just cursing his earlier decision to call for a ride rather than drive himself to the airport when he nabbed a taxi.

Stole it, you mean. The look the other guy gave you couldn't have been any more threatening.

But in all fairness, he was the more deserving of the two. His scruffy appearance more than verified this. He'd also be willing to bet the other guy had an easier past few days than he had. Hell, no doubt he was returning home after a week of long lunches and high-priced dinners with rich clients. So, the few extra minutes he had to wait for the next available taxi wouldn't kill him.

After he gave the driver directions, he took out his phone. The closer he was to home, all he could think about was Stephanie. He owed her an explanation why this journey he'd gone on was something he had to do. And how it changed everything.

He wanted Stephanie with him when he opened the envelope from his aunt. So, no matter what he found, he could fall into that every-thing-is-going-to-be-all-right feeling. The one only she could give him.

He gazed down at his phone. He had hoped she would have responded, if only to let him know she received his text. But after the way they parted, he really didn't have the right to expect this. For all he knew, it was possible she didn't even want to see him again.

Frustrated, he ran his hand down over his jaw. The ultimatum he had thrown at her now seemed so wrong.

He groaned.

You're a fool. You need to stop blaming her for your insecurity. If you don't, you're going to lose her.

And if this were to happen? He would have no one to blame but himself.

After he stuffed the phone back into his pocket, he leaned his head back against the seat and closed his eyes.

He wasn't in the right frame of mind to think about this.

At least not now, he wasn't.

Evan had the door open to his condo before the taxi driver even pulled away from the curb. After he threw his bag on the floor, he momen-tarily contemplated taking a shower. But it took only one look at his bed and the prospect of sleep won him over. He pulled off his boots, and after emptying his pockets, he fell on the bed, still dressed.

A slow smile working its way over his face, he closed his eyes.

Within seconds, he was out.

CHAPTER 33

I'm ready to risk it all.
You... Me... Everything...
~ Anonymously Yours

The sky had been full of threatening clouds all day. Now the forecast was calling for late afternoon and evening thunderstorms. At the sound of thunder, Stephanie glanced out the window, watching as a streak of lightning flashed across the sky.

She folded the last of the towels just out of the dryer and turned the TV on to the cooking channel. For a short time, she watched the co-hosts joke around with each other as they whipped up an entire romantic dinner for two in the magic of TV time.

Rolling her eyes, she grabbed the remote and turned off the TV.

You don't need this right now. And come on, no one is that perfect. This only happens on TV, remember?

She had contemplated going on a run, but the weather put a quick stop to that idea.

And even though it was late when she finally finished her baking marathon, when she went to bed, sleep had eluded her. Tossing and turning, it had been near dawn before she finally dozed off.

So, she was now running on pure adrenaline. This meant any little thing could be enough to set her off. But not in a good way…

She glanced over at the clock. It was almost five.

And you still have heard nothing from Evan.

She frowned. She wasn't sure if she should be concerned or mad at this point. Her fingers drumming on the countertop, she cast a calculating look at the two large containers of cookies in front of her.

She shot another glance at the clock. Enough was enough… she couldn't wait any longer. If she did, she was pretty sure she would go crazy.

She packed some cookies into a smaller container. Then she changed into her favorite pair of jeans and the new lacy white top she had purchased from the Chic Boutique. A little eye shadow, a touch of mascara and her new lipstick, Kiss Me Now, were her only make-up.

She was smiling as she slipped the lipstick in her pocket. Recommended by Livy, Carrie's sister, the shade was much bolder than what she normally wore. But since Livy swore by it, claiming good things always happened when she put it on, why not test it out?

It does look pretty good. Maybe you just need to get used to it.

She had it all planned out. She would drive over to Evan's condo. If his car was there, she would knock on his door, using the cookies as her excuse. She needed his opinion, she would tell him. She thought she may have goofed up the recipe. Even though they still tasted okay to her, she wanted to know what he thought.

And yes, this was the absolute truth. When she was mixing the dough, she thought she had forgotten to add the vanilla. So, she'd added more.

Now, any talented baker would tell you there was no such thing as too much vanilla. But she was pretty sure Evan didn't know this. And if she thought about it? That this even happened was all because of him. If he'd leave her alone, stop hanging around in her head, she probably would've paid more attention to what she was doing. And her cookies would be perfect.

But you're certainly not going to share this tidbit of information with him.

And if it turned out he wasn't home?

She wasn't going to worry about that until she got there.

CHAPTER 34

Evan opened his eyes, slowly taking in his surroundings.
Relieved to find he was in his own bed, he closed his eyes again, comforted by the familiar sounds of home.

The neighbor's dog was barking as usual, and he could hear kids playing basketball in the park across the street. If he wasn't mistaken, there was also the faint rumbling of thunder in the distance.

A sudden flash of lightning lit up the room. This was followed by an even louder rumble of thunder, a sign the storm was moving closer.

He reached for his phone from the nightstand. The time—four-fifty-three—jumping out at him from the screen.

This meant he had slept for almost fourteen hours straight.

He hauled himself off the bed and, after giving a long stretch, he made his way to the bathroom.

A sorry sight greeted him in the mirror. He definitely had a homeless look going on. His shirt was wrinkled and his hair had taken on a life of its own, sticking out in all directions. A quick swipe down over his jaw confirmed he was also in need of a shave.

Once that was taken care of and he took a long, hot shower, he'd be good to go.

He pulled out his razor and got to work.

Stephanie pulled into the empty space next to Evan's car and turned off the ignition.

For a few minutes, she stared at the door to his condo, the number one-twenty-five repeating over and over in her head.

All the confidence she had going for her only a short time ago?

It had disappeared.

And her plan?

It didn't sound all that great anymore.

It was only when a group of kids ran by, yelling as they passed a basketball between them, she glanced over at the container of cookies on the passenger seat.

Just get out of the car. It's too late to back down now.

A drop of rain hit the windshield, followed by another. When the drops began coming faster, she grabbed the container of cookies off the seat and got out of her car. A flash of lightning, followed by a loud rumble of thunder, sent her running up the steps to Evan's condo.

She hit the doorbell.

Then, huddled close to the door to avoid the rain, she waited.

She hoped this wasn't mother nature's way of giving her a preview of what was to come.

Evan had almost finished shaving when the doorbell rang. Since he wasn't expecting anyone, he ignored it. He was splashing water on his face when it rang a second time.

Damn...

He turned off the water and grabbed a towel, mumbling to himself as he headed for the front door. His guess was one of the neighbor kids was selling something for another fund raiser. He'd swear a different kid hit his house every month.

But he only had himself to blame. He never should've given in the first time they came to his door. Instead, he was still waiting for his first issue of Photography Illustrated. But now, almost a year had passed and not a single magazine had turned up in his mailbox.

He had placed the order with this cute little first-grader. Missing her two front teeth, she had conned him with a sales pitch way too impressive for someone her age.

Yep, she reeled you right in.

He shook his head. Not anymore. He was on to these pint-sized fast talkers. Ready to do battle, he gave his face one more swipe with the towel and yanked open the door.

His mouth falling open, he almost dropped the towel.

Stephanie...

Stephanie's plan was to hit the doorbell one last time. If Evan didn't answer, she would leave. But just as she raised her hand, the door flew open.

Faced with his shocked expression, her smile was tentative.

He answered this with a frown.

This was enough to send her into a panic. Dropping her gaze to the container of cookies she was holding, she told herself to breathe. Then she lifted her head and gave him another smile, this one more desperate.

Her voice came out all shaky. "Hi... you're home."

She closed her eyes.

Duh... this is pretty obvious, isn't it?

She swallowed. "What I meant to say, I'm glad you're back... that you're okay. Your text didn't say where you were going or when you'd be back. So, even though it's none of my business, I couldn't stop thinking something had to be wrong that you left so suddenly. I began to worry... wondering..."

Her words trailing off, she dropped her gaze back to the container. She needed to stop babbling. From experience, she knew the more she said, the less sense she would make. This is what got her into trouble in the first place.

After what felt like a very long and tense silence, she lifted her head. She shrugged. "So, that's why I'm here. If only just to say hi."

Finally, he spoke.

"Hi."

Yep, this is all he gave her.

Just… Hi.

Seriously?

In his defense, he was still trying to get over the shock she was standing in front of him. He could only imagine how hard it must have been for her to show up unannounced. Especially after everything he accused her of the last time they were together.

Yeah, the possibility she might never want to see you again was something you've been trying not to think about.

But here she was, the message in her eyes stirring a faint hope inside of him.

He took a step back, his intention to ask her to come inside.

But she thought he was about to ask her to leave. Or worse yet, close the door, leaving her standing on the steps. This had her shoving the container at him, her words tumbling out in a rush. "I brought you some cookies. I made them last night. The children named them Cinnamon Chocolate Chipperdoodles. They're the same cookies you had at the hospital. I guess I wasn't paying attention when I made the dough, because I couldn't remember if I added the vanilla. So, I added more, and now I'm worried I might have added too much. I was hoping you could try them and tell me what you think."

She shrugged, brushing the hair back from her face. "If you'd rather not, it's no big deal. I understand. Though it's always nice to have a second opinion."

He took the container from her. After gazing down at it for a few seconds, he nodded.

Again, he had nothing to say.

She was at a loss. Nothing was turning out the way she'd planned. After the initial shock of finding her at his door, she had hoped he would at least smile when he saw her. He'd invite her in and they could talk. Maybe it would take a while, but they would eventually figure out what had gone wrong.

Then they would be all right.

If only he would give her some kind of sign. But she saw nothing.

So, her only option was to leave before she broke down and made a fool of herself.

She swiped at a raindrop on her cheek. Or it could have been a tear, she wasn't sure. What she did know, if Evan's silence continued, more tears were inevitable.

She was mumbling as she began backing away. "Okay, then… I thought we could talk. You know… about what you said. But maybe it would be better if I left."

But the realization, by leaving, this could be the end of them, she searched for something more to say.

The photo wall… tell him you would still like to help.

She sent him a bright smile. "But if you're still working on the photo wall, I would be more than happy to help."

Evan had come to life.

What are you doing? Are you crazy? You don't want her to leave.

But here he was, like the idiot he'd become, sending her the message he did. While forcing her to stand in the rain.

He groaned, running his hand through his hair. "Wait… stay." He stepped aside, waving her inside.

When she hesitated, he smiled. "Please?" It wasn't a big smile, but it was enough.

She didn't notice how he pulled back to avoid touching her as she slipped past him. This was because he knew even the slightest contact would have him pulling her into his arms and kissing her like a man possessed.

Trying not to even think about this, he skirted around her into the kitchen. After he set the container on the counter, he turned to her.

She sent him a timid smile. Then she jammed her hands in her pockets, going out of her way to avoid even looking at him.

The tables had turned… now it was Evan who was out of his comfort zone. He didn't like what was happening. It was all wrong. The woman standing in front of him wasn't the Stephanie he knew. The caution in her features when she looked at him was something he didn't want to see.

And *you're the reason for this. You took a good thing—no, an amazing thing—and let it slip right through your fingers.*

So, now he needed to make things right.

He decided to go with a casual approach. Massaging the back of his neck, he glanced over at her. "Sorry about my appearance. I've been in these same clothes for the past two days. But when I got home last night, I was too tired to do anything but fall into bed. So, I was about to take a shower. Then I was going to fix something to eat."

He shrugged. "I don't know if you want to wait... you probably have somewhere else you need to be..."

Stephanie wasn't sure what he was trying to say. Was he asking her to stay? Or was he hinting he wanted her to leave?

Her gaze darted around the kitchen before coming back to him. "If you'd like, I could make you something to eat while you're in the shower. It won't be anything fancy and it all depends on what I find in your kitchen, but I'd be more than happy to do this."

He was searching her face, the intensity of his gaze making her more nervous than she already was. Tempted to ask what he was looking for, but afraid of what his answer might be, she shrugged. "Unless you'd rather I left?"

"No." This came out so fast and so loud, it surprised both of them. Trying to make light of this, he smiled, shaking his head. "No, no... of course not. It would be great if you were to stay. And whatever you make, I'm sure I'll like it. I'll try not to be too long."

She watched him leave the kitchen. Then, leaning against the counter, the frantic beat of her heart echoing in her ears, she tried to sort out what happened.

There was something different about Evan. Almost as if he was afraid of her, yet wanted to devour her at the same time. And though she found this overwhelming, the possibility of where this could take them filled her with such longing.

Never had she known such a desperate need to be with someone. The knowledge she would agree to anything he asked both frightened and excited her at the same time.

If this was love, and she was pretty sure it was, she was ready to dive right in.

She heard the shower turn on. This meant she needed to get to work.

But there was one little problem. She may have exaggerated a bit, leading Evan to believe she could cook.

And this wasn't true.

Her cooking skills were limited. No matter how hard she tried, she always burned or over-cooked whatever she made. She had only one dish she would consider her signature and easy meal fix. This would be grilled chicken with rice and vegetables. Far from gourmet, it was the one foolproof meal she could always fall back on.

But it was a whole different story with baking. This was something she did well. In fact, not to brag, but she considered herself quite the expert. She was never happier than when she was whipping up a new cookie recipe for the children at the hospital.

A search through the refrigerator and the kitchen cupboards turned up none of the ingredients she needed for her signature chicken dish. So, working with what she found, she decided on tomato soup and a grilled cheese sandwich.

But wasn't this what they called comfort food? So how could she go wrong?

You can't mess up the soup. And as long as you don't burn the sand-wiches, you should be fine.

Evan was having a hard time believing Stephanie was in his kitchen, let alone making him something to eat. The possibility she might change her mind and leave had him beating his all-time record for taking a shower and getting dressed.

This was even after his indecision about what to wear.

He was not one to dwell on his choice of apparel, but Stephanie looked so pretty in the frilly white top she was wearing. So he went with his favorite pair of jeans and a dark navy Henley.

After running his hand down over his jaw, he took a long look at himself in the mirror. Thank God he'd shaved before she showed up. Otherwise, who knew what a mess he might have made of his face.

He slapped on some cologne. Then, thinking he overdid it, he tried to scrub some off with a towel.

Peering more closely into the mirror, he grabbed his comb, dragging it through his hair. He frowned. How the hell had it gotten so long? He looked like a shaggy dog in dire need of a trim. Then, after almost poking himself in the eye with the comb, a sign he needed to settle down before he did some serious damage, he turned out the light and left the bathroom.

Think about it… she's here, isn't she? So, this has to mean something.

And to be honest? It no longer mattered why she was here. Only that she was. If she wanted to talk, this is what they would do. He would talk the night away if necessary.

Even though, if he had his way, he'd rather settle everything with a kiss. A passionate, mind-altering kiss. One long enough to erase all the accusations still unresolved between them.

He would do whatever it took to bring back the magic.

With one last look in the mirror and with what he hoped came across as a confident smile, he headed for the kitchen

Stephanie was feeling very pleased with how everything had turned out.

Okay, so maybe the sandwich was a little dark on one side. But it was more than edible, which was what mattered.

Silverware in hand, she turned to set it on the island, to find she was face to face with Evan.

It was the night of the masquerade ball all over again. Jumping back, she let out a little shriek.

But this time she held on to the silverware.

A slow grin came over his face. "I need to remember how easily you scare. Why is this? Did Jason play a lot of pranks on you when you were a child?"

Encouraged he seemed to be in a better mood, she smiled over at him as she placed the bowl of soup on the counter. "I'm sure he did, but nothing bad that I remember. He teased me a lot, though. Then I would cry and he'd get into trouble."

Her face crunched up in thought, she then shook her head. "Poor Jason."

She glanced over to see Evan was studying her with the same

intensity as he had earlier. Almost as though he was trying to figure her out.

But she could understand.

She was thinking the same about him.

Tucking a stray curl behind her ear, she nodded over at the bowl of soup. "I hope you like tomato soup and toasted cheese sandwiches. I should have been honest with you, and told you I'm not the best cook. I always seem to burn everything. But I didn't this time. So, I'm feeling quite proud of myself."

He took a seat at the island. "Everything looks great, and I'm starving."

Then he glanced over at her, an almost shy expression on his face. "This is nice. I can't remember the last time someone cooked for me. Thank you."

She laughed, ducking her head to hide she was blushing. "Oh, I don't know if you can count a toasted cheese sandwich as cooking."

She glanced over at him, happy to see he was smiling. Little did she know this was because of her laugh, and how happy it made him.

Encouraged, she was about to sit next to him when she noticed a long piece of thread in his hair. She reached over to remove it. "You have this—"

He flinched, jerking his head back to avoid her touch. But again, this was only pure survival on his part. He was trying so hard to keep his distance. He wasn't hungry for only food. He hungered for her—to the point this was all he could think about.

A stunned look on her face, Stephanie dropped her hand to her lap. She took his reaction as a sign the thought of her touch was repulsive to him. Whatever happened while he was away, whatever he had been searching for and the answers he'd received, was enough to change how he felt about her.

And most of all, what he wanted with them.

She slid off the stool, speaking in a whisper. "I'm sorry. I didn't mean... I was only trying to remove a thread... I didn't..."

"Stephanie..." He groaned, shaking his head.

And this was what finally did her in.

She became angry. Whatever he had to say? He might as well not even waste his time. Because she'd be willing to bet, any excuse he came up with, she'd already heard it before.

So why would she belittle herself any further by sticking around? To feel worse than she already did?

You get it. It's obvious he doesn't want you here.

He opened his mouth. To promptly shut it when she began shaking her head. "No, no, no... you don't need to explain. I realize now I shouldn't have come. And now, it's best I leave."

Trying not to cry, she nodded over at the sandwich and bowl of soup. "You should eat those before they get cold."

She grabbed her purse and took off, almost in a run for the door.

And why wasn't Evan trying to stop her?

He was in shock. So much so, he couldn't have moved even if he tried.

He didn't understand.

Why did she leave? What had he done?

Yes, he honestly didn't know what happened.

It was when the door slammed shut, this was enough to send him diving off the stool and sprinting after her.

Because if there was one thing he was sure of...

He would be making the biggest mistake of his life if he let her go.

CHAPTER 35

I love you
and that's the beginning
and end of everything
~Anonymous

Evan put his arm up to shield his face from the rain.

It was coming at him so hard, he couldn't see a damn thing.

As predicted, the storm had moved in with a vengeance. Traveling in waves across the parking lot, blurring everything in its path, the heavy rain was relentless. Lightning flashed across the sky, each crackling streak followed by a rolling boom of thunder enough to shake the ground beneath him.

A huge streak of lightning lit up the sky, momentarily making it as light as day. This is when he caught sight of Stephanie. Huddled next to her car, from what he could make out, she was searching for something in her purse.

"Stephanie..." His yell lost in the long roll of thunder that followed, he ran down the steps, waving to get her attention.

She ignored him.

Or, he'd like to believe, she didn't see him. Undeterred, he splashed his way across the parking lot to reach her just as another huge streak of lightning flashed across the sky.

He crouched over her, trying to shield her from the rain. Even as close as he was, he had to shout to be heard. "Stephanie... come on. You need to come back inside."

She continued to search through her purse, refusing to look at him. Then, her voice barely audible, she responded. "I thought I put my keys in my purse. But I can't find them. Don't worry, I'll be fine. Go back inside before you get wet."

His laugh bordered on hysterical. "Before I get wet? I think that's already happened. And the longer we stand here talking about it, the more wet we'll get. So, let's go back inside. Please..."

She began checking her pockets. "No, I'm going home. I never should have come. I don't know what I was thinking."

Her words coming between gasps, this is when he realized she was crying, her tears mingling with the rain.

He groaned, moving even closer

"Stephanie..."

She held up the keys. "I found them." After she pushed back the wet hair blowing in her face, she hit the remote to unlock the car. Still refusing to acknowledge him, she reached for the door handle. "Goodbye, Evan."

He didn't even hesitate. In one quick move, he had her pressed between him and the car. Framing her face in his hands, he captured her mouth in a bruising, demanding kiss.

He poured everything he had into the kiss. It was a kiss to let her know she wasn't going anywhere. Not as long as he had his say.

He soon realized he had no reason to worry. The keys Stephanie had been searching for?

They slipped from her fingers and landed right in the middle of a big puddle.

And she didn't even notice.

But it didn't matter, as any thoughts she had of leaving were no longer an option. The storm forgotten, the fire racing through them was one not even the heavy rain could extinguish.

Wrapping her arms around Evan, Stephanie held on tight. This is what she wanted, what she had been waiting for.

And it was so, *so* much more than she ever could have imagined.

Evan took a breath before claiming her mouth in another kiss. This explosion of passion—and this was the only way he could think of to describe what was happening between them—was enough for him to know he was finally at the right place and time for this second chance at love.

All because of the woman he was holding in his arms.

He didn't care about the rain… in fact, once his mouth had connected with hers, he didn't even notice it was there. Nor was he worried about the thunder, still rumbling in waves around them.

But the lightning?

This was a whole different story. As much as he'd love to throw all caution aside and let the kiss carry them through the raging storm, he wasn't stupid.

Lightning wasn't something to be ignored.

Careful not to get caught up in her eyes, afraid this would only lead to another kiss, he grabbed her hand. "Come on… we need to get out of this storm. It's not safe."

He ran up the steps to his condo, taking her with him.

No sooner were they inside, Evan pulled her back into his arms. As far as he was concerned, the kiss they shared in the parking lot had been only the beginning. And there was no way he was going to let things end there.

He had wanted her from the moment he opened the door and found her standing in front of him, looking so pretty in the white frilly top she was wearing. So, he had no plans of letting her go. This is where she belonged… with him, and in his arms.

His hands sliding in her hair to pull her closer, his whisper brushed over her mouth. "My God… what have I done? I'm such a fool. I should have kissed you like this long ago."

Without waiting for a response, his mouth covered hers in another kiss. Taking her moan as an invitation for more, he slipped his hands under her top. His fingers skimming over the silkiness of her skin, he felt a shiver race through her... everywhere.

His lips slowed. Nuzzling his face in the curve of her neck, his whisper settled right below her ear. "You're cold..."

Stephanie was hanging on for dear life. Clutching the wet fabric of his shirt in her hand and her face buried against the hard wall of his chest, she was utterly helpless, unable to move.

Not that she wanted to...

"Stephanie?"

When she lifted her chin to look up at him, he was gazing down at her, a question in his eyes. Another shiver racing through her, she ran her hands languidly down over his shirt. "Yes... we should get out of these wet clothes."

He went still against her. After holding her gaze for a prolonged moment, he lowered his head, his lips brushing over hers in a kiss. Once, twice, and then a third time. Soft, feathery kisses. Enough to bring his name from her in a soft moan.

He didn't even hesitate, gathering her up in his arms. When she wrapped her arms around his neck, he kissed her again... a long, sweet kiss, lasting until they reached his bedroom.

There he came to a sudden stop, overcome by a sudden uncertainty. This wasn't because he was new to this. Of course not. He had been with a woman before. He knew what to do.

But this was different. This was Stephanie.

There was something almost sacred about loving her, being loved by her. The spell she'd unknowingly cast had him ready to do whatever she asked. And once they took this ultimate step, there would be no turning back.

He laid her on his bed. Trailing his fingertips down the curve of her jaw to cup her chin, his deep voice rumbled through her. "I want to make love to you. I've wanted this since the first moment I saw you."

When her answer was to reach up to him, in one quick move, he pulled his shirt up and over his head and tossed it to the floor. Then he was on the bed beside her, the kisses he gave her, now even more passionate, more demanding.

Together they struggled out of their wet clothing, his mouth never leaving hers. And once the barriers were removed, his hands were everywhere, leaving behind a trail of heat wherever they touched.

It was when his lips slowed, leaving hers, she opened her eyes. Gazing down at her, he dropped the softest of kisses to her mouth.

Nothing had prepared him for this moment. In his mind, and yes, also in his dreams, the love they shared was gentle. Nothing like this desperate hunger, this need building inside of him, leaving him craving more.

More of everything, as long as it was with her.

And Stephanie?

Never had she experienced a passion of this intensity, this desperate need for someone to love her. Mesmerized by the way his muscles flexed under her touch, her hands roamed over him, every-where. He had her beyond thinking about anything except how much she wanted this with him.

After he lowered himself over her, he closed his eyes. He wanted to remember everything about this moment. Her soft curves beneath him. The eagerness of her response to his touch. And her eyes... filled with a desire mirroring what he knew she could see in his.

For a long moment, they didn't move.

Then he dipped his head, his breath brushing across her jaw before his mouth captured hers in another kiss.

He whispered her name.

When her lashes fluttered open, he pressed a soft kiss to her mouth. "Now?"

"Yes, now... Please..."

His gaze locked with hers, with one sure push, they became one.

He stilled, his eyes searching. "Stephanie? You—"

But her kiss had him completely forgetting what he was about to say.

And now, nothing mattered but the love they had to share.

A love that was a long time coming.

CHAPTER 36

The storm had moved on, leaving behind only an occasional rumble of thunder and flash of lightning
A gentle rain was now falling.

Inside Evan's bedroom, all was quiet. His eyes closed and a faint smile on his face, he didn't want to move. He wanted to stay like this for just a little while longer.

But this wasn't entirely true. He wanted more than a just a little while. The possibility of keeping Stephanie with him forever was becoming more appealing with each passing moment.

Stephanie's soft sigh had him opening his eyes. After he pressed a slow kiss to the hollow at the base of her throat, he lifted himself to his elbows to gaze down at her.

She looked absolutely beautiful.

Her hair was still damp from the rain, framing her face in wispy curls. Her eyes closed, her lashes rested against her flushed cheeks. And her lips looked swollen from his kisses.

A faint smile curved his lips. He didn't think it was a coincidence her lips fit so perfectly with his.

She had the look of a woman who had been thoroughly loved.

That he was responsible for this, a fierce longing swept through him, the need to know she was his. He rested his forehead against hers, his request a husky whisper. "I know I will always be yours. Tell me you'll always be mine."

Her eyes still closed, a faint smile touched her lips. "Yours... for always."

A frown suddenly flitted across his face. Tracing her lips with his fingertip, his voice was hesitant.

"*Hey...*"

Her lashes fluttered open. With every emotion shining in her eyes, she gazed up at him.

"*Hey...*"

His voice came out all gruff. "Why didn't you tell me? I would have—"

She pressed her fingers to his mouth. Her eyes searching his, she struggled to find the right words. "I knew you would think you needed to be careful. You'd hold back, afraid to love me." She reached up to give him a lingering kiss. "I wanted to know what it was like to have all of your love."

Closing her eyes again, her words trailed off in a whisper. "Even if it was only for tonight..."

A tenderness filling him, he rested his forehead against hers. "I will always be gentle with you. But loving you here, like this... it's a whole different gentle. I couldn't hold back what I feel even if I tried." He shook his head. "And this is not just the beginning. I'll be right here, for as long as you want me."

He smiled. "Remember what you promised? To be mine, for always?"

He watched her eyes become even brighter with the tears she was trying so hard to hold back. And even after taking a deep breath, her voice was still shaky. "I was so afraid you weren't coming back. I know you said you would, but after the meeting about the puppy, I was afraid you'd never want to see me again."

Her eyes pleaded with him to understand. "I know it seemed like I was siding with Noah. But I wasn't. What I said came out all wrong, and I would have given anything to take it back. But you seemed so angry, your mind made up."

He groaned, closing his eyes. "I'm so sorry. I have no excuse for the way I acted. In my mind, I knew I was accusing you of something you'd never do.." A wry smile tweaked the corner of his mouth. "Believe me, Elenore was more than quick to let me know what a fool I was."

"Elenore?"

He chuckled at her surprised expression. "Yes, she made it very clear I was in the wrong. And I needed to get my act together." He dropped another kiss to her forehead. "She has high hopes for us. And I agree with her. But then I think I've felt this way since the first time I saw you."

He hesitated, his eyes searching hers. "You've been like a healing light in my darkness, making me believe good things can happen. And if I get a little crazy, it's because I don't want to lose you."

She lifted her face to his, her words brushing over his mouth like a vow. "I have no plans of going anywhere. Unless it's with you."

"Good. I'm going to hold you to this." Settling next to her, he tucked her close. After he linked their fingers together, bringing them to his mouth for a kiss, he gave a long, contented sigh.

The soothing sound of the rain, holding her in his arms, and her heart beating so close to his... all of this was heaven to him. Especially after the chaos his life had been over the past few days.

This was a reminder he owed her an explanation. He cleared his throat. "I need to tell you why I left."

She shook her head against his chest. "If you don't want to, I understand."

"*Ah...* but sweetheart, I do." He pulled her closer before taking a deep breath for his next words. "It appears my life is more intertwined with Elenore than I ever could have imagined."

She leaned back, searching his face. "With Elenore? What do you mean?"

One look into her beautiful eyes, and he was pulling her back for another kiss. They had him ready to promise her anything. If she asked for the moon and all the stars in the sky, he'd find a way to give them to her.

He smiled down at her. "I'm sorry, but I'm still trying to believe you're actually here. And I can kiss you whenever I want." He play-fully tapped her nose with his finger. "And, miraculously, you're not mad at me because I did something stupid again."

Her mouth quirked up in a teasing smile. "*Umm...* I promise to never be mad at you again."

He burst out laughing. "Something tells me this will never happen. I'm bound to goof up, somehow."

This time, she was the one to initiate the kiss. Then she frowned. "Elenore sent you off on some special errand, didn't she? I told you how demanding she can be. She—"

He interrupted her. "No, this is different. In fact..." He pressed another kiss to her mouth before he threw aside the comforter and left the bed. He smiled down at her. "Stay right here. I'll be right back."

True to his word, he was back within seconds, He was holding an envelope, along with half of the toasted cheese sandwich she had made for him.

Settling next to her on the bed, he sent her a sheepish smile as he raised the sandwich to his mouth. "I'm sorry, but I'm starving." He took a big bite, and closing his eyes, a groan of pleasure escaped him. "This is by far the best sandwich I've ever had."

Her look was skeptical. "I find that hard to believe."

He nodded, holding it out to her. "It is. Here, take a bite."

With him watching, she took a bite of the sandwich. After she swal-lowed it, she shrugged. "It tastes okay? Like your ordinary toasted cheese sandwich?"

Taking another bite, he shook his head. "I beg to differ. It's amaz-ing?" About to pop what remained in his mouth, he raised an eyebrow. "Sure you don't want another bite?"

She laughed, shaking her head. If he said it was amazing, so be it. Maybe she was a better cook than she thought she was. "No, it's all yours. I want to hear more about Elenore."

After he popped the rest of the sandwich in his mouth, he started right in on the reason for his trip. How Elenore, through the informa-tion he gave her during his interview, suspected her husband had been the driver responsible for the deaths of his parents. Through her lawyers, she found his uncle had passed years ago, and the only information available for his aunt was an Atlanta address. So Elenore suggested he check it out. If only to give him closure.

There it is again. That word... closure. It seems like every time you turn around, someone is telling you this is what you need.

And now? He hoped to God he'd never have to hear the word ever again.

He went on to tell her how in less than twenty-four hours he'd traveled to Atlanta and back. Only to learn his aunt had passed, leaving behind an envelope he hoped held the answers to some of his questions.

He reached for the envelope. Tracing his name typed on the front with his finger, his voice was gruff. "So, this is what I came home with. Not what I expected."

He shook his head. "Doesn't seem fair, does it? My aunt's life is now reduced to this... a single envelope."

Since he wasn't one to share his feelings about the past, Stephanie knew how hard it had been for him to tell her all of this. She wrapped her arms around him, and after pressing a kiss to his cheek, she spoke, her voice unsteady. "Oh, Evan... I'm so sorry. But you did the right thing by going there. Otherwise, you would always wonder."

He rested his cheek on the top of her head. "You were all I could think about after I left the bank. This is when I decided I wanted to wait until I was with you to open the envelope."

He shrugged. "I think I'm afraid of what I might find."

She gave him another hug. "I'll do whatever you want."

After a slight hesitation, he broke the seal on the envelope and shook the contents out onto the bed. There was another envelope with his name on it, a bank book, a small velvet drawstring bag and a bundle of papers tied with string.

Evan looked at Stephanie, his expression uncertain. "I guess I should open the envelope first?"

At her nod, he pulled a folded sheet of paper from the envelope. Opening it, he read it aloud.

Dear Evan,

I can only hope you are reading this letter, that it finally landed in your hands. But first, I want you to know I'm not looking for sympathy, only the chance to explain.

The past few years I have been sick and have now accepted I have little time left. It was a close friend of mine who convinced me to try contacting you. I had hoped to talk to you in person, but I guess time was not on our side.

It is not your fault I waited so long to write. And it's not because of you I never came back for you as I had promised.

No, this is all on me.

When I left, my plan had been to get settled, get a good job and a nice place to live. This would give me the chance to prove you should live with me.

But I was too late. You were already in the foster care program and nothing I could say or do would convince them you'd be better off with me.

Yes, I never should have left you with your uncle. But if I had taken you with me, he would have fought me every step of the way. His drinking turned him into a very bitter man.

I did not mean for your life with us to turn out like this. When you were born, the wife of the man who caused the accident took care of all the hospital bills and gave us a more than generous sum of money for your upkeep. When your uncle started using the money for gambling, without his knowledge, I began investing whatever I could in your future. I continued to do this even after I left. The amount is in the bank book included with this letter. I know this can't make up for what happened, but I hope it helps even a little.

Your parents... Know that they were so much in love. And so excited when they found out they were pregnant with you. I remember you as a carbon copy of your father, with your mother's sensitive and caring personality. With this combination, I'm sure you have turned out to be a wonderful person, both inside and out.

Tied up with string is your birth certificate, your parent's marriage license and a few other items that might interest you. You will also find your mother's engagement ring and your father's wedding band in the small velvet bag. Maybe when you get married, you can give the engagement ring to your future wife. Your father had it custom designed for your mother. It is a beautiful ring.

So many times I've wished things could have been different. But now my only wish is you can forgive me. And you have the good life you deserve.

Your Aunt Mary

P.S. Elenore Cromley is the name of the woman who set up the bank account for you. Even though we were all devastated when the accident happened, and she had lost her husband, she was so concerned about you. I later learned she had even offered to adopt you. Maybe someday you'll get the chance to talk to her. If you do, please tell her I'm sorry. And thank you.

Evan was silent. There were so many emotions running through him — anger, grief, sadness, regret—just to name a few.

He was also feeling guilty. Dragging his hand through his hair, he groaned. "I should have tried to find her long before this. If only to make sure she was okay. What's wrong with me?"

Struggling to her knees next to him, Stephanie framed his face in her hands. She was shaking her head. "No, no… Evan, listen to me. There is nothing wrong with you. After the childhood you experienced, it's understandable you blocked so much out of your mind. This letter should give you peace of mind knowing what happened. And now you can let it go."

Her gaze holding his, she waited, watching as a smile touched his lips. He gathered her against him, his whisper falling right below her ear. "Now I know why I wanted you here with me."

After pressing a kiss to her forehead, he reached for the bundle of papers. His birth certificate and his parent's marriage license were there as promised. After reading the birth certificate, Stephanie looked over at Evan in surprise. "Your birthday is on Tuesday. Why didn't you tell me? I remember asking you about this the night of the masquerade ball, but the only information you offered was it's in the spring."

He shrugged. "Yeah, I know. I guess my birthday has never been that much of a big deal. With moving around so much, starting all over with new people, it was easier to pretend it was just like any other day. It was only when I met Kelsie, I realized what a big deal it is for some people. But after losing her, I found it hard to celebrate anything."

The expression on Stephanie's face was a combination of sadness and disbelief. Not that she was big on birthdays. No, for her, the extra attention could be overwhelming. But to ignore the day completely? Her family and friends would never allow this.

Well, you are going to make it up to him. From now on, you'll make every birthday one he'll always remember.

After surprising him with a kiss to his cheek, she leaned closer to get a better look at the photograph he was holding, taken on the day of his parent's wedding. She smiled. "Wow, you do look exactly like your father... so handsome. And your mother was beautiful. They both look so happy."

He nodded. "She is beautiful, isn't she?" His smile was wistful. "I often wondered what they were like. In my mind, I always pictured them like this. Not bitter and unhappy like my aunt and uncle."

The only other item a newspaper article about the accident, Evan bundled it back up with the photographs and certificates.

He shrugged. "Since I already know what happened, I don't need to see this right now."

He picked up the velvet jewelry bag, shaking his head. "I can't believe my aunt was able to keep these rings from my uncle. If she hadn't, I'm sure he would have sold them."

He shook the rings out into the palm of his hand.

Stephanie gave a small gasp before she glanced over at him. "Oh my gosh, the engagement ring is gorgeous. Was your father an artist?"

He read the inscriptions inside the bands before he shook his head. "I recall my aunt once telling me he was a photographer."He handed Stephanie the rings. "Both rings are engraved with the same words."

Forever yours, Forever my Love.

She sighed. "It sounds like they were very much in love."

After he put the rings back in the jewelry bag, he leaned over to give her a kiss. He was smiling. "I believe you're right."

He hesitantly picked up the bank book, holding it in his hand. After he finally opened it, without a word, he handed it to Stephanie. Then he leaned back, closing his eyes.

"Oh, Evan... "

Stephanie's reaction had him shaking his head, his voice choked. "This isn't right. She should have used this money for herself. She could have lived in a nicer place, maybe even had better care. I wish..." After a frustrated sigh, he was silent.

Stephanie closed the book and gently laid it on top of the bundle of papers. She reached for his hand, and after a brief silence, she spoke. "I think she did what she had to do in order to make peace with what happened. Something tells me she was so proud she could leave you such a generous amount. Consider it as her gift to you, a way of showing her love."

When he opened his eyes to see the tears in hers, he buried his hands in her hair, pulling her closer until their lips touched.

And then he kissed her like he was never going to let her go.

He hadn't intended for the kiss to turn into something more. But the passion that flared between them, each kiss more desperate than the last, was bigger than the both of them.

He wanted to lose himself in her, block out the world and everything but her.

She responded by opening her arms and her heart, letting him know she would always be there for him.

With the sound of the gentle rain in the background, they loved each other with everything they had.

For Evan, it was a healing love.

For Stephanie, it was the love she had always dreamt she would have.

Yes, the magic was back.

And it was even better than before.

Evan came up behind Stephanie and, wrapping his arms around her, he rested his cheek against hers.

She was making him another sandwich.

He had finished the other one, along with a handful of cookies. But he insisted he was still hungry.

His whisper tickled her ear. "Tell me you'll stay here with me tonight. I'll even sweeten the deal and make breakfast for you in the morning."

Placing the spatula on the counter, she turned to him. Linking her fingers behind his neck, she pressed a kiss to his mouth. "How can I pass up a deal like that?" She kissed him again.

"Though I would have stayed even without the promise of breakfast."

His lips brushed over hers. *"Mmm...."* I'll have to remember that. I just know I'm not ready to let you go."

He suddenly lifted his head. "Is something burning?"

"Oh, no..." Whirling around, Stephanie found that, yes, something was definitely burning. After she removed the smoking pan from the burner, she shrugged, laughing. "I tried to tell you, I'm not a good cook. That first sandwich must have been a fluke."

She took two more slices of bread out of the bag. "Let's try this again."

He reached over to turn off the burner before he pulled her back into his arms. "I have a better idea."

One kiss led to another... and then another... the sandwich completely forgotten.

But when she made one for Evan much later, according to him, it came out perfect.

CHAPTER 37

You're nothing short of my everything.
~ Unknown

T he long awaited grand-opening celebration of the new community center was less than two hours away. After Evan slipped into his tuxedo jacket and adjusted the collar, he tried not to be too smug as he checked out his reflection in the mirror.

But, hey… come on. The grin coming back at him was proof he was looking pretty good.

A few weeks ago, the thought of a tuxedo had been enough to put him in a lousy mood. But now here he was, smiling about it, eager for the night ahead.

You would wear one every day of the week if this is what Stephanie wanted.

He picked up the bow tie from the counter and put it in his pocket. There was no reason he couldn't tie it himself, but the memory of Stephanie's worried expression on the night of the Cleveland Elite Awards dinner was still with him. This had come about when she commented on how it looked like he had mastered the art of tying it on his own and would no longer need her help.

To be honest? He wanted her help. He didn't know what it was, but there was something almost sensuous about this simple task. Making it hard for him to think about anything else except how he wanted to pull her into his arms and kiss her instead.

So, the way he saw it?

The job was hers for as long as she wanted to take it on.

He checked his watch. If he left now to pick up Stephanie, he would be forty-five minutes early.

He realized this probably wasn't a good idea.

But you miss her. More than you imagined possible.

Was it really only a little over six hours since she left him? Because it felt like much longer.

Too long....

His mind made up, he grabbed his keys and headed for the door.

Stephanie gave her lashes one last swipe with the mascara wand. Now she only needed to figure out how she wanted to style her hair.

She gathered it up on top of her head and, after a critical inspection in the mirror, she styled it in a loose French twist.

She sent a nervous glance over at the clock on the nightstand. Evan would be here in about forty minutes and she was still waiting for Sophie to drop off her dress.

This was supposed to have happened almost an hour ago.

So, when her doorbell rang, she thought it was Sophie. Pulling on her robe on as she went running out of the bathroom, she threw open the door.

"Yessss... finally you're here. I've been—"

Her words came to an abrupt halt when she saw Evan.

He chuckled before he leaned in to press a kiss to her cheek. "*Wow*... this is quite a greeting. But I like it... I like it a lot."

He handed her the single red rose he was holding in his hand. "For you."

Before she could respond, an SUV came to an almost screeching halt in front of her condo. They watched as the door flew open and Sophie jumped out, carrying a garment bag.

She was out of breath when she reached them. "I'm so sorry I'm late. We had a minor episode at the boutique. A mother-of-the-bride had a melt-down when her daughter told her she didn't like the dress she had picked out."

She shook her head. "Aunt Louise was still trying to calm her down when I left. But I don't believe the dress was the problem. The two of them have some unresolved issues going on. Since Aunt Louise loves drama, she is in her element. She'll straighten them."

She turned to Evan. "Hi, I'm Sophie. I'm so happy to meet you. I've heard a lot about you from Steffi. But don't worry, it's all good."

She peered more closely at him. "You're rocking that tux, but you do realize you're missing something, don't you? Where's your bow tie?"

He cleared his throat, giving an embarrassed laugh as he patted his jacket pocket. "It's right here. I haven't quite gotten the hang of tying one yet."

Then he gazed over at Stephanie. "And I don't know that I ever will."

One glance at the color rising in Stephanie's cheeks, Sophie knew what Evan said went far deeper than his knowledge of how to tie a bow tie.

She was grinning as she turned to leave. "Well, on that note, I'm heading back to the boutique, my mission here accomplished. Have a wonderful time at the grand opening. I know you'll be the best-looking couple there. Bye..."

After she drove off, Evan followed Stephanie inside. She turned to him, the intensity of his gaze sending her heart beat soaring, her words catching in her throat. "I'm sorry... I guess... well, I wasn't expecting you yet. You're early."

He only got in a nod before she rambled on. "And Sophie... you heard what she said, why she was late. I was worried something had happened to her."

She was backing away from him, the garment bag clutched to her chest. She nodded down at the bag. "I shouldn't be too long. I only have to slip into this, and I'll be ready."

But he was having none of this. Before she took another step, in one swift move, he took the garment bag from her, draped it over the chair and pulled her against him. He brushed a stray curl back from her face. "Hey, it's okay… I know I'm early. But this is because I couldn't wait to see you."

A smile tweaked the corner of his mouth. "But I was hoping for a kiss. A hello-I-missed-you kind of kiss." His voice dipped to a husky whisper. "Or even two. If only as proof the last two days haven't been a dream."

After they shared a kiss, one that was more than enough to prove what they had was definitely very real, he buried his face in her hair, his low groan rumbling in her ear. "I've got an idea. Let's not go tonight and say we did. I'll even keep the tux on if you'd like."

She laughed. "The bow tie, too?"

He nodded, patting his pocket. "Yep, the whole deal. I've got the tie right here. I bet no one will even miss us."

She shook her head. "You know that's not true. And as much as I like your idea, I'm looking forward to the evening. I can't wait to see the photo wall."

She untangled herself from his hold and picked up the garment bag. "I won't be long. I promise. And then I'll do your bow tie."

After pressing a quick kiss to his cheek, she disappeared down the hall.

Evan couldn't seem to stay in one place.

He had been serious… very serious… when he told Stephanie he would be more than happy to skip the grand opening.

Remember, he had no desire to mingle with the high society of Cleveland.

Again, this wasn't his thing.

And after the kiss they shared? This had him even more reluctant to spend the next few hours with about a hundred and fifty people he didn't even know. He groaned, just thinking about this.

His hands shoved in his pockets, he wandered into the kitchen to get a drink of water. This is when he realized Stephanie was talking to him from her bedroom, something to do with Elenore. Only able to make out bits and pieces, he walked down the hall to stand by the bedroom door.

Stephanie was standing in front of the mirror, trying to pull the zipper up the back of her dress.

Unaware Evan had come into the room, she made a face at herself in the mirror. She was mumbling to herself. "Seriously? Why didn't they put the zipper on the side of the dress? This would have made things a lot easier."

She tugged at the dress, trying to pull it up even higher to get a better grip on the zipper.

When that didn't work, she groaned. "I give up."

Evan didn't even hesitate. Coming up behind her, he wrapped his arms around her. His breath brushing across her skin, followed by the kiss he pressed to the back of her neck, sent a shiver skittering through her.

Aware of this, he rested his chin on her shoulder. His eyes meeting hers in the mirror, he smiled. "I hope it's okay I'm here. But I couldn't hear what you were saying. And after watching your struggle with the zipper, I thought you might need my help."

His steady gaze had her chattering non-stop. "No, no... it's fine. I was telling you about the call I got from Elenore about fifteen minutes ago. She was worried the excitement might be too much for some of the children." She gave a little laugh, shaking her head. "I wanted to tell her it was a little too late to worrying about this. Instead, I reminded her the plan was to allow the children to stay for only the first hour. So, there shouldn't be a problem. I think she felt better when we ended the call."

He nodded. "*Hmm*... I'm sure she did."

Her hands covering his, she sent him a smile. "And you're right. I could use your help with this zipper."

Zipper? What zipper?

Now that he had her in his arms, the zipper was no longer his first priority. Instead, he pulled her closer. "You look absolutely gorgeous, by the way. Zipped up or not. I'm a lucky man to be your date for the evening."

The huskiness of his voice, along with the kiss he pressed to the nape of her neck, had her leaning back to smile up at him. Taking advantage of this, he pressed a slow trail of kisses along the line of her jaw.

Another shiver skittering through her, everywhere, her response was a breathless muddle of words. "Thank you. I asked the children what color my dress should be, and out of all their suggestions, this was the winner."

She smoothed her hands over the shimmery gold fabric of the skirt. "Some of their suggestions were pretty wild. Purple polka dots and red and white stripes, to name a few. I had to do a lot of fast talking." Smiling at the memory, she was unaware she had completely relaxed against him.

For Evan, this was a moment he knew he would remember forever.

It was official.

He was totally and madly in love with her.

You are hers… body, heart, and soul.

Between the intoxicating sound of her laugh, the way she felt so right in his arms and the memories of all they had shared the past two days, the need to be with her had now escalated to the point he couldn't think of anything else.

The way he saw it, this time belonged to them.

Everyone and everything else could wait.

Proof of this was the perfect view in the mirror of her bed behind them. The fluffy white pillows and comforter were an invitation to seize the moment, give into this passion so quick to ignite between them.

So, it was understandable the last thing on his mind was her zipper.

A slow smile traveling across his face, he held her gaze in the mirror. "Correct me if I'm wrong, but I believe it's more than acceptable to arrive fashionably late to an event."

He kissed his way up the slender column of her neck, his words coming in a groan against her mouth. "I want to make love to you. Right here. Right now."

"*Evan…*" She closed her eyes. "I… but we…"

"*Hmm…* I know what you're going to say. You're worried about the event. And how everyone is counting on us to be there. As we will be. But I think they will understand if we were to arrive a little late. In fact, I bet Elenore would be the first to approve of this."

Before she could respond, he turned her around to face him. His fingers sliding slowly through the French twist she'd tried so hard to perfect sent the bobby pins flying, her hair tumbling to her shoulders.

She closed her eyes, surrendering to the soft kisses he pressed over her eyelids and across her cheeks. When she arched up against him, her hands sliding under his jacket, a groan came from low in his throat. His lips slowed, his hand drifting to the zipper that had brought them to this moment.

As he slowly, *so slowly* eased it dow, his deep voice rumbled through her. "Tell me you'll always be mine."

"Yours for ..." The rest was swallowed in his kiss.

And she was lost... falling into him all over again.

Evan pulled his car up to the main entrance of the hospital, joining the line of cars there for valet service. He almost dove out of the car, his goal to open the passenger door before one of the high school seniors working the valet came over to them. He wanted to be the one there for Stephanie.

Yes, he knew his behavior was immature. But give him a break. Only a half hour ago, Stephanie had been in his arms, her cheeks flushed, her lips swollen from his kisses. The memory of the love they shared still so fresh in his mind, he considered it a miracle they'd even made it to the hospital.

With Stephanie's hand in his, they made their way inside.

The first person they saw was Elenore. In conversation with the volunteers as they checked in the guests, she glanced over in their direction. When she saw them, her relief was obvious.

Her look was searching as they made their way over to her. Then she smiled. "*Ah...* it seems the two of you have finally figured it out. It's about time." She nodded over at Evan. "I think we can all agree we've learned so much in these past few weeks. Beginning with how precious life really is."

In an impulsive move, Stephanie gave her a hug. Then she laughed. "I'm afraid you got a lot more than you bargained for when you took us on. Thank you so much for keeping the faith."

Elenore watched Evan re-claim Stephanie's hand, pressing a kiss to her fingers. She shrugged. "Who am I to stand in the way of true love?"

She gestured towards the crowded room. "Now go... mingle with the guests. The photo collage is a big hit, and everyone is waiting to meet both of you."

She winked at Evan. "I have a feeling your career as a photographer is going to have some big changes."

CHAPTER 38

The grand opening of the community center was a complete success,

Surpassing even Elenore's expectations.

This was even after Oreo, who had been allowed to stay for the event, ran off with a guest's shoe. Not used to wearing high heels, the woman had kicked them off under the table, hoping no one would notice.

She hadn't bargained on Oreo deciding to steal the show.

Even after it took three men and most of the children at least ten minutes to catch the little dog, the over-all consensus was this unexpected chase had only added more fun to the party.

Evan, Elenore, and Stephanie had made their speeches—with Evan's coming in as the shortest of the three, but drawing the longest applause—and now the disc jockey was taking requests.

Evan was definitely the man of the hour. With so many requests for photo shoots, his head was swimming.

But now, after escaping a long conversation with the owner of a venue in the downtown area, he was searching for Stephanie

He wanted to dance with her…

He finally found her. She was dancing with one of the board

members they'd met at Elenore's dinner party. Making his way over to them, he arrived just as the song ended.

The relief on Stephanie's face was obvious. "Evan, you remember Mr. Freeman from Elenore's dinner party, don't you? He tried to teach me the cha-cha, but I'm afraid I've stepped on his feet way too many times."

Mr. Freeman laughed. "No problem. It's been a pleasure to have such a beautiful dance partner. And please, call me Ed. Mr. Freeman makes me feel even older than I am."

Evan laughed. "Okay, Ed. But do you mind if I take over from here? I haven't danced with Stephanie yet, and this might be the last song."

Wiping his perspiring forehead with a handkerchief, Ed nodded. "Sure, I'm going to get something to drink." He turned to Stephanie, giving a slight bow. "Again, it was a pleasure, my dear."

"You're just too good to be true,
I can't take my eyes off of you…"

After listening to the words of the song, Evan reached for Stephanie's hand. *"Ah…* this song is perfect, everything I'd like to say to you. So, may I have this dance?"

She went right into his arms, and resting her head on his shoulder, they danced.

After a brief silence, he chuckled. When she gazed up at him, he sent a nod over at Elenore. Seated at a table, watching the action on the dance floor, she had also kicked off her shoes.

His words brushed across Stephanie's cheek. "I see Elenore has finally slowed down. She must be exhausted. She's been on the move ever since they opened the doors. Every time I turned around, she was introducing me to someone, giving me way too much credit for what I do. And because of this, it looks like I'll have enough jobs to keep me busy for a long time."

She smiled. "I'm not surprised, because the photos are amazing. I'm so happy for you. And so proud."

He noticed the tears pooling in her eyes before she rested her head back on his shoulder. This had him worried. The smile was promising.

But the tears? These could go either way, but since they just popped up out of nowhere, he had a sinking feeling they were leaning more towards the negative.

Maybe it was something he did? Something he said? Or had he unknowingly insulted a guest?

These were the only possibilities he could think of, since he'd made it a point to be on his best behavior around her friends.

He sighed… as usual, he was clueless.

Thinking it might be best if he kept talking, he pressed his cheek to hers, the hint of a smile in his whisper. "Ah… look at us. The more we dance, the better we're getting at it."

Proof of this, he twirled her around before pulling her back against him. He sighed. "You in my arms… this is all I need right now. If I had my way, I'd keep you with me like this forever."

She stilled against him, and lifting her head, she searched his face.

Uh, oh… maybe you went a little too far?

He started rambling. "Have I told you how beautiful you look tonight? Not that you aren't beautiful all the time. But tonight…"

She pressed her fingers to his mouth, shaking her head. Then she gazed right into his eyes. "I love you."

Caught off guard, he could only stare. Yep, these three little words, coming at him so unexpectedly, had left him speechless.

This had Stephanie in a panic.

Oh my God… what have you done? You've probably ruined everything. Quick, say something to make it better.

Her words were barely audible. "It's okay, I understand… you don't have to say anything. I didn't mean—"

Her frantic expression was enough to kick his mind right back into gear, his response coming in a long groan. "I love you, too."

Then, right there in the middle of the room, and in view of everyone there, he captured her mouth in an all-consuming and passionate kiss.

Yes, the magic was definitely back…

It was the sound of silence that had Evan lifting his head.

The music had stopped, and all eyes were on him and Stephanie.

He grabbed her hand, and almost in a run, they left the room. His plan was to head for the stairs, the only place he knew they could have some privacy.

Once he'd closed the door behind them, he took in his arms. A look of awe on his face, he gazed down at her. "I love you, too. And have from the beginning. It only took one look into your eyes… your beautiful eyes, and I was yours."

He shoved his hand through his hair. "I don't know what happened out there, why I reacted like I did. I think you took me by surprise. But it was a great surprise. The best. And one I'll never forget."

He groaned. "I'm sorry. I know I'm acting crazy, but I think… well, I'm just so happy."

She was half laughing, half crying as she reached up to stroke his cheek. "It's okay. I understand. I think I surprised myself, telling you when I did. But it suddenly seemed important I tell you what I've known all along. And this is that I've been in love with you since the first moment I saw you."

His mouth hitched in a teasing grin. "Hmm… you sure had a strange way of showing this. You had me so I didn't know what to think. There was only one thing I was sure of, the more time I spent with you, the more determined I was to never let you go."

He pressed a kiss to her forehead. "I love you Stephanie Bennett. Only you."

"I love you, too."

Encouraged by the brilliance of her smile, he grabbed her hand. "Come on, let's tell Elenore we're leaving. I believe our work here is done."

> *"At long last, our love has arrived,*
> *And I thank God I'm alive.*
> *I can't take my eyes off of you…"*

CHAPTER 39

I am absolutely, definitely, positively,
unquestionably, beyond any doubt, in love with you…
~Unknown

It was another beautiful May morning, and Elenore had already been in her office for over an hour.

The sound of someone clearing their throat had her looking up from her computer. Standing by the door, Evan lifted his hand in a wave. "Good morning."

She sent him a genuine smile. "Good morning, Evan. Please, come in."

He strolled into the room, smiling. "I hope this is a good time?"

She nodded. "It's perfect. Have a seat. I was just going through all the emails I received about the event on Saturday." She sent him a glance over the top of her glasses. "You're the person who should be reading these, as most of them are rave reviews about the photo wall."

She closed her computer. After resting her chin in her hand, she proceeded to study him.

This making him uncomfortable, he cleared his throat. "So, you wanted to see me?"

She smiled. "Yes, with everything going on, I haven't been able to talk to you. Did you go to Atlanta? And, if you did, what happened? I want all the details."

He sighed. "Unfortunately, I was too late. My aunt passed away shortly after she tried to get in touch with me. But I did get to talk with a friend of hers. She gave me the key to a safe deposit box my aunt had left in my name."

After filling her in on what he found in the envelope, he shrugged. "So, it seems the story ends there."

Her hand going to her mouth, Elenore shook her head. "Oh, Evan... I'm so sorry. I hope this gave you the answers you needed. If only for closure.."

Again, enough with the need for closure. You're beginning to think it's overrated.

With a wry smile on his face, he shrugged. "I'm fine with it. Like I've said before, I think I turned out pretty good on my own."

She nodded. "Yes, you have. But this doesn't make up for what happened. Your aunt and uncle were supposed to use that money to give you a normal and happy childhood. They gave me every reason to believe they would do this."

She picked up a folder from her desk, holding it out to him. "I did a lot of thinking after you left, and I decided I need to compensate you for what you lost. I want to give you an amount comparable to what I originally gave your aunt and uncle, with more to cover inflation. You'll find everything you need to know in this folder. Please, take it. I owe you this."

Evan held up his hand, shaking his head. "You owe me nothing. If anything, I am indebted to you for finding my aunt. And giving me a chance to show off my photography skills. But most of all, your trust in me to get the job done."

He reached into his pocket and pulled out the bankbook from his aunt. He pushed it across the desk to her. "My aunt left me this. In her note, she said it was to make up for the money my uncle used for his gambling."

He nodded. "Go ahead, open it. You'll see I'm going to be more than okay."

After Elenore opened the bank book, she looked up at him, a shocked expression on her face. "Evan... this is unbelievable. How was she able to accumulate such a large amount?"

He shrugged. "I don't know. She wrote she invested whatever she could of the money without my uncle's knowledge. I only wish she had used it for herself... a better place to live and maybe even better care when she got sick."

Elenore sighed. "This was probably her way of making peace with herself. I'm sure she felt she was to blame for a lot of what happened."

A faint smile tweaked Evan's lips. "Stephanie said the same thing."

"*Ah*, yes... Stephanie." Elenore tilted her head, a thoughtful look on her face. "I notice you always refer to her as Stephanie. Is there a reason for this?"

After a slight hesitation, he smiled. "From the very first moment I met her, I knew I could never call her anything but Stephanie. Everything about her... her beauty, her personality, and even her laugh... they're all perfection. I swear she is an angel in disguise."

He chuckled. "Maybe a very feisty angel. Either way, a nickname just didn't seem right."

Sitting back in her chair, Elenore shook her head. She was smiling.

This had Evan smiling, too. "What?"

"So, when are you going to ask her to marry you?"

After a brief silence, he gave a long sigh. "You know me too well. If I could, I would marry her today. So I could whisk her off to where no one could take advantage of her." He shook his head. "Like now... she told me she had to go into work early because she promised to cover for someone."

A wistful smile touched his lips. "Just for a little, I would like to have her all to myself, with no one asking her for help, fill in for them... the list goes on and on."

He shrugged. "This may sound selfish, but..."

Elenore nodded. "I know. And I'm afraid I just might be one of those people you're talking about. But she is a giver, through and through. And she will never change. Nor should you want this."

He nodded, a resigned smile on his face. "I know."

After taking time to think about this, Elenore became all business-like. "Well, when you do pop the question—and don't wait too long to do this—my gift to the both of you will be a honeymoon like you just described."

He laughed. "This is a gift I will accept with pleasure."

Coming to his feet and slipping the bank book back into his pocket, he extended his hand to her. "Again, thank you for the opportunity to be a part of such a great project. It was more than a pleasure to work with you."

Her grip was strong, her expression sincere. "I want you to know I think of you as the son I never had. So, please… don't be a stranger. Keep in touch. And let me know when you make it official with Stephanie."

He smiled. "I will."

At the door, he turned back to her. "The money you were planning to give me? I have decided to start up a program that would match children with a pet to help them recover from an injury, illness, or any other life altering situation. If you would like to donate, or even get involved, let me know. I'm still in the beginning stages with this, but I'd like to get this up and running as soon as possible."

She smiled. "I will be more than happy to help. Oreo has already shown how beneficial a program like this can be. And I've grown quite fond of the little dog."

She suddenly laughed. "I even caught Dr. Davis playing with her the other day."

Evan grinned. "That's great. I can't ask for any more than that, can I?"

On his way to the elevator, Evan was happy to see Stephanie was at the nurses station, typing something on the computer. He came up behind her, and wrapping his arms around her, he pressed a kiss to the top of her head.

She leaned back to smile up at him.

"Hi…"

This gave him the perfect opportunity to give her another kiss. This one to her mouth and lingering much longer.

"Hi…"

He chuckled. "I like your reaction so much better than the first time I saw you sitting here."

She smiled. "I know. You had me so I couldn't even think straight, even back then."

"Hmm… I like the sound of that. Because you do the same to me."

He glanced down at his watch. "I wish I didn't have to, but I need to go. I have a meeting with a potential client. But, I'll see you later tonight?"

She nodded. "And remember to keep tomorrow night open because I'm taking you out to dinner for your birthday."

He reached over to tuck her hair behind her ear. "You don't have to do that."

She grabbed his hand, holding it to her cheek. "I know I don't. But I want to. I already have the night all planned out."

"And are you going to tell me what this plan is?"

She shook her head. "Nope, it's a surprise."

"As long as I'm with you, I'll be happy." He leaned in to give her another kiss. "I'll see you later."

She watched him walk over to the elevator before he turned back to her, mouthing the words… *love you.*

She responded in the same.

After the elevator doors closed, Stephanie leaned back in her chair, a dreamy smile on her face. It wasn't until the screen saver popped up on the computer, she sent a guilty look around, thankful to see she was alone.

You need to stop thinking about him. Or you won't get any work done.

A determined look on her face, she signed into the computer.

And even though Evan had already looked up the address of where he needed to go, he couldn't remember what it was. He was shaking his head as he scrolled down through his messages, searching for the address.

You need that honeymoon Elenore promised. Soon, you need this.

This is what love can do to a person…

CHAPTER 40

I choose you.
And I'll choose you
over and over and over.
Without pause,
without a doubt,
in a heartbeat.
I'll keep choosing you.
~Unknown

"Stephanie?"

At the sound of Evan's voice, Stephanie gave one last swipe through her hair with the brush.

Then she went flying out of the bathroom and down the hall.

To run right into him.

He laughed, gathering her against him. *"Whoa...* once again, I didn't expect such an enthusiastic greeting. But I'm beginning to get used to it, liking it even more."

He nuzzled his face in her hair, his next comment a husky whisper. "And if I remember correctly, what happened after that was a time I'll never forget. In fact..."

She pulled back from him, shaking her head.

But she was smiling "Oh, no, you don't… we need to leave. We can't be late."

He pulled her right back into his arms. He found that whenever she was near, this was all he wanted. The need to have her close, to touch her, was so strong he couldn't fight it.

Nor do you want to.

He was smiling as he gazed down at her. *"Hmm*… exactly what do you have planned that we can't be late?"

She made a face at him. "I guess you'll just have to wait and see." Then she surprised him by wrapping her arms around him, giving him a kiss that left them both breathless.

When he opened his eyes, she was grinning up at him. "Happy Birthday." She traced his lips with her finger."I love you."

"I love you, too." Then he groaned. "But you have to know you're making me crazy, don't you? And, wait a minute… shouldn't I be the one to decide what we do? Since it is my birthday? If so, my vote would be to stay right here with you."

She slipped out of his arms, shaking her head. "Nope, no can do."

She reached for his hand. "Come on, let's go."

After Evan unlocked his car, Stephanie reached over and grabbed the remote out of his hand.

"Hey…" Surprised, he glanced over at her.

She pointed to the passenger door. "Since it's your birthday, I will be driving. So, get in."

After a bit of good natured grumbling, he did as he was told.

She handed him a blindfold. "Now I want you to put this on."

He gave her a long look. "You're kidding me, right?"

"Nope, this is all part of the surprise. So, go ahead… just put it on."

After he did this, she peered more closely at him. "Are you sure you can't see?"

A slow smile curved his mouth. "I'm not sure. Move closer…"

When her face was only inches away, his fingers catching her chin, he captured her mouth in a kiss.

He leaned back in his seat, a smug look on his face. "Nope. I can't see a thing. But as it turns out, I don't need to."

She was smiling as she went to start the car. Then she dropped her forehead to the steering wheel. "Oh, no... something tells me we're about to get a lecture."

Mrs. Sloan, her next-door neighbor, was standing in front of the car. Her arms crossed over her ample chest and a huge frown on face, her voice came at them, loud and angry. "What do you think you're doing? This is a family neighborhood, not a place to live out your hidden fantasies. You ought to be ashamed of yourself."

Now it was true Evan couldn't see. But he could hear.

And what this woman said had him sort of mad.

He reached up to pull off the blindfold, but Stephanie put her hand on his arm. "No, ignore her. That's what I do. Because even though I've told her I work nights as a nurse, she refuses to believe me. I don't even want to know what she thinks I'm doing."

"*Hmm...* then we should give her even more to think about." He reached over, and pulling her into his arms, he claimed her mouth in a passionate kiss.

"Scandalous... just scandalous." This said even louder, Mrs. Sloan turned on her heel and went marching down the sidewalk.

Stephanie groaned. "Now look what you did. Who knows what she'll do now. But I'm going to forgive you because it's your birthday."

His only response a big smile, she sighed. "I can't help feeling sorry for her. I don't think she has any friends. Maybe the next time I bake cookies, I'll take some to her. It's worth a try."

Evan was shaking his head. "And this is one of the many reasons why I love you. You always see the good in everyone."

After she started up the car and pulled out of the parking lot, she glanced over at him. "Are you excited?"

"Yes, I am. Out of curiosity, how long will it take us to get to wherever we're going?"

"Not long."

"*Hmm...* That's good to know." A smile tweaked the corner of his mouth. "You look beautiful in pink, by the way."

She sent him a suspicious glance. "Are you sure you can't see anything?"

"Nope, like I told you, I don't need to see you." He grinned, pointing to his head. "I have all of you up here, every second I've spent with you."

"Well, thank you. You look very nice, too."

He chuckled. "And now I know you're blushing. But that's okay. My plan is to keep you blushing for the rest of our lives."

She was silent. Which had him a little worried.

Maybe he had said too much?

He cleared his throat. "Hey, are you still there?"

"Yes, yes... I'm still here. Concentrating on my driving, that's all." This was as far from the truth as she could get. Her mind had grabbed on to what he said and darn, if it wouldn't let go.

For the rest of our lives? Did he really mean this?

Almost in fascination, she glanced down at the hand he put on her arm, a huskiness in his voice. "And yes, I meant every word."

She nearly swerved off the road.

Omg... he can read your mind?

This had her next words coming out all breathless. "Sorry about that. I must have hit a rough patch or something."

He started to laugh. "Of course, it's amazing how something can sneak up on you when you least expect it."

Now beyond flustered with the way their conversation was going, and maybe even more confused, she was more than relieved to see the sign for The Glass and Grape.

She put on her turn signal. "It looks like we're here."

He smiled. "That's too bad, I was enjoying our little conversation. And, just so you know, this is turning out to be one of the best birthdays I've ever had."

He didn't need to see to know there was a big smile on her face.

"You're doing just fine. Only a few more steps and we'll be there."

With Evan still wearing the blindfold, and Stephanie guiding him, they were now standing at the entrance to The Glass and Grape.

She was laughing.

While he was grumbling. "I feel like we've walked a mile."

She patted his arm. "I think you're exaggerating a little. It's been about fifty feet at the most. You only have to go up these three steps and we'll be there."

This accomplished, she was grinning as she pushed open the door before she looked up at him. "Okay, you can take off the blindfold now."

Evan pulled it off, met by a loud cheer.

"Surprise!"

He was promptly surrounded. Everyone wanted to shake his hand and wish him a happy birthday. Or to ask if he had really been surprised.

To which he could honestly answer with a yes.

Everyone was there…

Jason and Darcey, with Jason holding Madeline Rose. She had headed right to him as soon as she saw him. This gave Abby the opportunity to bring in the cake.

Joe and Beth, with Joe grinning from ear to ear.

Elenore, who was more than happy to be holding a sleeping Natalie, giving Carrie and Chris a much needed break.

Hannah, who had come with Sophie since Sean, Chester, and Kevin had a game.

Sophie, her attention on Trevor and Hudson, who were jumping up and down with excitement.

Livy and Sam, who had brought Gracie and Bella, since Jake couldn't leave the restaurant.

And even Jack. After all, he had been completely serious when he said he only wanted Stephanie to be happy.

It was only after Evan had greeted everyone, he pulled Stephanie against him and pressed a kiss to the top of her head. He shook his head. "I can't believe you did this for me."

She grinned. "There was no way I would let your birthday go by without a proper party. Are you really surprised?"

Before he could answer, there was a tug on his pant leg. He looked down to see both Trevor and Hudson were gazing up at him.

They began clapping their hands and chanting. "Cake, cake, cake..."

Sophie came running over to pull them away. "I am so sorry. They have been talking about this all day. They love Abby's cakes."

"It's okay." Squatting down next to them, Evan nodded. "I agree with the both of you. Who doesn't like cake? But I think I'm going to need help blowing out the candles. Can you do this for me?"

Almost knocking him to the floor in their excitement, they grabbed his hands and pulled him over to where Abby was lighting the candles.

After everyone joined in to sing a very loud and enthusiastic version of Happy Birthday, with the joint effort of Hudson, Trevor, Madeline Rose and Bella, the candles were all blown out, the promise of wishes granted.

The cake was a success, with Abby giving all the credit to Stephanie for her suggestion she make it entirely out of cookies. And the gifts were all opened and admired.

Someone called out for a speech.

His glance going to Stephanie, Evan held out his hand. Once he had her hand tucked in his, he gazed around at all the smiling faces. "I can't thank you enough for coming here to celebrate my birthday. Stephanie has told me so much about every one of you and how much you mean to her. And now I can see why, with how you have all gone out of your way to make me feel so welcome."

He paused, sending Jason a wry smile. "Well, maybe everyone wasn't very accepting at first. But I'm hoping this has changed."

A slow grin spreading across his face, Jason shrugged. "Hey, what can I say? It's my job to look after my little sister."

Stephanie rolled her eyes. "Jason..."

Evan smiled down at her. "Hey, it's all good. Everyone needs someone to look after them."

His expression turning serious, his gaze traveled around the room. "If any of you had asked me what I wanted for my birthday this year, my answer would have come in a heartbeat. Because I've found there is only one thing, or one person, I need. This would be the woman who has brought so much joy and love into my life. The one person I want to spend the rest of my life with."

Here he stopped to gaze down at Stephanie. The love shining in her eyes was all he needed to know what they had believed all along was finally theirs.

Magic...

Their magic...

He reached into his pocket and pulled out a ring. Aware of Stephanie's gasp as he dropped to one knee, he was smiling as he gazed up at her. His voice was deep... and so, *so* sure.

"Stephanie, I promise... and I mean this with all my heart... you will always be the love of my life, my better half and the reason for everything I do. As long as I have you, there will always be magic in my world... our world."

When her hand went to her mouth, tears already falling down her face, he had to stop and take a big breath to get out his next words. "So, Stephanie Bennett, marry me so we can keep this magic going forever."

In the hushed silence that followed, Stephanie could only nod. It was only after Evan put the ring on her finger, she finally choked out a yes before she threw herself into his arms.

As birthdays go, this one was definitely at the top of the list.

After Evan closed the passenger door, he ran around to get into the driver's seat. He glanced over at Stephanie.

Her head resting against the seat, she smiled at him.

Momentarily taken in by the love shining in her eyes, he swallowed.

"Happy?"

She reached over to stroke his cheek. "So, *so* happy. I love you."

Catching her hand in his, he brought it to his mouth for a kiss. "I love you, too." Then he hesitated, his gaze searching, before he shook his head. "I hadn't intended to propose to you like I did. But with everyone there, it suddenly seemed right."

She smiled. "It was perfect."

He traced the ring on her finger with his. "And I wasn't sure how you would feel about the ring once belonging to my mother. If you—"

She slipped her hand from his, pressing her fingers to his mouth. "I love the ring. It's beautiful, and even more special because it was given to your mother with so much love. But you could have given me a ring made of string and I still would have been happy. That I have your love is more than enough."

He leaned over to give her a kiss before he started the car. "There's something I want to do. Something I promised myself I would do if I ever got the chance to see you again."

He grinned over at her. "Never had I thought we would be at this point."

"What is it?"

He shrugged, a hint of mischief in his smile "I guess you'll just have to wait and see."

"*Evan...*"

He held up his finger. "*Ah, ha...* remember, it is my birthday, which means I can pretty much do whatever I want. Right?"

She laughed, shaking her head. "Oh dear, what have I done? But it's okay. It's only fair, since you have a lot of birthdays to make up."

After he blew her a kiss, he began talking about the party and asking her about her friends. They even checked on the score of the baseball game, happy to find it had already ended with Kevin's walk off home run.

To her surprise, he pulled into the parking lot of The Regency.

Ignoring her puzzled glance, he left the car before she could comment. Even after he opened her door, he put his finger to his mouth, shaking his head.

The sky above them ablaze with a million stars, he led her to the middle of the empty lot. After typing something on his phone, exactly as he had on that magical September night, he set it down on the pavement.

The same instrumental version of *The Way You Look Tonight* began to play. The familiar notes of the song rose over the deserted parking lot, floating through the night air.

It was the perfect invitation for a dance.

Evan watched as the breeze gently rifled through Stephanie's hair, the silky strands luminous in the moonlight. He reached out to smooth it back from her face.

Again caught up in the love shining in her eyes, his voice was deep with emotion. "I never thought I would get another chance to fall in love again. But from the very first moment I looked into your beautiful eyes, I knew I would always be yours. But never in my wildest dreams did I think you would agree to be mine. Then, here in this very parking lot, we shared a dance. And with you in my arms, this is when it all became real."

He held out his hand. "So, will you share this dance with me? Like you did on that amazing night?"

She went right into his arms.

And they danced... her head on his shoulder, his whispered promises falling like stardust in her hair.

It's been said, history never repeats itself. But, in this case, it came pretty darn close.

Because once again, on the uneven pavement and under the light of the moon and a million stars, the dance they shared was far more beautiful than they could have ever imagined.

> *"When I'm so awfully low,*
> *When the world has turned cold,*
> *I will feel a glow when I think of you,*
> *And how beautiful you looked tonight."*

* * *

It's Time to do Some Baking!

No doubt, you've already figured out Stephanie's cookies would be the recipe chosen for this book. You might remember Jason's comment Stephanie was a chocolate chip girl all the way. So, it was a sure bet chocolate would be involved.

Some say they taste just like Snickerdoodles, but with an added twist. Others claim they're a kicked-up version of chocolate chip cookies.

Either way, most agree the recipe captures the best of both flavors, all in one delicious and addicting cookie.

Ask Evan, he'll vouch for this.

Stephanie's Cinnamon Chocolate Chipperdoodles

For Cookies:
1/2 cup un-salted butter, room temperature
3/4 cup sugar
1 large egg
1 teaspoon vanilla
1 teaspoon baking powder
1/2 teaspoon salt
1 teaspoon finely grated orange peel
1-1/3 cups bread flour
3/4 cup mini chocolate chips
(These work the best, providing a sprinkling
of chocolate in each bite)
For Coating:
2 tablespoons sugar and 1-1/2 teaspoons
cinnamon, well-blended

Instructions:
Preheat oven to 375°F.
Line cookie sheets with parchment paper.
Beat butter and sugar until smooth.

Add egg, beat until well blended.
Beat in vanilla, baking powder, salt and
grated orange peel.
Add flour, beat until well-blended.
Stir in chocolate chips.
Scoop dough into balls (I used a
1-tablespoon cookie, scoop for each cookie)
then roll in the cinnamon/sugar mixture to
coat.
Place on prepared cookie sheet, about
2-inches apart.
Using the bottom of a glass, flatten
cookies slightly.
Bake 7 to 9 minutes for soft cookies,
10 to 12 minutes for crisp cookies.
Cool for 1-2 minutes on cookie sheet
before moving to a cooling rack to cool
completely.

Yield: 3 dozen cookies

Enjoy!

A sneak peek at where it all began...
A Million Decembers
Book 1 - Chapter 1

Nicholas—formally known as Nicholas William Edward Hanover III, a title he revealed only under the most dire of circumstances—found himself in a decidedly foul mood.

Because, *come on...* the transatlantic flight had to be the worst he'd ever endured, and he had survived his share of airborne nightmares.

He glanced down at the American woman whose fingers were locked around his arm in a death grip, her face buried deep in his shoulder as though the storm that had ambushed them mid-flight could tear her away at any moment.

Lightning flashed again, painting the cabin in stark white before the interior lights flickered and dimmed. A sigh escaping him, Nicholas, patted her hand with what he hoped passed for gentle reassurance. He was not particularly fond of the turbulence himself, but years of constant travel had taught him that pilots could handle far worse. Hadn't the captain said as much over the intercom?

Still, sympathy had its limits and this woman had begun testing his from the instant she'd dropped into the seat beside him at Heathrow.

What's with American women? he wondered, not for the first time. *Must they always be so... forward?*

She'd chattered non-stop from the moment the wheels left the runway—sharing her life story, the whole unabridged edition. Along with a long and drawn out rant about her rude taxi driver to Heathrow.

Not to be heartless, but he couldn't have cared less.

After takeoff, he'd hauled out his laptop. Making a big production of signing in, he'd kept his eyes glued to the screen, typing furiously as if he were sealing a multimillion-pound deal. When, in truth, he had merely been catching up on his personal emails.

He'd foolishly thought this would signal his disinterest, prompting her to bury herself in the celebrity magazine peeking from her bag, catch a movie, or even doze off.

He would've been happy with any of these.

But yeah, you guessed it... his hints had been entirely lost on her.

Instead, her chatter persisted, and leaning over the armrest into his space, her voice became louder, her laugh even more shrill.

Resigned, he'd slammed the laptop shut, leaned back in his seat and closed his eyes. And finally, there was silence... a sweet, blessed silence that lasted perhaps ninety seconds.

But almost as if the universe decided to mock him, the turbulence struck in earnest. Every jolt and bounce brought on another of the woman's piercing screams, her nails digging into his arm like claws.

And that, more or less, was how he spent the rest of the flight.

When the flight attendant's announcement for landing finally drifted through the cabin, he shot a glance at his seat-mate.

Her head thrown back against the seat, and her mouth wide open, she was lost to the world. But even in her sleep, she hadn't let go of his arm. Gently prying her fingers free, and fastening his seatbelt, he raised the shade. The reflection of his scowling face in the rain-streaked window said it all.

Not exactly a pretty sight.

Below, Chicago O'Hare was a blur through the downpour, the waves of Lake Michigan churned restlessly, a dismal shade of gray. Early December in the Midwest, this was to be expected, yet somehow seemed ominous. He hoped it wasn't an omen.

As the plane began its decent, he leaned back once more and closed his eyes. He was more than ready for this leg of the journey to end.

Good Lord, you are so ready.

Hopefully, Chicago was ready for him.

At last the wheels touched solid ground, Nicholas gave a long stretch before kneading the stubborn knots from his neck until the tension finally began to ease. This small relief lasted only a heartbeat—until he caught the heated gaze of his former seat-mate. She looked ready to pounce.

You need to make a swift exit—very swift..

He gathered his belongings for a swift exit, but luck evaded him once again. She latched on to his arm again and leaned in with a breathy offer to buy him a drink for his "strong, manly presence" during their "terrifying ordeal." Then, batting her lashes, she waited.

Good Lord... really?

He declined. Firmly, he did this.

He turned to leave. But she insisted he wait. After a slow search through her cavernous bag, finally pulling out a pen and what looked like a crumpled fast-food napkin. With deliberate care she printed out her name and number, then informed him this in case he later decided to take her up on her offer.

With her eyes tracking his every move, he tucked the napkin into his overcoat pocket. Then after a polite smile and narrowly avoiding her attempt at a more amorous farewell, he fled.

Moving at a brisk pace, Nicholas tried to ignore the twinge of guilt nagging at him. But in his defense, this woman's abrasiveness behavior had waved red flags from the start.

His sister Claire—happily married, mother of twins and forever fretting over his single state would no doubt lecture him later bout his impossibly high standards and unwillingness to commit. Yes, she agreed it was wonderful he was so successful at what he did. But after a long day at work, he couldn't cuddle up with contracts and year end profit reports, could he? And as much as she hated to remind him, he wasn't getting any younger.

Hmm... you wonder what she'd think of the real reason for this trip.

But enough of that. Right now, he was a man on a mission, focused on three simple priorities. One, baggage claim. Two, a taxi. And three, the hotel. Only then could he slip back into the normal routine of his life.

Was this too much to ask?

He didn't think so. But first, there was something he had to do. Stopping at the first trash container he saw, he pulled the napkin from his pocket and dropped it in without a second glance.

He felt better already.

From only a few feet away, the woman watched this, wondering if she should be insulted, or just plain out angry.

Then, with a defiant toss of her head, her lips curved into a small, private smile. Okay, maybe this was a bit of a setback as far as her plans went. But she wasn't worried.

At least not yet, she wasn't.

He obviously had no idea who he was dealing with. If he had, he'd know she always got what she wanted.

And right now, she wanted him.

Settled within the quiet confines of the taxi and en route to his hotel, Nicholas exhaled a long breath of relief. At last, he was back in control, a feeling he was most comfortable with in his hectic life.

The city a blur past the rain-streaked windows, he pulled out his phone and scrolled through the week's itinerary. He'd scheduled one meeting for today, his plan to use the remaining time to catch up on calls and emails, enjoy a quiet dinner in the privacy of his room, and turn in early.

A perfectly civilized plan. Then as he double checked the details of his meeting he realized the time difference here in the states had completely slipped his mind.

This meant his day was only just beginning.

Dragging his hand through his hair, he stared down at his phone.

How the hell did you forget something that basic? It's not like you've never traveled to the states before.

He massaged his forehead, the familiar restlessness pressing in again. His mind had been... well, unreliable lately. He refused to dwell on the reason. Not now.

He slipped the phone back into his pocket and, resting his head against the cool leather seat, stared out at the rain. In his preoccupied state, he didn't even notice it was still raining.

It was falling harder than ever.

After Nicholas checked into his room and he'd made a few calls, he wandered over to the window, taking in the glittering hustle of Michigan Avenue.

The city pulsed with life even under the gray sky, yet the restlessness that had traveled with him from London refused to loosen its hold. He felt trapped, as though the elegant hotel room had become a beautiful cage.

Maybe what he needed was some fresh air, inclement weather and all. A brisk walk before his meeting might clear his head--stop him from turning over and over the real reason he'd scheduled this trip. The one-in-a-million chance at a new beginning that could quietly change everything.

He scratched his head, a wry smile on his face.

You've got to stop reading so much into this. You know damn well this a one in a million shot.

A glance at his watch showed he had a little over an hour before his meeting. If he left now, he'd have plenty of time to get in a decent walk.

He exchanged his sweater for a shirt and tie suitable for his business meeting and shrugged into his overcoat. After slipping his room key into his pocket, he was out the door.

Yes, a walk and fresh air should do the trick.

About a block from Nicholas's hotel, Anna Jameson emerged from the fashionable boutique to find the rain of earlier had now turned to sleet. Ducking her head against the icy pellets stinging her face, she jammed her hat down even harder on her head.

But she was smiling.

Not even the wild and unpredictable Chicago weather could dampen her mood.

Nope, not today. Not with a check tucked deep inside the bag she was carrying. A check written out to her as a generous down payment for one dozen of her original designed and hand painted ornaments.

She peeked into the bag to make sure the check was still there.

Yep. There it was.

She tilted her face to the sky—there was no getting around it, she was going to get soaked. She pulled up her collar, about to make her move when a powerful gust of wind came whipping around the corner of the building and slammed into her, grabbing the bag right out of her hand.

Before she even realized what happened, the bag took off, sailing up into the air like a runaway kite. Left staring open-mouthed at her now empty hand, it was another gust of wind, this one even stronger, that was enough to shock her back to life.

"*Oh no, no, no—my bag—*" she cried, already sprinting after it. "If you can, please grab it."

Yes, she was screaming like a lunatic. But she didn't care. She needed that bag. A sample ornament and her designs were inside, along with the check.

Oh my God… the check!

The wildly dancing bag suddenly changed course, heading in the direction of the late afternoon traffic, bumper to bumper down Michigan Avenue.

Zig-zagging her way through the crowded sidewalk, she was only inches away from catching it when—unbelievable as this sounds, because who could even make up something like this—she collided with an enormous pile of fragrant evergreen garlands coming from out of nowhere.

Ommmph…

"What the…?"

The impact was enough to send her flying backward onto the sidewalk, her hat sailing through the air. Her head struck the pavement with a sharp crack that echoed in her ears. And as if this wasn't enough, the garlands came crashing down, one by one, to land on top of her.

And then, nothing—

The world went completely black.

This is only the beginning of a beautiful collection of love stories. Available in both paperback and ebook through all your favorite independent and on-line bookstores.

ABOUT THE AUTHOR

L. B. Joyce lives in Chagrin Falls, Ohio. A freelance artist by day, with designing Christmas ornaments her specialty, she's also a writer by night.

She loves getting lost in a good book, has redecorated almost every room in her house more times than she'd like to admit, loves baking up a storm in her kitchen, hates housework with a passion and will drive just about anywhere because of her fear of flying.

To keep up with the news about the series, Twelve Months, Twelve Love Stories—A *Million Decembers, For the Love of July, February's Angel, Promise Me November, An Unexpected June, A January to Remember, September's Moonlight Serenade, Goodbye Heartbreak, Hello May,* and *March, a Song and a Dance*—check out the links below.

Along with the new series, Holidays in White Oaks Valley - *A Grand Slam Kind of Christmas, Book 1.*

Check out the website/blog at: lbjoyceauthor.com

Facebook: @LBJoyceAuthor

Send an email: lbjoyce12@gmail.com

Inspiration from the following:

Can't Take My Eyes Off You - Robert Crewe, Bob Gaudio
The Way You Look Tonight - Composer, Jerome Kern. Lyrics by Dorothy Fields.

Cover: Tracey, at Soxsational Cover Art

www.ingramcontent.com/pod-product-compliance
Lightning Source LLC
Chambersburg PA
CBHW070538120726
47909CB00007B/2178